DESERT KILL

Beth,
Enjoy Santiago's
first AZ adventure
Ron Wick
6/17/18

RON WICK

DESERT KILL
Ron Wick

a GlenEagle publication

Copyright ©2014 Ron Wick
Printed in the United States of America
All rights reserved.

* * * * *

* * * * *

Disclaimer
This is a work of fiction, a product of the author's imagination. Any resemblance or similarity to any actual events or persons, living or dead, is purely coincidental. Although the author and publisher have made every effort to ensure there are no errors, inaccuracies, omissions, or inconsistencies herein, any slights or people, places, or organizations are unintentional.

* * * * *

Credits
Author photo courtesy of Linda Mismas
Cover photo courtesy of Shutterstock Photo
Editing and cover design by harveystanbrough.com
Formatting by Debora Lewis arenapublishing.org

* * * * *

ISBN-13: 978-1499631760
ISBN-10: 1499631766

For their critiques,
edits, and valuable guidance and motivation
this book is dedicated to Hjordis "Jeri" Arnold,
Gail O'Hara and Myrtle Norwood

PROLOGUE
Seaside Oregon: Spring Break

The radio was turned up loud. "Hello Pismo, Redondo, Manhattan, Lake Havasu, Rocky Point and all beaches east. We're broadcasting live at the sandy, slightly overcast bikini week long party where there's enough skin and booze to warm any heart; the spring break party that can't stop. This is Sound Man at Seaside. Let the party grow as the discs, play pumping out really good sound to...."

He toyed with the hair on the back of her neck. "Sound Man's a little loud for this moment. I knew earlier today when I saw you playing volleyball we were meant for each other."

"Was that when I dove for the ball and lost my top in the sand?"

"No, Barb, sorry I missed that. It was when you flashed one of the cameramen."

"That was fun too. They can't use it."

"The fun side of Spring Break?"

"It's all fun, but yeah, tease the news guys."

"He could've been one of the guys doing a Girls video, the ones you see advertised on late night TV."

"I didn't think of that, but what the hell. The guys watching those aren't looking at faces either and I didn't sign anything."

"It's nice out here tonight even if the air is a little cool," he said.

She stroked his thigh. "Sound Man's hot and you're not exactly cold to my touch. Bet you're hotter than he is."

"I should be. This old bod is surging."

They kissed. "I like being with someone a little more mature, not so caught up in the party scene."

He ran a hand across her hard belly. Her flesh jumped at his touch. "You're warm, soft. There's something about a naked woman on a blanket-covered lanai that just captivates me."

"Kiss me."

He moved his hand upward, brushing the warmth of a breast and burying his fingertips in her cleavage. "You excite me."

"Could it be you're naked too and looking for the Promised Land?"

He kissed her again. "Could be."

"That's why I'm here: parties, people, action."

"Sex?"

She stroked his chest. "Definitely sex. I bet couples are on half the lanais at this hotel as we speak doing whatever."

"Or maybe down there. I see a fire or two on the beach."

She looked south. "I don't see anything much toward Cannon Beach."

He pulled her closer, nuzzled her ear. "Come here. Every nerve in me is alive."

She wrapped her thigh around his hip, teasing his groin. "Mine too."

"Don't rush. We have all night."

"It already seems like all night."

He kissed her neck, ears and throat, rolled her onto her side and pressed against her back. "Let me feel your warmth. Can you feel my strength?"

She shuddered. "It's not strength that I'm feeling, but it's better."

"A chill?"

She reached behind her back and touched him where he was probing between their bodies. "Not a chance. Now... I want you now."

"Not yet. Let's take our time, enjoy each other, and share."

"Now," she moaned, "or do old guys need more time?"

He kissed the back of her shoulder. "No, I'm ready."

She arched her back and rolled onto her knees. "We're ready. Punch my ticket. Do me. Do me now, Backdoor Man."

He ran a finger down her spine as they joined in frantic first sex. "Every muscle in your back is tight."

"Not for long."

That's right, lift your head.

She moaned. "More! Faster!"

He quickly took her chin in his right hand. Suspended in their coupling he pressed the back of her head with his left hand, jerked her chin to the side. A whimper escaped her throat as the cracking bone echoed in his ears.

"That was classic, absolutely perfect. Now I'm spent."

He withdrew, stood and looked at the limp flesh beneath him. "Your ticket has been punched, you demanding bitch."

He stepped into the room, took a beach towel from a backpack, returned to the lanai and covered her. Back inside he showered and dressed. He returned to the lanai, rolled the body into a blanket, and repacked the towel. He went to the lobby filled with boisterous partygoers and borrowed a wheelchair from near the unoccupied concierge station

Back in the room he parked the chair beside the body. "This will work nicely, little lady," he mumbled. "A walk on the promenade with a half-drunk co-ed in a blanket is spring break gone silly. If anybody asks I'm just taking you back to your friends."

He stepped to the lanai and took one last look over the beach. "You were so right. The south end of the beach is dark and deserted."

Wheeling the chair to the door he paused, dug into the backpack and extracted a garden tool and small jar.

The walk south on the promenade was trouble free. At the end he lifted Barb from the chair and carried her into the darkness behind a dune. He pulled her left arm out from under the blanket, found her ring finger and snipped it off at the base. He dropped it into the jar. "Gotta keep the collection growing, Kid. Now I just gotta clean the room and I'm outta here with the early light."

He walked to the wheelchair and looked back toward the dune. "Bitch, sex is spontaneous, not something on short order. All I wanted was to make a sketch and share some comfort. I hate women who try to order me around."

* * *

A news flash came through the radio the following morning. "We interrupt Sound Man for this breaking story from Seaside. Crime tape separates a large area between Seaside and Cannon beaches where the body of a co-ed was discovered early this morning. Her name has not been released pending notification of next of kin. A large crowd of party goers are hovering nearby as investigators gather evidence. A touch of evil descended on our beach last evening. The only information we have currently is a young woman was killed, her body left against a dune as if sleeping, a bloody hand resting on the gray flesh of her belly. Authorities have made no further public statements at this time. Now back to the Sound Man."

Day One

Wearing a loose bathrobe, Michelle Santiago looked out the large picture window at Kalaloch Beach on the Washington coast. "We've got a pretty good breeze going this morning. The ocean is gray, rolling, restless."

Chance Stewart stretched as he stood by the small table in the kitchenette, then moved toward the counter. "It is. Want a cup of coffee?"

"Please. Just leave it on the table. I have to dress and dry my hair."

"It's hot. We'll let it cool."

She walked across the room toward the bedroom door, stopped beside the table and kissed his cheek.

He said, "I like your outfit. You'll bring out the beast in me."

She licked her lower lip. "I'll take your beast. It's been a great beginning to our first vacation together. The ocean is everything you said it'd be." She arched an eyebrow. "I like your jeans with no shirt look too. Let that tummy ripple."

"With you here it's much more than just physical."

She nodded and sipped the steaming coffee. The robe fell open, exposing a perfectly proportioned thigh. "I hope so."

He smiled. "The flesh you're showing isn't wasted, Madam."

"Madam? You know, Chance, if you're this glib now what were you like before?"

"You don't want to know."

"Think we've got TV reception this morning?"

"I doubt it. In fact, I hope not. The beach and you are enough for me."

She shrugged. "It's been a few days. Just want to know what's going on. We've been kind'a isolated."

"True, but we're on vacation. I love it."

She said, "You know, I'm falling in love with you."

"We'll give it some time. I feel the same way."

She looked toward the windows. *You didn't say you love me.* "Could we run up to LaPush today? I'd like to spend some time on the beach just walking."

"You mean like a tourist?"

"A touron."

"A touron?"

She nodded. "Cross between a tourist and a moron, not a care in the world."

He laughed. "Sure. We haven't been there since we caught Gunn almost a week ago. How about I fix some breakfast while you get dressed? Then we can eat and run."

Santiago moved off toward the bedroom. She dropped the robe as she passed through the bedroom door. Stewart watched his partner and lover, his breath taken away by her beauty. He called after her, "You know, Babe, what you're doing to my body ought to be illegal."

"What you do to mine is, but some laws were made to be broken."

He began cooking breakfast. The sizzling sound of bacon and the rich odor of hickory filled the cabin while Santiago showered and dressed. She applied green eye shadow, accenting her deep brown eyes and dark complexion, then rejoined Stewart.

He watched her cross the room. "Skin-tight low riders and a powder blue turtleneck, you're pushing all my buttons."

"Buttons are made for pushing."

He dished up the plates and put them on the table. She began eating. "Looks good. Smells good."

"You're the most beautiful woman in the world: smooth dark skin, Bambi eyes, silky brown hair to your shoulders. You're easy on the eyes, Babe."

She laughed. "Is something wrong? Do I have egg on my chin?"

"No. I'm just watching you, thinking how lucky I am to be here with you."

"We're both fortunate."

He cleared his throat. "I know Santiago is Spanish, but you're obviously a beautiful mix of cultures."

"My dad is a third generation Barcelona import with some Scandinavian tossed in. Remember my sister, Jill? All blonde. Our mom is a mix of English, Spanish and a touch of the islands."

"Beautiful," he said, "just beautiful."

"I think they more than qualified me as part of the great American melting pot."

"I know what you mean. My folks are from all over Europe with a touch of Sioux."

"At least you're part native."

"We're both natives," he said, "of Seattle. Considering the number of people migrating to the northwest these days that puts us in a minority of our own."

"Could be. Haven't thought much about it."

"Two more glorious days together. What else could we ask for?"

A lifetime together. "Don't know. Like you said, one day at a time. We'll see where it leads."

He walked around behind her chair as she took her last bite and kissed her neck. "This sure beats chasin' bad guys."

Turning, she looked into his crystal clear blue eyes and kissed him. She glanced toward the bedroom. "We'd better get going or we'll end up in there again."

"I hope so."

She cocked her head and frowned. "What's that?"

"Your cell phone. Mine's turned off."

"I thought mine was too."

She went to the bedroom, dug into a travel bag and pulled out her cell. "Santiago."

"Mitch? It's Nikki... Nikki Braun."

"Nikki, I haven't heard from you in ages. What a nice—"

"Mitch, I need your help." Her voice began to break up. "I know I'm calling out of the blue and you're on vacation, but it's Lindsey."

"Lindsey? Claude's daughter?"

"She's missing."

"Have you called the police?"

"No. She's twenty years old. There's no sign of foul play."

"How do you know?"

There was a slight pause. "Claude's people looked into it. We haven't heard from her in three days."

"Where does she live?"

"An apartment near ASU, but nobody has seen her."

"Has she taken off before? I mean, you remember our days at the U Dub."

"A few times, but she always tells us where she'll be and who's with her."

"Have her credit cards been used?"

Nikki began to sob. "No."

Claude Braun came on the phone. "Mitch?"

"Claude, what's going on?"

"I don't know. Lindsey's just disappeared. At first we thought it was another of her flings, but she's always called us."

"Does she have a boyfriend she's serious about?"

"She's serious and not serious about all of her admirers, and yes, I know I've been much too free with her while she grew up. If you're thinking she ran off to get married, I doubt it. She's always said she wants a big wedding and the two of us to give her away."

"And the police?"

"She's a legal adult. She can do what she wants. Obviously I don't want to compromise the company if she's just running around."

You mean social image. "But?"

"She's the most precious thing I have. She means everything to me. We need to find her and bring her home. We need to know she's all right."

"Do you think she's been kidnapped?"

"We don't know. We've had no contact or demands. God knows I'd give 'em the company to get her back."

"Of course I'll help. You know how close Nikki and I are."

"Yes, I do. There is another consideration. As you know I'm in a very sensitive business."

Santiago's eyes followed Stewart as he entered the bedroom. "Are you talking about the possibility of industrial espionage?"

"It's a consideration. We do some sensitive work for the government and we are developing new products for the consumer market that some of our competition would give anything to have first."

"I'll help in any way to find Lindsey."

"I know and I wouldn't expect you to get mixed up in company business. I've talked with some people. You can take a personal leave if you choose, no questions asked. I'll pay all of the expenses of course."

Money talks. "Will you put Nikki back on?"

"I'm here. Please, please help us!"

"I'll be there by tomorrow, but first I have to talk with my boss."

Stewart left the room and returned carrying his cell phone. He watched Santiago, a look of concern on his face.

Nikki said, "Oh God, thank you! You've always been like my sister. I just didn't know who else to turn to."

"I'll be there Nikki, but remember, I'm a cop. Some things I can't do outside of my jurisdiction."

"I know but just you being here will mean so much. Your direction and advice are worth their weight in gold. We're terrified. I feel so empty, helpless, even alone."

Braun came back on the line. "I'll do whatever is needed. Call us after you talk with Captain James. I'll arrange everything."

You know James? "I'll call ASAP."

"Thank you," he said. "And Mitch, let me give you Nikki's cell number. We want to keep the house line as free as possible just in case."

After the call she glanced up to see Stewart watching. He said, "I'll check the ferry schedule. We should be able to catch one around noon into Edmonds."

"Chance, I'm sorry about this. I have to help."

"Not a problem. I can see you and Nikki are close."

"She's like a sister. When some students were trashing my reputation at the U she stood up for me. It seems like yesterday. A few of them were bent out of shape because I worked as a dancer on the Sea-Tac Strip. Not only did Nikki support me, she went to work at the same place."

"Now that's a friend, but the cops down there aren't going to like you working their turf. You know how we feel when someone comes in."

"I know, but I won't be doing police work."

"So you say, but I know you. You'll do whatever it takes to help your friend. I'd do the same thing."

She said, "God, I hate leaving like this."

"At least you won't need to pack many clothes. It's warm in Phoenix and getting hotter."

"You wouldn't want to come along, would you?"

"I'd go anywhere with you in a heartbeat, but my kids are coming in next week for a few days, their yearly visit."

"You'll be here with them for another week?"

He nodded. "James gave me the extra week because of the kids. I forgot to tell you. They're only here for a few days."

"They'll enjoy the ocean," she said.

"Maybe after they leave I can fly down."

She took a deep breath and stepped to the closet. "I'd better get ready."

Stewart said, "I'll phone ahead and see if James is available."

Moments later Santiago emerged, suitcase in hand. "I'm ready. Is James in?"

"Yes. He's expecting you."

"I thought he might be after what Claude said."

"Mitch, I'm sorry. I should've told you about the kids."

What else should you tell me? "We'll talk about it later. I have to get going. Nikki needs me."

The drive to Kingston was long and quiet. From the moment they left Kalaloch until they arrived at the ferry terminal, Santiago was on her cell phone or lost in thought. Waiting in the loading lanes Stewart asked about Nikki.

"When did you last see your friend?"

"Nikki? It's been a couple of years. Not since the wedding. I was her bridesmaid."

"Her husband's got a daughter who's twenty?"

"From his first marriage," she said.

"How old is he?"

"Fifties."

"That's a gap."

She laughed. "He likes 'em young."

"Is Nikki as good lookin' as you?"

"Better. She's an easy 10."

He stretched his legs. "Well, the attraction is understandable. What happened to the first wife?"

"She died several years ago. Nikki said Lelani was the love of his life, her and Lindsey. Not much seemed to matter to him after she was gone."

"Until your friend came along."

She shook her head. "No, actually he remarried the first time a couple of years after his first wife died. He needed an escort. You know, business, appearances, a trophy."

"But they split?"

"She was pushing thirty and he met Nikki."

"A new playmate?"

"Yes, but Lindsey and Nikki have really grown close. Maybe it's the small age difference, sort'a like my sister Jill and me."

"But?"

"Now Nikki's pushing thirty. That's old in Claude's world of women."

"Sounds like a strange man."

He's not the only one. "Nikki says he's reserved."

"Is she happy?"

"Far as I know she loves him deeply."

"You were in college together all four years?"

"At the U of W. We were looking at law or business, something to make our fortunes. She met Claude at a seminar. He gave a talk about the impact of high tech on the future of business."

"And she earned her degree in husband?"

"Something like that."

"He sounds wealthy."

"He is. Owns a company called DataFlex. Develops software for the consumer and does government work. When we talk, Nikki and I seldom mention his business."

"I've heard of the company. So you two just talk girl stuff, huh?"

"Whenever we get the opportunity, which is not often."

"But she knew she could depend on you."

Santiago was quiet for a moment, staring. *Where are you Lindsey? What would I do if Jill disappeared?*

He said, "Penny for your thoughts."

"If it is a kidnapping the first twenty-four hours are crucial. It's been three days."

"True, but they've had no word. They don't know Lindsey's been kidnapped. You're worrying and you haven't even left yet."

"I know, but how would you react if it was one of your kids?"

"The same way. I'd fear something bad has happened but pray for the best."

"Well, that's what Nikki and Claude feel."

"And what are you feeling?"

She shook her head. "Tense. Nikki's the closest friend I've ever had. Want to walk the deck when we board? I need some air."

"Sure. I hope Nikki knows how lucky she is to have a friend like you."

"She'd do the same for me."

"You'll find her. I just wish I could help you."

She looked out the window at the other cars in the holding lanes. Her eyes were moist. "We do what we do... what we must."

A flagman waved them aboard.

* * *

T.J. looked around. "This is a cabin? High ceilings, four bedrooms, big kitchen, office, a living room, and all overshadowed by the Superstitions. I could live well in a place like this. How big is it?"

Lindsey Braun smirked. "Dad once said it was about thirty-five hundred square feet of living space. He's more into stats than me. We're on ten acres of desert foothills here."

"What does home look like?"

"MOS, just bigger," she said.

"This place is kind'a isolated out here on the Apache Trail. Is home as isolated?"

"No. It's just gated off from the world."

T.J. looked out the living room window. "I love the colors of the desert. More green than I expected."

"You're just like most of my friends from other parts of the country. They seem to think it's all sand dunes. Too many movies from the Imperial Desert."

"Will your dad's people be looking here?"

"I'm sure Dad's already had someone from the security office check the place out after the first day just to see if I was doing a social thing."

"Have you in the past?"

"Sure, that's why we stayed at your place the first two nights and you kept going to work. Now they don't have a clue where to look. This will be over before they think of looking here again."

"Right, only a couple of days you said."

"Four, maybe five."

He hefted two small suitcases. "Which room?"

"Last door on the right is my room."

He moved toward the hallway. "Nice place. A guy could get comfortable here in a hurry."

Lindsey made coffee and was at the kitchen table when T.J. returned. "So you like it here?"

"Oh yeah."

She ran a finger around the handle of the cup. "Where did you grow up? I thought you said Washington. Isn't the eastern half desert country?"

"Yes, but I was raised on the west side in Sequim. That's on the Washington peninsula, inside 101. It was a sleepy farming community, the only place around that needed irrigation. Now it's become a retirement center with wall-to-wall RV's."

"Sounds small and crowded."

"It is, and not much of an attraction. Most of the kids growing up there can't wait to leave."

"Why?"

"Who wants to be in the service side of the tourist-retirement industry? If you wanna make money, Sequim isn't the place for a young person."

"So you did what?"

"Graduated and went to Seattle. Then up and down the coast. Now I'm workin' my way through school. Between business and high tech there's money to be made."

"You want to be wealthy?"

He looked around the cabin. "Doesn't everybody? Rich works for me, but I'd settle for comfortable if this is it."

Lindsey shrugged. "I guess most people want to be comfortable or rich, but there's something to be said for having a family too."

"You've got both."

"Not really. I don't even have any close friends, the kind that would risk it all to help in a crisis except for you, and we've known each other for what, three weeks?"

"Something like that. Man, I gotta say it. Your old man's idea of a cabin is something else."

"He likes his creature comforts."

"Creature, hell. This is nicer and bigger than the house I grew up in."

"He calls it his Lost Dutchman getaway."

"He ever go looking for the mine?"

"No."

He smiled. "This place sure redefines roughin' it. I like your bedroom, too, a master suite."

"So do I as long as you're sharing it with me."

His face reddened. "It has been nice, hasn't it?"

"Yes."

"You know," he said, "it's been three days already. Don't you think it's about time to give Dad a call?"

"Close. He's had long enough to know I'm not just running around."

"How do you mean close?"

"We'll call tomorrow. Even in my wildest moments I always called him. He's always treated me like an adult from the time I was fifteen, even when I just wanted to be a kid."

"He let you do anything?"

"Anything. I had money, cars, even birth control. He personally took me to our doctor so I could get started. He told me the day would come when I would give in to temptation, and it did."

"And he wanted you prepared... smart man."

"He didn't want me pregnant, especially by a man he didn't approve of. Bad for the company image and the future of the family."

"Free rein—now that's something teens dream about."

"It's harder to live with than you think. You're on your own almost all the time. At first it's kind'a cool, but it doesn't take long to realize you're just out of their way. Half the clubs in Scottsdale either thought I was over twenty-one or just didn't ask. Money talks."

"What about boyfriends? It had to be a rush for them."

"My boyfriends, if that's what you could call them, were all older guys, in their twenties, whatever. God, some were even married."

"Married?"

She nodded. "I remember the first married guy I was with. It was exciting to me, like I was a real woman. I felt so mature. Later, I just felt used."

"How'd you meet them? I mean, you were in high school, right?"

She nodded. "Private, of course. I met most of my dates at the country club. You know—the pool, the workout room, social events, Dad's business parties."

"But you were just a kid."

"I always looked older. I liked men wanting me. I suppose Dad just saw it all as business. I was his chip off the old block or something."

"That's living in the fast lane."

"It was probably child abuse but when you're the daughter of Claude Braun, CEO of DataFlex, the rules are different and the gold diggers are on the prowl. They find you."

T.J. laughed. "Until you started ASU."

"True, but even then a couple came out of the woodwork. Most college guys are different. They're on the prowl but it's a testosterone thing, wannabe stud muffins. By the time I started school I wanted my own friends, people to like me for me, not for Dad's money. I'd bet half the kids I hang out with don't even know who my dad is, much less care."

"You're probably right. So how did we end up here in the middle of the desert playin' house and terrorizing your old man? I mean, the first time I saw you was in Las Vegas. It was bright lights, tons of people, gondolas, Dad and Mom."

"Yep, the Club Rio."

"And that skin-tight black leather jumpsuit. God, I couldn't take my eyes off you."

"I noticed. You said you'd been on a trip to the coast and I was just hangin' out."

"But you were meeting your dad and mom later for dinner and a show."

"Yeah, he was doing a presentation for some investors and wanted the family image."

"Good image... sexy image in the jumpsuit. I'm still surprised at how young your mom looks."

"You mean Nikki? She's not Mom. She's wife number three in Dad's trophy collection."

"How old is she?"

"Twenty-eight."

"And he's—"

"Fifty-two. After my mother died he did the escort thing for business purposes, and maybe a little servicing. Then he decided it would look better if he had a wife. The first trophy was Donna."

"Another young hottie?"

"She was the ultimate eye candy. Probably a good roll in the hay bimbo. She was probably a whole lot like I am today. That's pathetic, isn't it?"

He ignored her question. "Where'd she go?"

"He always said out to pasture. She got too old for him."

"Just like that?"

"He never loved her. His only love has always been my mom. When she died it was like something inside of him died."

"How old were you when that happened?"

Lindsey was quiet for a moment and looked out the living room window. "Ten."

"And then came the trophy collection?"

"Yeah, but Nikki is more than a trophy. I mean, she started out like Donna, but she's much more now. She and Dad were together even before Donna was out of the picture. They got married about six months after the divorce."

"Sounds like a soap opera starring your hormonally disabled dad."

"At first I didn't like her either, but over the last couple of years she's really become my second mom. She loves both of us. She's not some money grubbing cock crazy bitch."

T.J. laughed. "Don't hesitate to be completely candid. Seriously, what's the problem now? Why this stunt?"

"Dad's shopping for a new trophy. I want to bring him and Nikki closer and maybe make him realize we really are a family."

"So here we are while you play counselor-matchmaker for your dad."

"For a few days. If it works I'll be forever grateful."

"And if it doesn't?"

She looked at the bedroom and wet her lips with the tip of her tongue. "Even if it doesn't work out the way I'd like, at least I got his attention."

"Mine too. We could get in a lot of trouble."

"Not a chance."

"You said you're demanding a million dollars ransom?"

"Yeah, in hundreds," she said. "Nice size, not too bulky."

"A million bucks? And he'll pay it?"

"Without a doubt. Of course I'll give it back when this is over."

"Of course," he said. *A cool million... man what could I do with that kind of money.*

"And don't forget, Love, you get five thousand for your efforts... in addition to other perks."

"A tidy sum and the perks are great. It'll cover most of my expenses for next semester. Won't he object?"

"Once he realizes what this is all about he'll be pleased with what I've done. He's always said, 'Lindsey, we have to believe in ourselves first.'"

"A million dollars is a lot of money."

"Not to him."

"Well, we'll see how this plays out."

"You know, it's so good to have a friend that'll help make a difference."

"Friend? I thought we were lovers?"

"You know what I mean. I'm not ready to settle down yet and neither are you."

"No, I suppose not." He was quiet for a moment and watched her. *I could sure put a million bucks to good use.* "You're right about not getting in trouble. He wouldn't prosecute his own daughter."

"Don't worry, T.J. At least two things will come out of this: one, he'll want to keep the whole thing quiet and out of the papers, and two, he'll have me talking to my letch shrink. I just hope he and Nikki become a couple again. Then I'll be happy."

"So the urgency is Dad shopping around."

She looked across the table, sat up straight and arched her back. "I think one of my girlfriends is coming on to him. Like I said, he likes 'em young. Nikki is a mother-sister to me. I need his attention now, not later. They're my family."

* * *

Ray House was alone in the Security Director's office at DataFlex Corporate Center in Chandler, Arizona. He watched the screen centered on the credenza behind a large oak desk, viewing documents of various security operations currently in progress by associates within the division. A red flasher lit up the private line beside the mouse pad. He checked the caller ID, then answered the phone. "Hello Claude."

"Ray, I want you to send Sam Evans to Seattle. Have him meet Michelle Santiago at the plane.

Arrange first-class seating for them so they have privacy while they talk"

"Sam knows how to handle a conversation. He'll keep it private."

"Use U. S. Airways. They have a couple of flights out of Seattle in the late afternoon and early evening."

House brought up the file labeled *Lindsey Braun – NEED TO KNOW ONLY*. "Will do, and having Evans brief her before she arrives may yield some insight into what is so far a blank page. Maybe she'll find something we can use."

"I hope so," Braun said.

"Me too. Sam's been over the data with a fine-tooth comb and we still have nothing of substance."

"I know," Braun said, "but Santiago is a pro trained in crime, not industrial espionage. Just make sure she has everything she needs... everything."

"Of course."

"And make sure only you and Evans know why she's really here."

House said, "I've already got her in the system as a new associate brought in for a special assignment, just as we do with all new employees during probation."

"Good."

"Claude, we've worked together for twenty years. Looking at this operation, doesn't it seem like something is out of sync? Industrial or criminal, we should've heard something by now."

"I've thought the same thing. Far as I know, kidnappers usually move quickly to their demands. On the other hand, if it's related to business we could be dealing with representatives of a foreign corporation or even terrorists."

"Maybe someone is moving her out of the country first," House said.

"Lord only knows at this point, but you're right, something is strange. Last night Nikki and I were afraid she'd been in an accident and hurt, and nobody knows who she is. I just keep second guessing myself."

"It's frightening, I know, but we'll find her. We'll get her back."

"I'm terrified for only the second time in my life. I'm not sure I could handle the loss of Lindsey. I haven't done well with the loss of her mother."

"You did the best you could."

Braun's voice began to crack. "Looking back at it, I haven't been a very good dad either."

"Don't beat yourself up, Claude."

"I know. I just want her home, alive and healthy. Get Evans to Seattle. He'll work well with Santiago, certainly better than most of our crew would."

"How so?"

"Sam's middle-aged, married, faithful to his wife and loyal."

"All of our operatives are professional and loyal. They're—"

"And single. You haven't met Santiago. She's Nikki's best friend and I'd still like to be a tattoo hidden on her somewhere."

"A hottie?"

"A smart, sassy, beautiful woman. Christ, I'm so down even that doesn't get my interest. Find Lindsey, Ray. Bring her home."

* * * * * *

Santiago arrived at Captain James' fifth-floor glass-cage office five minutes ahead of the appointed time. He glanced up from his cluttered desk and muttered, "Damn, you're good looking. I hope Stewart knows how lucky he is."

Santiago stopped at the desk of Tina Satin, his secretary, to wait.

James stood and gestured for her to come in. When she opened the door, he said, "You're a few minutes early, Mitch."

"It's that kind of a day. New suit isn't it?"

James' face reddened. "Yes."

"I bet Tina likes it," she said. "Thanks for taking the time to see me. I know it's crowding you, especially when I'm on vacation."

He waved a hand. "Taking the time, me taking the time? My God, the governor calls the mayor, the mayor calls the chief. Who am I to stand in the way? Here in this office we only solve local murders."

"I didn't know about Claude's contacts either."

He sat down and folded his hands on the desktop. "I didn't know you were so well connected."

She ignored the sarcasm and took a seat. "Captain, I need your help."

"Sorry for the agitation, Mitch. You said this morning you wanted to take a personal leave. Apparently people in high places want you to have it too. What's going on?"

"A very close friend has a daughter missing."

"Have the authorities been notified?"

"No. Her father, Claude Braun, is a software designer and manufacturer. He wants no involvement from the authorities... at least not yet."

"Has she been kidnapped? Any messages, contact, anything?"

"Not so far. She could just be off running around. Lindsey is a rich little girl who lives in the fast lane according to her parents."

"How old is this little rich girl?"

"Twenty."

"Well, she's free to do what she wants."

"They know that, but they're still worried, scared something may have happened to her. Disappearing isn't her style."

"And her parents want you to find her?"

"Exactly. As I said, Nikki and I are really close. We were at the U Dub together."

"She has a twenty year old daughter?"

"Nikki's a stepmother, actually... Lindsey's second stepmother."

A smile crossed James face. "You can't go off conducting an investigation in another jurisdiction just because your friend's twenty year old daughter is having a fling."

"I know."

He pushed some papers around the desk and pulled out a folder. "Then tell them no. However, what you do on your own time is up to you. I have a request from the mayor's office—no, make that a command—for you to be given an unpaid personal leave if you ask."

"Apparently Claude knows many influential people."

"My chief agreed. The ball is in your court, Mitch."

"I want the leave. I told Nikki I'd help."

"Is Braun involved in government work?"

"Some. Why do you ask?"

He opened the folder. "Because I was also directed to complete some documents for a government security clearance. It's none of my business. Tell me to back off, but this leave sounds more like a front for a clandestine operation than helping a friend."

"I'm only going to help find Lindsey. I hadn't thought about government involvement."

"Ever hear of the Hughes Tool Company?"

"A little, when I was a kid."

"It was a big outfit. They did all sorts of top-secret, hush-hush work for the CIA, the military, and who knows who else. Those were the tabloid stories. Your situation looks similar. A wealthy manufacturer in top-secret work, a daughter that just drops out of sight and no ransom demands. Maybe she's on a fling—let's hope so—but maybe she's being held prisoner and the perps are biding their time."

Santiago nodded. "Or maybe she's been in an accident. Perhaps she's in a hospital and not identified. You've been watching too many spy movies, Captain."

"Good point, but local police could handle it better than you."

"Braun's company has its own security. I'm sure they're already working on Lindsey's disappearance since locals will delay for at least 72 hours."

"So why not have them or the authorities handle it and leave you out? I think it's something else."

"I know they don't want to compromise the family or the company. We both know how hard it is to conduct an inquiry with the press breathing down your neck. In his business it would be magnified tenfold, to say nothing of what the media could access because of the Freedom of Information Act."

"Perhaps," he said. "Mitch, you're one of the best detectives I've ever worked with. I just don't want to see you get in over your head."

"I know and I appreciate the concern. I'm only going to help my friend find her daughter. The government forms you mentioned are news to me. Perhaps I need a clearance to work in the security office at DataFlex."

"Just remember you're a Seattle Police officer first. Don't compromise yourself or us. We need you here."

"They need me too. I've committed to help them."

"Even if it costs you your shield?"

"It won't, but Nikki is like a sister. She's family."

"Mitch, after your last case you talked about leaving the force. This isn't just a way out, is it?"

"No, this is personal."

"Well, as I said when you came in, the leave is approved."

"Captain, is there any way I can do some investigative work in Arizona and remain within the guidelines?"

"Possibly, but without local involvement?"

"Yes."

"If your friend's husband has enough clout, get him to contact the U.S. Marshal for the region. Marshals can deputize any citizen to work on special assignments. As I recall, it can be outside the boundaries of local law enforcement. If I'm right you could be deputized, but keep in mind the Marshal's office would need to know what you're doing, and it would be public record."

"I may call the Federal Building in Phoenix tomorrow after I talk with Nikki and Claude. Thanks for the suggestion."

"Does Chance know you're taking leave?"

"Yes. He was with me when Nikki called. He's outside now, waiting. He's taking me to Sea-Tac when we're done here. I was already packed for our vacation on the coast."

"Phoenix is much warmer."

"I only expect to be gone a few days. I'll get whatever I need after I get there."

"You sound very focused. When's your flight?"

"U. S. Airways has two non-stops this evening. I'll try to get on the early one, but I had to arrange the leave first. Truth be known, I'd bet Claude already has me booked on both flights."

He looked at the young woman and smiled. "You were going either way."

"Yes."

"I just hope your loyalty isn't misguided."

"It's not. I have a feeling you'd do the same thing in my place."

"I know, I just hope the kid is out running around and okay."

"Me too."

The captain pointed at his phone. "You can call the airline from here."

"Thanks, but you're busy. I'll use one out there."

James got up and walked around the desk. "I don't like it, Mitch, but you do what you have to do."

A light knock on the glass door interrupted them. James looked up and nodded. His secretary sauntered in, walked past them and placed some papers on the desk. "Don't forget we have a late lunch at 2:15."

James smiled. "Not a chance."

Santiago's gaze followed the woman out the door. "Her skirt's a little longer isn't it?"

He laughed. "Yes. After you and Chance mentioned Tina and me meeting in the parking garage while negotiating your vacations we thought maybe she should tone it down a little."

They both laughed.

Santiago said, "Some things never change. If you've got it, flaunt it."

"Take care of yourself, Kid."

"I'll be home in a few days."

"I hope you're right. See you then."

She walked through the homicide division office to rejoin Stewart. "Government security clearance," she mumbled. "What have I gotten myself into?"

* * *

T.J. and Lindsey snuggled on the couch. "This plan of yours sure seems weird. I mean if your dad is so open, why not just tell him how you feel?"

"He doesn't think that way. It's like we're all totally 'independent units'—his words—and although we're a family in appearance, we function as separate entities."

"And you think this caper will change his point of view?"

"I know it'll make him move forward in the long-term grieving process."

"Grieving?"

"Sure. He's never gotten over my mom's death. To him other women are basically sex objects and show pieces. Like I said before, something to hang around with."

"And how does he see you?"

"An extension of himself. He knows every guy that looks at me is thinking about taking me to bed. That builds his ego."

"How do you like his attitude?"

Lindsey shrugged. "People are attracted to each other initially by something whether it's looks or behavior or whatever. I like men looking at me, wanting me. You said it yourself the first time we met at the Rio. It wasn't my mind or personality that drew your attention. It was the package: a babe in a tight leather jumpsuit. Your brain was between your legs."

"I guess you're right about that, but the attraction was mutual as I recall."

"Absolutely. Women are the same as men. I'm very physical, at least in the beginning. Guys are into tits and ass, and women do butts and brawn."

"Ah, so you check guys' butts."

"I like 'em firm and slim. A healthy bulge isn't a bad thing either. Bellies hangin' over belts are a real turnoff. You got my attention."

"I guess we all start somewhere."

"Dad always said body language speaks reams."

"So we're two physical animals in the desert trying to climb Maslow's hierarchy."

She pressed against his side and ran a fingertip around his cheek. "We're rising to the occasion."

They kissed. He said, "Rising yes, climbing the hierarchy I'm not so sure about."

She said, "How 'bout some background music while we climb the mountain?"

He reached over to the end table and turned on the radio. "The last few days have been bacchanalian if nothing else."

The radio blared to life. "Sheriff's office announced a hiker found the nude body of a woman some three hundred feet off Highway 87 near Rye south of Payson early this morning. Public Information Officer Dietrich Young said the young woman appeared to be in her late teens to early twenties. The body was rolled in a carpet. No other details are available at this time. The death is being treated as a homicide. On the national scene...."

T.J. switched off the news. "That's creepy—dead bodies in the desert."

"Bodies always get dumped out here. It's been happening for years. The big irrigation canals are another favorite spot."

He stretched out on the couch again. "Well, I guess there's less chance of being caught out here."

"For sure. Once a lady in Phoenix was observed dumping the torso of her husband in a trash bin. Nobody would've seen her out here. Bitch got caught. Duh."

"Well," he said, "we didn't need music anyway."

She laughed and looked at him with a coy smile. "Prudes would say I have the morals of an alley cat."

"Then both of us do."

"I think I'm normal and free to do what I want."

"The lady is a philosopher."

"The difference is people like us do what we feel. We don't bury our feelings and try to be something we're not."

He stroked the tight fabric of her jeans, caressing her inner thighs. "Well Babe, let's not talk this to death. You do look good in men's jeans."

She turned and kissed him, teasing his neck with the tip of her tongue. She unbuttoned his shirt, pulled it open and dragged the tip of her finger across his stomach. "I'm going to make you quiver and sweat."

"I feel it. This couch is awkward."

"Let's go down the hall."

He stood slowly. "Oh yeah."

She slipped out of her tube top.

A million dollar babe. His gaze rested on her full breasts and tanned torso. "You are so sexy."

They walked down the hall toward the bedroom, hand in hand, touching and kissing.

"Think I'll call Dad too. Let's make the call from bed," she said.

"Nice touch, Babe."

* * *

After leaving James' office Santiago made a reservation arranging a shuttle ride to the airport over Stewart's objections. She arrived at Sea-Tac two hours before the 5:30 p.m. flight. The driver dropped her off at the passenger loading area of the main terminal. She moved through security and rode the underground Satellite Train to Concourse B. The Phoenix flight gate had not yet opened but a fast food restaurant in the area was inviting.

She watched a young family a few tables away. *Will I ever have a family of my own? Will it be with Chance? I'd marry you today if you asked. Do you love me? Maybe it's just as well Nikki called. I need to think things through on my own.*

Finishing an early dinner of green salad and a diet soda she walked past the family toward the gate. The little girl smiled and waved, revealing the gap of a missing front tooth. Santiago waved back. The mother pulled the little girl back into her seat. The father seemed more taken with Santiago's tube top and Calvin Kleins than with his wife's reaction.

As Santiago approached the U. S. Airways gate counter a middle-aged woman asked, "May I help you?"

"Yes, I have a reservation for the 5:30 flight to Phoenix, Michelle Santiago. When I called they said I could check in at the gate."

The woman viewed the scanner screen. "Do you have some picture identification, Miss Santiago?"

She took out her driver's license. "Yes, of course."

"You've been upgraded to first class, Miss Santiago."

"I knew it. Claude is already at work."

"Beg your pardon, Ma'am?"

"Nothing... just talking to myself."

The clerk handed over a boarding pass. "Has anyone asked you to carry anything on board?"

"No."

"Have you left your luggage unattended?"

"No."

"Have a good flight."

"Thank you."

She took her pass and joined the others waiting. A few minutes later she boarded and took a first class seat next to a window. A stocky man in his forties took the seat next to her.

"Miss Santiago? I'm Sam Evans."

"Hello. Have we met?"

He showed her a company identification card. "No. I'm a DataFlex security associate. Mr. Braun sent me to brief you on your way in."

"He doesn't waste any time."

"They're very worried."

The flight attendant announced preparations for departure. A moment later she asked whether either of them would like something to drink.

Santiago looked past Sam. "Do you have Chardonnay?"

"Of course," the flight attendant said. "And for the gentleman?"

He smiled and looked at Santiago. "Diet soda. We can't drink on the job, you know. Company policy."

The plane backed away from the jetport and soon was rumbling down the tarmac. Another young flight attendant stood in the front of the first class seats and reviewed safety procedures while demonstrating the proper use of seat belts, facemasks, floatation devices, and the location of emergency exits. Santiago watched through the window as the satellite disappeared and the expanse of Sea-Tac rolled past. Traffic was light and the plane turned onto the runway without coming to a complete stop.

She said, "It's always a rush to be pressed into the seat. I love the powerful thrust of engines hurtling me into a new adventure."

"You fly often?"

"No, that's probably why I like the takeoff so much." She continued to watch out the window. *Goodbye, Chance.*

Evans reached into a coat pocket. "I have a list of Miss Braun's friends. It's not complete by any means but includes most of the individuals she has socialized with recently."

"Are you always this formal, Mr. Evans?"

"Mr. Braun views formality as part of professionalism, Miss Santiago."

"Please, call me Mitch."

"Of course."

She took the list. "Now Sam, let's have a look. Are these friends at ASU?"

Evans did not look at the list in her hand. "Not necessarily. Sierra Paradise has been a close friend of Miss Braun since high school."

"I'll want to talk with her immediately. Girls have a way of sharing things with each other."

"Then there's Mario Spears. He dated Lindsey a few times until about three weeks ago."

"What happened then?"

"He went to work for DataFlex."

"We'll talk," she said.

"T.J. Johnson is a part-time student Lindsey originally met in Las Vegas, also a few weeks ago while on a working weekend with her parents."

"Do they date?"

"Not really. They hang out with a group. Good friends."

"And Cliff Arnold?"

"A bouncer at the Bramble Bush."

"the Bramble Bush is...?"

"swallowed. "A gentlemen's club."

"In other words a strip joint."

Sam's face turned red. "Yes."

"Doctor Rich?"

"Her psychiatrist."

"Psychiatrist?"

"Miss Braun, Lindsey has been in therapy off and on since her mother died. She was quite young at the time."

"Yes, I know the history."

She pointed at the last name on the list. "Doug Straight?"

"A born-again Christian."

"Student?"

"No. His mission is to save humanity."

"Have they dated?"

"No. He hangs in her circle of friends."

"Are any of these friends from wealthy families?"

"Sierra's folks are wealthy by average standards, but certainly not by Mr. Braun's."

She laughed. "If Claude is the standard I doubt any of us are beyond poverty."

Evans joined in for a moment, then regained his composure.

"Well, Sam, it's an interesting group except for Sierra. Does Lindsey have any other girlfriends?"

"Just casual. She has many casual friends."

"It would be nice to know who they are, something about them."

"Of course. We have a list at the office."

"Why didn't you bring it?"

"Let me caution you, Miss Santiago... Mitch. Some of the names on that list are very prominent. Mr. Braun is a cautious man."

"He wants to find his daughter. He didn't sound very cautious this morning,"

"He does want to find her, but some of those people are married men. You know what I mean."

"No, I don't know what you mean. I'm coming to Phoenix to find Claude's daughter, the stepdaughter of my best friend. She's a legal adult, has a wild streak, and is rich and spoiled. Don't give me this crap about special people."

"Miss Santiago, Mr. Braun is prominent in the community. He doesn't want to stir up trouble where it's not needed."

"Claude mentioned sensitive areas but he referred to government work. What you're saying is that I should look for Lindsey quietly."

Evans said, "Be discreet."

"Discreet... does Claude know you're telling me this?"

"He sent me."

The attendant returned to their seating area and reached across Evans' lap. "Ma'am, your Chardonnay."

"Thank you," Santiago said.

"Your diet soda, Sir. If you need anything else before I return, please buzz me. We're taking the drink cart out in a few moments."

Santiago looked at the man beside her and sipped the wine. "How long have you worked for Claude?"

"Mr. Braun hired me four years ago. I'd been involved with security work in the government but wanted to work in the private sector. It pays much better. I have two kids to put through college."

"Does your wife work?"

"No. She did but it's no longer necessary since I went to work for DataFlex."

"How long have you been married?"

"Twenty-three years this July."

"That's like a record now days."

"Thank you. Have you ever been married, Miss Santiago? I mean Mitch?"

She laughed. "No, I'm the eternal bridesmaid."

"I would think a woman of your age and profession would meet many eligible men."

"I have, but most are not interested in long-term relationships, especially marriage. I'm in a tough business. Mr. Right? I'm not sure I've found him yet. Sometimes I think I have, sometimes I'm not so positive."

"Mitch, I've been assigned to work with you on this project."

"I thought that might be the case since you're doing the briefing."

"All of the resources of DataFlex are at your disposal."

Is this guy a company man? "And that means?"

"The DataFlex security office can access anything police agencies can access. We also have extensive contacts in the private sector and in government."

There's that word again. "You sound like a privately run CIA."

He chuckled. "In some respects not a bad comparison, Miss... Mitch."

"And using all of those resources, have you found any clues as to Lindsey's whereabouts?"

"Not a one. That's why you were called in."

"Her credit cards haven't been used, her friends haven't seen her, and nobody has called regarding her disappearance. How long has it been?"

He pointed at the list on Santiago's lap. "Three days. We've also had surveillance teams keeping track of the persons listed here. So far, nothing."

"Even Doctor Rich?"

"Yes. And he has an open-door policy where Lindsey is concerned."

"And in the past she has always contacted home when she's off doing her thing?"

"Always."

"I assume she has a car. Has it been observed or found abandoned?"

"No."

"Something just doesn't seem right. Sam, if this is an industrial situation, like espionage, would a three day gap be normal?"

"That depends. A few hours would be more like it, the threat being implied. In the States we concern ourselves more with the threat than with actual hostage situations. However, overseas kidnapping is common in some areas. In Columbia it's a major business."

She said, "And this situation with Lindsey, does it appear to be related to business?"

"We're developing some software for the government that will be quite invasive. It's designed to monitor communications primarily in terrorist nations. If one of those countries has snatched her, they may be moving her out of the States before initiating their demands."

"So this situation with Lindsey could be related to DataFlex?"

"I didn't say that, but anything is possible."

She looked at the list again. "Great leverage. Any of these names attached to activist groups?"

"Only the last name, Doug Straight. Like you said, this kidnapping has a strange feel to it. I just can't put my finger on it yet."

"I know what you mean. I appreciate you coming out and briefing me on the way back."

"I'm looking forward to working with you. Mr. Braun and Ray House say you're one of the best."

"Thank you. Earlier you mentioned Nikki would be meeting me at the airport?"

"Yes. She plans on you staying at their house."

"But the cover is I'm coming here to look into the possibility of future employment, right?"

"Not exactly. Inside the company you're listed on the security data bank as a new operative on temporary or probationary assignment. That's a common status for new staff. Mr. House—Ray—has also arranged for you to have a private investigator's license issued to you via the company. We're appropriately licensed to do so. Your administrator in Seattle completed the necessary forms for us. To the outside world you're a friend of the family visiting and looking into a new employment opportunity."

"Doesn't that sound strange, inconsistent?"

"Not really. At DataFlex new operatives spend time in a probationary status while assigned initial tasks. They become regular staff members following completion of their entry period if they are successful. For this operation we need you in this status to provide you with proper credentials and cover."

"Good plan," she said. "We want to be consistent with company procedure. Tell me, does Claude have any connections with the U. S. Marshall's office?"

"DataFlex is connected to everything. Why do you ask?"

"I was playing with the idea of getting deputized so I won't break any laws or offend the local police authorities too much."

"You'll be legal. DataFlex will see to that. As for the locals, don't worry about it. They're not involved and they won't be."

"Tell me, Sam, are you a 9 to 5 guy or do you often work open hours around the clock?"

"I have a regular shift. Why?"

"Often during investigations I work all hours of the night and day. I think you may find working with me an eye opener when you compare the private sector to standard investigative work."

"I did security work for the government. I know the routine."

The flight attendant approached. "Could I get you folks anything else? Perhaps a refill?"

Santiago looked at the young woman. "That would be nice."

Evans said, "I think I'll have a bourbon and water."

The attendant said with a smile, "Off duty?"

A broad grin creased his face. He looked at Santiago, then leaned toward her. "New partner, new way of doing things."

Santiago said, "And we shall succeed."

The drinks arrived and they touched glasses. Santiago said, "To partners, if only for a few days."

"May I ask a personal question?"

"Sure."

"Why is your nickname is Mitch, a male name?"

"My dad wanted a son. He was a big fan of Mitch Ryder. The name has stuck since childhood."

"I like it," he said.

* * * * * * *

T.J. held a pre-paid cell phone and snuggled up to Lindsey on her king size bed. Their heads were bent toward the tiny speaker as Braun's phone rang.

Braun answered the house phone immediately. "Yes?"

"You've been waiting on my call. I have Lindsey."

"Is she all right?"

"For now, old man."

"I want to speak with her."

"In a moment."

"Please."

"First things first. To get her home will cost one million dollars in used hundreds, no cops."

"Of course, whatever you want. Just don't hurt my daughter. Please, let me speak to her."

T.J. laughed as Lindsey kissed his thigh. Sounding like a television host, he said, "Here's Lindsey."

"Dad? You and Mom help me. Please do as he says... as they say."

"We will. Are you all right?"

"Yes, so far. I'm just scared."

"We'll get you home, Honey."

"No police, Dad. He's serious."

"I know. Only Nikki, Aunt Mitch and I know what's going on."

T.J. came back on the line. "What about the security guys at DataFlex?"

"They've been looking for Lindsey because I thought she was on one of her adventures," Braun said. "We haven't called the police because we didn't want to embarrass her or the family."

"Good. Get the money together and send the security guys back to the office."

"Yes, yes... anything you say. Just please don't hurt Lindsey."

"I'll call again tomorrow with instructions." T.J. broke the connection, looked at his bedmate and grinned.

She said, "You were great, very convincing."

"So far so good. Who is Aunt Mitch?"

Lindsey slammed the phone onto the nightstand. "Shit. She's Nikki's best friend, and she's a cop."

An eerie stillness came over the room. T.J. looked at Lindsey. "I said no cops."

"Apparently Dad called her when I came up missing. Don't worry. It won't change anything."

"You're sure?"

She climbed off the bed. "Yes. I'm going to take a shower. Where's my bathrobe?"

T.J.'s excitement of a moment earlier turned flaccid. "This could be serious. I need a beer. I don't like this."

As she walked into the bathroom, she said, "You'll have to go get some. We finished off the brew last night."

He watched the door close, then called after her, "You don't need a robe. You're beautiful."

The door reopened. "You know, Dad bringing Mitch into this means he's taking it seriously. Go get the brew and we'll talk when you get back."

The door closed.

* * *

Braun looked at his wife, his eyes welling as he gulped air. "She's all right for now."

Nikki said, "Thank God."

His hands and left leg shook. "I need to sit down." He collapsed on the stuffed chair next to the end table in the living room and began wiping his eyes.

"Did you record the conversation? I'm sure Mitch will want to hear it."

"Yes." He shifted his weight, bent toward a small recorder and pressed a switch. "Listen. I want her back so badly, I'll do anything."

"I know. We both will. We'd better take the tape out and save it. Do we have others?"

He pointed at the entertainment center. "A box full. I should be using digital."

"You have the conversation," she said. "That's all that counts right now."

Braun reached for the phone. "I have to call Neal Burke and arrange for the money."

Nikki said, "Better use your cell just in case they call back. We need to get in the habit of leaving the phone alone until this is over."

"Yes, although I doubt we'll hear from them again until tomorrow. You heard the tape."

"Just a precaution, Claude."

He fumbled with his belt, feeling for his cell phone. "Christ, I'm shaking like a leaf. Will you dial Burke's office?"

"Sure," she said, taking the phone. "While you talk I'll fix you a drink. I think you could use one."

"Thank you." He took the phone back. "Thank you."

She patted his shoulder. "We both could."

He crossed his legs and drummed his fingers while the phone rang. "What's taking so long?"

A secretary answered on the fourth ring. "Mr. Burke's office. May I help you?"

"Put me through to Neal. Tell him it's Claude."

The phone clicked and the cheerful vice president of accounting came on the line. "Mr. Braun, how are you today?"

"Tired, tense, impatient. I need one million dollars in cash by tomorrow at 2:00 p.m."

"That's a lot of money."

"I want it in hundreds, and it has to be used bills."

"That will be difficult in so little time, Mr. Braun."

"Send people out. If it's not in Phoenix go somewhere else, anywhere."

Burke dropped the professional demeanor Braun habitually insisted on. "What's wrong, Claude?"

There was a pause, and then Braun said, "Nothing, just get the money. Bring it to the house. Bring it personally."

"What do I tell the staff?"

"Nothing. This is personal. Take it out of my account."

"How do you want it packaged?"

"I don't care. No, wait—put it in a duffle bag."

"This is very unusual."

"It's an unusual day, Neal." He swallowed a sip of bourbon and water Nikki had set on the table next to the chair. "We've been friends and associates for years. Nobody is to know about this. Someday maybe I can tell you, but not now."

"I'll get right on it. The money will be there by 2:00 even if I have to send people to half the banks on the coast."

"Thank you, Neal. You have no idea what this means to me."

After Braun broke the connection Nikki stood behind him and gently massaged the back of his neck. "You're more than tense. Finish the drink and try to relax in the hot tub. Sam called while I was in the kitchen and said they'd be in at 8:35."

"Not on the house phone?" he said.

She came around the chair and looked into his tired face. "No, on my cell... yours was busy. Get some rest if you don't use the spa. I'm driving into Sky Harbor to meet them."

"Will Mitch be staying here?"

"Yes."

He closed his eyes for a moment and took a deep breath. "Good. We'll get through this. We'll get Lindsey back."

* * *

Rosie's Bar and Grill is located on the Apache Highway heading east toward Tortilla Flat just a few miles past Goldfield. The building is a small structure, wind worn and sun bleached, its asphalt parking lot punctuated with chuckholes and worn white lines. T.J. climbed out of the air conditioned pickup and looked around. He walked past the few cars and a motorcycle and pushed open the weather-beaten wood door. The door slammed behind him. "Rosie, how you doin' in this den of iniquity? Man, it feels like a blast furnace out there."

"Yeah, but it's nice in here, T.J. Good to see you," the female behind the bar said in a harsh smoker's voice.

T.J. turned and scanned the room as his eyes adjusted. "Well, look who's here. Diego, George, it's been a long time since we worked the summer labor market and post office as holiday casuals together."

George waved. "T.J., join us."

"I'd love to. Man it's hot out there."

Diego said. "For sure. We're just relaxin' and talkin' about some of the strange things our women do."

T.J. chuckled, walked past a man at the bar and sat down. "You guys aren't alone."

Rosie brought another pitcher and a chilled glass. "It's like old times, boys."

"Thank you," T.J. said.

George filled T.J.'s glass. "Diego was sayin' his girlfriend dresses him when they go out. She doesn't like his taste in clothes. Don't think I'd let my woman get away with that."

Diego checked the door as it opened again. "Hey, it's Mario. Amigo, join us."

Mario joined his friends. "Man, I haven't seen you guys since last year."

As Rosie brought another glass, George said, "We know. You've gone big bucks now that you've graduated and forgotten your old friends. It's good to see you, man."

They shook hands all around.

George returned to the topic at hand. "You know, my girlfriend won't stay in the same motel room with me overnight. It's like we get two rooms, not even adjoining. Then we spend the night making love in my room. Early in the morning she goes back to her room, messes the bed, takes a shower, and checks out. She says that's proper."

Mario laughed. "That's strange, man. The last babe I dated was like hot to trot for two weeks. Then I met her dad, got a job in his company. I'm thinking this is cool, right? I'm on the inside track. Wrong! She was gone as fast as she came. So much for bangin' the boss's daughter. But I still have the job."

George said, "Maybe she figured you for a gold digger."

"Well, if so she was on the money. But man, she was a babe."

Diego laughed. "There's more fish in the sea."

Mario nodded. "Many more, and I have a better job than planting palm trees in the middle of summer."

Mario placed a twenty on the table. "Rosie, another pitcher, please.

T.J. was feeling a buzz from two brews on an empty stomach. The idea of Lindsey sitting in the cabin waiting for him brought a smile to his face. "You guys have nothing weird compared to my girlfriend."

"How so?" George said.

"She wants to punish her dad or some crazy thing, so she's hidin' out for a few days. Thinks it'll bring her parents closer together."

Diego belched and topped off everyone's glass. "It could work."

"We'll see," T.J. said, "but it seems an odd way to get attention."

Mario said, "Parents miss their kids unless they're like the one I mentioned. They'd probably be glad if she took a vacation. All she did was spend, spend, spend. Did anything she wanted."

T.J. said, "My girl cares a lot about her folks and it's not even her real mom."

Mario said, "Lucky parents."

T.J. finished his brew, stood and reached for his wallet. "Man, I gotta get outta here. A couple of more and I'll be completely shitfaced."

Mario said, "It's all on me, guys. You're still working to cover tuition and stuff. I have a good job at DataFlex."

T.J glanced at around the table. *DataFlex....*

Mario said, "So where's your girlfriend hiding?"

"A cabin in the Superstitions."

Mario looked around the table. "My last babe would'a gone to something in Scottsdale or Palm Springs or out on the coast that's really nice and spendy." They all laughed again.

Diego said, "And Daddy would pay?"

"Always. She could do no wrong in her dad's eyes. Sky's the limit."

"Well guys," T.J. said, "I'm outta here. It was fun seeing you, but I just came in to get a cold case and go back to the cabin and my little kidnapping victim." He turned and left after stopping at the bar.

George said to Mario, "I like the sound of your last chic."

The man at the bar finished his drink. He followed T.J. out the door.

* * *

Nikki Braun waited at Sky Harbor's Terminal 4, periodically walking over to the departure/arrival monitors, checking the screens. Flight 37, Gate A28 was on time. Twice friends she didn't see until they spoke greeted her. She paced back and forth in front of the passenger exit gate next to the security checkpoint. *I'm in a building full of people and I feel isolated. Come on Mitch.* She reached into her purse for a package of cigarettes. *I'd kill for a smoke. Damn public buildings.*

An announcement came over the PA system. "Flight 37 from Seattle in now arriving at Gate A28." Ten minutes later Michelle Santiago walked through the exit gate with Sam Evans.

"Mitch!" Nikki shouted from the waiting area. They hugged. "You look great. Thanks for coming."

The two friends hugged again and stepped away from the exit. "Of course I'd come. You're family." She looked around. "Is Claude here?"

"He's trying to regroup. The stress is a killer."

Santiago said, "Have you heard anything yet?"

Nikki's face turned ashen, her eyes dull. "Yes, a call came about an hour ago. She's been kidnapped."

Santiago glanced at Sam Evans, then said, "Have you called the FBI?"

"Not yet," Nikki said.

Santiago shook her head. "What are the demands?"

"A million dollars, tomorrow in used hundreds."

Santiago said, "Then it's past time to call the FBI."

Nikki said, "We need to talk with Claude first."

"Mrs. Braun," interrupted Evans, "I'll be out to the house shortly, but first I have to go to the office. There are some additional files Miss Santiago wants to review right away."

"That's fine, Mr. Evans," Nikki said. "We're going to freshen up first and then head for the house."

Santiago smiled. "I see you're the ever-on-top-of-it fashion plate, as always. The flight has left me a bit rumpled, but thanks for the upgrade. First class sure beats steerage." They laughed.

"We wanted you comfortable and undisturbed while Sam briefed you. Let's get your baggage."

She glanced at her carry-on. "This is it, but I'd love a cup of coffee. You do remember it's the lifeblood of Seattle, right?"

"Oh yes, and as I recall you're a double mocha with skim milk."

"You never cease to amaze."

They began walking. "Don't I wish, but truth be known you got me hooked on those too. Stephan's Café is just down the corridor."

Nikki put a cigarette in her mouth, looked around, then pulled it out and threw it in the trash. She looked at Santiago. "God, I'm as nervous as Claude is. I'm sure Mr. Evans filled you in on the other concerns about calling the authorities."

"Yes, but prominent names and family image don't count right now."

"I agree. So does Claude. He's much more concerned about national security and some new program his company has developed."

"Sam mentioned foreign governments on the plane but this sounds pretty straight up as a kidnapping from what you've said."

"I hope you're right in some ways," Nikki said as travelers rushed past them on their way to various gates. "We'll talk with Claude first. He's calling the shots. It's his daughter, by blood I mean."

Santiago looked at her friend. *We have laws dealing with kidnaps.* "This could be way out of my league."

"Claude doesn't think so. He talked with your Captain James. He says you're the best."

Santiago's face got red. "He didn't mention talking directly with Claude. It's warm in here, isn't it?"

"You and James have something going?"

"No. He's my boss. I've only been in homicide for two years, so I'm a rookie by his standards. His thing is a sexy secretary."

"Apparently you've had two really good years."

"Only because of my partner, Chance Stewart. He's a pro."

"Maybe we'll bring him down."

"I don't think so." *But a pleasant thought.*

"Don't rule it out, Mitch. Claude usually gets what he wants."

"The privilege of wealth?"

"Something like that."

They approached the café. Nikki gestured toward an empty table facing the corridor. "Let's sit over there."

A waiter came up, took their orders and disappeared, but not before giving the two women a careful once over.

Santiago said, "He reminds me of the old days. I don't think he ever made eye contact."

Nikki laughed. "Definitely a tit man. He sure has a nice butt."

"True. So tell me, how did you and Claude ever become permanent, anyway? I know about the seminar workshop, but obviously a lot happened afterward, and you didn't share much at the wedding as I recall."

"After graduation he invited me to Phoenix. It was pretty much a pronto thing and you were at the academy. He talked about the possibility of working for the company and maybe a little something more. Lord knows I didn't want to interview for jobs in Seattle and encounter someone who had been a client on the strip."

"Tell me about it. I just had a pair of detectives harassing me about our old part-time job. One of 'em even sent an old photo of the club's entry featuring a poster of us in the background."

"So what happened?"

"I talked with James. He already knew my employment history. He thought at the time I was brought onto the force it would make me a better cop, more understanding, empathetic of some of the people we deal with on both sides of the law. Besides, I'd broken no laws and I've never been charged with anything."

"And your partner?"

"Same thing. He thought it helped with my work in vice, an assignment I drew after a brief time on the streets. But hey, enough of this changing the subject. There has to be more about you and Claude."

"Well, he obviously brought me to Phoenix for something. I went to an interview setup through personnel in the legal department. Nobody at DataFlex knew about Claude and me. Anyway, when I went in I looked good but the interviewer was a middle-aged woman. The long and short of it was no job. As I left the office Claude found me and asked how it went."

"I told him it was no go. He introduced me the vice president in charge of marketing while we walked down the hall, telling him I was a friend of his from Seattle."

"Uh huh, and the fellow just knew what Claude was talking about didn't he?"

"To be sure. Anyway, the marketing VP, while never resting his eyes, said he thought I should be in sales and to come see him. I went to his interview the next day."

"And you already knew you had the job."

"Something like that. I mean, let's face it, I was sleeping with the boss." They laughed. "Claude sat in on the interview, which I think was to just see if I could get along with the VP because I had the job as his assistant when I left."

"So who was this man who fronted for you and Claude?"

"Marion Harris. He's no longer with the company. He was killed by a red light runner in Phoenix shortly after I went to work for him. Very sad. He had been one of the original founders of the company. Most are still with DataFlex although a few have retired."

"And the rest is history," Santiago said.

"Well, yes. Claude always laughed about the interview because I was wearing a business-like micro-mini at his suggestion."

"Sounds like an oxymoron to me."

"Whatever. I got the job and the boss."

"But he was still married, right?"

"Yes, to a woman he didn't love. She was eye candy, a trophy. I knew about her in Seattle when Claude and I became friends. Why the interest?"

"Because somebody has kidnapped your daughter, Claude's daughter. Could she be in it for revenge?"

"Not likely. Claude had a prenuptial with her. She got a million dollars cash, a nice house, and more when they split. She's set for life."

"So you two started seeing each other in Seattle?"

"Yes, you already know that. When I came down here we sort of picked up where we left off. He said it was over between him and Donna, that it had been over between them before we ever met in Seattle. Mitch, there's no way I'm a home wrecker."

"I know."

"He fell in love with me."

"You or your body. This sounds like a soap opera."

Tears formed in Nikki's eyes. "He and Donna got an amicable divorce and here I am praying to God we all survive a parent's worst nightmare."

"How did Donna feel about Lindsey?"

"It's my understanding she didn't like being a mother to a fifteen year old going on twenty-five."

"And Claude's view of Lindsey?"

"He thinks she's perfect, always has."

"And you?"

"She's a kid with everything you could give her, but rootless. She has no goals, direction or responsibility."

"How do you and Lindsey get along?"

"You're beginning to sound like a cop."

"And you can tell a Zebra by its stripes. I'm thinking about age difference right now. You two are only about eight years apart."

"Yes, and when I first came into the family we probably revolted each other, a kind of competition for Claude's attention. But within a few months we were very close. Lindsey loved to get me talking about my college experiences, dating, and especially our working at the Mr. Tease Cabaret."

"And Claude?"

She leaned back in the chair and looked Santiago directly in the eyes. "He was very pleased we hit it off, but I won't kid myself. Claude has a wandering eye. Even Lindsey told me he used to give the help days off when she and her girlfriends wanted to have a pool party so they could sunbathe in the nude. We both think her dad was home more than once, even if they didn't know for sure."

Santiago's face showed deep lines as she squinted across the table at her friend. *A pedophile?*

"It's not what you're thinking. Claude loves beautiful women. He's always loved them. It's not even a midlife crisis thing."

"How old is he?"

"Fifty-two."

"Twenty-three years your senior. That's a good chunk of time."

Nikki shrugged. "I've always been attracted to older men."

"I remember only too well. I danced the tables for ten spots; you were always pulling twenties, and sometimes a fifty."

Nikki sighed and smiled. "I've always looked at it as young for studs, old for rich."

Santiago laughed. "God, here comes the old LBJ line."

In unison they said, "I've been rich and I've been poor. Rich is better."

Several patrons were looking in their direction. Nikki said, "It's good to laugh if only for a moment."

"It is. Now I think it's time to head out."

"Good idea. I'll leave Nice Butt a Lincoln."

"You must like what you see."

"Young, firm and working. What more can we ask for?"

In the parking garage they approached a new jet black Mustang. "It's a good thing I travel light."

"I know. I thought about that after getting here. I kicked myself for not bringing the Caddie or the Lincoln."

"Well, the Mustang fits the image I have of you."

"Personally, I like my Corvette but I knew we wouldn't have any room in it. Claude said you could use this one if you like while you're here. You'll need a car anyway."

"Oh, I like it all right. Every visitor should have a Saleen on loan."

* * *

It was crowded and noisy. Even in the early evening the smell of bacon and eggs permeated Jake's Eloy Truck-O-Rama, a restaurant diesel gas shower overnight stop for big riggers. A plate hit the floor back in the kitchen but the crash didn't faze the patrons, consisting mostly of men in boots, jeans and t-shirts. A few tourists were mixed into the crowd, definite outsiders in gaudy shorts, brand-emblazoned polo shirts and pure white canvas shoes.

Yancey Quarterman looked at the entrance just as Lisa Fargo strolled through the door and smiled. "I like a woman who can saunter. You may be forty-eight but you look fine."

He nudged Chuck, the man on the stool next him. "You ever notice the way Lisa eases into a room with those 38s jigglin' and her hips swayin'?"

Chuck was already looking in Lisa's direction. "Oh yeah, she's a woman. She's jump-started more'n a few guys."

Quarterman nodded. "I know what you mean."

Chuck said, "It only takes twenty bucks; then it's pleasure supreme."

"Indeed. More women should take care of themselves like her. She's got a few lines around her eyes but she sure looks better'n some of those twenty year old skinnies."

"Yup," Chuck said. "Watch her tits. The AC's gonna get her. It always does. See how they stand-up? She is all woman."

Chuck sipped his coffee, then reached down and rubbed the front of his pants.

"Quit playin' with yourself."

"Hell, I bet half the guys in here are doin' the same thing, Yancey... even some of the tourists."

Lisa approached the two men and leaned over Quarterman, her full breasts rubbing the back of his shoulders. "You boys see anything you like?"

"Oh hell yes," Chuck said, "but isn't it a little early to be peddlin' your goods?"

In a husky voice, she said, "You know me big guy. If a man's ready, I'm ready. Right now I'm a cup of java short of a good time." She gestured toward the empty seat on Quarterman's right. "This taken?"

He said, "Is now."

She slid onto the swivel stool while rubbing against Quarteman's thigh, then blew him a kiss. "Your pants getting a little tight, Honey?"

He said, "Only so you'd notice."

She leaned back and kissed his earlobe, then reached under the counter and stroked his thigh. "How 'bout when you're done we go outside? I have a surprise for you that'll put you in orbit."

Quarterman looked at her and grinned. "You know I love surprises."

"I know. Now think of the slowest most enjoyable pleasure you can come up with. What I have in mind is better."

A young waitress approached the threesome. "Evening Lisa. The usual?"

"Not tonight. I want breakfast; waffles with whipped cream and peaches."

Chuck said, "God woman, how do you keep the weight off?"

"Exercise honey. You should know that by now."

The young waitress grinned. "Is that what you call it these days?"

Lisa looked at her. "You ought to try it, Kid. Sure beats $2.13 an hour plus tips."

The young woman's face turned crimson. "I'm not ready for that."

"Well Vicki, look around. I've slept with half the guys in this room and not one has ever complained. And keep in mind it's tax free."

Vicki walked away shaking her head. Lisa, Chuck and Quarterman laughed.

Chuck said, "And Lisa, who's the best?"

"Yancey. I do him for free."

Chuck stood and tossed a $2.00 tip on the counter for Vikki. "That's more information than I really want to know. Gotta get goin' or I'll never make Nogales on time. You two have a great night."

Quarterman said, "Will do."

Chuck waved as he walked out. Quarterman looked at Lisa. "Maybe I should charge you. Let's go outside."

She said, "On second thought, let's go to a booth. The surprise revolves around money but I need food."

They moved to a corner booth and Quarterman scanned the room. "Is this private enough?"

She looked directly into his eyes. "It'll do. There's so much noise in here no one can hear us anyway. I heard on the radio they found the dancer."

"Yeah, I heard."

She smiled. "That was fun."

"Y'know, Cuz, some folks would think we're just a little off center."

"But they don't know what a true thrill is. I loved the shocked look she put on when I came in naked and joined you two."

Quarterman nodded. "Shocked, yeah, but she sure picked up on the action in a hurry,"

"She was willing, to say the least. I think she'd been there before, Yancey."

He said, "Yeah, but she won't go there again."

Vicki delivered Lisa's breakfast and refilled Quarterman's cup. "Need anything else?"

Lisa said, "No, unless you'd like to cavort with us."

"Not hardly." Vikki turned and walked off.

He said, "Man, you're a bold bitch."

"Maybe, but a little young stuff in the mix is fun. I saw you watching her hips sway just now. And you sure didn't complain about some young stuff when you first came back from Columbia."

"I'm not complaining now."

"And Yancey, careful on that 'Cuz' stuff. Remember what you said about identity."

"Good point and it's only by adoption anyway. So what's this hot surprise?"

"I heard about a guy in Tucson that deals in porno films."

"A lot of people sell porn."

"But his are special."

"Like bondage and stuff? I'm not into porn movies. I like doin', not watchin.'"

"Me too, but he's buyin'. I thought we might try makin' a flick."

"You're kiddin' I hope?"

"Not just a porn flick, Yancey... a snuff pic. Look at the fun we had with the dancer."

"Her name was Trinity," he said.

She wet her teeth and lips with the tip of her tongue. "Okay, Trinity. Do you know how much a film of that would be worth? A chick getting iced during her climax?"

"Do you know how dangerous something like that would be?"

"Others have done it, the ultimate thrill flick."

"I heard 'bout one out in the 70s. Don't know if it actually existed, the real thing I mean. And look at the other side of the coin. We had fun doin' Trinity and there's no video record to use against us. Hell, I figure someday they'll catch up with me. It's really only a matter of time before somebody finally realizes I'm alive and back."

"You're right. I just wasn't thinking. No big deal. It was just something I heard about, the chance to make a score. You said it yourself last year when you looked me up. If they find you they'll kill you."

He smiled. "You got it, and there's no point rushin' it. My compulsion will get me soon enough if they have any brains. Money I have, and a lot more coming."

She looked around the room. "Maybe you do, but I don't. And you should drop the finger thing too."

"Can't. It's my signature, like an artist. It goes all the way back to 'Nam. Sometimes I'm just curious how long it will take 'em to make the connection. Or maybe they've guessed but don't want to admit it. My resurfacing could be a big embarrassment to the Feds. Who knows, maybe they really are dumber than stumps."

"And you're smarter?"

"It's a game, Lisa. It was a game in 'Nam, Cambodia, Laos, Afghanistan, Columbia, wherever. The MIA spook is alive and well. They're just too blind to see it. Now I'll play my last game, and then it's just time to retire." He rubbed his eyes. "I want more out of life than a few thrills and a Harley."

"You're not talkin' about another thrill kill are you?"

"Maybe, when the money part is over. I haven't decided yet."

"Money? How much?"

He looked around and lowered his voice. "A lot more than you ever imagined. Yesterday, dumb luck being what it is, I was at a bar near Apache Junction.

This guy is goin' on about his girlfriend faking her own kidnapping. Why she did it isn't important, but the old man is loaded. I followed the guy to a mansion in the middle of the foothills, the Broken Spur Ranch. Sure 'nough, he's got this babe ditched out there."

"Who is she?"

He leaned back in the booth. "Well, the new Camaro in the carport is registered to Claude Braun."

"Who's Claude Braun?"

"Shit, Lisa, you've got to know. He's a multi-billionaire in Chandler. He owns DataFlex."

"And you think the little honey is his daughter?"

"Yeah. Why not take over her action and get the big bucks? It'd be a snap."

"Will you kill them?"

"Maybe. I don't know. I see this as business, not fun and thrills. The money we get from this added to what I've already got will give us a lifestyle for the rest of your life that you've only dreamed about. We'll get the big money and head for Mexico. Just think of all the young studs you could nail then."

"You're nuts, Yancey. They'll get you for sure."

"Maybe, but life's a game. I've been playin' the dark side for thirty years. They haven't come close yet. Remember when I was on leave before goin' the 'Nam and you told me about that guy who raped you? Your folks didn't seem to care and did nothing. Well, that's where the game began for me."

She said, "It's also the first time we ever had sex. You killed him and I loved you for it."

His eyes glazed as if he were looking into a distant space shared by no other. "*We* killed him. Then I went to Asia. That's where killing became an art form. That's why I had to have a signature, something that told others who did it. Almost all of the spooks had a signature of some sort. We drove Charlie nuts. I loved it."

Lisa watched her cousin without saying a word.

Quarterman's breath was short and sweat covered his brow. "I didn't want to stop, never have. Maybe now?"

Vicki walked over to the booth holding a pot. "More coffee?"

He took a napkin and wiped his brow. "No... no thank you. It's gettin' warm in here."

"Yancey's just havin' a hot flash, Honey."

They all laughed. Vicki left after dropping the bill on the tabletop.

Lisa said, "Do you realize we're social rejects? The incest, murders, thrill kills—who'd believe it?"

He looked around the restaurant. "It's in the genes, Lisa. We live by our own rules, just you and me. They're the degenerates. They haven't got the stones to do what they want, take what they need."

Lisa nodded. "Y'know, we could make some good money on that porn flick."

"We'll make huge money on the kidnapping. Then I think retirement sounds good. I've always wondered what it'd be like to have my own bar or study art, maybe both."

"A change would be nice, but what about getting caught?"

"They haven't picked up on me yet. I like the idea of this being my closer. Besides, it's easy to get a new identity in Mexico."

"So you think this will be our swan song?"

"For now. Old habits die hard, but we're gonna have a ton of money. We'll be the other half of society down there... the upper half."

She laughed. "Our point of view will be different."

"Absolutely. Listen, I want you to go to Chandler for the next few days, rent a room at one of the motels on Chandler Boulevard or Arizona Avenue and let me know where you're stayin'. I may need some help on this caper. When we're done we just disappear."

"Where will you be?"

"Around. I'll be spending some time in the desert. I'm gonna ditch the bike when we're done here and take the pickup."

"We're gonna just walk away today and disappear?"

"You missing a day or two of work isn't news to Jake. Yeah, maybe we'll just disappear and never come back here. Who knows? We'll let it play out."

Lisa slid out of the booth and leaned toward his ear. "I best get to packin' a few things if I'm gonna be on the road. Yancey, I think we should kill' em when we're done."

"I know you do, but I just don't want a man with Braun's kind of wealth and influence tracking me for the rest of my years."

* * * * * * *

The drive from Sky Harbor was shorter than Santiago had anticipated. Nikki drove north on Squaw Peak Boulevard to Lincoln Drive, then west to Paradise Valley. Huge gated homes and estates appeared one after another. Nikki said with a chuckle, "Arizona's most exclusive neighborhood."

Santiago watched out the passenger window. "It's spectacular. I thought you lived in Chandler."

"No. That's where the DataFlex campus is located. Claude wanted to be a little out of the way and enjoy some privacy. Our home isn't much farther."

The five-acre Braun estate was surrounded by a six foot high adobe wall. Huge iron gates guarded the entry. Beyond the gates a lush oasis of palms and greenery was visible, the red tile roof of a large house appearing through the treetops.

"Well, there it is," Nikki said. "Home sweet home."

She flicked the remote. There was a quick flash, and then the gates opened and they passed through. A security man just inside the gate waved at Nikki.

"Home? This place is like a fortress."

"We have security on site, cameras and all that stuff. More now. I don't pretend to understand all the technology. Claude is in a sensitive business and we often have some high-level visitors, even foreign dignitaries."

"Did Lindsey have security people with her?"

"No. Outside of here we're just normal people. We're not high profile like celebrities. If you noticed coming in, several homes are gated. Privacy is the big thing."

The grounds around the house were well cared for desert landscaping centered around a small waterfall and manmade stream flowing among cactus, trees and rocks. A large circular drive two lanes wide came into view. It passed by the front door and a section veered off toward an eight-car garage. Nikki pulled into the building and shut off the engine.

"No point in parking in the sun like Ray."

"Ray?"

"Claude's security chief. That's his car sitting out there baking."

The women entered the house through an inside door and passed a laundry area, a bathroom and several closed doors. They came out in the kitchen. Braun entered from the hallway leading to the study.

He greeted Santiago with a hug. "Mitch, thank you for coming."

"I wouldn't have it any other way."

He turned toward the open study door. "Ray will get your bags."

"This is all I have. I came straight from the coast and caught the first plane out."

He said, "We appreciate that, and anything you need we'll take care of."

Nikki said, "Later, after we're settled I thought we'd go into town and get her a few things."

Santiago did not respond.

Braun and Santiago walked into the study. "Mitch, this is Ray House. He can bring you up to speed. Where's Sam?"

Nikki had followed them into the study. "He went by the office to get some additional files Mitch wanted to read."

"Good. It's been a trying day. Nikki, show Mitch to her room and give her a tour of the house. Then we'll go over what we know so far."

Santiago said, "Anything new on the phone call?"

House said, "No, not really."

Nikki led her guest through the kitchen and a large formal dining room to the front entry. They walked up a circular staircase to the second floor.

Santiago looked back at the main entry from midway up the stairs. "This would put a southern belle to shame."

House watched the women leave the kitchen. Looking at Braun he said, "I see what you meant. She is easy on the eyes. She could even tempt me."

Braun smiled. "She could tempt any man. I remember many years ago in Seattle. Nikki and I were seeing each other casually while I was doing some guest lectures. When I met Mitch for the first time I wanted to bed both of them." He shook his head slowly. "No way was it going to happen. That lady is one loyal friend. That was then, this is now. The circumstances are different but I'd still bet on the friendship."

House said, "It's always good to have a true friend. They're usually in short supply."

Braun looked around the study, his gaze stopping for a moment on Lelani's portrait. His face was ashen, his brow furrowed in deep, dark gashes. "I saw one of our tech trucks on the side of the garage."

House said, "Yesterday we installed recording equipment connected to the house phones. Our people will record every incoming call, with your permission."

"Of course. Did they catch the one earlier today?"

"Yes, an excellent recording."

"Good. All I have is a message tape. Can you trace a cell phone?"

"We can triangulate its signal for a location. However, if they're using a cell the chances are they'll keep moving around and it's probably a throwaway or stolen."

"Did you get a location on the call?"

"No. The special equipment wasn't in place at the time."

"We can't have lapses, Ray. This is too important."

House looked into his friend's face for just a moment but said nothing.

The two men went to the kitchen and Braun began to pace. "They'll call tomorrow with instructions. We're going to follow those instructions religiously."

Sam Evans walked into the kitchen. "It's tight here. You'd think they were trying to get the rest of the family."

House shot a look at Evans. "Don't be too lighthearted, Sam. This is deadly serious."

Braun walked to the slider opening onto the patio and pool area of the backyard. "Sam's right. We're guarding an empty henhouse. I hate waiting."

The women returned to the kitchen. Santiago said, "You have a beautiful home, Claude."

He snapped, "All for naught. Sorry, I'm just edgy, frustrated."

Santiago looked at Evans. "Are those the files?"

He handed them over. "Yes."

"Thank you, Sam."

She looked at Braun. "I don't mean to look a gift horse in the mouth but if I'm going to be in and out of the DataFlex compound for the next few days it would be best if I had a rental car."

Nikki said, "Why?"

Evans said, "I see her point. If the kidnapper is connected to DataFlex personnel it wouldn't take a rocket scientist to figure out the rookie's driving the boss's pride and joy Saleen."

Braun nodded. "Good point, Sam. Arrange a rental. We don't know who those bastards are."

Evans said, "What about housing?"

"Not necessarily a problem," Santiago said. The background check would indicate I'm a close friend of Nikki and have known Claude since his visit to Seattle several years ago."

House said, "It would seem appropriate then, to have her as a house guest at least temporarily. Officially Miss Santiago is—"

"Mitch... please call me Mitch."

House nodded in her direction. "Mitch is officially on six-month probation, the entry level status of all new security personnel."

"Sam told me on the plane."

"Good," Braun said. "Ray, I know you have some other business to take care of so you best be off but thank you for having the monitoring equipment installed. Does Sam have a list of the staff working the grounds and van?"

"Yes," House said.

Santiago listened and watched as the men talked, then waved the files. "I'm going to have a cup of coffee and look these over."

Nikki said, "Don't you want to freshen up first?"

I'm not here on a social visit. "I can do that after I read these. That way I'll have something to think about while I soak." She stopped at the doorway between the kitchen and main entry and looked back. "We'll find her. This evening I'd like to talk with you about Lindsey's friends, gain your ideas and views."

Braun said, "That will be fine. We'll talk whenever you're ready. Do you want Sam to come back?"

"No. We'll compare notes tomorrow morning at the office. Right, Sam?"

He nodded. "Looking forward to it."

"And you may have some new information too?"

"I told you on the plane we have the best connections going."

She said, "And we need to talk about bringing the FBI on board."

The three men looked at each other. Braun said, "We'll talk about that, but keep in mind what Sam mentioned on the plane. This could be a national security matter that requires the attention of the Agency. I have some other contacts I need to make first."

A quiet filled the kitchen for just a moment disturbed only by the drone of radio news in the background:

"Authorities announced this evening the identity of the woman whose body was found earlier on Highway 87 south of Payson as Trinity Durango, an exotic dancer at the Bramble Bush in Phoenix. Police continue to seek leads in the homicide. No further information is available at this time. Locally, the weather is...."

Santiago said, "Okay, we'll talk, but remember there are specific laws about kidnapping. Before I read these files I'd like to hear the recording of the phone call. Sam, want to show me where the van is located before you leave?"

He moved toward the door. "This way."

Nikki said, "Well, you're all so busy. I have a few things I need to get in town for Mitch so I'm going to run a few errands. I need some space."

* * *

T.J. popped the tab on a can of beer and took a long pull, looked at Lindsey with piercing eyes and softly said, "I don't think you sounded very convincing.

It was like telling your old man you were gonna be late. No urgency."

She sighed, picked up the open can, and sucked on the top. "He'll pay. He's worried sick. What's that sound?"

"Probably a rabbit. You sound bored."

"No... well, maybe. I'm working a plan to help my family come together. Critics I don't need."

"I know. I'm part of the plan too, remember? It's just I was thinking we gotta scare him a little. You know, bland is bland. God, you were literally laughing in the background. Not good for building fear."

"I want to get the little Miss Gold Digger out of his life. I'm number one, Nikki is number two and—"

"I thought Nikki already knew that."

"She does. She's my mom, part of the family, and my friend. Sierra Paradise, my best friend from high school, is the one who's pissing me off. We went through school together, double dated, everything. Now she's balling my dad and planning on being wife number four in his train of window-dressing trophies."

T.J. chuckled. "Ah, now the truth comes out. Your girlfriend is the motivation. Good luck on the kidnapping scheme, Kid."

"Yes, can you imagine me calling her Mom for the next five or ten years or until whenever he gets tired of her and finds a new toy? Hell, number five would end up a little sister at his rate."

"I only met Sierra once. I gotta admit calling her Mom never crossed my mind." He smirked, blue eyes sparkling. "Nope, Mom is not what came to mind."

"Men... your brains are between your legs."

"Well, I'm having a few other thoughts too. Not about the kidnapping, but about you. Your dark tan and almond eyes suggest a hint of Asian blood."

"My mom was part Hawaiian."

"So you're Hawaiian?"

"Not so you'd know. I'm watered down. Nothing very traceable."

Clearing his throat and looking around the kitchen he mumbled, "It's been hot today. I hope the AC holds together."

She laughed. "That's no sweat."

"So tell me about Aunt Mitch. You said she was a cop?"

"Yeah, and Nikki's best friend. I've only met her once. That was at the wedding. She lives in Seattle. If you think Nikki's hot you'll love Mitch. She is a babe. And as I recall she has some island blood too. We kidded about it while waiting for the bride and groom."

He dropped the empty beer can on the floor. "Yeah, so why do you suppose she's here? Not to find you?"

"Of course to find me. Dad and Nikki are bringing in help. They're not going just sit around. He'll do everything he can think of except call the cops. You already know his security's been looking for me."

"Yes, and that makes me nervous."

"Well, I didn't expect them to just sit on their butts. Would you?"

"No."

"Don't worry. Nothing has changed."

"What kind of cop is she?"

"Police!" she said. "How would I know?"

"Just curious, Babe. You know, traffic, drugs, vice, homicide?"

Lindsey ignored T.J. and looked toward the window. "The rabbit or whatever you heard earlier must be back. Did you hear it?"

"No, but I'll scare it away. God, we must be getting paranoid or something."

"Don't hurt it."

He crossed the room to the door, and opened it. "Jesus!"

He jumped back. Lindsey looked up and began to shake. A large man wearing fatigues and a black ski mask stepped into the cabin waving a .45 automatic.

In a harsh voice he said, "Sit and be quiet."

T.J. went back to the table and sat down. "What do you want?"

The pistol slammed into the side of his face and temple. He fell to the floor, unconscious, blood flowing from split flesh on his cheek. Lindsey sat stunned, silent, knees jumping, hands shaking.

The man in the mask watched Lindsey for a moment, his cold black eyes boring through her. "Like I said, don't say a word."

She nodded and placed her hands on the table. *Oh God, T. J.! Quit shaking. Who are you? What do you want?*

"Hands behind your head, Bitch."

She did as directed. He placed his weapon on the table and bound her with heavy gray tape, first around her torso to the chair, then each arm to the sides of the chair.

He grabbed her ankles. "Spread your feet." He bound each to a chair leg.

She kept watching him.

"You're a fine lookin' young woman. What's your name?"

Her lower lip trembled. "Lindsey."

"Well Lindsey Braun, it's nice to meet you."

"How did you know my name?"

The man shook his head. "You're talkin' without being asked." He slapped her face with the back of his hand.

Her eyes welled and her face turned crimson, the sting like a flame held to her flesh. He dragged T.J.'s limp form onto a chair and taped his hands behind him, then placed tape over T.J.'s mouth.

He looked at Lindsey. "Don't worry, pretty lady. Your boyfriend is alive. He's just a little messy."

He's bleeding and unconscious, you jerk.

He taped T.J.'s legs to the chair, then put his weapon in a leather holster connected to a web belt.

He went to the refrigerator and fetched a beer. When he sat down at the table he popped the tab, took a long swallow and wiped his mouth with the back of his hand. "Now, let's have a little chat."

He raised his right index finger and waved it in her face. "Whatever you do, don't—I repeat, don't—lie to me. I've been outside following the chatter and I was here earlier. Understand?"

She nodded.

"You can speak when I ask questions or give you permission, okay?"

She nodded again.

"Good."

* * *

At 10:00 p.m. Santiago walked out to the patio overlooking a large swimming pool and spa. Braun and Nikki were sitting on lounge chairs by a glass-topped round table. Braun was wearing off-white trunks and Nikki a florescent pink thong. "You guys look comfortable. This is nice, very nice. I've never been in a house with so many big screen TVs. It's like there's one in every room."

Nikki said, "They're Claude's addiction.

Santiago looked at Braun. You're a good looking man—trim, tanned and fit. More like a man in his thirties. No wonder women go for you."

Braun glanced at her, smiled and looked over the silver French bikini hugging her frame. "I like to keep up on the news. Join us. We can talk here if you don't mind."

Santiago was carrying a small notebook and a file folder. "Not at all. I've been reading over the notes about some of Lindsey's friends and I have some questions." She took a seat. "The evening air is really refreshing by the pool, even with the heat."

Nikki said, "The mister helps. Maybe later you'd like to take a dip and relax before calling it a night?"

Santiago said, "That or try the spa."

Nikki looked at the bikini she had picked up shopping earlier. "Does it fit, Mitch?"

"Like a glove, you can't tell? I'm surprised you remembered we wore the same size. I like the matching cover too."

Braun looked at her for a moment and smiled. "So where do we start?"

"Sam gave me background on some of her friends, the college crowd and Sierra. He didn't tell me anything about the group in this file."

Braun took a sip from a tumbler. "I know. I told him I'd handle these. They're much more sensitive. As I recall, you liked scotch water. Let me fix you a drink. Then we can get started."

Santiago watched Claude go to the bar. "Sam said you didn't allow drinking on the job."

"DataFlex doesn't, but this is way beyond work."

"Maybe, when we're done. A little stress reduction is good."

"Of course, fire away," he said and returned to his chair.

Nikki stood up. "I have to get something. You two start without me. Claude knows these people better than I do."

As she walked into the house Braun watched her every move and shook his head. "She's a beautiful woman, Mitch. I fear the stress of this is getting to her... to both of us."

"That's to be expected."

"Yes, I suppose so. Nikki knows about Lindsey's men, probably more than even I want to know, but she doesn't like to talk about them. The two of them have a very confidential, trusting relationship."

"Well, it's nice when the two main women in your life get along."

"Yes, although they're more like sisters than mother-daughter."

"Tell me about Doctor Rich. It says here he's been Lindsey's psychiatrist for close to ten years."

"Lindsey started seeing Greg just after her mother's passing. She was young, in an awkward stage of life, confused." His eyes welled as he spoke in a hushed voice. "It's hard at any age. Are your parents living?"

"Yes. In fact they're retired here in Arizona."

"That's got to be nice."

"It is. Please, tell me about Doctor Rich."

"They get together whenever she wants. They talk."

"How often?"

"It varies. During the past year they probably averaged twice a month. Accounting could tell you exactly."

"Does he report to you?"

He took another sip from the tumbler. "Good question and the answer is no. He did when she was younger. About five years ago he stopped the feedback. He didn't want to compromise the privacy of their relationship."

"Do you or Nikki see Doctor Rich professionally?"

"No. Nikki sees a counselor occasionally, an acquaintance she made through her charity work. She's a great advocate of having a confidant, someone she can talk to without having some 'friend' blabbing to a gossip columnist."

"And you go along with this?"

He took another sip. "Yes. Mitch, you know Nikki's my third wife. You know my background. I'm sure she's told you Lelani was the love of my life."

"Nikki loves you."

He was quiet for a moment and looked around. "Yes, and I love her in my own way. I'm a man of many appetites and interests. Often business keeps me away."

She pursed her lips, lines formed around her eyes. *So who are you screwing now?* "Let's get back to Doctor Rich."

"He's become a good friend of the family. He's forty-eight, married, has three children."

"How old are they?"

"Sixteen to twenty-three, all boys."

"And his clientele specialty?"

"Teens, young adults. Most are women. I have not a clue to who they are beyond Lindsey."

"How did you come to use his services?"

"Our family doctor referred him to me."

"Did you do a background check on him?"

"No. As I said, he came highly recommended."

Santiago made a notation. "Who is Eugene Paterno? The name seems familiar."

"The local hunk at the club. He's our resident tennis pro and stud service to the local trophies of limp partners. He tried the pro tour but wasn't good enough."

"And Lindsey dated him?"

"A few times. Mitch, let me be frank. Lindsey is a very liberated young woman. I don't judge her by any standards other than the ones I live by. I'm sure Nikki's shared our daughter's... how shall I say it... intimate friendships."

"Yes."

"She's really not unlike you, Nikki, or any other young woman today. I accept her behavior for what it is."

"We all have our baggage."

He sniffed and looked at the water immersed in light. "Can you smell the pool? The chlorine must be out of balance."

This has to be difficult for you but I'm not changing the subject. "I smell charcoal. Someone's having a late dinner."

"That too."

She looked Braun in the eyes. "You're right."

"About the chlorine?"

"About Lindsey. She's pretty much a normal active twenty year old woman in today's world, and rich."

"You know, it's not much different from what men have been doing throughout history."

"I know, including her dad as I recall."

"As I said, appetites."

"When did she have her fling with Paterno?"

"During her senior year."

"Was she eighteen at the time?"

He smiled and closed his eyes. "Not as I recall. I think she seduced him. A young woman can do that to a man."

"You went along with their affair?"

"Not really, but she's mature beyond her years. She knew what she was doing."

"Didn't you consider charging him with statutory rape?"

He crossed his legs. "And put my family through a public spectacle? Not a chance. She's been with several men, Mitch. You know that."

"Would Paterno try to extort money from you?"

"You mean mastermind this kidnapping? No way in hell. He's got a good thing going here and he knows it."

She wrote *local stud* in her notebook. "What about J. John Kenneth, III?"

Braun laughed and shook his head. "Our local Ivy Leaguer. He manufactures microchips in a small company. He's also the local playboy from a wealthy family and irresponsible as hell."

"Is he married?"

"No. At thirty he's still sowing his oats."

Not unlike you. "When did they date?"

"Last year. I think he wanted an inroad to DataFlex and thought Lindsey's bed was the highway to heaven and other riches. He didn't expect her to be wise to him."

"How so?"

He laughed. "Like many young suitors he talked to her about love and mergers in one sentence. Not all conversations should take place in bed. She dropped him."

"How did you find all this out?"

He laughed even louder and sat up. "She told me about it over breakfast the next morning. I remember seeing him a few days later at a corporate meeting. I told him Lindsey wasn't involved with the company."

"His reaction?"

"He said, 'So I've discovered.' I think he was taken aback that she could play as well as he could."

Santiago wrote a note about Kenneth wanting into the company. She stood. The chiffon cover opened, revealing her statuesque form, the silver French bikini barely covering her bottom, the triangles tight against her breasts. She pointed at the small refrigerator built into the patio bar and grill. "Is there a diet soda in there?"

He never took his eyes off her. "Of course. Help yourself."

She turned and walked to the bar. He rubbed the tight groin of his swim trunks.

When she returned and sat down, the cover hung casually over her frame. "It's a lot warmer than Seattle, but comfortable."

"Yes, it is."

Your daughter is missing and you can't take your eyes off my navel. This is bizarre. She pulled the top together. "You're staring, Claude. This isn't eight years ago."

"Sorry. I was just thinking how much you look like Lindsey, even with the difference in age."

Right, and I'm Mother Theresa. "Let's get back to her friends. Tell me about Harrison Rockford."

"Wealthy, married, about thirty-one. He had a short affair with Lindsey. I believe the attraction was mutual. He likes young beautiful women."

Again, like you. "And she was aware of him being married?"

"She liked him and knew he was married. Eventually, after a few months, she came to the conclusion he was going to stay married to the current Mrs. Rockford."

"How did Lindsey react?"

Braun emptied his tumbler. In a harsh whisper he said, "I think he used her. She saw quite a bit of Doctor Rich for the few months following the breakup."

"How did you feel?"

His nostrils flared. "Angry... very angry. I canceled all future business with his company."

"How did he react?"

"He didn't like it, of course. When I told him I didn't like my daughter being used he denied the relationship. He was more than a little shocked when I told him Lindsey had shared the affair with me after it was on the rocks."

"Did he make any threats?"

"No, no. When he realized I was privy to the affair he became more concerned his wife would find out. She's the money. He runs a family business but it's his father-in-law's company. The old man owns over fifty percent of the stock. No wife, no career."

"So you don't think Rockford would kidnap or threaten Lindsey?"

"Quite the opposite—I don't think he wants anything to do with us. She's young. She learned a hard lesson from him."

"Did he want anything from Lindsey?"

Braun stood and walked to the bar. "Nothing but sex. He's set for life if he doesn't get caught screwing around. Lindsey was just another notch on his jockstrap."

You're making your daughter out to be whore, or maybe the son you never had.

Braun laughed. "I don't think he liked the idea of being just another notch on her thong."

She wrote *possible revenge* in her notebook.

"I think that covers the list, Mitch. Now, how about that drink? I have some of the finest scotch available."

"Okay."

He poured a drink and handed it to her. She tasted the amber fluid and smiled. "You always could pour a good drink. This is excellent."

"It's Walker Blue."

"Blue? Never heard of it; Red and Black yes, but Blue?"

"Not too much in demand."

"Probably doesn't fit into the average man's wallet. It's very smooth."

"Yes it is, and it could fit your wallet, Mitch."

"What does that mean?"

"Walker Blue and many other advantages. All you have to do is come to work for DataFlex."

She chuckled. "What else?"

"Much as I would have liked more some years ago, nothing. I didn't get to where I am playing in my own backyard."

"And you love Nikki."

He raised his glass in a toast. "To Nikki and her best friend."

She made a note to check the background of Rich and Rockford. "Did you see the briefing notes Sam shared on the flight?"

"Of course."

"Any personal reflections you care to share?"

"I didn't like Cliff whoever," he said waving a hand. "Strictly blue collar."

"You didn't approve of Cliff Arnold?"

"I don't usually approve or disapprove of Lindsey's friends, but if she had gotten serious about him I would've checked him out. He just didn't fit into my perceptions of who I want in my family."

Bet it was fun growing up with your ego as a watchdog. "Did they date for long?"

"Only a few times. She saw the light and dropped him. Like I said, she's a young woman. She'll have many suitors before she settles down. Don't forget, there's a great deal of money involved. I'm sure you can appreciate my concern."

"And Mr. Arnold is just a bouncer."

"Exactly."

"When did they stop seeing each other?"

"Some time ago, probably a couple of months. Then there was T.J. We've heard about him but never met. I'm sure he's just another flash in the pan, more physical than study partner. God, I remember college like it was yesterday."

"What's his real name?"

"Sam has it. Here today and gone tomorrow."

"Do any of her boyfriends stand out in your mind?"

"Two. Doug Straight because he was so insulting, kept referring to our decadence."

"She dropped him?"

"He was a hanger-on with an attitude."

Santiago wrote *conflicting attitudes* in her notes.

"I don't think they were actually dating. He was one of those flaming liberals out to save humanity for God and all that rot. I asked her not to bring him around anymore. A man shouldn't be insulted in his own home, especially by riffraff."

Easy Claude, you're getting tense. "You said there were two?"

"Mario." He laughed. "Mario Spears, I liked. Bright, a geek, a good-looking kid, made his way up from the bottom. His dad is a construction worker. Mother was a Mexican immigrant. Apparently she came over as a little girl, probably an illegal. Anyway, Mario has character and a stiff backbone."

"You liked Mario?"

"Absolutely. He has grit."

"And Lindsey?"

"I'm not sure whether she's still seeing him, but we have him on file at the office."

"Sam said he works at DataFlex."

"He's a tech whiz kid. We recruit people like Mario. Once when he was visiting Lindsey I asked if he might be interested in working for me. He said he might, so I sent him an application."

"What was Lindsey's reaction?"

"To what?"

"Your interest in Mario."

"I didn't ask her. It was business."

"Has he been around lately to see Lindsey?"

"No, not since going to work for me."

"What does he do?"

"He's a program developer but he does many delicate jobs for Ray."

Delicate—what does that mean?

Braun tilted his head. "I'm sure I smell a touch of chlorine. The damn chemicals have to be out of balance."

Santiago ignored Claude's comment. "How's Mario doing at work?"

"Quite well."

Nikki returned to the patio. "Are you two still talking?"

Santiago glanced at her, then back to Braun. "Is Mario working in the same building where the security office is located?"

"Yes. You don't think he's involved in this, do you?"

"I'm suspicious by nature, Claude. Right now it's an open field. Anything is possible."

Braun glanced at the television and raised the volume as the reporter repeated an earlier news bulletin.

"Police announced this afternoon the woman found yesterday south of Payson near Highway 87 has been identified as Trinity Durango, an exotic dancer at the Bramble Bush. While no details were forthcoming, authorities have classified the case a homicide and are looking into similar crimes, one a thrill kill at Seaside, Oregon a few months ago."

Braun turned off the set. "Oh, Jesus... that's where Cliff Arnold works."

Day Two

At 2:05 a.m. Quarterman left the cabin, his prisoners taped and gagged in the kitchen. He drove several miles into Phoenix and called Braun using a pay phone. Five rings later, at 2:56, Braun answered.

"Hello," he said rousing himself from sleep.

"Braun?"

"Yes. Who is this?"

"Your daughter's keeper."

"I thought you were calling later today, this afternoon?"

"Plans change. The price is the same but a few details need attention. First, get the cop out of the house. Nothing happens while she's there."

"Cop?"

"Don't give me any shit. Aunt Michelle. You were told no cops."

"She's a friend of my wife. She's in town for a tryout at DataFlex. She's not involved."

Quarterman paused, then spoke in a harsh whisper. "Crap! Send your wife's friend to a hotel. You know I have to punish you for bringing her in."

"She's not—"

"I said don't shit me! Tomorrow... I mean later today... you'll receive a package. It'll show you how serious I am. I want the cop out of there in the morning."

"She'll be gone."

"Where will she be staying? I'll need to make sure."

"The Oasis Hotel and Golf Resort. All of my business guests stay there. Now, can I talk to Lindsey?"

"No. She's sleeping. You will tomorrow after the package arrives. Then we'll get down to instructions."

This is a different voice. "I'd really like to hear her voice."

"You will, later. All you have to remember for now is she's paying your freight."

"Please, she's just a child."

Quarterman waited for a moment as the sound of a motorcycle passed. He glanced across the street at a flashing neon sign. *Stray Cat Gentlemen's Club.* He nodded and smiled. "Not if you consider what she and her little playmate have been up to. Now, do as I say or it will get worse."

"Of course. Please, please don't hurt her."

"Should'a thought of that sooner." The connection broke.

Braun climbed out of bed and slipped on a bathrobe. Nikki, now awake, looked at him, her face ashen with deep lines in the shallow light from the nightstand. She took short breaths. "Was it him?"

"No, a different voice. I'm going down to the van."

He left the room as Nikki climbed out of bed.

The DataFlex operative was on the phone when Braun entered the security van. "We've got a fix at Van

Buren Street and 5th Avenue. Get there, now! It's a payphone."

Braun said, "He's in Phoenix using a pay phone?"

"Yes, but he'll probably be gone by the time we get our people on site."

"Damn! Why a pay phone?"

The technician said, "He probably doesn't have a safe cell phone. I'll call Mr. Evans."

"Good. Call Ray too. I'll get Mitch."

Braun turned to leave the van and ran into Santiago as she came in.

"Nikki told me the kidnapper just called."

Braun's eyes welled. "Yes. He's threatened to punish me for bringing you here. He said, quote, 'Lindsey will pay the freight.' He said we'll get a package later today. This is terrible."

Santiago said, "Oh God... anything else?"

"He wants you out of the house."

"Of course."

Braun looked at the technician. "Please, play the tape."

The technician pushed the playback switch.

Santiago listened, then said, "It's definitely a threat and a different voice. Now we know there are at least two of them. I'll get my things together."

Braun looked at his watch. "You're not leaving now?"

"No. Later this morning I'll move to a hotel, something closer to the DataFlex campus. He's watching us from somewhere. The good part is, you maintained my cover. Even if they suspect otherwise, they're not sure."

He said, "They ought to be smart enough to figure that out. Meanwhile, House's office will make hotel arrangements."

"Thank you."

"Mitch, when we talked earlier Lindsey did use the word 'they.' And like you said, the different voice confirms at least two kidnappers."

"Yes, but he said nothing to explain the delay, a straight money deal. The other thing that stands out is his reference to 'playmate.' The first caller never mentioned a second person. Possibly he's a second victim."

"I'm not sure, but it could be T.J. Sam said they haven't been able to locate him for the last few days. More important, what kind of package is he sending?"

Santiago looked at Braun and the technician. "It could be anything; a piece of clothing, jewelry, hair. Probably something personal to reinforce they have her. Hopefully not like the Sinatra kid years ago."

Braun said, "I don't recall a Sinatra incident."

"His kidnapper sent his ear."

Sweat formed on Braun's face and tears filled his eyes. "No, God... please, not that."

"How did they pick up on me? It had to be something in the first call? Lindsey must have told them, or maybe her friend."

Braun said, "The kidnappers might have heard Lindsey and her friend talking."

Santiago looked at Braun. "Claude, try to get some rest. Today is going to be long, intense and painful. You need to be ready."

"What did he mean by 'plans change?'"

"I don't know. For now I'm assuming he's referring to me."

Braun said, "Could be, but you know what they say about assuming."

"I know only too well. Try to get some rest. I'll be down here for a little while longer." She turned to the technician. "Would you play the tape again, please?"

* * *

Santiago left the Braun residence at 7:30 a.m. The rented Chrysler Sebring convertible had been delivered sometime before she awoke. She drove to Chandler, enjoying the fresh air and the whipping wind. Arrangements had been made for her to move into the Oasis Hotel and Golf Resort near Baseline and Interstate 10. Throughout the drive she kept a close eye on the rear view mirror hoping to spot a tail but found none. *He's pretty good if he's tailing me.*

Approaching the hotel entry she was impressed by the adobe walls surrounding the grounds, the rich green lawn, and size of the main building entry. *It looks Roman.* A golf course wound around the east side of the facility, providing a natural barrier from the freeway. The Oasis was built in a cluster of three buildings, each appearing to have a courtyard. As she pulled into the covered registration area a young man opened her door.

"Are you a guest?"

She stepped out of the car. "I have a reservation."

"I'll take your bags in Ma'am. The concierge will hold them for you until the rooms are available later today. Allow me to show you to the registration desk."

"Thank you."

"Your luggage, Ma'am?"

She smiled at him and pointed at the flight bag. "I travel light."

Walking through the entry approaching the registration desk Santiago took note of the opulent surroundings. "You know how to pick 'em, Claude. This is a resort. Too bad I won't get to take advantage of it."

The clerk behind the counter stepped forward. "May I help you?"

"Yes, you have a reservation for Michelle Santiago."

"Welcome, Miss Santiago. We didn't expect you this soon. I did tell the secretary at DataFlex your suite would be available at 3:00 p.m. I'm very sorry for the confusion."

Santiago said, "No confusion. I haven't been in contact with the office this morning. Can I register now and just pick up a key later?"

"Of course. The DataFlex secretary said you are Mr. Braun's personal guest."

So much for low profile. "Do you need my credit card or identification?"

"No Ma'am. We have been instructed to send your billing to DataFlex. It's routine whenever Mr. Braun has guests."

"His guests stay here often?"

The clerk looked at the flight bag in the bellman's hand. "Some do. I see you're traveling light. We can store your bag until things are ready if you like."

"That would be fine."

Santiago next drove to DataFlex on Chandler Boulevard. The campus was spacious and fronted by a rich green manicured lawn. A security officer greeted her at the gated entry.

"Good morning," he said approaching her from the gatehouse, clipboard in hand. "Do you have an appointment?"

"No, I'm a new employee in security, Michelle Santiago."

He scanned the clipboard. "Ah, yes. We've been expecting you. Drive to the building on your far left. You'll see an entry marked *Security*. Mr. Evans will meet you outside." He paused. "Please park in a guest slot. Mr. Evans will assign you a permanent space." He stepped back and motioned her through the gate.

The husband, the house, the company—I'm impressed, Nikki. No wonder this guy swept you off your feet. Two young men were playing one-on-one in a basketball court near some picnic tables as she approached the parking area. Sam Evans was standing outside a closed steel door, his stocky silhouette in sharp contrast to the younger men as she pulled into a guest slot.

"Morning. I see you found your way."

"Yes, thank you. Anything new on the call last night?"

"No. A woman in suggestive attire was using the phone when we arrived. It was across the street from a gentlemen's club. Our man was either long gone or just watching us squirm."

Santiago said, "Having the cops on board would've been nice, a much quicker response time. So what's on tap first?"

"I'll show you around, get you established in our office, and assign the proper credentials so you can get in and out of here. Then we'll start by interviewing Spears since he's on site, unless you have another preference." He turned and punched in an ID number on a keypad beside the door. The lock clicked. "You'll be assigned a number inside."

They walked into a small lobby area with a glassed-in guard station.

Evans said, "We have a lot of sensitive documents here."

She nodded toward the booth. "Impressive. Bulletproof?"

"Way beyond. For our purposes only the guard can operate the door into the office area. What we have here is a high-tech fortress."

They approached the armed guard completely enclosed in the booth. "Ted, this is Miss Santiago, our newest recruit. I'll accept responsibility for her entry."

The guard pointed at a space on the counter and said through a small speaker, "Please sign the electronic clipboard, Miss Santiago." He then gave them access through the door.

Evans said, "This way, Mitch."

Following Evans into the secured area, she said, "Once inside it looks pretty much like most office areas."

"It is."

"Are all the offices this secure?"

"Secure, yes. This tight, no." He scanned the room and gestured with his hand. "We'll go down the right side aisle. You've been assigned to train with me in a private back office rather than a cubicle. It's not unusual and will raise no questions."

"Good." She continued to look around. "It's not a very large area, is it?"

"Big enough. This is our operations center. Most of our work is done in other facilities or the field."

"It doesn't look nearly as friendly as the compound coming in."

"Most work areas are informal except for security. DataFlex's workforce consists primarily of creative, intelligent individuals. Mr. Braun wants them happy and motivated. Most employees in development, production, maintenance, whatever, refer to us as The Guys in the Box. Part of our job is to ensure their privacy and comfort."

"Quite a contrast."

"Not really. It's our box and they can't come in." He smiled. "But we can go into their buildings. In here we do paper work, communications and Internet monitoring. It only gets dicey when we have a special project going or high-profile visitors. Then it can get really tense."

As they walked down the aisle Santiago looked around. "The cubicles look a little larger than most I have seen."

"They are a little larger than usual. They also have more equipment."

They reached the end of the aisle. "Offices surrounded in glass. Reminds me of home."

"The first suite is where Ray House and his Administrative Assistant Jessica Rodriguez work. The middle office belongs to Link Andrews, and the end one is mine. The other operatives work out of the cubicles."

"You and Link are the ranking guys?"

"No, we're all operatives here. Like any operation, some people work the more sensitive tasks. That's Link and me."

"Will Link be working with us?"

"No. He's on the east coast right now on another assignment."

They approached the end glass door. It had no name or identification. Evans smiled and opened the door using a punch code. "Now we'll get you taken care of so you're free to move about without a shadow."

* * *

Quarterman walked into the desert cabin, turned his head to the side, then looked at the two figures taped to their chairs. "Well, well, well, good morning. Whew, it smells like shit in here. I need more than a ski mask."

Lindsey looked at the bulky man. *Gray hair sticking out from under the ski mask.*

He stepped next to Lindsey and gazed into her eyes. "I promised your daddy a package this morning."

Package?

"You two are interesting. I see more anger than fear in your face, Darlin'. All I see in your boyfriend is fear. Personally, I like a fighter."

He went to the backpack he'd left on the counter the day before and took out a cassette recorder. He placed a tape in the unit and held it next to his ear. All was quiet. He walked to the table and set the recorder down in front of her and dropped the backpack on the floor.

Lindsey's gaze never left him. *What now?*

He pressed the Record button and reached toward Lindsey's face. She leaned away from his hand.

"We're goin' to make a little tape."

Lindsey tried to twist in the chair. *Don't touch me, creep.*

"That's it, Kid, fight me to the end." He tore the tape from her mouth, raised his index finger in front of her face and waved it. "Remember the rules. No talking except when I say so."

She nodded.

"Would you like a drink of water?"

"Yes."

"I suppose we should give him one too?"

Her voice was a whisper. "Yes."

Walking to the refrigerator he retrieved a cold bottle of water. Looking at the two prisoners he broke the seal and took a deep swallow. "It's good; wet and cold."

Walking back to Lindsey he held the bottle to her lips. She took a large swallow, some running down the sides of her chin onto the front of her shirt.

T.J. looked on.

Quarterman removed a large folding knife from the pouch and snapped it open. She said, "Oh God, what are you doing?"

He looked at her and grinned from behind the mask. "No talking, Kid... but I'll cut you some slack this time. I like watching you twist and squirm and I want Daddy to hear what's happening."

"Thank you."

With a quick slash he cut the tape binding her left arm to the chair. She stretched her arm and fingers.

He glanced at T.J. "It would probably help if I freed the other one, but not now. Get some feelin' in your hand. I'll give lover boy a drink."

Lindsey opened and closed her hand several times.

Quarterman tore the tape from T.J.'s mouth, held the bottle of water over his lips and laughed. "Sorry fella, I seem to have reopened the cut on your cheek."

T.J. gulped the water until the bottle was empty. Most of it spilled down the front of his shirt.

Quarterman looked at T.J. and spoke in a harsh voice, "Lover boy is a pig, Lindsey. He drank all of your water, but I bet he remembers the rules, don't you, Boy?"

T.J. nodded.

"Well Lindsey, let's see what I have here."

He picked up the roll of tape, grabbed Lindsey's arm and taped it, palm down to the table until she couldn't budge it. "I think you'll need a little more water so you can talk to your old man."

She looked at her arm taped at the wrist, her hand and fingers still free. The open knife was on the table just inches away.

Quarterman provided another bottle and held it while she drank. "After all, we want Daddy to hear you, don't we?"

She nodded.

"Speak up. It's okay."

"Yes."

He looked at the cassette recorder. "This is for bringing in the cop, Braun."

He picked up the knife waving it in front of Lindsey's face. Spitting on the blade Quarterman smeared the saliva with his fingers. "It cuts smoother wet. Always did."

She leaned her head away from the blade. "What are you doing?"

"Making Daddy pay," he said continuing to wave the blade back and forth. "Making Daddy pay, just making Daddy pay."

"No! No! He'll pay!"

Quarterman laughed loudly. "I know."

T.J. said, "Please, don't hurt her."

"Good. You're man enough to speak, but you're too late. Daddy broke the rules"

Quarterman looked at Lindsey's hand. "Let me see. I think I want this one."

Lindesy said," You don't need to do this."

Quarterman grinned, placed the blade's point between her middle finger and ring finger, the cutting edge against the latter.

She began to sob. "No! Please."

T.J. shouted, "Don't do that!"

"Oh yes," he said. "I must."

He raised her middle finger as high from the flat table as possible. Carefully he placed the sharp tip under the finger.

Lindsey shrieked, "No, no, no! You're crazy!"

"Could be, but who's to notice?"

He bent her pinky as high as it would go over the back of the blade. The knife cut into the flesh of her ring finger.

"Please! I'll do anything you want! So will my dad!"

"I know he will." Quarterman laughed, she cried, and T.J. became quiet. "Come on, kids. This is your chance to make some noise. We want Daddy to know you're alive. He'll be getting this tape as part of a little package."

Lindsey glared at the man in the mask. His lips were pursed, almost purple. Sweat had formed on the part of his upper lip she could see.

"Braun, listen carefully. Your little girl is paying for your stupidity."

She screamed, cried, shrieked. "Oh God, *please* don't do this!"

Her eyes filled with tears. Blood spurted onto the table, a puddle collecting under her left hand. The bone cracked as the appendage slid free. The amputation was complete.

Lindsey looked at her hand and continued to shriek from deep in her throat. Tears covered her cheeks. Looking at her tormentor she suddenly became silent. *Don't make a sound.* Her lips trembled. *Stop shaking.* She ground her teeth until a few small pieces of enamel wedged beside her lower gum.

Quarterman looked at the young woman and smiled. "You're tougher than I thought. I like that."

Staring at her tormentor, she bit her lip. The muscles in her face became stiff. Her body vibrated. *I can control myself.*

Quarterman looked at T.J. "You could learn something from her, Boy."

T.J. puked the water out of his system.

Quarterman said, "Jesus, it already smells like shit in here."

Lindsey didn't make a sound.

"You'd be proud of your little girl, Braun. She's a soldier, plain and simple."

He took a towel and wiped their faces dry, then re-taped their mouths. Putting a leather glove on his left hand he removed an empty cigarette box from the pouch. He speared the finger with the tip of the blade and dropped it in the box. He went to the refrigerator and dug through the freezer. "It's a good thing you have ice. That hand is gonna start throbbing." He grabbed a mixing bowl from the cupboard.

Walking back to the table he shouted at the recorder, "I love it, Braun. The crying, screaming, blood, pain. Hope it's all clear enough for you to hear. I haven't had this much fun in years."

Placing the ice and mixing bowl on the table, he used a phone book and magazines to build a pedestal beside Lindsey's chair on the floor. He placed the bowl atop the pile. In a softer voice he said, "I'm gonna free your arm and put your hand in the bowl with ice. Understand? Then I'll tape your arm to the chair leg to keep it in the bowl."

She nodded as tears streamed down her cheeks.

"You'll be okay for a while, Kid. Just pray your old man does what I tell him."

Lindsey glared at her captor.

Quarterman laughed loudly. "I see nothing but hate in your eyes. You'd kill me if you had the chance. Most of 'em never knew."

Lindsey stared at him but made no sound. *You're an animal.*

Quarterman looked at both prisoners, then the recorder. "You spoiled brats enjoy sittin' in your piss, shit and blood. I have errands to run. Maybe, when I get back I'll fuck you. Sort of a last treat for you and Daddy."

Quarterman removed the blood-smeared glove, switched off the recorder and took the cassette out of the unit. "Let's clean this baby." He picked up another washrag and wiped the box clean. "I'll just wrap these in a rag for now. You won't mind will you?"

Lindsey watched him through tear-filled eyes. Her hand was beginning to throb. She could feel every pulse. *I will hurt you badly if I ever get the chance.*

Quarterman placed the items in his backpack. "You know, I didn't figure out which one of those good looking women hanging around your old man was the cop 'til this morning when I followed her to a hotel." He picked up the backpack. "There're just too many women at your house, Kid. Oh well, don't do anything I wouldn't do." He walked out the door.

Lindsey tried to wiggle but couldn't move. T.J. watched from across the table. They continued to look across the table at each other, buried in their own thoughts, the sound of the air conditioner their only company.

* * *

Evans and Santiago were in his office. "It took longer to get you processed than I anticipated, Mitch. It's almost 10:00. Do you want to take a break, interview Mario now, or head back out to Braun's and wait for the package?"

"Let's do Mario while we're here. Then I'll head back. I can't get into my room until 3:00 this afternoon."

"Do it."

As they approached Spears' cubicle they passed several operatives in the Security Program Development Division, all in shirts and ties. Spears was facing one of two screens in his cubicle and feverishly working a keyboard while mumbling.

Evans said with a nod, "As you observed earlier, Mitch, we're not too casual."

"Sam, you need to lighten up. You sound like a walking policy manual." They both laughed.

Mario glanced to his side and minimized the screen. "Mr. Evans, to what do I owe the pleasure?" He checked out Santiago from head to foot.

"I want to introduce you to Michelle Santiago, a new operative in security."

He stood, a leering smile filling his face. "A pleasure indeed."

She extended a hand. "Mr. Spears."

"Mario... all my friends call me Mario, and I certainly hope we'll be friends."

"Mitch is in training mode. One of her assignments is learning our background verification procedures. She'll be interviewing several staff members with varying lengths of service in the company and from various departments."

Spears continued to look at her. "Am I'm one of the subjects?"

"Yes. I'm also one of her subjects." Evans pointed at the screen, redirecting Mario's attention. "Were you working on something special?"

Santiago said, "We didn't mean to intrude. Sam is showing me around."

"It's classified. You never know who's going to walk in." He paused and looked back at Santiago. "Sam is an excellent guide around here but if you're new to the area and want to know where the hot spots are, I'm your man."

"Sam, I'd like to interview Mr. Spears now. Is that a problem?"

"Not at all. I have to see someone a few slots down. I'll wander back when I finish." He turned and left.

Spears removed some boxes and papers from the other chair in the cubicle. "Please, sit down."

"Thank you." The mint green mini climbed as she seated herself and crossed her legs. She opened her notebook. "I see you're a graduate of ASU."

"Yes, computer science. I just finished."

"Congratulations."

He looked briefly into her eyes. "Thank you."

"Tell me how you chose to work at DataFlex."

"By chance, actually. I was dating Lindsey Braun. We went out a few times. I met her dad. Once, while waiting for her to get ready, we talked. I guess he liked what he heard. A few days later I was offered a job."

"Do you think Lindsey helped you get into the company?"

He looked around the cubicle. "I doubt it. She's... how can I put it? She's a party girl. Doesn't give jack about the company."

"Self-centered?"

He kept watching Santiago's hemline. "A total narcissist. I could get you something to drink. Water or a soda?"

"No thank you." *You might try eye contact.* "You said you were dating the boss's daughter."

"It was a short fling." He leaned forward and looked into her face. "You have beautiful eyes."

"Thank you." She sat straighter in the chair. "A short fling?"

"Can I be honest with you?"

"I hope so."

"I dated her a few times to meet her dad. DataFlex pays really well. The competition to get in is huge. Intense."

"So you used Lindsey?"

"Yes, but she used me too."

"How?"

He smiled, brilliant white teeth a high contrast to his dark complexion. "She's an animal, a real turn-on, know what I mean?"

Santiago smiled. "She's intimate but wild."

"A sexual athlete. This isn't going to be in the report is it?"

"No."

"She's also a ball buster."

"You don't seem to be complaining."

His voice became husky. "Hey, I'm young. I appreciate beautiful women. We've just met and I like you. Lindsey was all right, but I like a woman just a little more mature than a twenty year old party hardy, if you get my drift. You know, a relationship that's meaningful and intimate."

"So when was the last time you saw her?"

"About four weeks ago. I had the job but no way could I afford that chick."

"You knew her from school?"

"Yes. She hung around with a lot of different guys. But hey, you're here to find out about me, right?"

"Right. Lindsey just happens to be part of your recent past. There isn't much about the relationship on file."

"I hope not. It was totally physical, and expensive."

"Where did you two go?"

"Mostly a strip club. The place turned her on."

"I'm sure she wasn't the only one. What was it called?"

"The Bramble Bush."

"That's the place where a woman whose body was found murdered yesterday worked."

Spears took a deep swallow. "No shit? I have to start following the news."

Santiago leaned forward and held out a piece of paper from the notebook. "Is this current?"

Spears stared at the scoop neck of her blouse and his eyes dilated. "I beg your pardon," he said, looking up.

She waved the paper. "Your information, is it current?"

He took a quick look and sat up straight. "Yes."

She waved toward his computer. "Sam says you're a true whiz on these things."

"Really? I didn't think he noticed."

"He says you can do virtually anything from creating new programs to accessing files, including those that most people can't get into."

"I've had my moments, but nothing illegal you understand."

"Of course." Santiago adjusted her position in the chair. She wet her lips, teasing her teeth with the tip of her tongue. "So tell me, how did you become so good?"

He slid his chair closer to hers, crowding the space. "It's easy when you're a genius. Let me show you. What do you think the Internet is used for most?"

"My guess is porn."

"You're on the money. Now, can you access porn on your server at home?"

"I doubt it. Haven't tried."

"Lady, everybody tries... well, almost everybody. Let's access your provider." He gestured toward the keyboard.

She said, "Show me."

"Type in Erotic Nude Celebrity."

She did as directed. "It says they can't open the page."

"Okay, type in Nude Celebrities." She repeated the process with the same result.

He said, "This is a turn-on, isn't it?"

She licked her lower lip. "Not really." *It could be if I were looking for something like a younger brother or a horny hunk.*

He began to wring his hands. "Enter Sexy Models and watch." The screen changed its graphics. "Okay, we went into something that won't let us in. I'll just put in Sexy Celebrity Wallpaper Screens and we'll mess with it after we get refused."

Santiago stood, pushing her chair out of the way. Spears moved toward the screen. She leaned casually over his shoulder. "Show me something different than a skin show. Your hormones are racing way too fast."

"What do you want to know?"

"I'm told personnel records are confidential and subject to limited access. Is that true?"

"Yes."

"Are you cleared to access those files?"

"No, but it's no big deal. I could if I wanted to know something, for work of course."

"Of course." She rubbed a rock-hard leg against his upper thigh and leaned even closer. "Let's look at my file."

Spears feverishly worked the keyboard. Santiago watched as her file appeared in less than twenty seconds.

Spears cleared his throat, "Let's see what they've got on you. Ah, a student at the UW, graduated with a 3.21 GPA, that's respectable." He stopped chattering for a moment. "Well, well, the lovely Michelle was an exotic dancer before graduation and joining Seattle's finest." He grinned.

Her face reddened. "DataFlex has everything... very thorough, and fast."

"This stuff is from the Seattle Police Department. It says here you're currently on leave and have just completed a successful murder investigation."

"Anything else?" she said, bending closer to the screen.

"You socialize with Chance Stewart, your partner. Reason for the leave is personal." He looked at her cleavage, then her face and swallowed. "I thought you worked here."

"I do, but I'm just on a tryout, remember? I have to decide whether I want to be here."

A questioning look appeared on his face. "It says you're staying at the Braun residence."

"I am until later today when I'm in a hotel. To satisfy your curiosity Nikki Braun is a very close friend."

"Close is good." He smiled. "Strange... it says your assignment is confidential."

"I'm new here, remember?"

"Yeah, but the folder is empty."

"Well, it's my first day. Maybe Sam hasn't had time to put anything in it yet."

"Update, it's called update. I could help fill your file. Would you like to get together after work for a drink? I could show you around."

"I'm sure you could but as things are now I can't. Thank you, Mr. Spears." She turned toward the cubicle entry. "If I have any questions about programs, input or output, I'll get back to you." She walked out of the cubicle.

"Please do." He watched her leave. "Oh please, screw my brains out," he whispered.

Santiago met Evens coming toward the cubicle. "Done with the interview?"

She nodded. "Oh yes."

"So what do you think of our newest genius?"

"Your genius needs someone to lay him." They laughed. "He can access a personnel folder within seconds."

"That's interesting."

"He was trying to make an impression. Anyway, let's keep my current working file empty."

"No, we'll just fill it with data on interview assignments." Evans glanced toward Spears booth. "Mario thinks he's God's gift to women. I'd bet a year's salary he's more interested in your relationship with Braun than anything else right now."

"I think he has something a little closer to home in mind. We know he can follow the investigation if we put the data on file. We need to be very careful. He's a suspect at this point."

"Okay."

"Can we throw some numbers into the budget portion? They were blank. He just didn't notice. He was too overcome with my background as a dancer."

"I'll bet, but yes, we'll add scale for starting operatives. Anything else?"

"I'm going back to Braun's and wait for the package. It's my understanding Sierra Paradise often comes to their pool for a swim so I'm hoping to connect with her too. See what you can get on Cliff Arnold. That way we'll have some background to build on when we talk to him tonight at the Bramble Bush. While you're at it, see what we have on the other names I've gone over, the ones we didn't talk about on the plane. I'll call when we have something out there."

"You sound worried."

"I am. We don't need a package of anything. Hopefully the murder of the dancer at the Bramble Bush has nothing to do with Lindsey's disappearance."

He said, "Probably a pissed client."

"I hope so. Oh, and bring some flash cash. Those places are expensive."

"I will. Are you going to Lindsey's apartment too?"

"I want the authorities to go through it first. Forensics can find many things I'd miss and her place is a potential crime scene."

* * * * * * *

Lisa Fargo opened the room door at the Geisha Motel on Arizona Avenue south of Elliott

Quarterman looked her in the eyes and grinned. "Do they put a mint on the pillow?"

"Hardly, they don't even leave the porch light on if they have one that works." The robe she wore slid open, revealing her nude form. "Welcome to the Chandler slums."

"I gotta tell'ya, Cuz, you look good." He stepped toward her. "Are you ready for the Oasis Hotel and Golf Resort?"

"That's a classy place but not quite yet."

"You'll have to get ready."

She pulled him into the room and snuggled close to his chest. "I've been here a couple of days alone. No young guy in the valley can hold a candle to you," she said in his ear, tearing his shirt open, then off.

"Let's go in and close the door, Lisa."

Once inside she ran a long pink fingernail over his firm belly stopping at the belt buckle. "Look what I found." She unfastened the buckle and the buttons of his jeans. "You're bulging, and I like men that don't use underwear."

He pulled Lisa toward a chair by the bed. "I guess there's no big rush. Santiago can't get in her room 'till 3:00, so neither can we. I just want to be there when she arrives."

She pressed him down on chair and began pulling his boots off. The socks and jeans slid free with no resistance. "Who's Santiago?"

"The lady you're going to keep track of at the hotel."

Lisa stood, stepped to the bed, dropped her robe to the floor, and stretched out on her back. "I'm ready. Let's rock 'n roll."

Quarterman joined her on the bed. "We've been doin' it longer than most married couples. It must be our off-center family genes."

She brushed a hand over his belly. "You're eager, I can tell."

"Not as much as you are." He slid an arm around her shoulders. "First, let's talk business."

"Now? You're kidding."

"No, no. I have your attention. This is exactly the time and place."

"Can't we just—"

He held a finger to her lips. "Did you get some new clothes?"

She pointed to the closet. "Yes, and they cost you."

"Where?"

"Fashion Center here in Chandler."

"Good. When you leave here go back and get a red bikini, size 6. I want it gift wrapped. Have the clerk put it in a separate bag by itself just in case you happen to find something else you want, perhaps a new bikini, but not a thong." He kissed her neck. Whatever you do, don't touch the package."

"Why?"

"I'm sending it to Santiago." A smile crossed his face. "I just want to see what she's got and establish who's in command. Now listen carefully. Take a cab to the hotel. Arrive at the Oasis between two and two-thirty. A bellman or someone will greet you at the curb. Give him the package. Tell him you're from DataFlex and this is a gift for Michelle Santiago, a guest checking in sometime today. Give him ten dollars and ask that the package be placed in her room on the bed before she arrives. Wear your usual sexy clothes, preferably one of those low-cut tops with a push-up bra and big sunglasses. All he'll see and remember other than the tip are tits and cleavage. You won't even get out of the cab."

"Then what?"

"Have the cabbie take you back to the mall. From there come back here in your car, change into something less distracting, lose the glasses, check out, and return to the hotel as a guest. You have a room reserved under the name Brooke Meredith."

"You'll have to pay an extra day on this room."

"That's okay. When you get checked in at the Oasis go to the salon and have your hair and nails done."

"Charge it to the room?"

"Of course. It's critical for you to blend in as an affluent guest. You're a beautiful woman and you'll be noticed. I want you elegant and provocative, not hot and trashy. If anyone asks, you're there finalizing your divorce. That would explain hanging around the hotel waiting."

"And you'll be joining me?"

"Not exactly. I'll be checking into a suite of my own."

"But—"

"Your job is to keep track of Santiago at the hotel. You might even visit her room if needed. I'll let you know more later."

She licked his chest and rolled her eyes, looking into his face. "What about us?"

His body tensed. "When we encounter each other at the hotel it'll be as strangers, new acquaintances. We'll play it by ear."

"And the red bikini?"

He brushed a hand over Lisa's breast. "Like I said, it's for Santiago. I'm going to have some fun with her."

She cuddled into his bare flesh, kissed his throat and rubbed a knee against his groin. "I'm here now, and I'm ready."

"We're both ready."

"Take me from the backside like we did the dancer." She rolled onto her belly and rose to her knees.

He touched Lisa's shoulder, ran the edge of his hand down her spine and up again. He touched the side of her throat and whispered, "The dancer... yes, we liked the dancer, didn't we?"

"Yes," she said.

Quarterman took a deep breath. Sweat covered his body.

A chill surged through Lisa. "You're so quiet."

An odd smile creased his face as he looked at the back of her head and stroked her windpipe. "What would it be like to have the ultimate climax with you?"

"What'd you say?"

"The dancer... you said you wanted to do it like the dancer." He took her chin in his hand.

"That's not what I meant."

He gripped her chin tight, pressed the other hand against the back of her head.

"No Yancey! Please!"

"For just a split second you felt the thrill and fear of the dancer, didn't you?" He released his grip. "It was exciting you. I could feel it. You shuddered and squirmed when I touched your throat."

"You're scaring me, Yancey."

"Sometimes I scare myself. Look, I've lost it. I'm not even hard. I'm really tired... drained."

She rolled out from under him, went into the bathroom and called back, "What were you thinking?"

"So many things... Braun, a teenage girl I saw at the swap meet, and always Santiago. She's the most beautiful woman I ever encountered."

"You're not making sense. You've never been near her."

"Close enough."

"She's a cop."

"She's a challenge, my most beautiful adversary. I want her." He yawned and stretched out on the bed. "I'm so tired... so very tired."

Lisa repeated, "You scared the crap out of me for just a minute when you had your hand on my throat. Silly me." She looked into the bathroom mirror. *Good, no marks.*

"Sorry, but I know you like it a little rough."

Lisa came back into the room and began dressing.

"What's the rush? I thought you wanted to play around?"

"You lost your hard-on, remember? And I have shopping to do."

"Right... and I'm tired."

Lisa finished dressing while Quarterman remained on the bed.

"So are you going to tell me about the girl at the swap meet?

"I saw her yesterday. She hardened everything I have... tongue, muscles, lips, everything. She made me swell with energy."

Lisa narrowed her eyes looking into his face. "What did you do about it?"

"Walked bowlegged. The swap meet was crowded. No way was I gonna hit on a teenager." He shook his head. "She gave me a hurt that wouldn't go away."

"You're always horny but this one sounds younger than what you usually go for?"

"Yeah, just a kid. I bet she's got the football team jumping. Jesus, I'm getting excited just thinking about her. I'd like to have kids someday but not a daughter that looks as sexy as she did."

"Do I hear guilt in your voice?"

"Age, Lisa. I'm passing into late midlife. I didn't think I'd live this long."

"Well, you can lounge around naked but I have shopping to do. I'll see you at the hotel around 2:30."

"Yeah." He stretched shaking his arms. "Ever feel like you just didn't want to move? I really am beat... and I don't know why."

"You?"

"I ache all over."

"Maybe you're getting sick."

"I don't think so. I hope not, but I'm listless as hell right now." He shook his head. "I'm even having trouble sleeping at night. Must be gettin' too tired."

"Something on you mind?"

"Just this operation. You'd think with a million on the line I'd be wired."

"Just keep thinkin' about that little teen tart and Santiago," she said, opening the door.

"Oh yeah, but I better get going too." He rolled off the bed with a grunt. "In a while I need to give Braun a call and see how he liked the package. Now listen carefully. If for any reason I'm not at the hotel when you get there just check in using the alias. I'll join you in the pool area around 4:00."

"You have something else going?"

"Just business. I have a couple of hours to pick up a rental car and some clothes. I gotta get a makeover too. Next time you see me I'll be sophisticated, uptown."

* * *

It was almost noon when the young woman walked through the patio door carrying a beach bag. Her jeans were tight fitting washed denim slung low on her hips. The waistband appeared fashionably cut and frayed, making them hang just a little lower. A short pink tube top and canvas shoes completed the ensemble. Straight blond hair hung below her shoulders, framing a deep tanned face with large, light blue eyes offset by full dark brows.

Santiago watched the young woman cross the patio toward her and the pool. *Sexy, trashy. I'm sure guys go for this one. Nice placement of the tear on the hip. Show a little more skin, Honey.*

Her steps were slow, casual, a broad smile on her face, a dental-ad mouth surrounded by glistening pink lip gloss. "Hello, I'm Sierra Paradise," she said extending a hand.

"It's a pleasure. I'm Michelle Santiago. Thought I'd catch a few rays while visiting Nikki and Claude." *You are a sexy little vamp. What a difference a few years can make.*

"Nice to meet you. Lindsey and I are friends." She stepped out of her shoes and pulled off her top, shaking her hair free, then peeled off her jeans. "Don't the roses smell great?"

Santiago said, "The roses are nice." She looked at the young woman. "I work with more than a few guys who would like your swim attire. The lime green really sets off your tan nicely. It looks good on you."

Sierra flashed a grin and glanced up at the master bedroom windows overlooking the pool. "Thanks. You know how it is being young and single. I like your French cut. I have a couple of those too."

"I'm not surprised. They work."

Sierra stretched out on one of the lounges in the shade with a clear view of the master suite widows. "Don't want to get too many rays. It's pretty warm this morning. So where are you from?"

"Seattle."

"I bet you love the sun down here."

"Yes I do."

Sierra glanced toward the windows again. "Is Nikki around?"

"She was, but I haven't seen her lately. She said something about going shopping."

"Oh."

Santiago said, "I haven't seen Lindsey today, either. Have you?"

"No, but she's hot for some guy right now."

"A college campus can do that to you. So many men, so little time."

"She attracts them like fleas." Sierra laughed and glanced toward the master suite again. "For now I'm sort'a between guys, if you get my drift?"

"I surely do. So you don't see Lindsey too often."

"Not for about three or four days now, anyway. Don't you love the pool and the setting? It's really nice of Claude to let me use it whenever I want."

"He's always believed things should be enjoyed." *And I'm sure he enjoys you.* "Lindsey must really be hung up on her latest conquest. I got in yesterday and she hasn't been home yet. I haven't seen her since Nikki and Claude's wedding."

"That's where we met," Sierra said. "You were Nikki's maid of honor."

"Yes. That was the last time I was in Phoenix."

Sierra smiled. "I remember. You guys went to school together."

"We had a lot of fun at the UW."

"Yeah, Nikki said you guys are best friends."

"Like sisters."

"Like Lindsey and me, same thing."

"So who's Lindsey's current man?" Santiago said.

"T.J.," she said with a shrug. "A student. Personally, I like men a little more mature."

"Around my age?" Santiago said.

"You're not that old. I like a man that's a little older, but buff." She glanced toward the master suite again and patted a well-shaped thigh. "I'm not giving it away to some pizza delivery guy. I want a man who's caring and sensitive."

"Caring and sensitive sounds more like rich when you take away the pizza," Santiago said.

"That too, and I may have found one."

You have if he plays. "It's hard to find one of those available. I've been trying that approach for a couple of years. Perhaps it's because I want a commitment too."

"With a body like that you don't need to try very hard," Sierra said with a laugh.

"Maintenance is tougher at my age, but only if you want someone permanent."

Sierra smiled. "I doubt that."

Santiago walked to the edge of the pool and sat down. "I'm going to try the water." She slipped in.

"Me too," Sierra said.

Santiago said, "This is great."

Sierra stood, went to the pool edge and dove in. When she surfaced a skimpy pair of triangles were on her head. "I hope Claude isn't around." She tossed the halter onto the deck and glanced at the house. "The damn thing always comes off when I dive in." She pushed off the edge and swam on her back across the pool.

Nikki, I've met the competition. Santiago watched Sierra. "That's one way to eliminate tan lines."

"For sure... we skinny-dip all the time, but it's okay. We're the only ones here during the day."

"We?"

"Yeah, usually it's just Lindsey and me. Claude's at work and Nikki's doing her shrink thing or community leader interested citizen bit, shopping... always something. I shouldn't have said shrink. You know, she goes to a counselor or something, probably for drinking. So does Lindsey, although hers is an old letch... but her dad doesn't know it."

"Lindsey told you that?"

"Sure. She likes him in her own way. They've been doin' the deed for years." Sierra pushed off the side of the pool still on her back.

"It doesn't bother her?"

"Are you kidding? Nikki told us about some of the stuff you guys did. We just started a couple of years earlier. It's today's world. My mom said she got my dad through sex in the beginning. How did she put it? Oh yes—sex sells," Sierra said.

"What about commitment, emotions, feelings?"

"Come on, you guys were a strippers. Nikki told us. Besides, I figure the other stuff, like commitment, will come with time. As I said, I think I've found the right man, but now I have to sell him on it."

"I hope you're right. It's just that you and Lindsey are so young. But then, Nikki was only twenty-two when she met Claude for the first time."

"From what Lindsey tells me, Nikki and her dad were hot and heavy even before he divorced his last wife."

Don't go there. "You're right. We did some crazy things and fortunately we survived. I'm sure you will too."

"Well, at least I've made it this far and found the man I love. I did start young, though. God, like fourteen the first time I got banged. You know, that first time you feel so scared, then like such a woman. It was my math teacher. He hit on me all the time. After we did it I aced the class without cracking a book."

"I think that's called rape. Didn't you feel used?"

"I figured I was using him. Every man wants sex. They'll give anything to get it." She smiled as the water lapped at her body. "Take his cock and you got him."

Santiago shook her head. "A lot has changed in the last couple of years: AIDS, more STD's."

"Nothing has really changed except it's talked about more openly now. Even old guys can't get enough. I had a thing with a guy who was seventy-eight. He was a lousy fuck but he loved getting head. Go down on him and you had him." She started to laugh but swallowed some water. "And he did great tongue work too. I could'a had him for a sugar daddy but he died."

You're a prostitute and you don't even know it. "Well Sierra, it's been nice chatting with you, but I have things to do. I stayed here last night but since I'm trying my hand at working for DataFlex I don't want to set tongues to wagging about sleeping at Nikki and Claude's house."

"I know what you mean and Claude is a bit of a flirt."

Santiago boosted herself out of the pool and returned to the lounge chair. Toweling herself off, she sat down for a moment to let the sun finish the job. Sierra swam to the end of the pool and walked up the steps, the sun washing her topless form. She walked over to the shaded area where her clothes were strewn, checking the lanai windows as she went.

You're a beautiful young woman. I'm sure Claude is enjoying this show. "I'll be seeing you," Santiago said as she stood and moved into the house.

"I'm sure," Sierra said as she dragged a lounge out into the sun and stretched out.

So much for too many rays. Santiago walked through the patio door into the house to

wait for the package.

Sierra was spreading sun tan lotion on her naked torso.

Santiago smiled as she walked through the kitchen and loudly said, "Nikki, the water was great." She looked back. Sierra was grabbing her clothes and putting them on much faster than they had come off.

* * *

Sam Evans approached the Chief of Security Office alone. Ray House said, "Where's Santiago? Too early for lunch isn't it?"

"She went back to Braun's to wait for the package and talk to Sierra Paradise if the kid comes for a swim this morning."

"So what kept you here?"

"Mitch asked me to run background checks on the other list of names, the ones Braun had at the house last night. I was going to check with you first, but you weren't available so I went ahead and got started."

"Good. Check 'em. Be thorough. Claude wants his daughter back. He told us to give Santiago all the support she requires, no strings attached. He meant it."

"We are. I've had a team working on it for an hour."

"By the way, how is our wonder cop to work with?"

"She's as good as advertised, a real pro," Evans said.

House rolled his eyes. "She seems to flash a lot of skin, don't you think?"

"She's young, and way beyond attractive. I think she dresses a bit provocatively but consistent with today's styles." Evans' face turned a slight pink. "She really knows how to use it, too."

"How so?"

"I monitored the interview with Spears. She had him eating out of her hand. He was hittin' on her like crazy. She just kept probing, always comin' back to the topic at hand. Mario wants to show her the local hot spots and she gets him goin' on his sex life with Lindsey. He asks her out for drinks and she gets him to break into our programs, the ones nobody can get into," Evans said.

"Our programs? That's impossible," House said.

"Think again. He pulled up her confidential personnel file." Evans smirked, "You know, the one he can't get into? And he showed it to her."

"Why?"

"Ego, Ray. She asked him about breaking into sites, programs and files. He goes to porn, but she steers him to our records. Now we know for sure one of our suspects can track anything we put into the files about this case."

House scratched his chin. "True. That's also grounds for termination, you know."

"I think Mitch wants Spears kept in place. If he is involved we have an inside track."

House nodded. "I see what you mean. She is good."

"I don't know how she is with women but from what I saw her do with Mario, she could get any man to talk. Trust me, she knows what she's got and how to use it." Evans smiled.

"So again, tell me, what's it like, working with her? Every man in security is jealous of you."

"Like I said, she's a pro. So am I. Besides, she's not available. And even if she were, we're not."

House raised an eyebrow. "Come on, Sam. You must think about it."

Apparently not as much as you. "I'm like Jimmy Carter. I think he said something about lust in his heart. Well, that's where mine will stay. I'm quite happy in my own relationship. Isn't that why I was assigned to work with her?"

"That and you're one of the very few Claude has absolute confidence in, and I do mean absolute."

In all my years here I don't believe I've ever heard you be so informal with the boss's name. "That's nice to know. I hope he still feels that way when we're done. Oh, one other thing—even if we were available I think Mitch would want someone a little less long in the tooth."

"You never know, Sam. You just never know."

* * *

Santiago came into the Braun's kitchen area after changing into shorts and a blouse. "It's almost 2:00 p.m. Nothing yet?"

"Nothing," Nikki said. "Maybe he's changed his mind."

Santiago said, "I doubt that. If anything he's playing this for all it's worth. It'll get here. Anytime is too soon. I'm sure he followed me this morning, but I couldn't pick him up."

"Traffic on the 101 is pretty intense during morning rush."

"So I noticed. What's the deal here anyway? Is the speed limit set at a minimum, not maximum? I was doing 75 and everyone was passing me. And the motorcycles—God, they're everywhere."

"Yeah, but they get through traffic. It's not like the northwest, Mitch. Riding is a year round sport here. As to speed limits, we locals like to think of them as suggestions." They both laughed.

Santiago said, "He could have been on a bike. We know there are two males involved, but the tail today could have been a woman. Maybe I wasn't paying close enough attention. I hate waiting."

Nikki lit a cigarette. "So how was the rest of the morning?"

"I thought you quit smoking before you got married? At the airport I thought it was just nerves."

"That was a long time ago. It's not easy being Mrs. Claude Braun." She stuffed the butt out in a clean ashtray on the counter. "Let's get back to your morning."

"Busy. I tried checking into the hotel but I can't have the room 'til 3:00. Then I met a couple of Lindsey's friends."

"Who?"

"Mario early this morning at the office and Sierra just a little while ago."

Nikki said, "She was over for a swim?"

"You could say that. She jiggled in, stripped to a thong and got wet. Oh yes, and she lost her top as soon as she hit the water."

"Yeah, the girl likes to show her stuff. Sort'a reminds me of us a few years ago, the old turn 'em on and tease 'em."

"She's a beautiful young woman and very forward."

Nikki forced a chuckle. "No shit. Sierra knows what she wants."

"Rich and old," Santiago said. "Apparently she's got one on the hook."

"I know," Nikki said softly. "Only too well."

"And you let her get away with it?"

"It's not her, Mitch. It's Claude. You haven't forgotten how I met him."

"No."

Nikki's eyes welled. She took a deep breath. "It's something he has to decide. He's like a lot of wealthy, powerful men. I love him and Lindsey, but he has to decide who or what he wants. I knew the score coming in. It's different being the wife."

"The wife?"

"Eight years ago I was the other woman. You just don't think it can happen to you. God, I need another drink. You?"

"No thank you."

Nikki walked out to the patio bar and called back, "So what else happened today?"

That was a sudden change of pace. "Not much. Sam and I are going to the Bramble Bush tonight. They don't open 'til 5:00 p.m."

Nikki came back into the kitchen. "Gonna talk to the bouncer?"

"Yes." *About Lindsey and the stripper whose body was found.*

"It's a college crowd. Believe it or not I felt really old when we went there."

"You were there?"

She nodded. "Claude and I went. He was into eye candy. No surprise there. But hey, so was I. Lindsey wanted us to go. Once was enough, but what a thrill."

"You're only a couple of years older than the college crowd."

"Tell me about it. One of the things I didn't expect was to be groped by every guy in the place." She laughed. "What is it you cops say? Oh yes, expect to be patted down. It's like everyone was copping a feel."

"And you?" Santiago said smiling.

Nikki laughed and shrugged. "When in Rome."

"Well, at least you didn't feel abused."

"Oh no, but I have to warn you. The stud muffin dancers start without their shirts, showing nothing but promise in tight pants and six-packs; then they get down to those little tiny jock straps and it's all a rush."

"Don't you mean male thongs? Some things never change."

"There's a difference? All I know are those guys come with a package, no question about it. I loved it."

Santiago said, "Sounds like it."

Nikki peeked over the tumbler in her hand. "We had the best sex ever when we got home that night. We could hardly keep our hands off each other on the drive."

Great, just what I need to hear. "So what can you tell me about Doctor Rich?" Santiago said changing the subject.

"Not much. Lindsey's been seeing him for years. Why?"

"Just piecing things together. Sierra mentioned him, said Lindsey had a thing for him."

Nikki took another sip. "Probably, Lindsey's got a thing for every man she sees. Now, could the good doctor be interested in Lindsey? Oh yes."

Santiago said, "Do tell."

"Nikki!" Braun shouted from the living room. "It's here. The package is here."

Santiago stood and turned toward the living room. "Oh God... Nikki, prepare yourself. This could be harmless, but it could also be very bad."

* * * * * * *

Sam Evans read the background report slowly in a near whisper. "Well, Dr. Rich, you seem to have a jaded past." He looked up at Clark Hoffman, the associate responsible for the report. "Good job."

Hoffman said, "I thought you'd want to see this right away. Is he someone we're thinking of bringing into the company?"

"No. We're just doing a background check." Evans pointed to the screen. "You see the list of clients?"

"Yes. Is that our Lindsey Braun on the list?"

"One and the same. Of course I don't need to remind you this is confidential."

"I understand, Sir."

Evans shook his head. "Look at this. Accused of molesting a client in '89, sexual assault in '91, rape in '92, and all of the charges were dropped. I'll be damned."

"When you get further into the report you'll see he also made a cash settlement with a female client in '95, but he made no admission of guilt."

"There it is; sex with a minor. Not much info with it. Clark, any chance we can find out who these victims were?"

"Probably... we've accessed some very sensitive files in the past."

Evans said, "You mean we hacked into someone's system."

"Precisely. They won't know who we are or where the data went. In fact, unless they monitor the program really closely they'll never even know we were visiting,"

"Good. This is really sensitive."

"Does Mr. Braun's daughter still see him, this Doctor Rich?"

Evans rubbed his hands together. "Yes, she does. Can we access Rich's files right now?"

"Of course. If he has them stored on his hard drive we'll be able to take a look." Hoffman paused for a moment. "However, if he's like the people in the Lava Incident last year, he may still keep his most confidential data in hard copy only."

"Understood," Evans said. During a recent industrial espionage case he was almost caught breaking into Lava Industries. "Go ahead and probe his files. I want to see what else he has, not just on Lindsey Braun, but anyone. Obviously he isn't the white knight we thought he was."

"Are you sharing this with Mr. Braun?"

"Possibly. First I want to talk to Ray House."

"Shall I forward the information to Mr. House?"

"No. Print it, but don't save it. We don't want someone else's confidential files in our system. You and I are the only two people who know about this."

"Mr. House will make three of us."

"And that's all who will know for the time being," Evans said. *Us and Santiago.*

* * *

Quarterman found the lobby of the Oasis Hotel and Golf Resort luxurious. He seated himself on one of the many overstuffed chairs arranged throughout the spacious lobby along with large glass-topped brass tables, lamps, and couches. Holding a newspaper and facing the drive-up area he checked each vehicle as it arrived. As a white and black taxicab drove in, he began folding the newspaper. The car came to a stop and the bellmen went to the cab. Quarterman looked at his watch. "Finally... 2:10."

A young man and woman stepped out while the bellman held the door. He turned the paper over and glanced at the headlines again. "Damn it." *Where are you, Lisa?*

A gray cab approached the entry with a blue haze behind it. "Yeah, that'd be the one you'd get."

He put the paper down and stood as a middle-aged man wearing a business suit got out. He took another look at his watch. "Jesus... its 2:13, Lisa."

He picked the newspaper up again. *Hurry up, Cuz. She'll be here soon. I need to get into that room.*

A red and black taxi approached. The bellman went to the door. When he opened it, Lisa leaned out, handed him a package, said a few words, and handed him a bill. The bellman lingered for just a moment, then turned and walked into the lobby.

A smile spread across Quarterman's face. *Well Son, was it her tits, the tip, or both?*

The cab pulled away as he stood, dropping the newspaper on the table. The young man walked to the front desk, spoke with a counter clerk, got a pass key, and went to the elevators. Quarterman followed. Together they waited for the doors to open.

The young man said, "Nice day isn't it, Sir?"

The doors opened and an Asian couple exited. The bellman stepped aside inviting Quarterman's entry. "Yes, it is. Thank you."

Following Quarterman onto the elevator, the package held flat on his left hand, the young man pressed five on the panel. "Floor, Sir?"

Quarterman glanced at the panel. "Fifth, please."

"Same as me."

They rode in silence. When the door opened on the fifth floor Quarterman stepped out first and looked in both directions down the hallway. The bellman turned left while saying, "May I help you find your room?"

"No. It's that way."

Quarterman followed the young man, but several paces back. He paused at another door when the bellman stopped and inserted the keycard at room 5004, then entered. Quarterman sprinted to the open door and peered in. The sitting room was empty. Whistling came from the bedroom. He entered, opened a louvered closet by the hallway door, stepped inside, and closed it. A moment later the bellman walked out of the bedroom to the door and exited. The door latched with a quiet click. *That was close. I'm getting too old for this stuff.*

Opening the closet door he stepped out and looked around. "Nice suite... a mirror image of mine." He went to the table beside the small couch and lifted the telephone receiver. Reaching into a pocket he extracted a small package, opened it and removed a tiny voice-activated microphone transmitter. Using a handkerchief he removed the voice cover, put the device in the phone, and replaced the cover, wiping it clean of prints.

He placed another device behind a picture suspended on the wall opposite the couch, then walked into the bedroom. "Well, let's see. We'll put one of you in the phone and the other under the base of the lamp on the nightstand. Bless those paranoid souls who make Private Eye stores possible."

The package was in the center of the king size bed. He removed an envelope from the inside pocket of his lightweight blazer. "And for you, Miss Santiago, a greeting card. See you at the pool, Aunt Michelle." He took one last look around, then started back to the sitting room, pausing at the bathroom door. "One under the edge of the counter would work."

At the exit he pressed an ear against the door and listened, then opened the door just a crack, checked the hallway and stepped out of the room. Using the handkerchief he closed the door. *We're almost neighbors.*

Quarterman returned to the lobby and went to the lounge. The room was full of light with one wall of windows opening onto the pool. He took a seat at the bar with a view of the check-in counter.

A bartender approached, her hair a mass of long blond perm touching her shoulders. "Good afternoon. Just arrive?"

You have enough cleavage displayed to excite a dead man. "How can you tell?"

"Only the business types wear coats on a day like this and most of them have ties. Can I get you something?"

"Oh yes," he said, staring at her chest. "Tanqueray and tonic, two limes." He watched as she went to the workstation. *Nice... very nice. Don't see black mesh very often these days except in Las Vegas.*

The woman returned with his drink.

"Jackson's your man," he said. "Keep the change."

"Thank you."

"Thank *you*." He took a sip of the gin. *Nice smile even if your teeth are tobacco stained.* "So tell me, what time is check-in, generally?"

"Three, but you can usually get in by half-past two if you're just waiting and have a reservation."

"No. I checked in last evening but I have an associate arriving, probably around 4:00." He took another sip and swallowed, placing the tumbler on the bar.

"Another?"

"No thank you. Think I'll go change into something more comfortable."

She said, "Try the pool. It's really nice."

"And it will get better I'm sure, but right now I have a call to make."

They both laughed as he left the lounge.

* * *

Braun was in the middle of the living room holding a standard sized manila envelope when Nikki and Santiago walked in. Nikki went to Claude's side.

Santiago's brows went up. *There go the fingerprints.* "Claude, please put the envelope on the coffee table. We want to preserve any evidence that might be on the surface."

He did as she directed. "Damn! Of course. I wasn't thinking. Sorry."

Santiago said, "How did it get here?"

"Some kid on a bike came to the gate and handed it to the security man. The kid said a big guy gave him $10.00 to drop it off."

Santiago stared at the envelope. "Do we know who the kid is?"

Braun's gaze never left the envelope. "No. Just a boy, probably ten or eleven."

"Did security get a description of the man from the boy?"

"Not much. Just that the fellow had gray hair, was big, and looked older."

"How old?"

"The kid said forty or fifty."

"To bad we don't know the kid's name," Santiago said.

"I know. My man tried to get his name but as soon as the gate started to open the kid took off like a shot. You'd probably like to talk with him?"

Santiago nodded. "I would. Right now let's see what we've got. Nikki, do you have some cooking tongs and a sharp thin-bladed knife?"

"In the kitchen. I'll get them."

Santiago bent over the package. Her nostrils flared. "Oh, Jesus... Claude, this could be unpleasant."

"I know. I smelled it too."

Nikki returned from the kitchen. "Here's the knife and tongs."

"Nikki, I want you and Claude to sit down together on the couch."

"Why?"

Braun said, "Let's do as she asks. The package has a very strong odor when you get up close."

Nikki sniffed. "I don't smell a thing."

He held out his hand. "One of the hazards of smoking, Dear. Please, join me."

Santiago dropped to her knees beside the table and picked up the envelope with the tongs. She slid the knife blade into the seam of the envelope and slit it on the fold. After she shook the envelope a few times the bloodied cigarette box and a cassette tape in a plastic carrier fell onto the tabletop. Dry blood splatters covered the opening of the small box. The odor of the rotting flesh filled the room. Her stomach turned as the taste of phlegm crept into her mouth. In a whisper she said, "This is bad." She held the box with the tongs and pushed the lid open with the knife, then looked inside the pack. "Oh no."

She held the box out across the coffee table.

Braun peered in, then jerked back in a reflex action. "The bastards! Those dirty, rotten sons of bitches! I'll kill 'em if I ever get my hands on 'em." Tears filled Braun's eyes. He sat straight, rubbing the tops of both thighs. "How could they do this?" He wiped his cheeks with the palms of both hands. "God, Lindsey, I'm so sorry."

Nikki leaned forward and looked into the box and her face lost its color. Covering her mouth, she stood and ran from the room.

Santiago said, "We'd best open some windows and doors. The odor is gagging us."

Braun looked into the cigarette box. "Can we save it? Maybe it can be reattached when she gets home."

Santiago shook the finger out of the small box as a few flakes of tobacco fell onto the table. "Let's put it in the refrigerator. Can you get me something to put it in? Then we'll call your doctor. I don't know if it can be saved. Probably depends on the time of exposure or something."

Braun headed toward the kitchen mumbling "Rotten bastards."

Santiago called after him, "I'll open the windows."

Braun returned, tears streaming down his face. He handed Santiago a bowl filled with ice. "My baby... my poor baby. What was I thinking?"

Santiago placed the finger in the bowl and snapped the plastic lid closed while burping excess air from it, then took it to the kitchen and placed it in the refrigerator. When she returned Braun was on his cell phone.

Braun's voice was a near growl. "I want them really bad, Ray, but first let's get Lindsey home. I'll do whatever it takes. These guys are mine." He saw Santiago returning from the kitchen. "Talk to you later, Ray." He broke the connection. "Mitch, will you help us get them?"

"I'll help get Lindsey back of course, but first we should contact the authorities."

Braun began pacing. "Yes. I don't want anything to happen that will jeopardize Lindsey more than I already have. He said yesterday we'd receive instructions. We'll follow them to the letter, whatever he wants. After we get her home safe, we go after these animals."

Nikki returned from the bathroom, taking a place on the couch. "Sit with me, Claude. I want to hear the tape."

He moved to his wife's side and they joined hands. "Are you sure you're up to it?"

"I don't know. I think so. Yes. Whatever is on it, I need to hear. Lindsey is our daughter. Her suffering is ours."

Braun said, "Yes, she is." He placed his arm around Nikki's shoulders.

Santiago looked toward the entertainment center. "Does the stereo have a cassette player?"

Braun reached for the tape. "Yes."

"No, no," Santiago said. "I'll put it in the unit."

She picked up the tape with the tongs and crossed the room. The receiver popped open with the touch of a button and she dropped the tape into the slot, pushed the door closed, and pressed Play.

The speaker came to life. Braun stared at the unit as Quarterman's voice echoed through the room. "Your little girl is paying for your stupidity," followed by a blood-curdling shriek. Braun gripped Nikki's hand, his knuckles turning white. "Oh my God," he said, breath short, echoing his daughter's plea.

The couple looked at each other as the dead, cracking sound of bone snapping filled the room. Braun said, "I'm going to be sick."

Santiago remained in front of the entertainment center, her attention focused on the speakers.

The voice on the tape continued, "You're tougher than I thought."

Tears ran freely down the couple's cheeks. Braun swallowed. "I hate the taste of bile."

Nikki released her grip and rubbed her eyes, her hands in fists. "Why? Why?"

Santiago shook her head, the hair on her arms bristling. They listened to the remainder of the tape in silence. Santiago asked, "Who's the boyfriend?"

Braun said, "Probably T.J. We've been monitoring her friends since she came up missing. Ray reports we haven't been able to locate him."

Santiago pursed her lips. "But it could be someone else?"

He said, "With Lindsey anything is possible."

Nikki said, "It also means the kidnappers have two prisoners. Does anyone know the boy is even missing?" A silence fell over the room.

Braun straightened his back. "If it's a money thing the kid is probably a victim of circumstance. We don't know T.J.'s family, if indeed it's him. We've got to get them both home."

Santiago handed Nikki some tissue. "Do you have anything you can take to help you relax? Claude, let's call the FBI."

"It's already been done. House did it while we were listening to the tape."

Santiago said, "Good."

"Mitch, I want you to remain in charge."

She said, "They usually run things their way, working with local agencies."

"I know, but they'll cut me some slack. We'll continue in our role as well."

Nikki nodded, but she never took her gaze from Claude's face.

Braun said, "I don't want anything to jeopardize Lindsey's coming home. I—" Taking a tissue from Nikki, he brushed his eyes. "This is so goddamned gut wrenching. I've never felt so powerless."

Nikki said, "What do we do now?"

"Wait," he said. "We wait. It's their move. Lord only knows when they'll call again, or which one."

Santiago said, "We still have to get in touch with your doctor about the finger."

Braun reached for the phone. "Yes."

Nikki said, "Use the cell, Honey. Remember?"

"I forgot. Yes, the cell. When I'm done I'm having a stiff drink to quiet my nerves. Nikki?"

"Yes."

"Mitch?"

"No thank you. I have work to do, and Nikki, if you're going to take medication I'd skip the drink. They usually don't mix very well."

Nikki said, "Right now nothing is mixing well, Mitch. It's like I have a cement mixer in my gut."

Braun said, "We all do, but she's right. You take a pill and try to relax. I'll call the doctor and wait on the kidnappers."

Santiago said, "I'm going to the hotel. They're probably watching the house and tailing me."

Braun nodded. "Good point."

"I see you have the capability to duplicate the cassette. Any blanks?" Santiago said.

"Yes. In the cabinet, right side."

"I'm going to copy this and leave the original here for the authorities. We don't need to handle it anymore than we already have although I doubt they'll get any prints. I want Sam to hear this. The man on the tape made several references that implied a military background."

Braun looked at his trembling hands and wiped sweat from his face. "Jesus, I'm sweating like a pig and shaking like a leaf, but I feel paralyzed."

Santiago looked into Braun's face. A chill ran down her spine. "I'll get you that drink, Claude. Your eyes are vacant."

The telephone on the end table rang.

* * *

Yancey Quarterman moved between the Oasis Hotel buildings using an elevated pedestrian walkway and took a stairway to the ground level after crossing over the main driveway to the parking lot on the north side of the campus. He looked back at the five-foot high stucco walls of the walkway. "Man, that sky bridge is hot. A little shade and breeze would fit the bill."

He'd stolen a cell phone from a woman earlier in the day, taking it from her pocket as she browsed products in a card shop. He studied the faceplate. "I don't think any two companies make the damn things the same."

He punched in Braun's number, twice having to start over because his fingers overlapped the small buttons. He looked at the faceplate to check the number. "I don't believe it. How can your line be busy?" He pressed Off and returned the cell to his pocket, then walked across the parking lot.

He watched as cars slowed and stopped in the afternoon commute on Baseline Avenue. He reached for the cell phone again, pressed redial and waited. "One more time, Braun." He continued to watch the road while waiting. "Man, is the traffic always this heavy?"

A shaky man's voice answered. "Hello."

"Braun?"

"Yes."

"Did you get the package?"

"Yes, you bastard!"

"Careful, Braun. You don't want to say or do anything stupid."

"Let me talk to Lindsey, please."

Quarterman chuckled. "No can do. She's not with me at the moment. She's under wraps, so to speak. Bet her stub hurts a bunch."

Braun's voice began to break. "Why did you do that?"

"I told you on the tape. Now let's get down to business. I don't want to tie up your phone."

"I've been keeping this line open just for you."

"Hmm... it was busy a few minutes ago."

"A damned salesman from some AC outfit called. It's the only call we've had since—"

"Not interested. Here's the deal. We'll make the exchange tomorrow. Is the money ready?"

"Yes. When? Where?"

"Don't rush me. I'll let you know just a few minutes before it happens. Oh, and get another million ready just in case something goes wrong. Call it insurance."

"Insurance?"

"You never know, Braun—inflation, stupidity, a last-minute change of plans. As a businessman, you know the value of being prepared."

"I have the money. That's not a problem."

"Good. Now, has Aunt Michelle left yet?"

Santiago looked at Braun and shook her head.

"Not yet," Braun said. "We only received the tape and cigarette box a half-hour ago."

"Tell her to get moving. She has a date at 4:00. And Braun, she's definitely involved now."

Confusion crossed Braun's face. He looked at Nikki and Santiago. "I don't understand."

"You don't need to. She'll get instructions at the hotel."

The muffled sound of metal crunching crossed the parking lot. Quarterman watched as cars lined up behind an afternoon fender bender. Horns began honking and angry shouts filled the distant background. "Don't you love rush hour traffic?"

"What are you talking about?" Braun said.

"Just being amused by the traffic in front of the Oasis Hotel, Braun. That little tidbit ought to save your folks some time trying to triangulate this call."

A BMW convertible pulled into a nearby parking space. A young woman in tight-fitting shorts and a halter top got out of the car and walked across the lot toward the same stairway he had used. *Nice ass.* "Just be ready tomorrow, Braun."

"I'll be ready."

"Good. You know what I'm thinking about just this moment?"

"No."

"I'm thinking about fucking the eyeballs right out of Lindsey's head."

Laughter was the last thing Braun heard as the connection broke. Quarterman took out the handkerchief, wiped the phone clean, and dropped both in a trash container as he returned to the stairwell.

* * *

The phone on his desk only rang once before he answered. "Evans."

"Santiago. The package is here. It's Lindsey's finger and a cassette tape."

"Shit."

"It's pretty bad. Claude and Nikki are taking this very hard."

"That probably explains the urgent call I have from House. A secretary just walked in and handed me a note saying he's on another line."

"Yeah, Claude was on the phone almost immediately to their doctor after we played the tape. Then he called House."

"Doctor?"

"To see if anything can be done to save the finger."

"What about the tape?"

"Brutal. I'll have a copy with me at the hotel. That's where I'm heading now. Most important, the kidnapper just finished talking to Claude. He says the exchange is tomorrow, but also wants another million available. He called it insurance."

"That's a little odd. Directions?"

"None until just before the exchange. I'm thinking two parties, one a wild-goose chase, maybe."

"Could be. Look, I'll meet you at the hotel. You'll be getting there around 4:00."

"Hopefully a little quicker. The man said he was calling from the hotel and that I have a date."

"In that case I'll definitely be there. If nothing else I'll have your back, no pun intended."

"Appreciate it."

"And sometime this evening I'll fill you in on Dr. Rich."

"Right, and I haven't given up on the Bramble Bush tonight. Guess that will depend on what's awaiting me at the hotel. See you later."

After breaking the connection she went to Nikki at the patio pool bar. *My friend has a drinking problem.* "Nikki, can I borrow a few clothes?"

"Sure. Let's go check the closet." She placed a large tumbler on the bar. "I probably shouldn't drink this anyway, but I want to."

"I know. It's been a bad day." They walked back into the house and down the hallway.

"What would you like? Something sexy? Club stuff? Corporate bitch? I have it all."

"Definitely club since I'm going to the strip joint tonight. A mini but not a micro. Maybe a cocktail dress. Nothing real tight or too short."

"You don't want one of those come-fuck-me numbers like we used to wear?"

"Not this time. How much of that tumbler have you emptied?"

"Not enough," Nikki said. "Think he'll rape her?"

"I hope not. She's been through enough. The whole family has."

"I've always wondered what it would be like, being raped."

God, the stress and fear... anything for a diversion. It's getting to you. "I hope you never find out. I worked a couple of rape cases. At best, they were ugly. Where's Claude?"

"In his study on the phone arranging for more money."

"Well, I'm out of here. Come on. Walk to the den with me while I let him know."

As they approached the door it opened and Braun stepped into the hall. "The money is ready." He looked at Nikki, then took her hand. "Come on. I think you need a little rest."

Santiago said, "I'll call you later. Both of you try to get some rest. You're going to need it."

* * *

Santiago entered suite 5004 in a rush and glanced at her watch. "3:49 and I have a 4:00 o'clock date? What did he mean?" She checked the phone message light. "No calls. Good."

Her flight bag was already sitting on the couch. Picking it up she went into the bedroom and saw the gift-wrapped package and card on the bed. "Chance, you romantic. I haven't even called you yet."

Removing the card from the envelope she smiled at its cover. The caricature of a smiling cactus looked back at her. "Welcome to Phoenix."

As she opened the card her smile disappeared. Glued cutout letters read, *Aunt Michelle, in the package you will find a red bikini. Put it on and be at poolside by 4:00 p.m.*

She checked the clock radio; 3:51. She undressed and slipped into the red bikini. Looking in the mirror she mumbled, "Doesn't cover much. The triangles could be larger. They barely cover my nipples. I could use some carpet tape about now. You'd like this, Chance."

She grabbed a towel from the bathroom and wrapped herself while heading for the door. Snapping it open she found Evans, his hand raised as he prepared to knock.

"The tape is in my purse. Play it and just stay here 'til I get back. I'll explain later."

"No need. Where are you heading?"

"The pool at 4:00," she said and raced down the hallway to the elevator.

"Great legs, great everything," Evans mumbled as he walked into the suite.

He crossed the room, passed through the bedroom, came to the lanai slider, moved the curtain and peered out. "Damn, wrong side of the building. Listen to the tape, dummy."

* * *

As Quarterman walked into the pool area of the Oasis, he spotted Lisa Fargo embracing the sun on a lounge, her oily flesh gleaming. He gestured toward an empty chair only a few feet away with his right hand. "Is this taken?"

"No," she said glancing up, shading her eyes. "I thought you'd never show."

"I'm Lance Norton," he said extending a hand. "And you're obviously a guest here too?"

"You know I am."

He leaned toward her and quietly said, "It's a pleasure to meet you, Miss...?"

"Brooke... Brooke Meredith."

"That's better," he said in a whisper.

In a voice just loud enough for those in the immediate area to hear she said, "Yes, I'm just here for a few days."

He looked at the pool. "How's the water?"

"Fine," she said. "You sound different, like a guy in a movie."

A waiter appeared. "Would the gentleman like a cocktail?"

"Please. Tanqueray and tonic." Quarterman looked at Lisa. "Would you like to join me?"

"Yes, thank you. I'll have a vodka martini with olives and an onion."

"They'll be here shortly." The waiter left to continue his round.

Quarterman moved his chair closer to Lisa. "Remember, we're strangers." He paused for a moment. "I'm here on a business trip."

"I'm finishing a chapter in marriage, just waiting around for my attorney. You know how it is." She laughed. Then more quietly she said, "You're so different."

"It's a cover."

"You've done this before. My cousin is a man of mystery."

"Many times. The one piece looks very nice on you."

"Thank you." She looked at Quarterman's lean frame. "I don't think I've ever seen you in trunks before. Nice image. They look good on you."

"Strangers, Brooke. We've never met before. Remember that. Santiago will be coming here in a few minutes. When she does I'll point her out. Remember, I just want you to keep an eye on her when she's on site."

"I know my job."

The waiter returned, placed coasters on the small patio table, and put the drinks down slowly while surveying Lisa's cleavage. He handed Quarterman a twin receipt.

"I'll put it on my room," he said, signing the slip and adding a five-dollar tip.

"Thank you, Sir... Mr. Norton."

"My pleasure." Quarterman raised a glass and looked at Lisa. "To the wonderful people I meet in my travels." As they sipped, the waiter departed.

"I didn't know you could be so suave," she said. "I kind'a like it."

"In my profession a man must blend into many settings."

"Your profession? All these years and I don't even know you."

"We don't need to go there. Let's just say I've been more than a mercenary these last several years."

Lisa nodded toward the building. "I'm in 1103. It opens onto the pool."

"Good."

"Where are you located?"

"Suite 5009." He glanced upward. "Way up there. Remember this—if you must reach me, call my room and leave the message, 'This is your broker.' I'll get back to you. One never knows who will hear those messages. If I call you I'll leave a message using Lance Norton. Got it?"

"Sounds easy enough."

"Did you get any shoes?"

"Yes, two pair and a nice cocktail dress." She sipped the martini. "It's conservative but elegant. How about another round?"

"Not today. We're working, remember?"

"How could I forget? Do you want me to approach Santiago?"

"No, just blend in. If you encounter her keep it simple. I just want to know when she's here and who she sees."

She nodded toward a young couple with their chairs snuggled together. "They look happy."

"That they do. He looks like a jarhead, probably on leave."

"Jarhead. That's not a very nice thing to say."

"Trust me, it's a complement. He's in really great shape."

"I don't recall you ever lookin' at guys before, but he is a hunk."

"He's a Marine if I've ever seen one."

"Or maybe just a jock."

Quarterman shook his head. "Look at the tattoo on his bicep... eagle, globe and anchor." Quarterman took a sip from his drink. "That's what I want someday, and soon."

"A tattoo?"

"No, just to be with a woman that has eyes only for me. To be a couple lost in our own world. I have to admit I haven't done much to get there yet."

"No, but you've had an exciting life... strange, but exciting. You've been everywhere."

"Yeah, mostly as a fugitive or a mercenary. I'm thinking it will be nice to settle down in the time I have left. It gets tiresome traveling all the time."

"You mentioned that earlier. Mexico, maybe a bar and grill, right?"

"Something like that. I just want to experience what life is as a normal person before they catch up with me."

She took a sip of the cocktail. "You have some strange habits that will need changing."

"I know, but maybe with the right woman...."

Lisa checked the young couple again. "She's a lucky girl."

Quarterman sat up straight and glanced at his watch. "There she is, right on time."

"Where?"

"The red bikini coming through the gate. Don't you recognize it? You bought it."

"I see her, red string and showing a lot of really smooth skin." She paused, tongue teasing her teeth. "And you tell me no thong. That's close."

He stood up. "Lots of skin, no wire. It's just one way of letting her know who's in charge."

"Are you goin' over and meet her?"

"Not exactly. Just a phone call from my room." Then in a louder voice others could hear he said, "It was pleasant meeting you, Mrs. Meredith. Perhaps we'll run into each other again before your business is complete." Quarterman left the pool area.

Lisa took a final sip of her drink and said in a soft voice, "Where are you comin' from, Yancey? First you're tired, now you're talkin' about settlin' down."

She looked across the pool at Santiago stretched out on a lounge. "You're nothin' but trouble, Bitch. I can feel it."

* * * * * * *

The Oasis Hotel pool was in keeping with the other appointments of the facility. Santiago walked in and took a lounge located on the shady side. She looked around, searching for a face watching her for too long. *Great, a red string bikini... every man in the place is either glancing or just flat staring.* Five men and three women were using cell phones. A barman approached her from behind carrying a hotel phone.

"Miss Santiago, I have a call for you if you choose to take it."

"Yes, thank you."

He left immediately.

"Hello?"

"Welcome to Arizona, Aunt Michelle. I see you got my package."

She looked around the area again. "It was hard to miss."

"Don't bother trying to figure out which guy is me. I'm not in the pool area, but I can see you very clearly. I like what I see."

Santiago sat up. The pool was enclosed in a courtyard of four buildings, five floors each. "So why are you calling me?"

"I figure you're here to find Lindsey. I feel it in my bones."

"Mr. Braun invited me here because I'm considering working for his company."

"I like the sound of that, very professional. I read about you in the Portland papers, or maybe I heard the kids talking about you nailing some professor for killin' a bum and a teacher."

"You know who I am," she said, thinking of the just-completed Cashland case. "Actually, you invited me into this drama," she said searching the lanais. "You know I was at the Braun's when they played the tape because you called. So why the charade and the red bikini?"

"Control, Bitch. I want you to know I'm in charge and I'm watchin' you. Right now I'm enjoying watching you squirm, checking the balconies, the two guys with binoculars on the fourth floor."

A chill shot up Santiago's spine. The hair on her neck and arms bristled. "How do we know Lindsey is still alive, that what you imply is true?"

"Lady, cut the crap. Jesus, do all cops talk like that? Imply, my sweet ass. Look, how about I send you another finger?"

"Okay, okay, let's assume she's alive. Braun wants to talk to her before payment."

"Good. I'm glad to see we're getting somewhere. Tomorrow before the exchange he'll get a call with directions. He'll get to talk to her then. Did he tell you I told him to get another million ready? He may have to pay something for bringin' you in."

"I thought that's what the finger was for?"

"The price could go up."

"I heard the call. Same breakdown in bills?"

"Not necessarily. It's his insurance the kid makes it home."

"A second payment?"

"Anything is possible. It could assure she doesn't have another negative experience."

She wiped sweat from her arms while cradling the phone. "Fair enough."

"Is it hot down there?"

"Yes."

"I like the look of you covered in sweat."

Lust always sounds the same. "You do? Judging from the guys down here I don't think you're alone. I'm sure they thank you for the gift too."

"It's not a gift, just a fringe benefit because of the time and place."

"Really? A perk for whom? I'd bet you can't get any without being a thug."

"I'd watch my mouth if I were you."

"Okay, all we want is Lindsey and her boyfriend returned."

"Don't forget you're a cop. I haven't."

"I'm on leave. New job possibility, remember?"

"You keep sayin' that. Enjoy the sun. We'll be talkin' tomorrow. That reminds me, I need the number of your cell."

She swallowed, then gave him the number complete with the Seattle area code.

"I'll be callin' when I'm ready. Make sure it's charged."

* * *

Santiago returned to her room, not bothering to use the keycard but just tapping on the door. Evans opened it and stepped to the side. "How did it go?"

"Strange, odd, frightening," she said, dropped the towel on the couch and headed for the bedroom. "Did you listen to the tape?"

"Yes. What kind of a man could just cut the finger of a kid?"

She returned to the sitting room in white shorts and a pink tube top. "Who knows—psychopath, sociopath, someone who's just evil.... God, I felt really naked down there."

Evans smirked. "You were close."

"I'm not a prude, but if I'm going to show that much skin I want it to be by choice, not chance or coercion."

"So what did he want?"

Santiago paced the room. "He wants to intimidate me. He emphasized who's in charge. 'Control' was the word he used. The package in the room was his way of showing me he can get anywhere he wants, whenever he wants. On the tape he made several references that implied a military mindset, at least to me."

"For example?"

"He said something about Lindsey being 'tougher' than he thought, and the phrase 'being a real soldier' caught my attention."

"I noticed those comments too, but the ones that bothered me implied a potentially deadly background, especially when he said something about not having 'this much fun in years'... really spooky. Another one that really set off the bells was 'most of 'em never knew.' That's a really loaded phrase."

"Sam, we need to know who these guys are, especially the older one."

"I agree. When I leave here I'm going to the office. We're only a few minutes away. I want to get some things started. That'll give you some time to get dressed for the Bramble Bush. I'll be back in half an hour, maybe forty-five minutes. Okay?"

"Sure. I need to call my partner anyway. I told him I'd keep him posted. Does your wife know where we're going tonight?" She smiled. "You know, a room full of naked women dancing around and maybe a few naked men too?"

He laughed. "Not exactly. I told her I'm working late. We'll have dinner, just the two of us, when I get home."

Santiago grinned. "That should be some dinner."

"Do they really have naked men dancing there?"

Santiago raised an eyebrow. "According to Nikki they do. That's a twist on most clubs."

Evans blushed. "Sounds deviant."

"Only to men. But back on task, did you find anything in the background checks of Claude's special list?"

Evans stepped toward the door. "Some. I'll fill you in on the way to the club. I'll see you shortly."

"Wait up. I'll ride down with you. I have some clothes in the car for tonight, unless you want me going this way?"

He stopped and laughed as the empty elevator opened. "I'll wait, but most of the audience would probably prefer the shorts."

She said, "What are you checking on?"

"Nothing. Just some loose ends, an idea or two."

Partners are supposed to share. "Well, I have something. Remember Spears tapping into my personnel file?"

"How could I forget? House didn't believe it."

"While you're at the office would you check my file and see if my cell number is listed?"

"Can do. Are you expecting him to call you?"

The doors opened in the lobby and they exited passing by Lisa Fargo. "No, just curious. The man on the phone wanted my cell number."

When Lisa spotted Evans and Santiago she whispered, "God, you'd think she would have a better looking younger partner than him."

She walked into the hotel restaurant just off the lobby for an early dinner, and a hostess greeted her. "One for dinner?"

She grinned. "For now."

* * *

Quarterman smiled at himself in the mirror, his chiseled naked frame defined in high contrast shadows. He tossed the cell phone on the bed and glanced a final time out the slider toward the pool, then looked at the wall mirror. "She's already gone. You've got needs... big needs."

He dressed in tan slacks and a mint green polo shirt, then slipped on a pair of canvas shoes, no socks. He checked his image one more time. "I think it's time to meet, Sugar."

Leaving the room and walking down the hallway he wondered, *Will I encounter Santiago?* At room 5004 he paused for just a moment. All was quiet. He boarded the elevator. "We'll meet. The recorder will pick her up."

He rode the elevator to the lobby and went directly to the parking lot. As he opened the door of the new rental Cadillac a wave of hot air rolled out of the car. A backpack was on the passenger seat. "Chocolate," he hummed, "oh, sweet chocolate."

It took only a few minutes for the car to cool down with its engine purring and a soft breeze flowing from the AC. Driving through the parking lot he approached the exit onto Baseline. "Thank God they have a light here. It would take a saint to let me into this traffic."

He made a right onto Baseline and moved across the three-lane highway to the left turn lanes, passed under the I-10 overpass, and waited for the next green light. Then he followed I-10 into Phoenix. The traffic was slow even as the rush hour wore down. Chase Field, home of the Diamondbacks, slid by on his right, the top open for a bit of natural light on the grass. He turned north on the I-17 exit and drove to Indian

School Road, then west to 7th Avenue. He pulled into a small older motel just across the street from the Stray Cat Gentlemen's Club. Two late model SUV's were the only vehicles in the parking lot. "This will do nicely."

The small office of the Cut 'N Go Motel was wallpapered with XXX film posters, a flat rate occupancy per room sign stating $50.00 per night, checkout at 11:00 a.m. and flyers from several fast food services that delivered until around midnight. The registration area was surrounded by wire mesh windows with a small slit in the middle bottom where items could be exchanged.

A man wearing a turban, a western shirt and tight jeans came through a curtain suspended on the wall behind the counter. He said in a soft, strong voice with a Middle Eastern accent, "A room for the night?"

Quarterman pushed a $50.00 bill through the slot. "Yes."

The man pushed a card and pen through the small opening in return. "Please complete the registration card and include your license plate number. We have many people attempting to use our parking lot during the evening hours."

Quarterman gestured toward the door. "I'll need to check the plate. It's a rental."

The man followed his glance. "The Caddie?"

"Yeah."

"We don't get many of those here. It won't be a problem Mr...." He studied the registration card. "Ah, Mr. Smith."

"I come from a big family."

"Yes you do."

Both men laughed and exchanged glances. The clerk pushed a key through the slot. "You're in number 7, a few doors down on the left. Checkout is 11:00 a.m."

"Thanks. I saw the sign."

"Would you like to rent some videos? We also have coupons for several of the delivery restaurants."

"No thanks. In fact, I'm taking off for a while. I may have a friend with me when I return."

"Our fee for the room is a flat rate. No charge if you have a friend in."

Quarterman realized he hadn't put his watch on before leaving the Oasis. "Do you have the time?"

"6:41."

"Thanks. See you later."

Quarterman returned to the car. The return trip to the Oasis was much quicker. The evening rush had subsided and he was driving against that which remained. He looked at his eyes in the review mirror. *I'll get a little rest and then it's off to the Stray Cat. It's been a long day.*

His tires thumped against the lane markers. He refocused his attention on the road after swerving into the lane on his left. A man waving a beer bottle from the window of a pickup truck next to him was jacking his jaws and glaring daggers. He threw the bottle, barely missing the Caddy's windshield as it flew over the hood. Quarterman smiled and speeded up, pulled alongside, then ahead of the truck. He raised the middle finger of his left hand to the window. "A salute to you."

The truck came alongside again. The bottle-tossing passenger pointed to the roadside. Quarterman reached into the backpack on the passenger seat and rested his hand on the butt of a .45. *Not a good plan. They'd probably report a gun to the cops.*

He let go of the weapon, smiled again at the man in the truck and nodded. He slowed and the truck cut in front of him and pulled onto the I-17 shoulder. The traffic behind Quarterman backed up. Gunning the engine, he pushed the Caddie to 75 and filled in the gap in front of him. The cars behind him matched his quick burst. The truck disappeared in his mirror caught in the last gasp of the day's rush, stuck on the shoulder waiting for an opportunity to get back on the freeway.

Quarterman looked into the review mirror. "Dumb shits. *Lucky* shits."

* * *

Santiago showered after returning to the suite before changing into Nikki's party attire. It was more of a cleansing reaction to the call at poolside than late day refreshment. Wrapped in a thick bathrobe she poured a glass of Chardonnay from the hospitality bar and curled up on the sitting room loveseat to call Seattle.

He answered on the second ring, "Stewart."

She felt a rush of energy. "Hi."

"Mitch, how's it goin'?"

"Rough, very rough. They sent Lindsey's ring finger in a cigarette box today."

"Jesus," he said.

She made a face at the wine glass. "Ghoulish. Dry blood and the stench of rotting flesh."

"Why?"

"Punish Braun for involving a cop. Somehow they found me out."

"Any idea of how many?"

"At least a pair. We've had calls from two different men. The first sounded young and the second older. The older guy sounded mean, very threatening."

"So what's next?"

"First, they insisted I move out of Braun's place so I'm staying at the Desert Oasis Golf Resort Hotel."

"They let you stay around?"

"I don't think they were sure of why I'm here. Claude didn't blow my cover story last night."

"That's good."

"Maybe. I think the older man has other plans. Truth is, it doesn't matter much now. I just had a phone conversation with the older guy at the pool and he's put me in the middle of everything." The sound of children talking in the background came through the phone. "Sounds like a cabin full."

"Yeah. We came home. The kids want to go to the Seattle Center. You know the routine, rides and a pizza."

"I wish I was there."

"So do I. You know, they could be keeping you around just to hold over Braun's head."

"How so?"

"They can keep tabs on what you're doing."

"Compromise the investigation?"

"To a point, and threaten Braun. If anything goes wrong with the exchange it's his fault for bringing you aboard. Have they given any instructions yet?"

"No, but they doubled the ransom. Funny part is they didn't stipulate what form the additional money should come in. The first million they want in used bills, hundreds. Something else, they originally said we would get instructions today, now its tomorrow."

"That's not a good sign."

"My feeling exactly. They could be fighting among themselves."

"Possibly, especially if one wants to kill Lindsey and the other wants to get her home safely."

"Same thought I've had. It's spooky, Chance."

"How are your friends doing?"

"Well, they're not what I expected. Nikki seems to be caught up in trying to distract herself through shopping and booze, and Claude is still horny as ever. You'd think he'd give it a rest, but he's actually got some nubile bimbo hanging around the backyard pool. I'd expect him to give his wife a little consideration, especially now."

"He's definitely a piece of work, not too sensitive."

"Hardly."

"The ring finger, huh?"

"Yes. Why?"

"Strange."

"Sick is more like it," she said.

"No, I mean strange. While we were chasing Gunn around La Push the Seaside Police were looking for clues into the murder of a co-ed during spring break. They've notified all surrounding agencies about the homicide because they haven't got any leads, nothing. Odd part is one of the victim's finger's was amputated. I believe it was also the ring finger."

A chill ran up Santiago's spine. "Have they released the info to the public?"

"Not a word. But you know they're thinking serial killer."

"Was the victim sexually assaulted?"

"I'm not sure. As I recall the report said the victim had sex shortly before her death, but made no mention of it being forced. The cause of death was a broken neck. If you'd like the details I'll pull up the file and get back to you."

"I'd appreciate it. I hope the two incidents aren't related, but stranger things have happened. He did mention the Portland newspapers. Just give me a call when you get it together."

A soft voice came from the background. "Chance, we're ready when you are."

Who the hell is that? "I thought you and the kids were going to the center?"

He chuckled. "We are. The kids are a handful so I asked Amber to go along, kind'a help keep track of 'em."

Santiago's temples suddenly burned and blood pounded through her body. *I'll bet. Gone forty-eight hours and you're already back in the saddle.* "Well, call me when you have something if you have time."

"I will. Talk to you later."

Santiago walked over to the slider and looked outside. Even in the front of the hotel couples were walking, laughing and enjoying themselves. "You're all having more fun than me. Damn it! Damn you, Chance. I didn't even tell you about the call or the red bikini."

* * *

The faint outline of a full moon appeared in the still light evening sky as the Brauns sat on lounge chairs overlooking the pool. Nikki's eyes were bloodshot and her face flush. The tumbler near her right hand was empty except for the remains of a few pieces of ice.

She said, "I think I need a refill."

Braun said, "No, that's the last thing you need. We need to keep our act together for Lindsey's sake. They could call at any time."

She sucked the remaining ice into her mouth and crunched it. "Act, that's a good way of describing today. Mitch met Sierra this morning."

"Yes, I know. After she left I told Sierra she had to leave."

"You told her to leave? You ditched your whore?"

"Nikki, I know I haven't been the most faithful husband, but now is not the time."

"When is the time?"

"She's gone. I doubt she'll be back even after Lindsey gets home."

"And our future?"

He looked out beyond the stucco wall surrounding the yard. "One day at a time. Too many things are happening too fast. I need my world whole again."

"We both do."

"Look at the moon, Nikki. It's beautiful. Maybe we should have one more drink." He stood and picked up both tumblers. "All my life I've wanted things. Originally it was for my family. Somewhere I lost track of where I wanted to go."

"And now?"

He looked at the empty glasses in his hands. "Honestly? I feel suspended and helpless. My emotions are bouncing like they're on a bungee cord."

"You loved Lelani so much Claude, and Lindsey too. That love was good and healthy, but you need to make room for others in your heart. I love you and Lindsey. We're a family."

"I know."

She looked at her husband and the empty tumblers. "Love is much more than a physical relationship. It means trust, understanding, the joy of sharing big things and little ones... everything."

"I know, it's a lot of other things and maybe I haven't done very well with some of them. Right now I just want Lindsey home safe and sound."

"We both do, but what about afterward, when things are normal again?"

"Things will never be normal again. This whole kidnapping business is a cloud that will hang over us forever," he said.

She looked into Braun's tired eyes. "Lindsey being home can bring closure."

"That bastard being dead will bring closure. I want Lindsey home; then I want Santiago to find him and bring him down."

"She won't kill him, Claude."

"I know. It's just a figure of speech, but somebody could if she finds him."

* * * * * * *

Santiago and Evans drove north on Tempe's Mill Avenue, the hub of most ASU students' social life. From 7th to the Rio Salado Parkway where the historic Hayden Flour Mill stands they passed block after block of tiny boutiques, restaurants, bars, coffee houses, and groups of people milling about as evening encroached. The sound of loud music repeatedly filled the car, then faded. Walkers, skaters, bicyclists, and the occasional skateboarder cut in and out through the bunched traffic. Parking places were full and flashing neon filled the sky as the avenue's after-dark light show came to life.

Santiago said, "Reminds me of the U District, alive and friendly, people enjoying life."

"Yeah," Evans said. "It is now, but not the first time I saw it during '70s. Then it was all hippies and protesters. It was ugly."

"College kids all over the country were protesting according to my parents."

"Yeah, from their deferment-sheltered soapboxes. Mostly anarchists pushing their right of free speech while denying it to anyone who disagreed with 'em. It was free sex, drugs, and commies. Mill Avenue was Sodom and Gomorrah to some of us."

"You were here?"

"You bet. Government sent me. I was doing undercover work investigating possible terrorist groups, subversives, stuff being promoted by the Russians, Chinese, and VC."

"You were very young."

"Just out of college. They trained me and sent me here because I could fit in."

"Did you find much foreign involvement?"

Evans face became red, his knuckles and fingers white wrapped around the steering wheel. "Not as much as my superiors expected. Most of the stuff goin' on was home grown. It's past history now, nothin' like the terrorists and cartels we have today in the Middle East, Latin America, South America, Europe or even the States."

They stopped at a red light. A blind man was led across 7th by his dog while a young couple kissed on the corner, oblivious to all around them. Santiago nodded in their direction. "They're happy."

"Too public for me."

The light changed and they moved on. Santiago laughed. "You sound like a friend of mine from Yoder the first time she went to Alki Beach with us. Her idea of a bikini was a two piece swim suit with a waist at the navel."

"Alki? That in Seattle? I thought it always rained up there."

"It gets its fair share, but yes, Alki is in Seattle, the northwest version of a California beach, the college young adult crowd."

"Did she go back a second time?"

"Oh yes, and in a bikini. Even with Seattle weather she had a nice tan by the time she went home for the summer."

They approached an old cinderblock building. Evans said, "Here we are. If the parking lot is any indication, they don't have much of a crowd. Only four vehicles, all trucks."

"It's early, Sam. I'm sure the murder of Trinity Durango has slowed the regulars down too. You ready? Let's do it."

They crossed the parking lot. He said, "No windows."

"No free peeks, not at one of these clubs."

Evans held the large dark sun-dried wooden door open. "After you. This is one time you get to lead."

She smiled and nudged her way past him. "Sam, have you ever been to a strip club?"

Evans blushed. "Not really."

A small welcome sign hung behind a counter that restricted to single file those entering. A buff counterman checked identification and collected the cover charge. Another muscular young man stood at the other side of the narrow entry directly across from the counter, arms folded, biceps stretched tight.

She said, "Those guys are a nice way to caution the clientele that stupid behavior won't be tolerated."

Evans moved in front of her to the counter. He whispered, "One of 'em is probably Arnold."

The man behind the counter wearing s skintight tank top said, "Welcome to the club. That'll be fifteen bucks, the lady is free."

Santiago smiled at the counterman. *Not really.*

Evans paid the man as he looked at a small sign behind the counter. "Bramble Bush Gentlemen's Club?"

The counterman looked at Santiago and chuckled. "Some nights we have guys dancing for the ladies, still no charge of course. Sorry, no guys tonight."

Santiago said, "Win some, lose some. We're here to see Cliff Arnold if he's available."

The counterman said, "Who are you?"

She said, "A friend of Lindsey Braun. I'm in town for a few days and I thought I'd look her up, but she hasn't been around her apartment or her folk's home. Her mom said I might find her hanging around here, or maybe Cliff might know where we could connect."

The counterman paused. "It's been a tough day. Cops had all the employees here a couple of hours ago, and a few of the regulars that came by. You heard about the murder?"

"Yes, we did. Very sad," she said.

"Boss wants to keep a tight rein on staff talkin', especially to the press."

Evans said, "I don't blame him."

The man across from the counter looked at Santiago and said, "I'm Cliff. I'll have a break in a couple of minutes. Go on in. I'll join you when my relief gets here."

A middle-aged woman approached the door from the shadows of the club room. "Is anything wrong, Cliff?"

Arnold said, "No, Ma'am, just a couple of Lindsey's friends lookin' for her."

She looked Santiago over from head to toe and gave Evans a quick glance. "Really? You look like cops to me."

Santiago smiled at the woman. "You're close. I'm a Seattle cop on vacation. As I told Cliff, Lindsey Braun is a friend of mine. I'm in town and thought I'd look her up. Nikki sent us here. She said the Bramble Bush is one of Lindsey's hangouts."

The woman took a deep breath. "It is, for both of them. Like Cliff said, he'll be on break shortly. It's been a bad day. The murder of one of our girls has shaken everyone up."

Evans looked for a place to stand and said, "We can wait here in the lobby."

Santiago nudged him. "Oh, come on, Sam. Let's see what's goin' on. They don't bite."

"You sure?"

"No."

They walked into the main clubroom. Strobe lights flashed to the beat of loud music. A young woman appeared on stage wearing a thong, a silk blouse and five-inch stilettos. The color of her garments depended on which light was hitting her at any moment. Few patrons were visible in the dark room but two men were sitting at the stage bar waving dollar bills. The dancer straddled a pole in the middle of a small stage and slowly removed her blouse while teasing the two off their stools. When she came near the edge of the bar they put the dollar bills in the thong.

Evans sat down at a table on a wall near the back of the room, looked at the bar, loosened his collar and nodded toward the door. "Those two are sure a pair to draw to."

"They look pretty good to me."

He rubbed his brow. "You think so? It's warm in here."

She laughed. "It may come as a shock to you, Sam, but women are interested in men for more than intellectual stimulation."

Another young woman, all legs and flesh, approached their table. She slipped a cropped blouse from her shoulders and dropped it on the floor by Evans' feet. "Table dance?"

Cliff Arnold approached the table. "Not right now, Dottie. I gotta talk to these folks for a minute while I'm on break."

She bent over, brushing Evans' knee, and scooped up the blouse. "I'll be back, Handsome."

A man barely visible in the dark waved a twenty dollar bill at Dottie. "Over here, Honey."

Arnold pulled over an empty chair and sat down. "So you guys are looking for Lindsey? I haven't seen her for a few days, maybe a week. Wish she was around. She makes this place come alive."

Santiago said, "Any idea where I might find her?"

Arnold glanced at Dottie and smiled. "She's probably holed-up somewhere with T.J. They were hitting it off pretty good."

Santiago said, "Well, she gets around."

Arnold nodded. "I know. Wish I was T.J. We all do."

"All?" Evans said.

"Yeah... me, Doug Straight, Mario Spears. She's a great gal and T.J. seems to be more than the flavor of the month. They could be at his place."

Santiago said, "We tried there but nobody was home."

"T.J.'s a romantic kind'a guy. They could be somewhere like a love nest. They met in Vegas."

Evans watched the couch dance going on at the table near them and swallowed, then looked back at Cliff. In a higher voice than normal he said, "Can he afford a love nest, being a student?"

Cliff said, "No, but Lindsey can."

Santiago asked, "Are you a student?"

Cliff said, "Only of life and hard knocks." He shook his head. "I've thought about going back to school but money and time get in the way. I like to do a lot of things. I read a lot."

Evans said, "You folks were busy today."

"Really, Trinity not showing up for work for a day or two is no big surprise, you know, but murder? Christ, that has all of us shaking."

Evans turned fully back to the table. "Was Trinity popular with the clientele?"

Arnold chuckled. "Look around, man. What do you see?"

Evans surveyed the room. "I see naked women dancing like they're having sex without partners."

Cliff said, "Nah... beautiful women teasing the socks off these guys and making good money, that's what you see."

Santiago nodded and let a small giggle escape.

"Was she popular? Hell yes. All of them are. This is dreamland. Guys come here to fulfill fantasies. Well, most of 'em do. A couple of 'em hang around because it's home, like a neighborhood bar."

Cliff gestured toward the table on Santiago's right. "Jed is here almost every night. He knows all the girls, watches them dance, buys an occasional table dance... a true regular."

The man heard his name and looked over at their table. "How y'doin', Cliff?"

He nodded at the man dressed in jeans and a dirty work shirt. "About what you'd expect with Trinity's murder, Jed. These folks are friends of Lindsey's. They're looking for her."

Jed licked his lips. "Nice kid. Wish she worked here."

Cliff said, "I have to get back to work, guys. Hope you find her before you leave town, Miss Santiago. If she comes in I'll let her know you're looking for her."

Santiago said, "Thank you. Before you go, Cliff, did Lindsey have any friends among the other patrons?"

"Other than Mario, Doug and T.J. no, but every guy who comes here regularly was hot for her. A couple 'em tried getting on her good side but Lindsey's part of her own crowd. The club is just background, a place to hang out."

Evans asked, "Did she know Trinity?"

"Not really. Sorry guys, but I have to get back."

Jed leaned toward Santiago and Evans. "Heard you askin' 'bout Trinity and Lindsey. Nice girls, easy on the eyes. An older fella like me was hittin' it off pretty good with Trinity. Wanted to take her out, that sort of thing."

Santiago leaned toward Jed. "Did you tell the police about him?"

"They didn't ask."

Evans said, "Maybe you should give them a call, just in case nobody else mentioned him."

"Maybe I should. He was a big dude, mean looking, but he sure liked Trinity."

Santiago's eyes had adjusted to the lighting. She looked at Jed, his long white hair touching the shoulders held in place by a dark colored headband, his powerful forearms highlighted by the flashing lights distorting the images of a tie-dye soiled shirt. *Is this guy still in the '60s or '70s?* "What did he look like?"

"Like I said, he was a big guy, ruddy complexion. Hard to see in here. All the lights are on the girls." He laughed. "But they're better lookin' anyway, don'cha think?"

Evans said, "For sure."

Santiago asked, "How well did you know Trinity?"

"Not hardly at all, but she was a nice little thing."

Thing? "Did she ever talk with you?"

"Only when she was doin' a table dance, not very often. They're too expensive, the dances."

Santiago noticed her partner was caught up in the show at a nearby table. "I know what you mean, Jed. Just tell me what you recall about her."

"She was pretty sexy, seemed to be available, you know. The big guy liked her, like I said. Surprising she was interested since he was easily in his fifties, maybe even sixties, but his wallet always seemed to be full. They talked a lot but nobody could hear 'em. He bought couch dances all the time like he was keepin' her away from other guys."

Santiago nodded. "Did you know his name?"

Jed took a sip of his four-dollar soda. "Nope. Like I said, he looked really mean. He was always sneakin' pats on her backside, teasin' her, givin' her big tips."

Santiago nodded. "It's a tipping business."

Jed wiped his mouth with the back of a large hand. "He wanted somethin', but then don't we all?"

Evans turned back to the table. "Are we talking about Lindsey?"

"Jed was telling me about Trinity and a special fan she had. I'll fill you in later. Jed, did the big guy visit with any patrons or any of the other dancers?"

Jed took a deep breath. "Just Trinity. Terrible. I'm gonna miss her. We all are. Do you think he had anything to do with it?"

"That's for the police to find out, Jed. Like Sam said, give them a call."

He took another sip of the soda. "I might just do that. Gotta make these bastards last at these prices, and I sure can't handle booze anymore."

Evans waved a hand and a young woman, apparently a dancer doing her time as a barmaid, came over. He gestured around the table. "Three more, please."

"Thanks. That's mighty kind of ya," Jed said with a laugh. "You know, he always struck me as bein' kind'a dirty."

Santiago said, "Really?"

The conversation paused when the waitress dancer delivered chilled glasses of soda.

Jed continued, "He had the nasty biker image thing, you know."

Santiago watched Jed's unblinking eyes.

"You guys with the cops?"

"No," Evans said. "We're just looking for a friend. Mitch is always into crime stuff. She's a cop on vacation."

"That Lindsey is a pretty little thing, not like most of the crowd she hangs with."

Evans turned away from the floor shows and focused on Jed. "Really?"

"Really, most of 'em look at us regulars like perverts. To her, if she ever spoke at all, we were just people here havin' a good time, makin' ourselves at home. Most of 'em were like the one over there, just spoiled brats who think their shit don't stink."

Santiago glanced across the room. "Well, well, it's a small world."

Jed started shifting around in his seat, looking around the club.

She looked at Evans, again lost in the performance taking place near their table. "It was nice talking with you, Jed. Thank you."

Jed looked at Santiago. "Pleasure was mine. You know, you could probably get a job here if you wanted."

Santiago nudged Evans. "Well thank you, Jed. Sam, do you have a card?"

Evans reached in a pocket and pulled one out, holding it across the table, his eyes never leaving the dancer.

"Jed, take this. If you think of anything else or want some help talking with the cops just call us."

He again tilted the glass slightly toward her, and the card. "Thanks for the refill."

"You're welcome."

He turned back to his table and the staring state he had been in when they entered.

Santiago nudged Evans' arm again. He turned toward her. "Time to go?"

"Probably past it. I think I've lost you."

Sweat covered Evans upper lip and forehead. "This is really degrading."

Careful, Sam... I'm sure you've read my file. "I can tell you're into deep research, but take a moment away from your studies and look across the room."

Evan followed her glance, then gulped. "Well, Mario. Oh man, I hope he hasn't seen us. This will be all over the office."

"I doubt he's watching us. I'm done here. How about you?"

He stood. "Oh yes. You're ready to go? Good."

She nodded and stood. "I'm going back to the hotel and eat dinner."

"And I'm heading home."

Passing the exit they saw Cliff checking ID. He said, "Come again."

"We just might do that," she said passing a poster of the male dancers.

Cliff pointed at the man in the middle of the poster. "They call him 'The Counselor' and the ladies love him."

She said, "Safe bet." *Boss lady says Nikki comes here often and Sierra says Nikki has a counselor.*

They walked out the door passing a small line of patrons, all men, mostly young, lined up waiting with eager smiles and macho commentary. Evans said, "Who was the old guy you were talking to?"

"Jed. We were talking about Trinity and a man she seemed to be connected to in a professional sense. I didn't want to bother you with the conversation. You were involved in... what should we call it? Ogling or just plain fantasizing?"

He said with a sheepish grin, "Those girls are very athletic."

She patted him on the back and laughed. "Somehow athletic never crossed my mind. That's an interesting way to describe them. Better hope your research findings settle down before you get home. I don't think dinner is what's on your mind."

On their way back to the Oasis she filled him in on the details of her chat with Jed. Evans pulled into the loading area at the main door and the bellmen quickly opened the passenger door. Stepping out of the vehicle she looked back and smiled. "Get a good night's rest, Sam, and my sympathies to Mrs. Evans."

Santiago watched Sam drive out. *Right now I envy her.*

* * *

Before going to dinner Santiago went to her room to freshen up. She was greeted by the blinking message light on the end table phone. "Is it him again?" She lifted the receiver and dialed for messages.

"Hi Mitch, I have the Seaside details. Give me a call."

She dialed Stewart's cell and plopped down on the couch, kicking off her shoes and curling her legs beneath her.

"Stewart, homicide," he answered on the second ring.

She chuckled. "Santiago, kidnapping. Why didn't you call my cell number?"

"I did. I think your battery needs recharging."

"Could be, and it's not the only thing. What have you got?"

Stewart read from his notes. "The victim was Barbara Ratafia, a co-ed at the U of O doing spring break at Seaside. She had sexual relations before death but no forced entry. Cause of death was a broken neck. The body had been moved to the south side of the beach. The initial report noted she appeared to be sleeping, resting against one of the dunes."

"Do they know where the murder took place?"

"No, but they speculate either on the beach or at one of the condos. It was not where she was staying with girlfriends."

"Anybody see her prior to the killing?"

"Everyone on the beach saw her during an afternoon volleyball game. She was playing on one of the teams. The news people even got some footage of her."

"That could help."

"Maybe, maybe not. She lost the top of her bikini diving for a ball and drew a big crowd. If you'd like I'll send the clip down."

"Good idea. I might find a familiar face. It's probably a coincidence, but a dancer at the Bramble Bush was murdered a few days ago. Her body was found just off a highway by some hikers."

Stewart was quiet for a moment. "Was she mutilated? The finger could be a signature. I'll see what I can find on her."

"Do you always keep up on things around the country?"

"When I have a vested interest, yes."

"So it seems, and no, I don't have any details on her murder. We did talk to one of the patrons about her a little while ago. Did anything come in from other departments with a similar MO to the Seaside killing?"

"A couple of possibilities... one in Spokane and another at Pismo Beach."

"Co-eds?"

"Yes. Both were missing their ring fingers and had unforced sex prior to death."

"Broken necks?"

"Don't have all of the details yet, but I'll let you know."

"Sounds serial."

"My thought exactly. Sure seems to reinforce Seaside PD's scenario."

"Any suspects?"

"None. What have you got on your guys?"

"About the same, nothing concrete. The transfer is supposed to take place tomorrow. Claude is waiting for instructions, probably at the last minute."

"That's normal."

She bit her lip. "I talked to the kidnapper."

"Really? What did he have to say?"

"Not much. It was his way of letting me know he was in charge."

Stewart said, "In charge?"

"It wasn't what he said, it was his style. When I got to the hotel a package was on the bed with a card. Dumb me; I thought it was from you. Anyway, I opened it and found a red string bikini and a note that said 'wear this to the pool at 4 o'clock.' I followed the directions and received a call from him."

"Did you follow-up on how it got in the room?"

"Yes, a bellman delivered it after some lady dropped it off."

He moaned. "That would make three players."

"Yes, it would. The call was just to intimidate me, let me know he was watching me. In fact, he was watching me from somewhere during the phone call, probably from one of the rooms overlooking the pool. He made references about it being hot down there."

"Well, I bet he liked what he saw. It wouldn't take a blue pill to excite a guy watching you in a bikini. My bet is they'll use you to make the drop, Mitch. That way they know your location."

"And the second million?"

"Maybe a second drop after you're on the road out of play."

"I hadn't thought of that."

"As you said, they're keeping you around for something."

"Yeah. So how was the trip to the Seattle Center? I didn't expect to hear from you until tomorrow."

"This seemed pretty important. Amber took the kids while I went to the office."

So where is Amber? And do I want to know? "Handy having her around."

"She's just a friend, Babe. Anything else new?"

"Tonight when we were at the Bramble Bush I spotted Mario Spears, one of Lindsey's flameouts. He was across the room enjoying a table dance. I interviewed him this morning."

"Think he saw you?"

"I don't know. Probably doesn't make much difference. I doubt the kidnappers would be that obvious in following me. I asked Evans to check my file and see if my cell number is listed."

"Why?"

"The man on the phone demanded it, probably for tomorrow. If Mario's involved they would already have it."

"Good point."

"We did interview Cliff Arnold. He hasn't seen Lindsey for several days. He thinks she and T.J. are doing their thing."

"Sounds nice."

"I don't think Cliff is involved either, just a gut feeling. Everyone around the club is sure down about the murder of Trinity."

"Who?"

"The dancer who was murdered. You said you were going to check the police wires. Trinity Durango is her name."

"Think she's connected to Lindsey's kidnapping?"

"Not at this point, but I've given it some thought."

"Anyone else on your list of suspects thus far?"

"Just Doctor Hotpants... I mean Rich. It seems he's been scoring on Lindsey for some time now. She's a patient."

"Patient?" he said.

"Her psychiatrist dating back to her mother's death. We'll probably be talking with him tomorrow sometime depending on what all comes regarding the kid's return."

"So what's your gut feeling on the case so far?"

"Claude wants these guys, especially the older one. If they'd just taken the money and sent Lindsey home all would be done with, but cutting her finger off made it personal."

Stewart asked in a soft voice, "And what about you?"

"The one on the phone is making it personal for me. He's stalking."

"Has Braun contacted the authorities yet?"

"He said he did right after the package came. One thing is for sure, the wealthy play by different rules."

"No shit. Can you hold a minute? I have another call."

"I have to go anyway so we'll talk later. I haven't even eaten yet. It's probably Amber wondering what you're doing."

"I'll call again tomorrow. Take care of yourself."

She hung up the phone and looked around the room, slowly. *What if the kidnapper did get in here?* After a quick cleanup she headed for the hotel dining room. Standing alone waiting for the elevator she took out her cell phone and dialed Evans number. He answered on the third ring.

"Hi. Sorry to bother you. Have you made it home yet?"

"Just pulling in. Why? What's on your mind?"

"Is it possible to have some of your people check my room for bugging devices just in case the bellman who delivered the package is connected to the kidnappers?"

"I'll bring a team over this evening."

"I'd appreciate it. How 'bout we do this after dinner? I'm on my way to the dining room and I'm sure you have some adventures to share at home."

Evans laughed. "Right. It's been an interesting afternoon. Give me a call when you're returning to the room. I'll call the office for a team."

"Sorry about messing up your evening."

"Hey, that's why we get the big bucks."

They both laughed.

* * *

The hotel dining room was packed. However, the hesitant maître d' immediately found a table for Santiago after the passing concierge reminded him she was a guest of Claude Braun. She was seated at a table for two with a view of the lighted pool and was enjoying a chilled Chardonnay while awaiting salad and dinner when a middle-aged man approached.

"Pardon me, Ma'am. I don't mean to be forward, but may I share your table?"

She looked up and glanced around the crowded room. "Be my guest. It's a full house."

"Thank you."

A waiter approached with a menu. "The gentleman is joining the lady?"

The man responded, "We're sharing the table."

"Of course. May I get you something to drink?"

"Whatever the lady is having and another for her, please."

Santiago said, "Thank you, and waiter, our dinner checks are separate."

The waiter looked at the man. "Yes, Madam."

Extending a hand across the table the man said, "I'm Aaron Martin from Wichita."

"Michelle Santiago."

"I must say, Michelle, you've made me feel beyond old age by insisting on your own dinner tab."

"I don't want to be beholden to anyone. Besides, I'm here on an expense account."

"That's funny... so am I."

"And Aaron, nobody in this room could think of you as old."

"You're very kind. Are you vacationing or here on business?"

"A little of both."

The waiter arrived with two glasses of wine and departed.

Aaron raised his glass. "To the future."

She followed suit while noticing the diamond wedding ring. "And new friends. Is your wife joining you this week?"

"No. I'm sorry to say she passed away some time ago, God rest her soul."

"I'm sorry."

He blinked. "It's probably for the best. She was quite ill for a long time. And you?"

"Unattached, always a bridesmaid, never a bride... at least not yet."

"You're a young beautiful woman. I'm sure the right man will come along when you least expect it and sweep you off your feet."

It seems less probable each day. "I hope so, but there's no rush."

"Smart move, young lady."

The waiter returned and took Martin's order. "Madam, would you prefer your meal delayed until the gentleman's is prepared?

"I'd like that but I have another appointment."

"As you wish," the waiter said.

"Pity, but I'll be here the whole week at least. Perhaps we'll have another opportunity to visit over dinner."

"One can never tell. What business are you in?"

"Sales, fitness equipment. And you?"

"Homicide."

"Homicide?"

She watched his reaction as he choked sipping the wine. "In my real life I'm a homicide detective for the Seattle Police Department. I'm visiting here and toying with a career change."

She watched his reaction.

"I'd never guess you're a homicide detective or even a law enforcement officer. You're way too attractive for that."

"Well thank you. Apparently you practice what you sell. You look to be in pretty good shape."

"For an older man," he said.

"For any man."

"Thank you."

Santiago flagged the waiter. "I will delay my dinner until Mr. Martin's is ready."

His response was curt. "Of course, Madam."

Martin said, "Arrogant bastard, but thank you, Michelle. Eating alone is not fun, not when you do it most of the time."

"My appointment is open. I just have to call when I leave. Besides, I don't like eating alone either."

"I must say they don't make detectives like they used to. I recall rather portly fellows in threadbare suits and fedoras."

"Perhaps you've been watching too many movies. Today's officers are in much better shape than in the past, something a man in your business should appreciate."

"Oh, I do appreciate it," he said.

Dinner arrived and they ate while exchanging small talk. As the plates were removed Martin looked across the table and stroked his chin. "A nightcap before you depart?"

"Not tonight. I have work to do. But please have one on me."

She flagged the waiter, ordered a bourbon and water, flashed her keycard and said, "Put the drink on my bill, 5004, and add 20 percent for you."

Martin said, "This is different. Now who's beholden? I'll return the favor later this week. How did you know I drank bourbon and water?"

"Just a lucky guess," she said taking out her cell phone and speed dialing Sam Evans.

"You've got style, young lady."

"Sam, I'm ready. I'll meet you there." She snapped the case shut and stood. "Sorry to eat and run, but it has been a pleasure, Aaron."

He stood. "The pleasure was all mine, Michelle."

Walking across the lobby to the elevators she called Evans again. "Can you have someone do a background check on Aaron Martin of Wichita? He's about fifty, in good shape, well spoken, and somehow found his way to my table in the crowded dining room."

"I'll have someone on it immediately. We'll be at your room within the next half-hour."

"Thanks, Sam."

Lisa Fargo sat a small table just inside the lounge door and watched Santiago leave the dining room and walk across the lobby. "Bitch."

Her current escort's jaw dropped open. Then he flagged the cocktail waitress and ordered another round.

* * * * * *

Claude Braun retreated to his den after putting his intoxicated wife to bed. He sat down in an overstuffed chair and looked through a window overlooking the circular driveway. After several deep breaths he stretched his legs while twisting his back. Across from him displayed as the centerpiece of a cherry wood paneled wall was an oil painting of Lelani. His gaze never left the portrait as he rubbed the back of his neck.

"I still love you so deeply," he said. "Tomorrow we get our little girl back home. This is all so wrong. The life we planned together for Lindsey and us was lost."

He drummed the fingers of his right hand on the armrest, shuffled his feet, and crossed his ankles. His eyes welled. He closed them and visualized the young family all smiles and happy. "What happened to us? Where did the future take us? I failed you and Lindsey. How?"

The veins on his forearms stood out. He watched them pulsate. The muscle tissue was defined by shadows. Removing the cell phone from its belt clip he punched in a number. Neal Burke answered his private line.

"Is the money ready?"

"Yes, Claude. One million dollars is at your house in used bills."

"I mean the second million."

"Of course. It's in the security vault here at the complex. Other than having it ready I don't know what to do with it."

"Neither do I," Braun said. "We wait."

"Claude, I transferred funds around so the money came from your personal account and not the company. You did say this was personal?"

"Yes. Did you put any backup funds in my account just in case I need more?"

"Another four million, Ray House suggested I have a reserve ready. He was quite mysterious about its destination, but then all of this seems strange."

"All you need to know is to have it ready if I need it. Ray was doing his job. Good anticipation."

"Claude, what's going on?"

"Nothing I can share right now. Just keep doing what I ask and everything will be fine. It has to be."

"Are you okay, Claude?"

"Just be at your office by seven tomorrow morning. Clear your calendar."

"What will I be doing?"

"I don't know yet. Just be ready."

Braun looked around the den at a desk photo of Lindsey and Nikki. "Don't even leave for lunch. It could be a long day."

"Claude, I'll help in any way I can."

"I know. Sorry I snapped at you."

"If it's a legal matter we have some of the best corporate attorneys in the country on retainer."

"No, it has nothing to do with the company, but thank you."

Braun scanned the books on one wall shelf passing over those on business to his favorites: Ludlum, Clancy, an assortment of mysteries and suspense thrillers. "Neal, if I wanted to electronically transfer funds to another country how long would that take?"

"Given the account number and destination, only a few minutes. And Claude, keep in mind once you transfer the money it's gone. Why?"

"Nothing, just a crazy idea going through my head. Getting the money back wouldn't matter either. Someday I'll tell you about this. Nikki and I appreciate your help, Neal. Thank you."

He hung up, but continued to look at the bookshelves, the picture on his desk and the portrait. It was deathly quiet. He punched the speed dial on his phone.

"House," came the abrupt answer on one ring.

"Sorry to call so late, Ray."

"It's not late, Claude. What can I do for you?"

"Can you arrange to track the transfer of funds from one bank to another electronically without others knowing?"

"Yes. We have the best people and equipment in the industry. Why?"

"I know it sounds crazy. Maybe I've been reading too many thrillers, but what if the kidnappers want to move the money, the other million, offshore, maybe move it someplace electronically."

House said, "Have you heard from them? The money is in cash, remember."

"Yes, the first million is here and the second is in the office vault."

House said, "That's in cash too."

"I know, but I just talked to Neal. He said you directed him to have additional funds available."

"That is correct. A demand for an electronic transfer is possible even though they instructed cash. I thought of it but I didn't want to alarm you."

"I appreciate that. You're always ahead of the game. I know the probability is minor at best. These guys sound like gutter snipes to me."

"It could be a cover, Claude. We just don't know."

"Do you have a team ready if necessary?"

"Yes."

"You sound hesitant."

"The most capable operative we have for this task is Mario Spears, and he's on the list of suspects."

"We have no others available?"

"Not as good."

"Use him. We don't need to tell him the if, and, or why. Have your backup available too, just in case he falters. Better yet, set up two independent teams. If they do transfer the money we could discover whether Spears is a player."

"I like your idea, Claude. I'll take care of everything right now."

"Yes, just in case."

House broke the connection and dialed Jessica Rodriguez at her home. A sleepy voice answered on the third ring.

"Yes, Ray."

"Implement the plan we worked out earlier today. Make sure Spears is on one of the two teams."

"Consider it done. Shall I contact Evans and Santiago?"

"No. We'll let this ride. They don't need any distractions tomorrow. Thank you."

"Anything else?"

"No. We'll see how it plays out. Good night."

* * *

Quarterman was sprawled out on the king sized bed, drifting in and out of a restless sleep. Staccato thoughts of Lindsey, the cabin, Lisa, sex games, money transfers, Mexico, Sugar, Santiago and the game raged through his semi-conscious mind. He twisted onto his side, and one arm flopped out, striking the nightstand and the Play button of the recorder he used to monitor Santiago's room. The sound of running water filled the room, and the memory of finding a dead GI draped over rocks by a small stream flashed through his mind. The right hand was cut off, and his sergeant was spitting and damning "Charlie" for leaving his signature. "He wasn't regular army," the sergeant had said. "He was a killer... a psycho like us." Then a rifle cracked and a small hole appeared in the sergeant's forehead, his brain exploding on the foliage behind him.

Quarterman sat bolt upright, wiped the sweat covering his face, and squinted into the darkness. The only light was a thin ray seeping through the curtains from the outside lighting around the pool five floors below. He looked toward the nightstand and the sound of the recorder and turned on the lamp. The sudden brightness was a shock to his eyes. *Must'a hit the switch when I turned over.*

He glanced at the clock radio. It was 9:01.

He shook his head. The sound of rushing water echoed in his ears, then quit. He reached over and turned the volume down. Taking a deep breath, he smiled. "What have you been up to today, Michelle?"

The voices of Santiago and Chance Stewart filled the room. He listened intently as they discussed the kids, Seattle Center, the case, and Amber. "Sounds like your boyfriend is playing around on you while you're trying to catch my ass. Friendship does have its price."

He stood and walked around the room, then sat down near the nightstand. "I don't like your pal looking into the Seaside incident. Serial killer, signatures, military mindset—very analytical, Aunt Michelle. You get extra points for picking up on the Portland papers."

The recorded call ended. He stood and had started moving toward the bathroom when a second call began. Standing naked in the dimly lit room, he listened as Stewart provided details about the killing at Seaside. He squirmed when the two detectives talked about Spokane and Pismo Beach. "You guys are thorough, I'll say that for you."

He listened further. His anger exploded when the conversation got to the Bramble Bush. "Damn it! I never saw Lindsey there. This isn't good."

He turned the player off, went into the bathroom, showered and shaved. Looking at the shaving cream residue on his face in the mirror brought a smile. "Maybe Chance is your man. He worked on your project while his kids were with Amber, but maybe not. There's always after hours when the kids are home and in bed."

The room phone interrupted his focus. "Hello?"

Lisa Fargo said, "The bitch cop had dinner with some guy in the dining room earlier."

"Probably the fellow she's working with."

"I don't think so. This guy was workin' the lounge earlier, hittin' on any woman seated alone."

Quarterman laughed. "A little competition? Did he hit on you?"

"No, I was occupied. My guess is he's a visiting salesman on a week long pass, expense account, a little wife at home."

"Did he leave with her?"

"No. He was having another drink when she walked to the lobby and made a call. Then she went upstairs."

"Just now?"

"No. It's been an hour or so. Like I said, I was occupied. You know how it is."

Oh yes, I know how it is, especially with you. "Well, maybe you'll get an opportunity to check this guy out a little... that is, if you have the time."

"I'll make time. He's still floating around the lounge. Otherwise, there's always tomorrow."

"Thanks for the call."

"Sure. What are you doing tonight?"

"Business, Lisa. I have an appointment and you have a task. Right?"

She laughed. "Yes, one I'm overqualified to handle."

"Work, work, work. We'll talk tomorrow." He broke the connection, looked out the slider facing the pool area, and said quietly, "I have to get dressed, Sugar. Do I need my backpack tonight?"

* * *

The cabin was cool to the flesh compared to the early evening heat. The air was stagnant and rancid with the odor of body waste, vomit, and their flesh locked in saturated garments. Lindsey had been pressing her tongue against the tape and wiggling her mouth. After what seemed like hours, the tape had come loose on the edge of her mouth. Eventually it separated from her chin. Soon, though it still clung to her upper lip and the right side of her mouth, it was loose enough to wiggle, and in another half-hour or so the tape lost its grip and dropped away, clinging to only one side of her mouth. In a weak voice she said to T.J., "Push your tongue against the tape. Work it. It'll come loose and you'll be able to breathe easier."

As T.J. began to work his mouth, the tape barely moving in the shadowy light, she said, "It'll take a long time to get it off. It seemed like forever to get mine off, but it worked."

She rubbed her chin against her the right shoulder, trying to get the clinging piece of tape off her face. After a few minutes, it dropped away. She smiled with satisfaction, then looked toward the windows. The air conditioner provided the only sound in the room. "I wonder what time it is. Thank God for moonlight. I'm so tired."

T.J. watched Lindsey as he began working to free the tape. *It figures, the little rich girl would get free first. You bitch. Your stupid idea has nearly gotten me killed. If that guy hadn't shown up I would'a taken the money and run.*

Once he'd freed himself of the tape, he took several deep breaths. "I'd kill for a sip of water."

Lindsey looked up. "You're free."

"Not exactly, but an improvement. I can breathe easier and speak a little."

She smiled. "My hand is throbbing and I'm sweating like a pig in a puddle of shit, but right now the sound of your voice makes my day. Does the cut hurt?"

"I hurt all over but nothing compared to what he did to you."

"Think we can get loose?"

"We can try," he said. "Man, I'm exhausted."

"I know. I fell asleep. What time do you think it is?"

"Wish it was time for someone to come and get us."

Lindsey said, "I'm gonna try to get the tape around me loose. Maybe it'll break."

"If we could get it started tearing, it would be easy to get free. The bad news is it doesn't break."

She said, "Do you have any idea who that guy is?"

"Not a clue. You?"

Lindsey started twisting, leaning toward the tape wrapped around her chest and the chair. "How would I know? We can die sittin' here."

"Someone will be here tomorrow."

"We hope! But do we know who or when?"

T.J. looked into the shadows on her face and began trying to loosen the tape binding him. "I don't want to see that guy again. I've been beaten and humiliated enough for a lifetime."

She said, "Keep working."

He watched Lindsey's shadowy figure struggle against the tape. *It's your fault. I hate you.*

* * *

Quarterman stood near the poorly lit service entrance to the Stray Cat Gentlemen's Club. "Sugar, remember me?"

The young woman glanced at the shadowy figure. "Well, the big tipper."

"You said to catch you on your way out, around 11:00."

"Give or take," she said with a smile. *No vice cop drops a Franklin to score a hooker.* "You mentioned an after-hours drink?"

Quarterman nodded toward the Cut 'N Go Motel. "I have a room across street. Would you join me?"

"Sure, but only one."

"Of course. You look even better in those jeans. What do you do, paint them on?"

Sugar laughed. "A girl's gotta show what she's got. You know my name and I never drink with a stranger, except at work."

"Yancey, and it's a pleasure to have you join me."
Damn, that was a mistake.

"You're a silver tongued devil, aren't you, Yancey?"
She laughed.

They crossed Van Buren, dodging traffic.

She looked at him with a coy smile. "You like
chocolate?"

"I like anything if the package is right." He opened
the motel door. "It's not much but it'll do for the
night."

She walked in and dropped her coat on the bed.
"I've seen worse."

He said, "The coat is a surprise."

"Don't know why I carry it around this time of
year."

"Neither do I. What was it you said? 'A girl's gotta
show what she's got,' right?"

"That's right."

He walked to a small table with two chairs. "I have
bourbon."

"Works for me."

"How do you like it?"

She laughed. "What, the bourbon? 50/50."

He said, "You have something else in mind?"

She sat down on the bed. "Well, a hundred is an
awfully big tip just for a drink later on."

"It was for the couch dance. Believe me, you earned
it."

She took a sip from the plastic water cup, lit a
cigarette and took a deep drag. "I try."

He watched as her breasts swelled. *Oh sweet Jesus, it has been a few days.* With each drag on her cigarette they expanded more, pulling the crop top higher and revealing the muscled flesh of her flat dark midriff.

He said, "You're in great shape."

"I'm in the action business. You won't see fat girls doin' what I do."

He smiled. "Wouldn't want to."

"So let's get down to it. You bring me here for a private couch dance, maybe something more?"

Quarterman sat up straight. "Yes, and maybe spend a little time together, maybe the night."

"Maybe," she said.

He placed two more hundred-dollar bills on the table. "And I tip well too. Want another drink? There's no hurry."

"Sure, but what say I get comfortable first?"

"Comfort is good."

She pulled the crop-top over her head, arms extended high. "Showtime."

His eyes feasted on her full, firm breasts, the dark nipples beginning to harden. Reaching over to the nightstand he turned on the radio. "Oh yes. This is gonna be a night to remember, Sugar."

She straightened and jiggled her breasts in Quarterman's face. "Let's find a rock station."

He said, "Not a problem. Anything you want."

She stood and stretched, reaching high overhead, then bent over, legs straight, the objects of his attention suspended beneath her. "You're not missing much."

"I don't even hear the music," he said.

She smiled, stood straight and began moving sensuously while slowly sliding the zipper of her jeans open. She spun, turning her back toward Quarterman and began working the skin-tight jeans over her hips and thighs, then stepped out of them, leaving them in a heap on the floor.

"No underwear. That's a nice touch."

"Figured why bother. It wasn't the G-string that caught your attention."

He stood while taking one last gulp.

She tore his shirt open. "I like to undress a man. You're looking' pretty good yourself."

"I try."

She rubbed his chest with the tips of her fingers, her long white nails teasing his flesh. The shirt slid off his shoulders to the floor. She said, "You're lovin' every moment of this... I can tell."

"I am."

She moaned and rubbed his crotch. "Um, you're big for a white guy. I like what I feel."

"So do I," he said in a husky voice.

She freed the buttons, opened the fly and stepped back. "Someone else is dressed for pleasure."

"Guilty."

She gently stroked his firm erection.

His back arched, hips involuntarily thrusting forward. His pants dropped to the floor caught on the tops of his boots. "Oh, God."

She looked at him and licked her lips. "You're still overdressed."

"Not for long."

He sat down on the edge of the bed and pulled the boots off, then the socks. The jeans landed in a heap. Stretching out on the bed he looked up at her. "Better?"

"Much," she purred, joining him.

He slid an arm around her shoulder and squeezed, bringing her close. "Sugar, what's your greatest sexual fantasy?"

"To fuck a guy until he dies having an orgasm made in steroid heaven."

"Ever do a threesome?"

She kissed his chest. "Sometimes... with friends for fun."

"Two men or two women?"

She ran a hand toward his groin. "Both ways. All this talk excites you?"

He kissed her throat. "You excite me. Want another drink?"

"I'll drink you," she said.

"Ever do it?" he said.

"What, suck a guy dry?" She smiled, licking her lips. "Often."

"Ever fuck a guy to death?"

"No, but I've come close a few times."

They both laughed. "I'll bet you have."

"Want to spend the night? I have to leave early but you can sleep 'til checkout."

"I'm here. You're here. You're huge and the tip is on the table."

"I've always wanted to screw a woman 'til she dropped, same scenario."

"Have you?"

He smiled. "Wouldn't admit it if I had. Would you?"

She explored his ear with the tip of her tongue. "Never. You've got great rocks."

"Let's enjoy tonight, maybe tomorrow night, maybe even a threesome."

They kissed hard as he pulled her on top of him.

* * *

The knock on the door was a light tap. Santiago pressed an eye to the peephole and saw Evans with two younger people, a woman and a man carrying a metallic case. She opened the door. "Hi. Thanks for coming over."

Evans motioned, indicating she should step outside. The two DataFlex technicians slipped past her into the suite following Evans hand signals. The man went into the bathroom while the woman headed through the sitting room to the bedroom. Evans reached past Santiago and pulled the door closed, but not quite tight. "We'll go in and chatter about the Gentlemen's Club for a few minutes while they work."

She nodded. Evans pushed the door open and they entered. Water was running in the bathtub while the man moved about the room waving a scanning device.

Evans said, "I see I caught you getting ready for a bath. Sorry about that. Can we talk while you're drawing the water?"

"Sure."

He said, "I thought we could compare notes on the visit."

"You mean about Arnold?"

"Yes. He seemed like a pretty decent young man, a roustabout."

"My impression too. He doesn't come across as the criminal type even though he has a record."

Evans smiled. "He seemed more interested in just knowing Lindsey."

Santiago tossed her head back and chuckled. "If he wants anything it's carnal knowledge."

He glanced about the room. "So it would seem, but then that place nurtures lust. Wouldn't you agree?"

She laughed as his face turned red. "Like a supermarket for real sex toys, Sam. Have you seen your wife yet?"

"Of course. We were getting ready to watch a little television, but I thought you and I should go over tomorrow's plan first, even if it is late."

"Television, eh? I doubt that, Sam."

He looked into Santiago's face with a smirk. "I can still smell the popcorn and anticipate getting home to taste the butter."

Santiago looked around. The young woman was holding up two fingers and pointing to the bedroom. "You lustful little devil. Well, it's a good thing you came over. Tomorrow will be busy. My plan is to do what they tell us. Not much to plan at this point, not 'til we hear from them."

The young man come out of the bathroom holding up one finger. The pair went to work on the sitting room. "I think so."

Evans and Santiago moved to the bedroom. He took a card and pen from his shirt pocket. "I have an address for us to check tomorrow," he said. He printed *Pull them?*

Santiago shook her head.

Evans held the card out for the tech team to view. They read the card while the woman held up two more fingers.

Evans said, "Better turn your water off or you'll be testing the overflow."

Santiago stepped into the bathroom. The tech team left, closing the door behind them before the water was off. She walked back to the suite's entry. "Let me see you out," she said walking out the door into the hall.

Evans whispered, "What made you think of listening devices?"

"Just an uncomfortable feeling: the delivery of the gift into my room and too many people coming and going when I'm not here."

He said, "The gift was delivered by an employee."

"I know, but the employee could have let someone else in, or someone else could have snuck in while he was in the bedroom. Any number of employees could have planted the devices." She looked back at the entry. "Housekeeping always leaves the door open when they're working in a room, probably a policy."

"You're right. Someone could have even slipped into the closet by the door."

"The older man sounds much sharper than the first caller," she said looking down the hall.

Evans said, "We can pull 'em tomorrow, after the exchange."

"Or we can leave them and maybe feed some info of our own their way."

Evans sniffed and smiled as a bellman pushed a catering cart past them, the aroma of cooked beef filling the hallway. "I like the info idea. Whatever, we'll know more tomorrow."

She said, "Do you think they'll know we found the bugs?"

"Yes, if they know we were looking for them. This pair is smooth, more sophisticated than I thought."

She said, "And very dangerous. See you at Braun's around 7:00."

She turned and walked back into her room, then closed and locked the door. *You can hear me on the toilet; so much for privacy.* She looked at the tub and dipped a hand. *Tepid... the pool sauna would have been nice but this will do.*

Reaching across the tub she turned on the jets and watched the water begin first to stir, then bubble and whirl around. After undressing she stepped in, sat down slowly and stretched her legs. "This feels good. Wish you were here, Chance," she purred. "I can do more for you than Amber ever thought of." *Damn, I can play a game with your head if you're listening, Mr. Red Bikini in Charge.* "Water, keep licking my flesh. Touch every private place I have. Oh, God, yes. This is so good."

Her voice was soft, throaty, sexy. She looked at her reflection in the mirrors surrounding the tub. *Too bad you don't have a camera.* "Whoever invented pounding bubbles had more than relaxation in mind." *I hope you guys are getting your rocks off on this. I am.*

She stretched over the edge of the tub, picked up her cell phone, and punched in Braun's number. He answered on the first ring.

"Claude?"

"Yes."

"Evans just left the hotel. We've been comparing notes on the interview this evening. We'll be at your place tomorrow morning by 7:00. Is that early enough?"

"Should be. If they contact me earlier I'll call you."

"How's Nikki doing?"

"Best as can be expected. She'll be better tomorrow when this business is over."

"We'll see you in the morning. It's late. Try to get some sleep," she said and broke the connection.

She sat back in the tub. "Well Chance, that broke the mood but I'll have happy dreams."

DAY THREE

The door flew open, crashing against the wall as the man in the ski mask burst into the cabin. "Good morning. I see we've made it through the night."

He eyed the loose tape hanging from T.J.'s mouth, then walked to the refrigerator and opened the freezer. He took out a small bag of ice and went to Lindsey.

He opened the bag while checking her bindings, dumped the bowl of bloody water on the floor, then filled it with ice. "This will ease the pain, Kid. Only a few more hours and then if Daddy comes through, you'll be home."

She looked at their tormentor with piercing, tear-filled eyes. Fine lines crossed her forehead. T.J. looked down at the table.

Quarterman looked at the empty bottles on the table. "Water?"

She nodded, lips moving but no sound coming forth.

He returned with a bottle of cold water and held it to her mouth. She took slow sips, some spilling. "No rush, Kid. I'll get to him in a minute."

Lindsey's nose curled as Quarterman breathed in her face. She turned her head away.

He looked up and sniffed. "Christ, it stinks in here. I imagine your old man will have the place fumigated, cleaned, painted."

Lindsey looked up at him, studying the ski mask.

He said, "You can talk. Hell, you've earned the privilege."

"You're in a good mood today," she said.

He looked at Lindsey in surprise. "That's not what I expected to hear, but yes, I am. It was a busy night and a busy morning. It's almost over."

He looked at T.J. and wiggled the bottle in front of him. "Water?"

T.J. nodded. Quarterman stepped around the table and tore the loose tape free from his cheek. T.J. guzzled the water again, choking as Quarterman held the bottle. "Man, you didn't learn anything yesterday. You're still a coward and a pig, boy."

Lindsey looked across the table at the man. "Are you going to rape me like you said yesterday?"

"Would you fight me?"

She said, "Yes."

"I thought so." He looked into her eyes. "No, I'm not going to do that. I just wanted to scare your old man. First man I ever killed was a rapist, lower than scum. I've never raped anyone in my life and I'm not startin' now."

She looked at her tormentor but said nothing.

"I'll say this for you little lady. You've earned my respect. You're brave, strong, and don't give in. I like that."

He circled the table and looked down at T.J. "I think you're worthless but I won't hurt you, either."

T.J. looked at the man, his eyes welling. "Thank you."

Quarterman laughed looking back at Lindsey. "Thank her, Asshole. I hope someday you find yourself a real man little lady."

Lindsey looked from the man to T.J. but said nothing.

Quarterman walked to the door. "I'll leave the tape off your mouths this time. Just hope the next person to come through the door isn't me. You know, little lady, it wouldn't surprise me if the wimp over there was thinkin' about stealing the money and maybe something worse. Your plan had to be a temptation."

He stepped outside, closed the door and stopped for a moment. "It sure is quiet out here this morning. Sugar, you were all I imagined and more. A man shouldn't be tired on the most important day of his life."

* * *

Lindsey and T.J. looked across the table at each other as the sound of the car faded.

T.J. said, "Think he's gone?"

"Sounds like it. I hope so. I want this to end."

"It was a dumb idea turned bad."

"I guess. Let's see if we can get free."

He said, "We haven't done very well at it so far."

"No, but now we can use our teeth. Maybe get a tear started."

"He was wrong, Lindsey."

"About what?"

"Me planning to take the money. I just got into this to help you out, friend to friend."

"I know. Don't worry about it. If you haven't noticed, he just doesn't like you."

"I've noticed. Hard not to."

"He's gone. We'll be out of here in an hour or two. Let's just keep trying to get loose. If nothing else it gives us something to do."

T.J. said, "Do you think he's really killed people?"

"Without a doubt. You heard him. I just pray he isn't the one coming back in a couple of hours. We need to get free."

* * *

Santiago and Evans arrived at the Brauns' by 6:50 a.m. Claude and Nikki joined them in the kitchen where coffee was already prepared. The four stood around, sipped from oversized cups and said little. Waiting.

At 7:01 Santiago's cell phone rang. "Santiago."

"Good morning," said the cheerful voice. "Is your phone battery charged?"

She looked around the kitchen at the three others, listening, their heads tilted in her direction, eyes boring holes in the small cellular unit in her hand. "Yes."

"Is the money in the car?"

"It's here with me in the kitchen."

"Have Evans take it to the car. Remember, I'm watching."

Evans picked up the duffel bag with the money and walked through the house, out the front door to the car. Santiago followed, the phone plastered to her right ear.

Claude and Nikki Braun stopped at the front door. Braun strained his neck, looking to see anyone watching the house. He looked at Nikki and shook his head.

Santiago said, "Okay, what now?"

The man on the phone said, "I want Evans to walk to the right front fender."

Evans did as directed.

After a few seconds the man said, "Now, have Evans take the cell phone out of his pocket and hold it up."

As Evans held up his cell phone Santiago looked around. "Can you see it?"

"Have Evans drop it on the asphalt and crush it."

Santiago relayed the message. Evans did as directed.

"Now, get in the car and drive to Highway 60. As you approach 60 ask for directions. Oh, and keep the connection open. I want to hear you two talking. If the connection is broken for any reason the exchange is off. Understood?"

"Yes."

Santiago drove the Sebring out the main gate, the duffle bag sitting behind the passenger seat. The Brauns watched from the front door. Nikki stood near her husband and slid an arm around his waist. He grasped her shoulder and they walked into the living room.

Quarterman laughed. *Great bluff.* He drove west on Highway 60 toward I-10. He placed the cell phone on the seat and covered it with a gray tinged towel from the Cut 'N Go Motel, then took a second unit and punched in Braun's number. It took only one ring.

"Braun here."

There was a pause, silence. Finally Quarterman spoke in a deep, raspy voice. "You have ten minutes to complete a transfer of funds to a bank account in the Cayman Islands. Don't worry about tracking the money. It will be moving about quite a bit in places our government can't follow. Understand?"

Yes," Braun said in a weak voice.

"Good. Call your people and tell them to do exactly as I direct. Any deviation and the deal's off."

"You said yesterday I would get to talk to Lindsey before the exchange."

The phone was still for a moment. "Well, I've changed my mind. Right now I'm following your cop and her escort down the road. If you want to delay the transfer and have me go back to where Lindsey is I could do so, but I haven't raped her yet. Are you sure you want me to see her again?"

"No, please don't. I'll do as you say."

"Give me the name and number of who will be handling the transaction."

Braun gave him Neal Burke's private number.

"Now call him. You have two minutes; then I'll contact him. The clock is running."

Nikki watched her husband punch in a number on the cell. His hand shook; he swore and punched in another number. He looked at Nikki. In a strained voice he said, "I misdialed."

Burke answered on the first ring. "Hello?"

"Neal, Claude here."

"Claude, I expected—"

"Not now. There is no time. In less than two minutes you will receive a call from a man. He will give you specific instructions to make a money transfer."

"Where?"

"I don't know, and I don't care. Just do as he says. No questions. This is a matter of life or death. Do you understand?"

Burke gulped air and looked around his office. "Yes, I'll do as he says."

Nikki's face was contorted, eyes bloodshot ovals surrounded by dark circles. "Claude, what's going on?"

"A money transfer, another million. I just felt it in my bones. I knew it was coming to this. Thank God Ray arranged for additional money in the account."

She said, "Can Neal do this?"

"Yes, he can. He must. There'll be no tomorrow."

"What now?"

"We wait. That's all we can do. He's talking to Burke. I'm sure the bastards are following the transfer. When it's completed we get Lindsey back. I'll call Michelle and let them know what's happening." He punched her number on his cell phone. "Damn," he muttered. "In use."

"Try Sam."

He punched in Evans number, listened briefly and slammed the phone onto its cradle. "He's turned off his cell."

A security guard knocked on the wall near the entrance to the living room.

"Yes?" Braun said.

He held out a hand, the crushed remains of a cell phone in his palm. "We found this in the driveway after Mr. Evans and the woman left."

They stared at the phone. "Thank you," Braun said, then walked over to Nikki and embraced her. "So that was the business in front of the car. We can't reach them. The bastards are smarter than I thought."

"Oh, God," she said.

"It'll be all right. We'll get our girl home, I promise." His eyes welled as they hugged. "And I'll kill them if I ever find them."

* * *

Evans picked up Santiago's phone. "We're approaching 60," he said. "What now?"

"Good. Head east," said the man, his voice breaking up just a little.

"We go left," Evans said. "Is he following us?"

"One of them must be, but I haven't spotted a tail yet."

"Evans placed his thumb over the tiny microphone. "Are the Feds tailing us?"

"I don't think so. Claude said he contacted them but he wanted no activity on their part until after the exchange. Far as I know, we're on our own." *Not the way to do something like this.*

Evans said, "I have 7:24. How long do you think they'll keep us on a string?"

"As long as they want. I don't like this."

"Have you ever been involved in a kidnapping before?"

"Vice and homicide," she said. "No kidnappings, and surely nothing like this."

"Like this?"

"I'm a cop. I work with cops."

"Yeah." He continued to hold a finger over the receiver of the cell phone. "The bugs we discovered last night, isolation, everything about this feels ugly."

She said, "It's odd working with ex-spies and not trained police officers."

"These guys started out like everyday criminals but now it's professional."

"You're thinking about the other million."

He shook his head. "It's everything. It's clandestine... the feel of it."

She smiled. "You'd be more familiar with that. I just chase regular bad guys."

"That's the first smile I've seen today."

"Well, maybe it's about time."

"I hope so."

Santiago was gripping the steering wheel so tightly her knuckles had turned white. "After we get Lindsey back I want to talk with Doctor Rich today. I'm sure she'll be in the hospital for observation and a look at the amputation. We probably won't be able to talk with her until tonight or tomorrow."

Evans reached down to the cuff of his slacks and pulled it up. He removed a small caliber automatic pistol from an ankle holster and passed it to Santiago. "This is a just in case gun."

He lifted his finger from the phone.

* * *

"Mr. Burke, I believe you're expecting my call? Mr. Braun just called you."

"Yes," said an agitated and sweating Neal Burke.

"I want one million dollars transferred to Grand Cayman Industrial Bank in the next ten minutes."

"Our bank isn't open yet."

"Doesn't make any difference."

"Of course. I'll need the account number."

"Put the phone down on the desk and go to your secretary station. A courier delivered an envelope with instructions this morning at 6:00 a.m. You have two minutes to get back on the line."

The phone cracked loudly in Quarterman's ear. Burke hurried to the door, opened it and was greeted by Jessica Rodriguez, Ray House's personal assistant. She smiled at Burke and passed a brown courier envelope to him without a word.

Burke rushed back to his desk and activated the speakerphone. "I have it."

"Good. Open it and follow the directions. I'll be checking for confirmation in ten minutes."

"That's a very small window."

The smell of diesel exhaust invaded the Cadillac as Quarterman sped west on Highway 60. "It's big enough. Quite frankly, I wouldn't want to face Braun if I was late with this item." He chuckled and broke the connection.

Jessica Rodriguez walked into Burke's office. Burke was on the phone giving directions. He looked up as the blood drained from his face.

She said, "It's all right, Neal. I know what this is about."

Burke nodded.

She asked, "Where are we sending the money?"

"Grand Cayman Industrial Bank."

She removed a cell phone from her cinch belt and forwarded the information separately to two tracking teams in different locations. Then she sat down on a sled chair, watched Burke, and listened. Ray House entered and took the other chair while giving Neal his undivided attention. He lit a Winston.

Burke finished within a few minutes and looked across the desk at the two visitors. He cleared his throat. By now the tight collar of his custom made dress shirt was drenched with sweat and discoloring. "There's no smoking allowed in the building, Ray."

"There is today," House said.

"What's going on?" Burke said.

"You'll find out later. Is the transfer complete?" House said.

"Yes."

House and Rodriguez stood. He dropped the cigarette into an empty water glass sitting on Burke's desk and they left the room, closing the door behind them. Burke watched while wiping his forehead. "Money, couriers, offshore accounts—this has to be illegal."

Looking out the office interior window he watched the two of them saunter through the area. "You'd look better in a miniskirt, Jessica."

The office was silent, empty, smoke hazed. He looked at the butt holder water glass, then scratched his head and checked the time. "Jesus, its only 7:36 and I'm exhausted. Now I wait."

* * *

Claude and Nikki Braun were sitting together on the couch in the living room. Sweat formed in the palms of their gripped hands. The grandfather clock ticked incessantly, punctuating each beat of their hearts. "I need some coffee, Claude. You?"

He took a deep breath while staring at the phone. "Sure. I hate that clock. The never ending sound. It's like water dripping."

Nikki went to the kitchen and returned with a tray, two cups, and a carafe. Her knuckles were pure white. She set the tray down with a clatter. "Sorry."

"Don't be. We're a little tense. If we weren't, something would be wrong with us." He paused. "There's probably something wrong with us anyway. Here, let me pour. Just come and sit by me."

In a weak voice she said, "Thank you."

"You're shaking. Are you sure you can hold the cup?"

She wiped her forehead. "Yes. No. Maybe... I don't know. Leave it there for a minute."

He said, "I think I'll leave mine too. It needs to cool."

Nikki took out a cigarette and began striking a match without success. "Damn it!"

He took the matches. "May I?"

"You hate lighting cigarettes for me."

"I've hated a lot of things, mostly myself of late."

"Don't say that, Claude."

He looked at the clock with a blank stare. "What time is it?"

She took a deep drag. "7:39."

Braun leaned forward and picked up his coffee cup, spilling some. "You're not the only one with the shakes."

"I'll get a rag."

"To hell with the rag. I'll get it later. Please, just sit with me."

Nikki stubbed out the cigarette. Braun placed his hand on her left thigh drumming his fingers, shifting his feet, crossing and re-crossing his ankles. "This reminds me of waiting for school to get out the last day before summer vacation when I was in the first grade. Time didn't move then, either."

She smiled, then leaned forward and picked up her cup. Some of the hot fluid dribbled onto the rug. "Shit."

Braun glanced at the spill, then looked away. "Come on, Sam, call us."

Nikki said, "I have to go to the bathroom or wet my pants."

"Then go."

"I don't want to miss the call."

"Just go. I'm here. We're not missing anything."

He glanced at the clock and Nikki left the room. He picked up his cell and began to punch in a number, then stopped. "No, they might be trying to contact us."

Nikki returned to the living room. "Anything yet?"

"No," he said tersely. "I'm sorry. I didn't mean to be short with you."

She patted his shoulder. "I know."

"You going to sit down?"

She began pacing. "I think I'll stand... keep moving."

"Can you hear the blood pounding through your head?" he said.

"I can feel it. Yes, I can hear it. You too?"

"Oh yes."

He waved a hand and inadvertently knocked over one of the cups. He smiled and looked at Nikki. "I think we'll get new carpet when we replace the clock."

Nikki said, "Will she be all right?"

"She has to be, Nikki... she just has to be."

"What will we do when they find her?"

"Evans will call House. The company copter, crew, and Ben Yount are waiting. They'll take her to his clinic."

"Not the hospital?"

"No. Lindsey doesn't need a bunch of reporters and cops bothering her. Ben has everything he needs at his clinic. You know that."

"Do we?"

"Yes. If her life is in danger he will change plans and take her to St. Joseph under an alias."

"Do the police know about the arrangements?"

"Nikki, the Feds know. House set it up with them. It'll be fine and best for Lindsey."

Tears filled her eyes. "I'm just so scared."

"We both are. Come back over and sit down. Right now hope and each other are all we've got." He held his hand out and she came to him.

* * *

Quarterman listened to the chatter of Santiago and Evans as he pulled into the parking lot of the Oasis Hotel. A cool breeze surrounded him, the AC making a barely audible hum. He looked around the parking lot, then at the cell phone. "I passed you guys out there somewhere going the other way." He laughed. "It's nice this morning, very nice. Not much action here." He tossed the dirty towel over the open phone again.

He called the Grand Cayman Industrial Bank on a different cell. The transfer was confirmed and immediately moved to a bank in Rio de Janeiro activating a preset, often-used sequence. Eyes narrowed, he looked into the rearview mirror. "It's a done deal."

He picked up the towel. "Michelle, are you listening?"

She picked up the cell phone. "Yes."

"When you get to the Idaho exit go left to Apache Trail. Then go east toward Tortilla Flat. You'll come to a restaurant called the Green Chili Café. Pull off the road and drive around behind the building. Drop the money in the dumpster, get back on the road and drive to the marina. When you get there, pull into the parking lot, shut off the engine and wait."

"Has Braun talked to Lindsey this morning?" she said.

"Lady," he said in a quiet soft voice, "I've talked with Braun. I believe he told you two to do as you're told. Otherwise you're just out for an early morning drive. Got it?"

"Got it." She ground her teeth and pressed the accelerator. The Sebring jumped to 85.

Evans said, "Take it easy. We don't need to get stopped now. What did he say?"

Santiago stared at the road. "Idaho, Apache Trail, Green Chili Café, marina, stop and wait."

"I know those locations." Evans sat back. "We'll be at Idaho in a minute or two." He opened the passenger window. "It's a nice morning. May as well take advantage of the fresh air now that we're away from Phoenix."

Santiago opened her window and shut down the AC. Her nose wrinkled. "It seems to be a bit more country."

"There are still a few dairy farms around. It all depends on which way the wind's blowing."

"Do tell."

Evans said, "Nikki Braun is a lucky woman."

"I agree. Family, financial security, and hopefully her daughter back shortly."

"No, I mean to have a friend like you. I'm not sure I know anyone who would just drop everything and come to my aid, not on a deal like this."

Santiago's face turned a light pink. "She's family, like a second sister. She'd do the same thing, no questions asked."

"You're both fortunate."

"I know. Now all we have to do is get the two kids back."

He pointed at the green highway sign ahead. "Idaho. Here we go."

* * *

Claude and Nikki Braun were still waiting on the living room couch, surrounded by expensive furniture, pieces of sculpture, the painting of Lelani watching their every move, the clock ticking incessantly. He turned to his wife, their faces only inches apart. "Jesus, it's 7:56. We should be hearing from someone, anyone."

Nikki said, "We will, any minute."

He said, "Look at the junk in this room. 'High end' the media calls it. It's high end, all right. Worthless." Braun ran a hand through his hair and looked into his wife's eyes. "Sometimes, right now, I wish life was simple like before the company got so big and successful."

"Why?" she said.

"Because we lived like normal people, Lindsey, her mom and I. Nobody thought about kidnapping the daughter of a struggling entrepreneur trying to start a software company."

Nikki said, "There goes the clock again."

He looked again at the grandfather clock. "I swear to God the thing isn't moving."

She reached for the package of cigarettes on the coffee table, then withdrew her hand. "It's moving. Time is just crawling. Where do you think Mitch and Sam are?"

"I haven't got a clue... out driving around someplace."

"Think Burke got the money moved?"

"That would only take a few minutes. We should know something by now. If the transfer didn't get done, we lose Lindsey." A lump filled his throat, pain stabbed into the windpipe. Tears formed again in his eyes.

Nikki embraced him, kissed his neck, and rubbed his shoulders. "Hope that feels better," she said. "I don't know which one of us is the more tense."

He smiled at her. "I don't think anyone could measure that right now."

He kissed her. "When this is over we ought to pack the kid up and go away for awhile."

Nikki laughed. "You haven't referred to her as the kid in years, but I like the plan."

"I mean it. We need to be more like a family. It'll take a while for Lindsey to recover, but it would be nice to just go someplace nobody knows us and relax."

"And the kidnappers?"

"Mitch, Sam, the government boys—they'll get 'em."

"No more revenge?"

"I want them, you know that, but right now I want my family... you and Lindsey. Right now I want peace."

* * *

"There's the Green Chili Café," Evans said, pointing to a small sun-bleached stucco building on the right side of the road with a dirt parking lot. "Let's find the dumpster." He looked at the cell phone. "Did you hear me? We're dropping the money."

The phone remained silent.

Santiago pulled up beside the container and Evans climbed out of the car, reached into the back seat and pulled out the duffel bag. "I suppose I should set it in the damn thing. Wouldn't want to toss it and have it come open."

He walked up beside the dumpster and reached over, released the bag and watched it fall to the empty bottom. He looked back at the car. "Guess the garbage pickup was today. That thing smells bad but it's empty."

"Come on," she said. "Let's go."

Evans got back in the car. "Funny thing, we're not all that far from the marina or Braun's desert getaway."

"The one that's already been checked?"

"That's the one. We'd better get to the marina," he said.

Santiago looked at her cell phone and said in a loud voice, "We don't want to keep anyone waiting."

* * *

Claude Braun stood, picked up the phone and began pacing the living room. "It's 8:01. Come on!"

Nikki watched as he moved about the room looking at the clock every few ticks, his breath labored like that of a much older man. "Now it's 8:02."

She bit her lip while watching her husband. "They'll call. I feel it. I've never seen this side of you, so vulnerable and tense."

She stood and walked to him, looked into his face, his eyes dark circles, moist. He reached out to her and they embraced.

He said, "Have you ever felt so empty? So helpless?"

"No."

They hugged again and stood very still. At 8:04, the cell rang. They both looked at his shaking white-knuckled hand holding the phone. He pressed the Receive button. The phone dropped to the floor. Kneeling, he leaned over it.

"Braun?"

"Yes," he said picking up the phone.

"The transfer is complete."

Braun sighed, looked at Nikki and smiled, nodding his head. "My daughter, where is my, our daughter?"

The voice laughed. "A little tension in the household?"

"Please, we've done as you asked."

"Directed," said the voice.

"Yes, directed. Please, where is Lindsey?"

"See? You don't give a shit about the boyfriend either, do you Braun?"

"No. Yes." Braun paused. "I guess not really. Where are they, please?"

"Call Santiago. Tell her they are at your cabin in the Superstitions." The connection broke.

"The cabin!" He entered Santiago's number. "Busy! The damn thing's busy! Oh Lord, help us."

He looked at Nikki, tears filling his eyes. "They're at our cabin, right under our noses. We checked it. We should've checked again."

He stabbed the digits of Santiago's number again. "Still busy." He looked at Nikki, his face turning dark red.

"Call House," she said. "Tell him where the kids are."

"Yes, we can get him and the doctor going. They have the chopper."

She took the phone from his quivering hand. "Here, let me do that."

He said, "Then we'll leave for the clinic. We'll meet them after they pickup Lindsey. We can try Mitch again on the way."

House answered on the second ring. "Hello?"

Nikki said, "They're at our cabin out by—"

"I know. We're on our way."

* * *

The voice was eerie and soft. "Michelle, can you hear me?"

Evans picked up the phone. "We hear you."

"Hang up. Braun wants to call you."

"That rotten bastard!" Evans said. "He just cut me off. Said Braun wants to call us."

Santiago started the engine. "I hope the fresh smell of the lake is an indicator of good things to come."

"So do I, Mitch... so do I."

Santiago drummed her fingers on the steering wheel. "8:08... feels like it should be noon. Why did I start the engine, anyway?"

"Just nerves. You're ready to go. We just don't know where."

The phone rang at 8:10. Evans took the call. "We're at the marina. Be there in ten minutes."

"Where to?"

He looked at Santiago. "The cabin! Damnit, I knew it! I felt it coming out here! Get back on the highway and head east! They're at the fuckin' cabin!"

A large tractor-trailer cut across the parking lot, snaking its way to the road. Santiago gunned the engine and passed the rig, cutting in front of it just before the entrance. The truck's air horn broke the morning quiet. She glanced in the side view mirror only to see a large burly man waving a one-fingered salute at them. Slowing she checked for traffic, then stabbed the accelerator. As the Sebring gained speed she laughed.

"What's so funny? He was really pissed," Evans said.

"You are, Sam. I've never heard you use such strong language... always the company man."

"I guess I forgot myself. Sorry."

"Don't be. Let's get to the fucking cabin in under ten. Better call House."

"Right, but I'd bet Braun already has."

* * *

Quarterman looked around the parking lot, shut off the Caddie and yawned. He saw his bloodshot eyes in the rearview mirror. "It's tough running on four hours sleep. I'm getting' too old for this. Time for a little rest."

He scooped up the two cell phones, wiped them clean and wrapped them in the dirty motel towel. "8:15 and it's already a great day."

He got out of the car, closed the door, stretched, and walked toward the stairwell dropping the towel in a trash container before heading up. "I'll be callin' you this evening, Michelle."

He hummed and walked across the sky bridge to the main lobby. "Now the game begins... my last game."

He passed an early morning couple coming out of the lobby. "Good morning," he said with a nod.

* * * * * * *

The Sebring held the road at high speeds on tight corners. The desert flew by sun baked with more than a small amount of green generated by the large number of cactus and other unique plant life.

"Slow down," Evans said, "we're almost to the turnoff. There, on your right where it says Broken Spur Ranch."

An open gate, traditional barbed wire fencing and what passed for a wide dirt driveway led toward a hill. Suspended overhead was the sign with the name of the ranch. On one of the posts supporting the arch was a private property notice.

Santiago followed the rutted lane to its crest with dense cloud of dust trailing them. "It looks really desolate."

Evans said, "Wait 'til we get over the little rise; then you'll see the cabin to end all cabins."

As the car nosed over the crest a large single story flat roofed desert mansion came into view. It was placed inside high walled grounds. The bleached ivory white stucco was almost blinding even in morning light. The iron gates were open.

"I don't see any cars," she said as they slowed to a near stop.

"If her car is here it's probably in the covered parking area. The wall is shielding it from our view."

They eased down the lane to the gates and entered the front courtyard complete with a cement driveway.

"There's Lindsey's car. Pull over by it. The company helicopter will need this space to land on," Evans said.

"A chopper?"

"House has it waiting with Braun's family doctor. They'll be here any minute."

"Good."

Evans said, "How do we go in?"

"Through the front door. The kidnappers aren't here. Let's hope the kids are." She paused for a moment. "When we get to the door, let's be careful and make sure they haven't left any other surprises for us."

The pair crossed the courtyard. The curtains were drawn. They checked the door and windows, the space around the entry, but found no wires or other indicators of danger. Barely audible murmurs came from inside. They looked at each other.

Mitch thought, *For the first time since I left Seattle I miss my Glock.*

They approached the front of the cabin. She tried the door handle, looked at Evans and whispered, "It's not locked."

He nodded, kicked the door open and rushed in, scanning the room over the barrel of his Glock. Santiago followed Evans holding the .22 caliber loaner, both moving into the shadows surrounding the entry once inside. The stench of fowl putrid air greeted them. The shaded windows allowed very little light into the room but enough to provide silhouettes of two heads over the divider separating the kitchen from the great room. The murmurs became louder. Evans rushed to the two young people. Santiago followed after clearing the area.

"Remember, Sam, this is a crime scene. Be careful. We don't want to destroy any evidence."

"Understood." He was at Lindsey's side. "Whew, I'd sure like to have a little Vick's for my upper lip right now."

Lindsey looked at Evans, then Santiago. "Aunt Michelle."

Mitch could barely hear her weak voice. "Get some water, Sam."

Lindsey said, "There's some in the fridge."

Santiago turned to Lindsey. "How's the hand? It's been a rough few days, I know."

Lindsey writhed in pain as Santiago freed her arms. "It's mostly numb, but it hurts when I move it. Other times it's just numb. Maybe I'm getting accustomed to it."

"Never. The doctor will be here any minute," Santiago said, circling around the table to T.J. and freeing him. She looked at his cheek. "That's a nasty cut."

T.J. said, "Yeah."

Evans brought two bottles of water to the table and opened them. He held one to the Lindsey's mouth and handed the other to Santiago. Lindsey reached out for the bottle with her right hand. Evans helped hold it for a moment as she drank. He watched her face, then released the bottle.

He said, "I'll open the windows. You kids could use some fresh air in here, even if it's hot."

Lindsey smiled and looked across the table at T.J. as he gulped from his bottle.

Santiago came around to Lindsey's side of the table and reached for the left arm still suspended in the bowl of bloody water. "Let me see your hand. You're going to be all right when this is over."

The quiet surrounding the room and courtyard was disrupted by the whine of a jet turbine as the DataFlex helicopter landed. Dust came pouring through the open door and windows. Lindsey's gaze shot to the doorway, intense and frightened.

Santiago said, "We're going to get you out of here. Your dad sent the doctor. Both of you are going with him to get checked and any receive any medical treatment you need. I was going to wash the wound and repack it in ice but I'd best leave that to them. They're the pros."

Evans met two men at the door, the older fellow carrying a medical bag. He had longish gray hair, a thick mustache and a deep tan. A younger man in a white polo shirt and pants followed him through the door. Evans trailed the two men to the table.

Standing behind the older man Evans said, "This is Ben Yount, the Braun family physician."

Santiago nodded at the man, who was focused on Lindsey.

Yount checked Lindsey's pulse, eyes, and the wound on her left hand. He removed a syringe from the bag. "This will deaden any pain and relax you, little lady. The wound looks uglier than it is."

Yount looked across the table at his colleague. "How is he?"

"Dehydrated, a bad cut on his cheek, probably infected. Vitals look good."

Yount said, "Let's get them out of here"

T.J. tried to stand but collapsed as his legs folded. Evans helped him stand and led him toward the door.

Yount's assistant said, "Take it easy, fella."

Yount said to Santiago, "I want you to support her under her right shoulder when she stands up. I'll support her left side. Sorry, Kid. We have no stretchers on your dad's bird."

Lindsey emitted a soft chuckle and smiled as they helped her to her feet and out the door.

Evans was talking to T.J. when they arrived at the helicopter. "I appreciate your help, Son. So does Mr. Braun. He will make it worth your time and effort."

Evans stepped back from the door so Lindsey could board.

Santiago gestured toward T.J. "What was that all about?"

"I asked him to keep quiet about everything that's gone on the last few days. The Feds have asked that we sit on it. I told him Braun will reward him for his efforts."

"You mean a payoff?" she said as the helicopter took off.

"He got caught up in something that didn't involve him."

Santiago looked around the courtyard. "Where are the cops, anyway? You'd think they'd be here by now."

As she spoke two black Suburbans came over the crest toward the cabin.

Evans said, "Well, here come the reinforcements. Mitch, the event is being handled by federal government agencies. They don't want locals involved."

"You mean FBI?"

He nodded. "And Homeland Security, an interagency operation. While we've been in the field their people have researched the incident. They have reason to believe at least one of the kidnappers has a background as a mercenary with a history of covert operations and terrorist activities. The government wants us to work with them."

The cars ground to a halt in a cloud of dust.

Santiago said, "The kidnappers are criminals, Sam. I thought Braun had contacted the authorities?"

"He did, and they're here now. If the kidnappers are not who they think, it will be turned over to the locals, but it could be a much bigger situation than we know. They need your help... *our* help... okay?"

I should've listened to Captain James. "For now, but I'm a cop first, Sam."

Four men get out of the vehicles, two from each. Three men entered the cabin, each putting on booties and gloves at the door.

She said, "They seem to know what they're doing."

"Mitch, they're FBI trained in crime scene investigation and collecting evidence."

The fourth man approached Evans and Santiago. He was big, mid-forties, dressed in dark slacks, a white shirt and a tie. His aviator style shades obscured his face except for dark creases framing an unsmiling mouth. His hair was short with a touch of gray.

She said to Evans, "This must be their leader. It looks like they all shop at the same department store."

Evans said, "It's like a standard non-uniform. I remember those days only too well."

Extending a hand the man said, "Mr. Evans, I'm John Stone. We're on a special operation. I believe Mr. House advised you of our involvement."

"Yes," Evans said. "This is Michelle Santiago. She's been assisting in the location of the victims."

Stone tilted his head. "Ma'am. I understand you've had direct contact with one of the kidnappers."

"I have. What does special operation mean?"

Stone ignored the question. Looking at Evans he said, "Is she cleared?"

"She's cleared."

"We're a deep cover layer of the Bureau. We handle covert operations, domestic spying, terrorist threats on U.S. soil in conjunction with Homeland Security. You'll be brought on board at a briefing this afternoon at 1600."

Stone glanced at the cabin. "For now we will treat the site as a crime scene."

Santiago said, "You know I'm a Seattle homicide detective, right?"

"I do, and as Mr. Evans has noted, you have been cleared to work on this operation. Your cooperation is most appreciated." Stone turned and faced the cabin. "Any evidence we find will be turned over to regular Bureau operatives if our subject is not involved.

Otherwise it will be a matter of national security. Do you understand?"

Santiago said, "Not really."

"You will, and after the briefing this afternoon the big picture will become much clearer to you. We are thankful for the help of both DataFlex and you. Please understand what we are doing here is Top Secret. Do not discuss the operation with anyone else. It could compromise national security, maybe even prove fatal."

She said, "What happens if the kidnappers, or one of them, is the man you're looking for?"

"Federal interests must come first. Rest assured nobody skates because of security. My people will take it from here. We'll see you at the briefing."

He turned and walked toward the cabin.

Santiago said, "I think we've been dismissed."

Evans said, "Yeah, those guys aren't exactly known for their people skills."

Santiago said, "Let's call the Brauns. I'd like to tell Nikki her daughter is safe. Then we'll visit Doctor Rich. Lindsey won't be available to us for several hours and we have work to do."

Evans gestured toward the black Suburbans. "What about their request?"

"According to my math we have at least three players; the young guy, the old guy, and the woman who left the package at the hotel. They are interested in only one. That leaves two. Right?"

"Correct," Evans said. "You look troubled."

"Think about it. Top Secret everything—no police, FBI deep cover, Homeland Security, a mysterious suspect that they seem to have a name for but aren't sharing. And I loved the way Stone said 'fatal,' before going into the cabin. I'd better get some answers, Sam. I don't like this arrangement."

"Why is it I get the feeling you're not as nice as you've been coming across? Could it be our guest detective is taking off the gloves?"

"Could be. We've got the kids back safely and now we're in pursuit. Who knows... I might have a surprise or two for Stone at the briefing."

* * *

Aaron Martin rolled over and faced a sleepy eyed Lisa Fargo. She looked at him, blinked and in a soft voice said, "Good morning. Last night was fun."

"Yes, it was."

She pressed a leg against him. "You're still sweaty."

He smiled and looked at his watch. "8:46. I think I liked watches better before digital timepieces were the rage. More important, I think I'd like to do this again tonight."

She said in a thick voice, "I'll be available. I'm available right now. When I first spotted you at dinner last night I thought maybe you were married to your young table partner or something."

He laughed. "At my age I could be her father. I'm a widower. Michelle, that was her name, had a free seat at her table in a very crowded dining room. I asked and she was kind enough to share it. I have eyes for only you, Brooke."

Right. "Most men like young hard bodies."

"I'll take experience and skip the cardiac any day."

She kissed his lips and felt the probe of his tongue. "So will I. Morning breath never tasted so good. I want more."

He said, "A leisurely morning? Me too, right here."

She gave him another kiss. "Let's shower together first and really awaken our pores."

"I like the way you think. You know my status. I assume you're unattached."

She said, "A little late to worry about that now."

"I wouldn't want some jealous type to come knockin' on the door."

"I'm footloose and fancy free, Aaron. Well, almost. I'm waiting for finalization papers and the settlement, but it's not a problem."

He rolled toward his side of the bed. "I know what you mean. A friend of mine lost three-hundred grand on one of those settlements, plus support. I guess that's the price of testing your dipstick on one of those toys while it's still attached elsewhere."

They both laughed and she said, "It's true. It's gonna cost my old man a half-million and change. I can't wait 'til it's a done deal."

"Do tell." He leaned over and kissed her left breast, teasing the nipple with his teeth and tongue. "Do you have plans for the future?"

"To live and make love, maybe in old Mexico. Who knows?"

He kissed her again. "Let's do that shower and freshen up. We'll take breakfast right here if you'd like."

"I'd like that... a champagne breakfast," she said.

"I wouldn't have it any other way. Would you like orange juice with a straw too? I'll call room service."

She teased her teeth with the tip of her tongue. "I can do things with champagne you haven't even imagined. As for the juice, skip it. I like flesh straws."

"Woman, I'm tinglin' just at the thought of breakfast in bed."

"I have a story to tell you about the real me. Do you believe in love at first sight?"

"I do now, Brooke. I do now."

"Lisa, call me Lisa."

"Lisa?"

She smiled "We'll talk later."

"You sound mysterious. I like that in a woman. I might even give you my class ring."

"That would be a first. I've never had one."

* * *

Santiago punched in Nikki's cell number. She answered on the first ring. "The kids are safe."

"How's Lindsey?"

"In pain, dehydrated. Doctor Yount gave her some painkiller. They're on the way to his clinic."

"Did you talk with her?"

"Hardly. We arrived just before the doctor. Her vitals were good. Both of their vitals were good. Are you and Claude on the way to Yount's clinic?"

"Yes, as we speak. Claude is calling Yount on his cell."

"At best she'll be semi-conscious judging from the injection. I'll see her later today or this evening when her head is clear if she can talk."

Nikki's voice was breaking. She stammered and cried. "I'm sorry. I'm being a baby. We're both crying driving down the road."

"Tears of joy," Santiago said. "Her friend T.J. was in pretty good shape too. He was dehydrated and had a gash on his cheek. Otherwise, not bad considering what they've been through. It looks like both kids will bounce back."

"Thank God. Where are you now?"

"We're still at the cabin, as you call it."

"Weird isn't it?" Nikki said. "Using the cabin for a hideout?"

"Yes. Sam's people checked it out a few days ago. Apparently they brought them here later."

"Mitch, Claude wants to know if you're coming to the house?"

"When we leave here we're going to Doctor Rich's office. Where will you two be around noon?"

"At home. We're going to see Lindsey for a few minutes but the doctor just told Claude she's out like a light and will be for several hours. Why?"

"I'll come by after I see Doctor Rich and drop Sam off at DataFlex. The three of us need to talk."

"Fine," Nikki said. "If there is a change I'll call you. Right now Claude wants to talk with Sam for a moment. Is he handy?"

"Sure." She handed the phone to her partner.

"Yes, Mr. Braun," Evans said.

"Where did you leave the money?"

"In a dumpster behind the Green Chili Café. We didn't see anyone following us either."

"Don't worry about that. You'll be passing the café on the way to Rich's office. Stop and take a look. I think the money is still sitting there."

"You're kidding."

"No."

Evans looked confused. "But if the money wasn't collected we wouldn't have gotten the kids back."

"The kidnappers had us transfer a million dollars to an offshore account. I suspect the million in the dumpster was a ruse. Just go take a look. If it's there bring it with you."

"If it's there wouldn't it be safer with an armed escort?"

"Maybe, but I doubt it. Besides, House and Stone don't want any more attention brought to this matter than is necessary. You had it in the car going out there didn't you?"

"Yes."

"Well, put it in the trunk coming in."

"And if the money isn't there?"

"Call me. I'll have Stone take his team out for a look."

"What about Lindsey's car?"

"It's there?" Braun said with surprise.

"Yes, in the covered parking area."

"I'll have someone pick it up. Don't worry about it, Sam. This is a good day."

"Yes, Sir. Mitch would like you to call Rich's office, kind'a clear the way for us. We should get there between 9:30 and 10:00 depending on the traffic."

"I'll do it as soon as we finish. "Let Mitch know I'll be at the briefing at whatever time Stone said it is."

"4 p.m. Mr. Braun."

Evans looked at Santiago. "Why are we going to Rich's place rather than the clinic?"

"As I told the Brauns, the kids aren't going to be in any shape for an interview. Besides, if the good doctor is involved he may tip his hand. I'd like to see if he's excited, happy, whatever this early in the morning."

"You think he's involved?"

"Don't know, but he could be. This way we'll get a feel for it, to say nothing of the fact the bastard needs to know we know about his escapades with Lindsey."

"If he's involved it could be dangerous. Keep my ankle gun handy for the time being," he said.

"Thanks. I felt naked pulling into Braun's place, but your .22 sure beat being empty handed."

Evans smiled.

She said, "Let's go take a look for the money and see if we can shake-up Doctor Rich."

Evans said, "It's going to be a long, long day."

"No shit," she said.

They both laughed walking to the car.

* * *

Santiago and Evans drove north at a crawl on Mill Avenue in the Tempe morning traffic of shoppers, students and an assortment of young people. Santiago looked for any available parking place. "You'd think Doctor Hot Pants would have his office in Scottsdale among the rich and famous. I said yesterday I like college towns. Apparently he does too."

Evans nodded. "Rich specializes with teens and young adults. Mill Avenue is their comfort zone."

"I'll bet most, if not all, of his clients are girls... vulnerable girls and young women."

"No doubt," Evans said.

She smiled and slipped into a parking place just vacated. "The gods must be with us."

Evans pointed to a well-maintained older structure with no outstanding signage. "In more ways than one... the two-story building just down the other side of the street is where Rich is located."

"Sam, when we get inside I would like to do the talking. I want his reaction to a few things I have in mind. Okay with you?"

He laughed. "I still can't believe we're just parking here with a million dollars in the trunk, but yes, I understand you wanting to jerk his chain. What do you call it? Good cop, bad cop?"

"Something like that. Let's go."

The second floor hallway floor was polished hardwood, about six feet wide with a carpet runner down the center. An elevator was at one end. The walls were painted light green with small tile implants of desert scenes. "How old is this building, Sam?"

"Probably early twentieth century. I'm sure these walls could tell many stories. Rich is at the end on the right."

Santiago reached out and opened the wooden door. Like many older building interior doors it framed a frosted glass window in the upper half. Lettered on the window were the words *Office of Doctor Rich.* The outer office area was small, furnished with a leather-covered couch, a few captain's chairs, the receptionist's desk, and a coat stand.

As they approached the receptionist, Santiago said, "Sam Evans and Michelle Santiago to see Doctor Rich."

The receptionist picked up the phone, dialed and listened for a moment, then replaced it in the cradle. "Go right in. He's expecting you."

"Thank you," Evans said as they entered.

Santiago followed Evans through the door, then stepped around him. "Doctor Rich, thank you for seeing us on such short notice."

Greg Rich was standing behind a neat, polished desk. The office suite was large, with several overstuffed burgundy chairs surrounding a glass coffee table. The walls were dark wood with some shelves. A few books were visible. Most shelves displayed photos of Rich climbing, hiking, swimming, and boating. A lone degree was framed on the wall directly behind the desk.

She said, "Nice office." *He's alone in every picture.*

"Thank you. I try to have a comfortable setting for my clients. They're all young people."

"So I've been told."

He gestured toward the chairs and walked around from behind the desk. "Please be seated. I hate barriers when I'm chatting with anyone." He took a seat across from them.

Santiago leaned over and took a notepad from her purse. "Do you mind if I take some notes, Doctor Rich? We're looking into a matter for Claude and Nikki."

He studied the exposed flesh of Santiago's upper thigh as her mini slid up when she took a seat and crossed her legs. "Of course not. What can I do for you? Perhaps coffee while we talk?"

"No thank you." *Very little eye contact here.* "We need some background on Lindsey."

He wet his lips. "Of course, Miss Santiago."

"In the last few months Lindsey has been in to see you on average about every other week, is that correct?"

"Sounds reasonable."

Evans sat quietly, watching the two interact and taking a few notes.

"What did she talk about? Did she have any particular concerns she brought up, maybe repeatedly?"

"Miss Santiago, you know about doctor-patient privilege. Claude and Nikki know about it. In her early years, until she was around fifteen, Claude would call and we would talk, but he and I agreed to honor Lindsey's confidentiality. It's important for her and for me. I have an ethical code."

"Yes, I'm aware of the code and the laws, and I'm aware of the need for privacy... especially when you're screwing the patient."

"What! How dare you say such a thing?!"

"According to my information you've been having sex with her since she was about fifteen."

Evans swallowed, his throat constricting; he remained quiet.

"About the time you stopped having your little chats with Claude if I'm not mistaken."

"I don't know what to say to such accusations. Did Lindsey tell you I was having a relationship with her?"

Santiago ignored his question. "Did Claude tell you what Lindsey has been through in the last few days?"

"Only that she had suffered a very painful negative experience. He said you could fill me in, but that she would better explain in her own words."

"Lindsey was kidnapped a few days ago. We found her this morning." Santiago watched Rich's reaction.

"That's terrible." He exhaled and looked across the office at the water cooler in one corner. "Just terrible. Is she all right?"

"She'll survive."

Rick looked Evans and Santiago in the eyes and gripped the arms of his chair. "I mean, I know she's alive or she wouldn't be coming to see me. I'm sure she's emotionally spent. This is terrible."

"She's been through a lot. Not only was she held prisoner, but she was mutilated."

"No! She's a beautiful woman!" He crossed his feet repeatedly and then took a package of cigarettes from a drawer beneath the table. "I quit a long time ago. This is shocking." He tossed the pack on the tabletop.

Santiago said, "Now, Doctor Rich, let's focus on our problem. We know about the relationship you had with Lindsey. I suspect you have had several such intimate affairs with the young women you're supposedly helping, but right now, Lindsey is my only concern. Do you want me to just turn this over to the authorities, or do you want to talk to us and skip the games?"

"I think I should call my attorney."

"By all means, call."

He stood, walked to the desk and reached for the phone. He looked back at the two visitors just as Santiago stood and took a cell phone from her purse. He said, "Who are you calling?"

"The Tempe Police. If you're contacting counsel, there's no reason for us to remain here. We'll let the authorities and press handle our end."

"Does Claude know you're doing this?"

"Claude knows I'll do whatever is necessary to get the information I want."

"Do the authorities know about the allegations?"

"I've already answered that, but when I finish my call, as you finish yours, they will. And the press will be interested in the payoff you made to another youthful client some years back, don't you think?"

Rich set the phone back in the cradle and faced his two inquisitors. Santiago sat back in the chair and re-crossed her legs. Rich's eyes still followed the flesh as it was uncovered by the climbing hemline. He wet his lips, then returned to his chair at the table. In a quiet voice he said, "Those charges were dropped."

"I know, after the payoff... the cash settlement with the victim."

"Accuser, not victim," he corrected.

"For now."

Rich wiped beads of sweat from his forehead. His face turned crimson, sweat soaked the collar of his dress shirt. He cleared his throat. "If Claude believed any of those rumors Lindsey wouldn't be a client."

She looked Rich in the eyes. "He doesn't know yet."

Rich took a long deep breath and looked at the tabletop. His voice became soft. "She's a beautiful woman, older than her years, more experienced and aggressive than any woman I've ever known. I love her. Oh God, I love her like a daughter."

Santiago laughed. "Most dads don't have sex with their daughters. There are laws that protect children from people like you whether you're the father, doctor, teacher, priest, man, woman, whatever."

Rich stood, walked around the office and came to a halt behind the desk. Santiago and Evans watched his every move as Rich rubbed the back of his neck, swiped a palm across his forehead and looked at the photo on the desk. "Miss Santiago, I believe we've gotten off to a bad start. There is no need for us to be adversarial. If you please, let's start again." He cleared his throat. "Of course I will help in apprehending the perpetrators of this heinous crime."

She looked at Evans, then back to Rich. "I was sure you would want to work with us. Now, when she was visiting during recent times did she say anything about someone stalking her, other than you?"

"I wasn't stalking Lindsey. Ours was a mutually happy relationship. She was mature beyond her years."

"I stand corrected," Santiago said. "You were, how should I put it, having sex with a minor you were helping or just banging the patient."

Rich said, "That's a very crude way to put things."

"Yes, perhaps it is, but accurate. I'm sure Lindsey had some help making those decisions. That's why she came to you, because she was young, impressionable, troubled, and vulnerable. I doubt her dad would pay two-hundred dollars an hour for stud service to his over sexed daughter."

"It began as a tryst, the melancholy reaction to her mother's passing and her father's loneliness. It became an infatuation for both of us. She was in love with her father and wanted to bed him, take the place of her dead mother."

"So you were just standing in for dear old Dad. What a guy," Santiago said. "What do you think, Sam?"

Evans smiled. "Sounds like the good doctor wanted to try a little young stuff on the side. It also sounds like a man volunteering to be neutered."

Rich winced.

Santiago said, "It won't fly with the cops, but this isn't what we came for. Did she ever comment about anyone following her, showing unusual interest, always being around?"

"No, no stalkers. She had many admirers, as you're probably aware."

Santiago said, "No concerns regarding any of her friends?"

"Only Sierra. Lindsey was quite stressed about Sierra's infatuation with Claude. The two girls have been friends since grade school... friends and neighbors."

"And this friend, Sierra, did her interest go beyond just *thinking* about Claude?"

"According to Lindsey, Sierra was interested in anything that wore pants, but yes, way beyond just thinking. Claude is a handsome, wealthy man, and he loves young women. It's common knowledge in Phoenix gossip circles that he collects trophies, not wives. His last one is a millionaire and living comfortably. The current Mrs. Braun will do likewise when he gives her the pink slip."

"And you think he's shopping?"

"Claude is always shopping, Miss Santiago. I'm surprised you haven't noticed. He's undoubtedly checked you out."

"Let's get back to Lindsey. You say she was upset about Sierra and her dad?"

"Quite so. She said she'd do anything to keep the current Mrs. Braun, Nikki, in the household. Sometimes she talked endlessly about how to get her father and Nikki closer together and Sierra out of the picture."

"What type of options did she explore?"

"Running away, talking with her parents, threaten to get married, drop out of school, change her lifestyle—pretty much an endless list of things."

"Kidnapping?"

"Yes, that too. You don't think she would fake a kidnapping and mutilate herself?"

"No, I don't."

A silence fell over the room. "You haven't said how she was mutilated. Was she burned, tortured? Will she be scarred?"

"The ring finger of the left hand was amputated."

Evans said, "So let's make sure I have this right. According to you, Sierra was the only problem Lindsey had?"

"No, Sierra was the root of the problem. The problem was how to keep her current parents together. Lindsey loves her father and Nikki. She sees the three of them as a family unit. She doesn't want that to change."

Santiago said, "One last thing for now. I expect Claude will be calling to vent his anger after he and I talk. When he does you will tell him you're closing the office."

Rich looked at Santiago with a shocked expression. "What?"

"You heard me. Claim health, family, whatever, I don't care. I doubt he'll be asking you for recommendations. But I do suggest you take his call. If you don't do as I say, I will forward all the information we have to the authorities immediately."

"This is blackmail."

"No Sir. It's your choice, Doctor Rich. Right now our concern is Lindsey. Claude doesn't even know about you yet."

"But he will?"

"Obviously, he's the one paying for the investigation. You can figure out that answer for yourself. We also need a copy of your log of Lindsey's calls and appointments for the last six months. Will that be a problem?"

His voice was weak. "No, I'll have the receptionist print it out while you wait."

Santiago and Evans stood to leave. As they watched, Rich picked up the phone and called the outer office, giving specific instructions to the receptionist. Then he turned, walked to the window and looked out onto Mill Avenue. Tears ran down his cheeks. The smell of fresh baked bread wafted through the office when he opened the window and the warm morning air flowed in. He shook his head. "I don't know what to do."

The office door clicked shut behind Santiago and Evans. Rich continued looking out the window. After a few minutes he saw Santiago and Evans cross the street and get into a car. He turned and looked at a small picture of his family on the desk. "I just don't know what to do."

* * * * * * *

Mario Spears punched Santiago's cell number with anticipation, then waited for her to answer.

"Hello?"

"Michelle?"

"Yes," she said. "Who is this?"

"Mario Spears. You interviewed me day before yesterday."

"Yes, Mario, what can I do for you?"

"It's what I can do for you."

"That sounds like a come on."

"Probably is, but seriously, I was tracking a money transfer this morning for Mr. House. He gave me your number and said I should call you. You don't mind, do you?"

"No, not at all. Do you know where it went?"

"Well, I tapped into a couple of programs and started to—"

"No, no. Please, I'm almost computer illiterate. Skip the jargon. Just tell me what you have."

"I think the money is in Phoenix."

The car swerved slightly, hitting the lane bubbles. "Phoenix?"

"I followed it to the Cayman Islands, Rio de Janeiro, Bogota, and back to Phoenix... I think."

"You're not sure?"

"99 per cent sure."

"Which bank?"

"Veteran's Trust. They have a few branches around the country. They're part of a consortium of small banks in various countries, probably little guys trying to compete with the multi-nationals."

Or a quasi-military network used by adventurers, mercenaries and crime cartels. "Does anyone else know about this?"

"Not yet."

"Good. Sit on it. This is very confidential."

Spears chuckled. "So I've been told... that and probably illegal."

"I owe you."

"I hoped you'd say something like that. How about we have a drink after work? Nothing serious. I'd just like to get to know you better."

"I'll get back to you on that. Maybe you can come by the hotel lounge later this afternoon or evening."

A horn blared in the background as a Ford 350 passed her.

Spears said, "Where are you, anyway?"

"Somewhere on Rural Road playing bumper tag. Sam and I have been up on Mill Avenue. It reminds me of the U District in Seattle but with lighter traffic."

"Mill's always seemed crowded to me with students, shoppers, whatever, but I've never been to Seattle. And yes, I will meet you in the lounge of your hotel later today. I'll be waiting to hear from you."

"Thanks, Mario."

"Thank you."

As Mitch ended the call, Evans said, "What was that all about?"

"Mario believes he has a trace on the money."

"Really? Where?"

"Phoenix. Ever hear of Veterans Trust Bank?"

"No. It must be small."

"We'll find out, but for now let's keep a lid on this until I can check a few things. Did you know about a possible transfer, the tracking?"

"No, but House probably did. He's a master of anticipation. If he thinks something might occur, he's ready."

Santiago frowned.

"You look troubled."

"Sometimes I feel like we're puppets on a larger stage and we don't have the script."

"I know what you mean. I've had moments when I'm sure House thinks he's still running operations for the Agency."

She glanced at Evans. "It's a strange way to work with a team."

"I know."

They entered Chandler Boulevard, heading for the DataFlex main gate. Mitch said, "Let's get you and the money taken care of. I have some things I need to do."

"Solo?"

"Yes, after I drop off you and your garbage bag, I have another source I want to check with: my partner in Seattle."

* * *

Santiago eased the Sebring into a parking space near the front entry of the Desert Oasis. She picked up her cell phone and jabbed in Chance Stewart's number. "I hope the battery still has a little juice in it."

"Stewart."

"Afternoon stranger... or should I say good morning?"

"Depends on your time zone, Mitch. What's up?"

"The kids are safe, but that's a long story. I'm calling because I want to call you in a few minutes."

"Have I missed something here?"

"My hotel room and phone are bugged. I want to stage a conversation, something to draw them out, especially the older one."

"What do you mean? You're going too fast for me."

"I'm not sure what all we have here. Some FBI types showed up. They think the older man is someone they want, but it's all buried in classified wrapping paper. They'll brief us this afternoon."

"Really? The detectives at Pismo ran into a stone wall on one of their inquiries too. Same thing, classified material, an MIA in Vietnam."

She said, "To add to the confusion we may have a fourth murder. The body of a dancer was found here a few days ago with the same MO."

"I don't like this, Mitch."

"Neither do I, but for now I'm stuck in the middle. What troubles me the most is could there be a link between the serial killings and the kidnapping?"

Stewart said, "Could be the events aren't related."

"I hope they're unrelated, but you know how little faith I have in coincidence of any kind. Things are just getting too close to home."

"So why let them know what you've got?"

"I want to shake 'em up. The older one has a prurient side I want to entice. We know our guy threatened to rape Lindsey, but he didn't. We know the killer may have had unforced sex with his victims before breaking their necks. We know both amputate the ring finger of the left hand. Now we have a link to the Vietnam era where an MIA used the same signature in his operations. We have the FBI sniffing around looking for their classified mystery man. And we have a guy stalking me who gets his rocks off watching me in a red bikini."

"A lot of possibilities, Mitch."

"That's why I want to nudge them. I want to manipulate the conversation. I'd like it to be provocative. I'd also like for you to give me whatever information you've gathered on the Pismo, Spokane, and Seaside murders."

"So you want to excite him, turn him on, and feed him data?"

She smiled. "You got it."

"We'll play it out," Stewart said. "I'll use an interrogation room for privacy. But take it easy on the sexy stuff. You're a long way from Seattle."

After she closed the connection, she said, "But you have Amber." She left the car and walked into the hotel lobby.

Several guests smiled as she passed them going to the elevator. She pressed five and watched the door close. *I didn't see anyone suspicious but the friendly smiles made me feel good.*

The room had already been cleaned by housekeeping. She went into the bathroom and began filling the tub. "I feel so dirty after being out there. A bath and change will do wonders," she said while looking around the sitting room. *I hope you enjoy this, gentlemen. I know I will.*

She dialed Stewart on the room phone and waited.

"Stewart."

"Hi. Do you miss me?"

"Is the Pope Catholic?"

"Know what I'm doing now?"

"It doesn't sound like work."

"I'm unbuttoning my blouse, slowly, like you do."

"Great visual."

"I just dropped it on the floor."

"Are you doing a striptease for me?"

"Oh yes, and more. My mini-skirt just joined the blouse."

"Absence makes the heart grow fonder, Babe."

Her voice was soft and suggestive. "It's not the heart I want to see and touch."

"I should come to the desert."

"Come, yes. Now I'm naked, just standing here all alone."

"And how do you look just standing there all alone?"

"Vulnerable. Hot. My nipples are hard as rocks."

His breathing became harsh. "Beautiful diamonds mounted on firm, full mounds."

"Chance?"

"Yes."

"I'm running my fingers down over my belly... my navel... low...."

He said, "I love to tease your flesh with the tips of my fingers."

"I love the touch of your tongue."

He squirmed in the chair and glanced at the mirrored window across the table from him. "Oh God, yes."

"Ooh," she moaned. "I want you. I want you now." She gasped and smiled. "No wonder people make such a good living at this. How much a minute?"

"I don't know, but I think I like it," he said.

"I'd rather be holding you, tasting your sweat, licking you all over. Just a moment. I need to shut off the bath water."

He glanced at the interrogation room mirror again. "Go for it. I need a cold shower."

"I'm back... are you still there?"

"I'm here. Am I *ever* here. You know, this reminds me of the women in the murders you asked about."

"How so?"

"All three were having or just had sex before they were killed. Not rape, but good old sex, and I don't mean on the phone."

She forced a laugh. "I like the sound of that. What a way to go."

"Yes, but then they had their necks broken, and then a finger amputation."

"That sounds so gross. You're breaking my mood, Love."

"Well, there's more. One of the detectives at Pismo Beach traced the ring finger amputations as a signature for a serial killer. He went through the FBI, military, other government and civil agencies."

"What did he come up with?"

"Mostly dead ends."

"Dead ends?" She sat down on the loveseat.

"One guy that did something like that is in prison, and two others are dead."

"Any other possibilities?"

"One. The Defense Department has an open file on an MIA with a similar MO, but they refused to identify him."

"Really?"

"The record, his record, is sealed. The Pismo guys are following up but haven't been able to break anything loose yet, not even the name."

"I wonder why."

"He must have been doing special assignments or something top secret. Like I said, the guys in Pismo are following it. This whole thing is out of my ballpark."

"Is that everything so far?"

"For now."

"It's getting chilly standing here naked and sweaty. I'm going to take a hot soak, just immerse myself in a warm bath and try to get back to where we were."

"I have to stand up straight and walk to my desk." He laughed. "Any idea of when you're coming home?"

"Soon, I hope. I'll know more after a briefing at 4:00. I miss what we had... what you have. Love you." She broke the connection without waiting for a response.

Lowering herself slowly into the hot water she moaned, "This is *so* good... not as good as a man, but good. Touch me, water. Invade my private places. I want a man... a strong, dominating man... someone who thinks he can control me."

* * *

In room 5004 Quarterman smiled as the tape recorder automatically stopped. "Little lady, I like your style. There was a reason that bikini looked good on you... should've been a thong. What a way to wake-up. I'm as excited as your boyfriend."

He called room service, ordered a carafe of coffee to be delivered outside the door, then went to the shower. Fifteen minutes later he was clean shaven and he'd changed his hair color to dark brown. He sat at the small lanai table overlooking the swimming pool and scanned the area for Lisa. He spotted her in a sunny corner, baking in a modest bikini he'd insisted she wear. "There you are. That'll ruin your sexy tan line in that for a few days."

He listened to the recording of Santiago again as he doodled on hotel stationary. He jotted notes and caricatures: *Aunt Michelle, MIA, Pismo Beach, Seaside, Spokane, move Lisa, seduce Aunt Michelle, leave and send farewell message.* He looked at his work. "I always wanted to be an artist, maybe in Mexico. That would frost you, wouldn't it, Santiago? To get banged by the guy you're trying to lock up? I love horny women; lust will be your downfall. You can live with it or me."

He smiled in Lisa's direction five floors below. "I think you're the only woman I've ever trusted and loved 'til now. You're family. Let's get you out of here before the fireworks start."

He called the front desk and asked for a connection to Brooke Meredith in the pool area, then waited as a waiter came carrying a phone paging her name until she waved him over, smiled, and took the receiver. He jotted *Michelle* on the paper again, then *Sugar*.

"Hello?" she said.

"Cuz, it's time to pack."

"What?"

He watched as she looked around, spotting him on the deck. "Don't wave. We've got the money. It's time for you to get out of here."

"When?"

"Now. I expect some people will be looking for you very soon."

"Me? I have plans for later."

"Change 'em. This is important."

"Okay. I'll go to Tucson and get a room at that place we used so often on Miracle Mile. You can join me there."

"No, they know us down there. Have you ever been to Yuma?"

"Only to drive through on the way to San Diego."

"Good. There's a motel just left of Exit 1 off Interstate 8, the Borderline. I'll meet you there in a couple of days. Register as Brooke Meredith so the credit card is good."

"All right, but why would anyone be looking for me?"

"I think they've figured out who I am. Your name is in my old service records.. And Lisa, don't tell a soul."

"Understood." She cradled the phone and stood up.

Quarterman watched as she walked out of the pool area. He checked his watch. "Briefing at 1600. I'd like to be at that meeting. I hope your boyfriend calls tonight, Aunt Michelle."

He stepped to the door and removed the privacy hanger. He stored the listening equipment, went back to the table and doodle paper. Picking it up he jotted next to *FBI* the word *WHO* in capital letters, then crossed out *Sugar.*

* * *

Santiago walked into the Brauns' living room as the grandfather clock chimed 1:30 p.m. "Boy was I glad you arranged for Doctor Yount to be standing by this morning. How's Lindsey doing?"

Braun shook his head. "Well as can be expected. It was like seeing her as a small child again: fragile, asleep, tucked in safe and sound."

"How about the hand?"

Nikki said, "Infected. She'll recover but obviously the finger didn't survive. We'll do something to make her whole again when she's feeling better."

Braun sighed. "I'm sure Doctor Rich will want to see her as soon as possible. He'll have his work cut out for him again. This has to be as traumatic as her mother's death, maybe more."

Santiago looked at her friends. "We need to talk about Doctor Rich. Some things have come to light you need to be aware of."

Braun looked puzzled. "Greg? He's helped Lindsey for years. What could—"

"First let's sit down."

The Brauns walked to the couch holding hands. Nikki said, "What's the problem, Mitch? She's known him longer than I've known Claude."

"In a nutshell?" Santiago said.

Braun nodded. "Please, we can't handle much more drama around here today."

"Sam Evans discovered that Rich has a background of alleged sexual abuse with some of his clients. He found a record of some allegations, cash settlements, and dropped charges following a payoff during our review of his records."

Nikki sat up straight. "You say alleged...."

Mitch nodded. "Yes. Then yesterday when I talked with Sierra, the good doctor's name came up again. According to her, Lindsey and Rich have spent a great deal of time having sex."

Braun said, "Lindsey and Greg?"

Santiago paused and rubbed her hands. "During therapy... since she was fifteen."

Braun said, "Lindsey's never shown any interest in him other than professional. At least I thought it was professional. She went to him whenever, you know."

"This morning Sam and I interviewed Rich. We wanted background on Lindsey's visits with an emphasis on concerns like someone stalking her, relationships with friends, that sort of thing. He was reluctant to share, citing confidentiality."

Evans walked into the living room and stood quietly.

Braun said, "Yes, he would be. Greg emphasized the same thing to me some years back."

Santiago said, "About age fifteen."

Evans smiled. "Then, if I may, Mitch gave him a lesson in hardball. She put the cards on the table and told him we wanted the information or she'd just turn our findings over to the authorities, immediately."

Braun gripped Nikki's hand. "What was his reaction?"

Santiago said, "Outrage at first."

Evans continued, "Yeah, he even wanted to call his attorney. Mitch said go for it and dug out her cell phone. He's dialing away at his desk and sees her doing the same thing. He asks who she's calling. She says the cops. He puts the phone down and does a giant about face."

Nikki said, "Did he admit having a relationship with our daughter?"

Santiago said, "Yes. He also gave us what little information he had but nothing that will shed any light on the kidnappers."

Braun looked at Nikki. "I feel I'm hearing some implications in that statement."

Santiago said, "There are some other issues that are not germane to this case."

Braun said, "Sierra's got to be one of those issues."

Santiago looked into the face of her friend, then Braun. "Yes. Rich was more concerned about whether you were aware of his affair with Lindsey. I told him you weren't yet but it was obvious you would know soon."

Evans said, "She also told him to shut down his business for whatever reason he could think of unless he wanted to run the risk of public humiliation, which he'll probably get anyway."

Braun said, "And the authorities' involvement?"

"I pretty much have to leave that up to the families of the girls, or the girls themselves if they're of age. The DA will know about the accusations, but whether he can do anything with the information really hinges on the individuals and state laws. I trust all are from prominent families and may force him to stay out of business or face the consequences. Whether any of them are willing to go through the legal process and expose themselves in court is quite another story."

Nikki said, "I'm sure. We'll have to give this some serious thought before we make a decision, won't we, Honey?"

Braun smiled and nodded. "After the last four or five days I'm inclined to do whatever Lindsey determines is best. If she wants to go after him, so be it. If nothing else I'm slowly learning I've been far too concerned with image along with a few other things. And if Lindsey wants to prosecute him, we'll do it whether or not the other families choose to do likewise."

Santiago said, "Of course he could deny the statements he made to us or even claim coercion. And we haven't talked to Lindsey yet. The bottom line is to keep her away from him now."

Braun said, "I agree, particularly in light of the inquiries now taking place."

"There's one other thing you need to know too. Doctor Rich said Lindsey was toying with the idea of staging a fake kidnapping to bring you two closer together."

Braun nodded and put an arm around Nikki's shoulders. "She's worried about her father's bad habits, and with good reason. When she wakes up we'll be letting her know we will be doing everything possible to change my bad behaviors."

Nikki kissed his cheek. "Enough said for now on that topic."

Santiago said, "Well, we got Lindsey home safe and almost whole. That's why I came down. I'm fighting with myself about staying on and going after those guys, or going home. I've even done a little baiting of the trap."

Braun laughed. "If you're baiting them you've already decided. I think the federal agents need your assistance. I'm sure they'll ask for it this afternoon."

"I'm pleased to hear that, and I've anticipated staying around for a few more days. We've learned some things through our own sources that lean toward at least one of the kidnappers being a serial killer. Even more meaningful to me, the older one has made it personal."

Braun said, "What new information?"

"I'll bring it up at the briefing."

Nikki said, "How personal has he been?

Santiago looked at her friends. "He's stalking me. Of course, that also means he's staying around for the time being. For now, I want to interview a couple more of your high profile associates, friends, whatever. They're still suspects in this 'event,' as Mr. House likes to call it." She looked at Evans. "And what brought you out here, Sam?"

"We received a call from a lady. She said she was a dancer at the Bramble Bush. She wants to talk with you this evening after she goes to work. With all the phone taps I didn't want to call and tip our hand."

Braun shot a look at Evans. "Phone taps?"

Santiago said, "It's a long story, Claude. You'll hear about them at the briefing." She looked at Evans, raised an eyebrow smiled. "Sam, what time are we going to the strip club tonight?"

Evans' face reddened. "Whenever you say as long as it's after 6:00."

Nikki said, "Why after 6:00, Sam?"

"That's when the woman comes to work. She doesn't want us at her home."

Santiago patted her backside. "Works for me, Partner. But first I need to get in a workout. I've been sitting, riding around, and munching for three days. Can't let it go to flab or they'll have me watching teen scene nightspots when I get home."

Nikki said, "We have a complete gym at the country club. I'm sure you'll find everything you need."

"I'm sure, but I don't think my routine would fit into that setting."

Braun said, "Why not use the DataFlex facility? It was built for our employees including the security team."

"I'll do that right after I do some shopping. Can't mooch your clothes the whole time I'm here. How about it, Sam? You feel like a workout?"

"After today, Mitch, I'd go anywhere with you."

"Good. How about 2:30?"

Evans smiled. "You're on."

Santiago looked at Braun. "When will we be able to see Lindsey?"

"Tomorrow morning. She's really sedated right now."

"And her friend T.J.?"

"Yount is keeping him at the clinic overnight, but you could probably catch him this evening if you want."

She headed for the door. "Later, Sam... first it's shopping."

* * *

At 3:59 p.m. Claude Braun, Michelle Santiago, Sam Evans, and Ray House were seated at a long table in the conference room adjacent to Braun's office. The large dark wood door opened quietly. John Stone entered, accompanied by a woman in her mid-thirties. Both wore navy blue pinstripe suits. Stone wore a white shirt and a red tie, the woman a knee-length skirt, a white blouse, and a short red tie. Santiago watched them enter, then looked down the table toward Evans.

Stone looked at his watch and went to the head of the table opposite where Braun was seated flanked by Evans and House on his right and Santiago on his left. He opened an attaché case and removed some papers. "It's 1600, time to start. I appreciate each of you being prompt."

Santiago scanned the group, noting Sam and Ray were in slacks and blazers with light print shirts and dark ties. Braun was in off-white slacks, white slip-ons with no socks and a pink polo shirt. The large gold Rolex covering his left wrist, a gift from Nikki on their first anniversary, sent out a constant stream of light beams from the metal and four large diamonds on the face. Santiago leaned to her right and whispered to Braun, "This looks like a stockholders' meeting—very formal except for you."

In a faint whisper he said, "And obviously you too. I think DataFlex needs to work on its inter-office image. It's way too straight for me anymore. Personally, I'll take your mini and stiletto heels over any lady who works here. I don't even recognize this skirt."

"I bought it today. It's not one of Nikki's."

Stone said, "Gentlemen, Miss Santiago, let me introduce Alexandria Hughes. She'll be providing critical data later in the meeting. First though, I want to thank Mr. Braun and his team for working with us on this highly confidential matter, providing support in a way only DataFlex could. I would also—"

"Mr. Stone," Braun said, "we're not here for a speech. Let's get down to it."

"Of course. All of us know of the events leading to this meeting. We have reason to believe one of the kidnappers may be an MIA who carried out classified missions during the Vietnam War. The perpetrator—"

Braun said, "Does the man have a name?"

"Yes, Yancey Quarterman. We believe Mr. Quarterman is the older man involved in the kidnapping of your daughter. The amputation of the victim's ring finger has always been his signature. We also believe he killed a woman, a stripper and probable prostitute, in this area recently."

Santiago interrupted. "Are you assuming the dancer was a prostitute or is it a fact?"

Stone took a deep breath and waved a limp hand. "Well, I actually said she's a 'probable' prostitute because of the situation in which she was found—all evidence pointed to her having been paid for sex—but yes, strictly speaking I suppose it's an assumption, Miss Santiago. Women in that business... you know."

"Yes, I do know, and Mr. Braun knows assumptions are not necessarily accurate."

Stone glanced first at Hughes, then at Santiago. "My apologies. I stand corrected. Thank you. Now, as I was saying, we also think Quarterman was involved in the murders of at least three other women in Pismo Beach, Seaside, and Spokane. We're not positive about the latter because of incomplete information."

He looked around the table, noting shock on the faces of Evans, House, and Braun. "You don't appear to be surprised about the murders, Miss Santiago."

"I have the same information. The only element I lacked was the man's name. It seems to be off limits to local police agencies, according to a detective in Pismo Beach."

"You're very resourceful. I'm sure that's why Mr. Braun brought you into the matter."

"Mr. Stone, please, can we stop the game playing? My wife and I brought Michelle into this matter because she is a highly trained and respected investigator who also happens to be my wife's best friend. Let's move forward together, shall we?"

Stone cleared his throat. "Very well. You probably have been wondering why my people are involved in this investigation rather than local authorities working with regular FBI."

Santiago watched Stone's eyes but remained silent.

"It's because Quarterman, while on special assignments for our government, carried out secret missions that we do not want made public in court. It's a matter of national security. While working for others, he carried out missions that could be treasonous. My mission is to locate and contain him for debriefing before anything else happens."

Santiago continued to watch Stone's eyes, then looked around the table.

Braun said, "Mr. Stone, what about a trial? This man, Quarterman, may be my daughter's kidnapper. He may have killed other women in the public sector."

Santiago said, "So when he is captured will he be turned over to local authorities?"

Stone looked down the length of the table. "If he's not Quaterman, yes, he'll be turned over to local authorities. If it turns out to be Quarterman he'll be tried by a military tribunal for acts against the United States."

Santiago looked at Braun. He looked at Stone and said, "Wouldn't this man be tried in the criminal court for murder and kidnapping even if his trial for those crimes took place after the military tribunal, assuming they are one and the same person?"

"If the kidnapper is Quarterman, it is my understanding once he is out of circulation he will not be made available for criminal proceedings. As I noted, the government does not want Quarterman in open court."

Santiago said, "What about the other two players? Quarterman's testimony may be essential in securing convictions."

Stone's jaw tightened as he ground his teeth. "I know of only one other possible participant, Miss Santiago... a younger man."

Santiago said, "A woman delivered a package at the Desert Oasis Hotel and had it placed in my room the day after my arrival in Phoenix."

Stone thumbed through a few pages of loose paper. "I don't have that in my notes."

Braun looked at Stone and Hughes. "As I said a moment ago, we've had a very sharp criminal detective working on this case with my people non-stop for the last three days. We have information you don't possess and vice versa."

Stone said, "Okay, bottom line, I—we—want Quarterman. I haven't a clue as to why he was involved in your daughter's kidnapping. Maybe for the money. Maybe chance or fate. Who knows? But we need him out of circulation. He is a security threat to the country for a number of reasons I cannot go into." He turned to the woman on his right. "Alex, would you brief the group, please?"

Hughes stood and spoke in a monotone. "Yancey Quarterman is a killer. He was an operative in Vietnam."

Evans watched Hughes. *Threat to national security. He's done some dirty work for the government, maybe even wet operations.*

Hughes said, "Like many serial killers he developed a signature, the amputation of the left ring finger of each kill. He began that practice in Vietnam. We have some data that supports our believe that he survived the fall of Saigon and escaped, probably to a third-world country. We're not sure. However, he or an individual using the same MO has worked as an assassin, a mercenary, and a terrorist for governments and drug cartels over a number of years, and that individual has always signed his work in the same way. The evidence is limited, but the signature has been consistent."

Santiago, hands folded, thumbs pressed against her mouth, watched Alexandria Hughes.

Hughes said, "In the last several months we believe he's resurfaced in the states for whatever reason, and is now killing women. He is older than most serial killers, who usually range in age from their twenties to thirty-five. Consistent with others he is white, has a high school education and comes from a dysfunctional family dominated by his mother. In his teen years his mother sexually abused him, using him as a partner in lieu of the father. We believe the women he has killed in some way trigger an association with his mother, probably in the realm of domination on their part and a rejection of his father's weakness."

Evans said, "Why didn't he kill Lindsey?"

"Because she is a fighter. We learned that from the tape. Even though he threatened Mr. Braun with her rape, he doesn't rape his victims. We think he allows himself to be picked up. If the interlude proves satisfactory and the woman is neither demanding nor dominating during sex, fine. Otherwise he may kill them, probably during his orgasm. We also know he likes women who are young. What we have is a dangerous, skilled killer who is active." She sat down, removed some sheets of paper from a leather attaché case and passed the stack around the table. "Please take one. The sheet contains two pictures. One is the identification photo taken of Quarterman when he enlisted in the army several years ago. The second is a computer generated picture of what he may look like today." She nodded toward Stone.

Santiago stood. "We have some information you might find both interesting and useful."

Stone stared at Santiago's mini, then slowly worked his way up to her face.

Santiago said, "First, the kidnapper has my room bugged, meaning we've had some communication.

Second, he—or possibly they—are stalking me. Third, the older one is easily stimulated sexually. Fourth, the killer would appear to have two signatures; the finger which has been consistent for several years and the broken necks of the murdered women."

Hughes asked, "How did you know he was sexually stimulated before this briefing?"

"Beyond the obvious he sent me a red bikini and insisted I wear it at the pool where he could observe me while we talked on a phone. During that phone call he demonstrated that he was watching very closely. I believe his sexual appetite is also why he went to the strip club where he picked up the young dancer and later murdered her." Santiago looked at Stone. He averted his gaze. She said, "We agree with John that the woman in this instance was a prostitute, based on interviews with some of the people who work at the club and a patron."

Stone said, "Let me get this straight. You've talked with the older man on the phone and he's heard you in your room."

"That is correct. He was also on the phone when we were making the money drop and finding the kids. I expect to talk with him again in the near future." She paused and took a deep breath. "And fifth, I believe the money transferred around the world this morning is right here in Phoenix at Veteran's Trust Bank."

Braun looked at Santiago, then House. "I thought you said we lost it in the Cayman Islands, Ray?"

House said, "My team did. Apparently Spears stayed with it and found a way to follow through. I had him report directly to Mitch."

Santiago said, "Finally, it came up this morning that we are dealing with a double kidnapping, the first a false effort masterminded by Lindsey for personal reasons and the second a real kidnapping carried out by Quarterman. If my guess is accurate we may be dealing with only two players: the woman and your man. The other man was Lindsey's partner in the fake kidnapping."

"Will you continue to help us, then?" Stone said.

"I came here to help my friends. For now I'm the strongest link to the perps, and of equal importance to me, he's made it personal." Braun smiled and House nodded.

Stone said, "My people will stay in the background, but we will have your back."

"Give me one operative to work with, to play the role of a love interest, definitely not in a suit. Sam, I want the bugs out of my room before I return to the hotel. I want Quarterman to come to me. I want to appear vulnerable, even available, but not to him."

"Available?" Stone said, looking her over again. "You think this will work?"

"Yes, if he stays around. One way to keep him around is tease him."

House nodded at Hughes and smiled.

Santiago fixed her emerald gaze on Braun. "Can you assign Spears to do research for me?"

Braun said, "Consider it done."

"And let's reassign Sam. On the surface we should all appear to be doing company work except for me. I'm sure Quarterman will assume my job is to find him for revenge on behalf of Claude. I want him to question whether I'm out of the loop, my work done."

House said, "You say 'appear.' Does that mean you want Sam to continue on the case?"

"Absolutely, and if I'm right, he can only follow one of us at a time. Can we freeze the money at Veteran's?"

House shook his head. "Not without a court order and that doesn't appear to be an option, is it Mr. Stone?"

"No, and I doubt it would make much difference. We suspect Quarterman has several million stashed around the country and in Europe." He looked at Mitch. "You're playing a dangerous game, Miss Santiago."

Hughes said, "Exactly. It could be he finds Michelle a challenging opponent. I wouldn't pretend to know what makes this sociopath tick, not yet."

Stone looked around the table. "I'll schedule another briefing for tomorrow at 1600."

"Mr. Stone, with all due respect, I may need more flexibility than your set pattern allows. I would suggest using whomever you assign to work with me to also serve as the liaison so our efforts are not abridged. We'll work out the details after we've met."

Stone said, "Very well. I'll be in touch with you this evening after the room is clear."

Hughes said, "Michelle, you're sure this plan will work? If it's Quarterman, this is very risky."

"I'm betting my life on it."

* * * * * * *

The meeting broke up at 4:31. Stone went to the door and left without saying a word. Alexandria Hughes walked over to Santiago and said, "We may need to talk about this man. Take my card. If I need to reach you I'll call here." Santiago nodded as Hughes left the room.

Evans said, "What was that about?"

Santiago waved the card. "Just in case we need to talk. You're heading home for dinner, aren't you?"

"After we sweep your room, if there's time. You?"

She said, "I want to talk with T.J. I might try the hot tub after the Bramble Bush and dinner. I'll meet you at the club around 6:00, right?"

Evans checked his watch. "Could we make it 7:00?"

"Not a problem. See you then," she said. Evans left the conference room with House.

Braun said, "What are you doing for dinner?"

"Probably starving 'til later. First I want to talk with T.J."

"I'll go with you. I want to check on Lindsey anyway. Nikki can pick me up at the clinic when we're done."

Santiago picked up her notepad. "Let's do it."

Twenty-five minutes later they arrived at the clinic on 24th and Camelback near the Biltmore Shopping Plaza. Yount's clinic was contained in a four-story building along with several other medical professionals. It occupied half of the first floor.

A receptionist greeted Braun. "Doctor Yount said you might be in this afternoon or evening." She smiled. "He's keeping one staff member on duty at all times because of the two patients. If you want to come in again later tonight just buzz the door. I'll be here to let you in." She smiled again and glanced at Santiago.

Braun said, "Appreciate your efforts, Janet."

Santiago stood beside Braun observing the interaction. Finally she stepped forward and introduced herself. "I'll probably be in again tomorrow to see Lindsey when she's awake."

Janet said, "Whatever Mr. Braun wants."

Santiago said, "Of course. For now I'd like to talk with T.J."

Braun said, "And I want to look in on Lindsey."

"This way, please," Janet said walking down a hall, her hips swaying lazily.

Santiago looked at Braun and whispered, "Claude, you're drooling."

He whispered back, "Changing is harder than you'd expect."

Janet waved toward a door. "The young man is in there. He is awake." She knocked and opened the door. "You have a visitor."

Santiago went in, closed the door. "You look healthy."

T.J. sat up in the bed and grinned. "I am. And you're Aunt Michelle."

She said, "We didn't get much opportunity to talk this morning."

"I'm more alert now. You can ask me anything."

"I want to know what happened during the kidnapping."

"Such as?"

"Was the initial kidnapping a fake?"

"Boy, you don't waste time."

"Time is something we don't have much of."

"Lindsey dreamed it up, you know."

Santiago said, "No, I don't know."

"To bring her parents closer together. She's pissed at a girlfriend for hitting on her dad."

"It's a two-way street, T.J., but I'm sure you know that too. So it was you who made the first call?"

He blushed. "Yes. We were in… ah, her room at the time."

"Did anyone else know about the plan?"

"Not that I know of. Lindsey is really good about being tight lipped."

"How about you?"

"Actually, I told a couple of friends of mine about the plan when we met at a bar in Apache Junction. But I didn't tell them who or where. We were just bullshitting about the weird habits some of our girlfriends have."

She took out a notepad. "And who were these friends?"

He shrugged. "Just guys I hang out with."

"Names?"

"George Eddy and Diego Palmas. We first met doing seasonal work first as laborers and then again as casuals at the post office."

"Just the two of them?"

"No, Mario Spears joined us later."

"The same Mario that works for DataFlex?"

"Yeah, that's him. He mentioned Lindsey while we were having a few brews, so I never mentioned her name. Apparently they had a thing for a week or two." He looked into Santiago's eyes. "Knowing Mario, he wanted into her pants and Daddy's company."

"It doesn't sound like he was alone, at least for the first part."

"No, I guess not."

"But that's not why I'm here. Anyone else know about the plan?"

"No," he laughed. "Other than Rosie the only other person in the place was some old biker, but he was at the bar. I doubt he heard anything."

"Can you describe him?"

"Not really. It was dark in there."

"Let's try to focus on him for a minute. You said he was older. It was dark, right? Try."

"I'm tryin'. He had kind'a longish hair... seemed to have some gray in it."

"Good, what else?"

"He was a big guy, or least he looked big sittin' at the bar." T.J. looked at Santiago. "Wait a minute. He left when I did, sort'a... out the door just a few steps behind me."

"So you did see him in the light?"

"Well, I wasn't payin' much attention. He came out right behind me and started his bike. I was already pullin' onto the road."

"Did he follow you?"

"I don't know. I think he was a few cars back for a couple of miles, but when I pulled off nobody was behind me. Well, nobody I saw. There was a lot of dust."

"How about sound? Did you hear a bike or anything after leaving the main road?"

"I was playin' a CD really loud. Do you think he's the guy who cut Lindsey's finger off?"

"Could be."

"That guy was scary."

"How?"

"Always wearing a ski mask. He seemed to know what he was doing. Had a backpack with everything he needed."

"Everything?"

"Duct tape, recorder, everything. Mean dude."

"Mean?"

"He told us no talkin' without permission. First time we said somethin' he just hit us."

"Is that how your cheek got cut?"

"Yeah." He reached up and felt the bandage on his face. "He liked Lindsey better'n me, said she was tough."

"He liked tough?"

"Yeah. Hell, I didn't want to get knocked around or have a finger whacked off."

"Neither would I, T.J. You did fine. Is the doctor going to let you go home tomorrow?"

"That's what he says. I feel good right now but, hey, if old man Braun is gonna send some cash my way I'll stay as long as he wants."

"Your loyalty has no bounds. Tell me, what were you originally getting out of this before the kidnapper come along?"

He smiled. "Lindsey for a week or so, maybe a couple of bucks for helpin' out.

"Nothing else?"

"Believe me, Lindsey is enough."

"I believe you."

T.J. quietly smiled.

She turned toward the door. "Well, thank you for your time."

"Am I gonna go to jail? I mean, I didn't really do anything, you know."

"I doubt you'll have a problem as long as you tell the truth. But you're right if you think helping those close to you can be costly." She stood a moment holding the door. "By the way, Lindsey is recovering nicely." She left the room.

T.J. looked at the door. "Shit... I didn't even ask."

* * *

At 6:51 p.m. Santiago arrived at the Bramble Bush and met Sam Evans in the parking lot. They entered the building together, passing a sign that read *Open at 7:00 p.m. this evening.*

Evans said, "Good thing we delayed."

"Back for the show?" Cliff Arnold said from his familiar post by the door.

"Not this time," Evans said.

Santiago held out her hand so Arnold could stamp it, showing the cover was paid. He gave her a once over and accepted the cover charge for Evans. "Maybe next time we can have a drink or something. Ladies are always free. I'll stamp him."

"Deal," she said. "Can you tell us where we can find Karen Gerard?"

"You mean Eve? Sure, when you get in the showroom just go to the far end of the bar. It's her space when she's not working. Does she know where your friend Lindsey is hangin' out?"

"Something like that."

Evans followed Santiago into the showroom and looked the area over until he spotted a lone woman sitting on a stool at the end of the bar. "Must be her."

"You're much more relaxed tonight, Sam. Are we getting accustomed to being surrounded by naked jiggling women?" Santiago laughed, then coughed. "What they need is a smoke eater. I thought smoking in here was illegal."

"It is. I guess nobody here complains," he said with a smirk. "I told my kids I was here yesterday."

"And?"

He rolled his eyes. "No big deal. I guess times change."

"That they do, but you're right, this is still not a respected business even if the girls start off dressed the same as rock stars."

They approached the woman. Evans said, "Miss Gerard?"

The woman nodded and took a deep drag on a cigarette.

"You called our office. I'm Sam Evans and this is my partner, Michelle Santiago."

"Jed, one of our regulars, said I should talk to you... said you're not cops."

Evans said, "We're private."

A door opened off to the side allowing the last light of the afternoon to fill the room as a delivery driver pushed a hand truck with two kegs stacked on it to the bar.

Santiago looked at Eve's face and the flesh of her upper arms, most of which was exposed except for a light cover-up. Her skin was like leather, and deep lines had formed around her eyes. "How long had you known Trinity?"

"Since she went to work here. Not very long. She was a nice kid, liked the business."

Santiago said, "What do you mean liked the business?"

"You know. I can see it in your eyes. She liked turning guys on. She was a natural. He'd come in here and sit down, and she'd be there in a flash. Always took him to the private room. I watched her work him once. She was good."

"Watched who?" Evans said.

"The older guy. She was hot for his wallet. That's why I called you. Nobody knows about him."

Evans said, "You watched them?"

She shrugged. "Somebody always watches. We get everything in here from bashful momma's boys too shy to look at the girls to studs pullin' out their cock and tryin' to put it somewhere, anywhere."

Santiago said, "And the man you last saw with Trinity?"

"Oh, she liked him. Like I was sayin', she'd put her bare ass right in his face, bury his mouth in her bush, unzip him and give him a hand-job while dancing, anything and everything. Her motto was keep the customer satisfied, and did she ever."

Evans looked puzzled. "What about the rules, laws?"

"Rules?" She laughed and took another drag. "There's only one rule here. We can touch them but they can't touch us."

Evans said, "Really?"

She pointed to the door of the private showroom. "That's why someone's always watchin', especially back there, to help if needed."

Santiago said, "So Trinity was doing this guy right here at the club?"

"Pretty much so. One night she kept at him 'til he came all over her hand, a real gusher. She laughed and laughed, lookin' at her cum covered fingers. He says 'Lick your fingers and I'll give you another hundred.' Lord, she sucked those fingers dry. That was the same night they left together. Haven't seen either one of them since."

Santiago said, "Was she tricking?"

"She worked anybody with tight pants and a bulging wallet here at the club. What she did after hours I don't know, but I'd bet she made more money then than the rest of us put together... I mean, those that do that sort of thing."

"Of course," Santiago said "But she liked the old guy?"

"Oh yeah, she was hot for him. He'd walk in and she'd just cum, I swear it. And he was old enough to be her father."

Evans smiled. "Aren't most of them?"

"You know it. We get the young crowd; the college boys and a few girls on weekends, but during the week it's mostly the graying of Arizona out there."

Evans jerked his head as loud music started playing, spotlights glared and strobes blinked. Eve dropped her cover on the bar and eased onto the small attached dance stage. She took hold of a shining pole reaching into the ceiling from the middle of the stage and looked right at Sam. "We're open for business."

Evans looked at Santiago. "She's kind'a old for this business isn't she?"

"Early thirties I'd guess," Santiago said. "But yes, that's old for this job. She's got a lot of mileage on her."

"She acted like she knew you, or knew you worked clubs."

"It's something I can't explain, but to another stripper or ex-stripper you may as well have a tattoo on your forehead. Some people say it's the same way with teachers, hookers, and cops."

"So are we ready to go?"

"Not a chance. When she comes off the stage wave a twenty at her. We'll buy a dance. I still have some questions."

The bartender announced the next act in a growling slow drawl. "A pair of twin sisters on stage as you'd like 'em in bed, naked and squirming."

Eve left the stage scanning the almost empty room and spotted Evans waving a twenty. She strolled toward him showing no tan line or leathery skin in the shadows, her belly flat and rippled. She reached for her lime green cover, then stopped. "You do want a dance?"

Evans stared at her breasts. "Oh yes."

She took the money and began her routine as the twins worked the stage. Eve gestured toward a table away from the bar, rubbing against Evans as she held the chair. "I thought you two would be gone when I finished. Sit, Sam."

Evans sat straight up in the chair as she ground her butt in front of his face and lap. Santiago sat across from them off to one side.

While Eve worked, Santiago asked, "Can you describe the man?"

"Bouncer type, big forearms, middle aged."

Eve turned and faced Evans. His eyes were fastened to her only garment, a thong. "You like this, don't you?"

He nodded as she slid the thong slowly off her hips and down seemingly endless legs. "Like the view, Handsome?"

His jaw dropped open as she tipped back toward Santiago, arms stretched above her head, legs spread.

Santiago said, "I don't think he's had this experience before. Yesterday was his first visit to one of these clubs."

"He's hooked. You know it; I know it."

"I think so. What name did the man use?"

"Lance."

"Any last name?" Santiago said

"No. The dude always flashed a wad of cash but he didn't go for any of the other girls, just Trinity. We hated her for it, but now we feel kind'a lucky." The music stopped and another announcement was made.

Santiago said, "Sam, another Jackson, please."

He dug back into his wallet. "Oh yes."

"I could'a used some of the cash Lance was always waving around. I'm gettin' out of the business and opening a card shop. I have a daughter. I'd like to do something a little more acceptable for her."

"Good luck," Santiago said. "Anything else you can tell me about the man?"

"Yeah. He wore an odd musk-like scent. It was unusual. And he had a lot of facial hair, scruffy, like unshaven for a few days, had a lot of gray in it. He always looked rough."

Santiago said, "We appreciate you calling the office."

"Hope you find your friend."

"We have. Now we want to know about the man she was with. Good luck on your new business," Santiago said.

Eve slid the twenty into her thong. "Thanks."

The music stopped, another announcement and Evans dug another twenty out of his wallet as Santiago watched. "I'm glad we came in separate cars. See you tomorrow, Sam."

She stood to leave. "Are the bugs gone?"

He nodded again, his smile growing, sweat forming on his brow.

* * *

The Braun residence, nestled in the southern portion of Paradise Valley, was a structure lost in shadows when Santiago arrived at 7:47 p.m. The gate guard let her pass after telling her the Brauns were home for the evening. She parked the Sebring at the front door.

Claude Braun opened the door before she had the chance to lift the brass knocker. "Hello, Mitch. Come in. Nikki's sleeping and I don't want to disturb her. The guard buzzed me you were here."

"How is she holding up?"

A smile crossed his face. "Yount has her sedated. Both of the women in my life are sleeping. It's a strange feeling."

"Have you seen Lindsey this afternoon?"

He led the way into the living room. "Yes, she was awake for a few minutes. Kept telling me she was sorry this happened. I tried to tell her it's not her fault but she wasn't very responsive. Probably the meds. Join me."

She said, "Remember earlier I mentioned the possibility of a fake kidnapping?"

"Yes. Caught me off guard with that one. Want a drink?"

"No thank you. I just wanted to see how everyone is doing and share what T.J. had to say."

"About faking it?"

"Yes."

Braun nodded. "I talked with him for a few moments while Nikki and I were there. He told me he'd seen you and what happened. Extreme isn't it?"

She said, "If you mean Lindsey staging the kidnapping, desperate might describe it better."

He took a sip from a tumbler sitting on an end table. "Yes it is, and this other guy coming in is really off the wall."

"I think he picked up on the plan at Rosie's out in Apache Junction."

"That's what T.J. indicated. So what's your plan for finding this man? Stone didn't have much to share this afternoon."

"I'm going to hang around the hotel. I want him to come to me, keep the area we're dealing with as limited as possible. You already know I want Sam and Spears on the job but low profile, like they're working regular company business. That way I'll look vulnerable."

"And you think that'll draw him out?"

"It should if we're right about the stalker issue. He could have someone at the hotel. Don't forget the mysterious woman who dropped off the package."

He smiled. "You mean tits and tips."

She laughed. "That's the one."

"Why didn't you go into detail this afternoon?"

"I don't think Stone wants to help us. He wants us to help him. He has no intention of letting the man go to trial before he gets his hands on him, if ever. That's my read."

"Mine too. It bothers me. I want revenge. I'd like him dead, but Stone's way won't bring closure. I like your plan. We'll just place personal business in your file in case someone noses around. It's unusual for a new hire, but you're a close friend of the boss and I don't have to explain anything to anyone." He chuckled. "Hell, they'll assume I have a new toy stashed at the Oasis. Odds are some already have."

She said, "How are you doing?"

"Haven't been into the office except for the briefing and just a little phone business since Lindsey was found. I'm spending a lot of time thinking about what kind of dad I've been, what's happening with Nikki, and always about Lelani."

"Don't beat yourself up. I'm sure others are more than willing."

"Oh, I know that, but I'm worried about Nikki. She drinks too much. This mess has really not helped in the least."

"She's under a lot of pressure and not just from the kidnapping."

"I know. I appreciate your candor. Most people wouldn't touch that issue but you're right. I'd like to say I know how it'll all end but I don't. Guess that's why I always go back to Lelani in my mind."

"Tell me about her."

He glanced down for a moment, then back at Mitch. "I loved her. She was everything to me. We met in high school, went to college together. Then we graduated."

"You didn't marry until after college?"

"No. We decided it was best to get through school and start our careers before making a formal commitment, especially starting a family."

"People can choose when to have children."

"Exactly, and we were both free spirits. If we had been apart going to different schools maybe in different states, who knows, we may have sought comfort elsewhere." He shook his head. "I doubt it, even looking back... not even me."

"Did you live together?"

"We were a couple, man and wife in all but the formal word. In those days I didn't look at women the way I do now. Funny part is that was the seventies. College was like a vacation to us, freedom to dream. There were no boundaries."

"What happened?"

Claude's hands moved back and forth on the tumbler. "Everything was good. We finished school, started the software business when PC's were just becoming the latest 'in' thing. The rest is history."

"No, I mean what happened to Lelani?"

"She developed cervical cancer. It was horrible, devastating. We had everything to live for including our daughter, a true love child. After Lelani died I was a different man. They tell me the grieving process usually takes a year. I don't think I'm at closure yet. When Lindsey disappeared it was like all the emptiness I felt before was back."

"Nikki will help. She loves Lindsey like her own child."

"I know, but it's not the same. After Lelani died I withdrew from life, business, everything."

"You must have done something right, the company survived and flourished."

"Thanks to the managers and a dedicated staff. For two years they ran DataFlex. Without them it wouldn't exist today. The advice Neal Burke gave me at the beginning was more of a key to survival than I thought at the time."

"What was that?"

"Make all the employees owners of the company through grants of stock. If after three years a staff member wanted to cash out their shares that was their choice. Today we have several millionaires on staff in any number of positions. It's important to have the freedom to choose what you want to do. They can."

She looked out through the living room window. "Millionaires? Must be nice."

"Our stock has split several times. All those shares granted split along with the others. It makes for a loyal and happy staff, to say nothing of wealthy."

"I know it's none of my business, but how did you change so radically?"

"It *is* your business, Mitch. You're a member of the family. After I returned to work I was expected to attend many social-business functions on behalf of the company. Most expected a couple. I went from escort services to trophy wives. Nikki has told you about how we met. I'm ashamed of myself but I admit to not being faithful. As you've surmised I've been interested in Sierra. We've had an affair if you want to put it that way. My daughter was more sensitive to her dad's bad habits than I thought. Now I'm afraid of losing Nikki and Lindsey both." He shook his head. "I may have already lost both of them."

"You might consider getting help for you and Nikki, not just Lindsey. The two of you need to talk with each other." She reached out and took his hands in hers. "Together you're a great couple."

"You're right, we are." He emptied the tumbler. "She has a confidant or counselor she gets together with occasionally. Maybe we both should."

Santiago said, "Perhaps, but both of you may feel more comfortable talking with someone new to each of you. I'd ask Nikki first."

"I will. How's the rest of your investigation going?"

She laughed. "For the time being I'm not going to talk with anymore of Lindsey's friends or flings. Near as I can tell they're not involved. The plan for now is be sexy but unreachable."

"You obviously can fill the role, and knowing you it will probably work, but don't put yourself at any more risk than necessary. We know this man is dangerous. Maybe Stone is on target; just get this guy out of circulation forever, however."

Santiago stood. "I'll be careful. Tell Nikki I was by. I'll talk with her tomorrow. It's late and I'm heading back to the hotel before the restaurant closes, maybe catch some bubbles in the spa."

"Have something here."

"No, remember the plan."

"Unreachable babe... I know it well."

They both laughed.

* * *

Sam Evans was home sleeping on his favorite rocking chair after the Bramble Bush experience. At 9:03 p.m. the phone sitting on a nearby end table brought him back to the conscious world. He looked around the room. "Nobody home, yet? Must be a shopping trip and a half." He picked up the phone. "Hello?"

"Mr. Evans, is anyone else at home?"

"Who's calling, please?"

Quarterman's voice was quiet and calm. "The man you and Aunt Michelle are trying to catch."

A chill ran up Evans spine. He squinted, lips puckered. He looked around the empty room and pressed the phone to his ear to control the quiver in his right hand. "What do you mean?"

Quarterman was perched on the roof of a condominium facing the Evans residence from some four hundred yards as he watched the lone figure in the living room through the rifle scope. "You know what I mean, so let's not waste time. I want you to do something for me."

Beads of sweat began to run down the sides of his face. "I'm listening."

"Good. Now, is anyone other than you at home?"

"No."

Quarterman brought the replica tiffany lamp into focus with the crosshairs fixed on the center of the lamp body and squeezed the trigger. A silencer muffled the report of the weapon.

Evans leapt from the chair when the glass base shattered. He dropped to the floor, losing his grip on the phone. "Holy shit!"

Quarterman's voice was calm. "Pick up the phone, Mr. Evans. If I wanted you dead, you'd be dead. Pick up the phone, now."

Evans crawled behind a couch blocking any view of him from outside. He peered over the back.

The voice became harsh. "Pick up the phone, Evans!"

Evans pulled the phone cord until the receiver was within his reach behind the couch. Carefully he reached out to it. Sweat poured out of every pore, short breaths caught in his throat, harsh breathing all that passed between the two men. His stomach was churning. *I'll never put my Glock in the gun safe again.*

"Don't bother looking for me right now. You can't see me. The bullet is a message. You or any member of your family can be a target. Do I make myself clear?"

A violent shudder pushed through his body. "Yes."

"I know you found the bugs in Michelle's room. I know they've been removed."

Evans was silent.

"Are you listening?"

"Yes, I can hear you."

"I want you to keep me informed of the investigation. Remember that your family is at risk."

Evans swallowed. "I've been removed from the inquiry. She's on her own, a break for a few days. When the kids were found her work was done."

"I doubt that. Braun wants revenge. She's the tool. I know about the suits coming in too. You were in the business, Evans. You know how it works."

"Yes, I know how it works and obviously you do too. She's out of it. I'm out of it. If the Feds are playing they think it's a security issue." Evans paused. "We both know government agencies don't want outside interference."

"So what is Michelle doing?"

Evans looked at a family portrait lying on the floor surrounded by shattered glass and pottery. Tears filled his eyes. "A few days rest and then heading home unless she decides to work for DataFlex. We're not looking for you any longer now that Lindsey is home."

"Cut the bullshit, Evans. If she's here, she's looking. Her masters may have changed, that's all. It's your job to keep me informed of what they find. Think family."

Evans' body became stiff except for the hand holding the phone, which shook almost uncontrollably. "Yes."

"I want two new bugs planted, one on the lanai and the other in the bathroom. Tell her to talk outside just in case new bugs have been installed you haven't found. I also want your cell number."

Evans gave him the number. "Where do I get the listening devices?"

"They'll be at your office when you arrive tomorrow."

"How did you get my home number? It's unpublished."

"Where do you think I got it?"

"The only listing is in the company directory."

"Very good."

Evans was silent. *How did you get into the system? An insider? No, you hacked into our system.*

Quarterman chuckled. "You sound worried, Sam. Look at this way. In a few days all this will be past history, no one the wiser. If you do as you're told, your family will remain safe."

"How do I know that?"

"I'm a man of my word. Ask Braun."

"I doubt he'd give you a vote of confidence."

"Perhaps not, but let's change the subject. How do you like working with the beautiful Aunt Michelle?"

Evans smiled. "A lot of people seem to ask that question. She's a pro."

"She's a very beautiful pro who doesn't mind showing her stuff. Come on, man, don't tell me you don't want to bang her. I'm the enemy and I want to."

Evans swallowed and licked his lips. "Like I said, she's a pro."

Quarterman laughed. "I'll bet she hardens you up. Just too much woman. She gets to me every time I see her."

Evans remained quiet. *How often have you seen her? How often have you been around her?*

Quarterman rubbed his thigh. "You should've heard her in the bath… absolutely outstanding."

Evans listened, shaking his head. *You're a psychopath and a pervert.*

"Enough for now, Evans. You have some cleaning to do and some explaining to the wife. That'll require careful planning." He laughed. "I'll be calling tomorrow sometime. And Evans, don't forget the bullet in the wall."

Day Four

Santiago was buried in the covers of the king sized bed flipping and flopping. Sleep escaped her even in the dark room. The phone beside the bed rang. She pushed the blankets off and stretched across to the far side nudging the small automatic pistol onto the floor next to the nightstand as she picked up the receiver. "Hello?" Her voice was sleepy.

Quarterman spoke in a soft voice. "Good morning, Michelle. You didn't look like any aunt I ever knew immersed in the spa last night."

A chill ran down her spine. *You are watching me. Good.*

"The light played beautifully on your warm flesh, little rays dancing over every curve and pore, teasing my hungry eyes, awakening my needs. The bubbling water made me jealous, touching every part of you, caressing your body."

"It's too early for an obscene phone call," she said glancing at the clock radio. "It's 8:13 in the morning."

"I've been up most of the night thinking about you. I saw a quiet, relaxed smile, your eyes closed. Were you thinking of someone special, weren't you? Maybe your partner in Seattle. Someone to share the moment, brush against and touch you... I was thinking that."

Santiago moved to the edge of the bed. "It's been a long three days. You've got the money, the kids are home safe. Why the stalking routine? My work here is done."

"You're very direct, Michelle," he said in a near whisper, "but I don't want to talk about that. It would be so easy to share the spa, maybe even a private spa where we could be naked and enjoy the pleasures of our flesh. The warm bubbles would tickle those special private parts of us. The jets could help us reach new heights as we explore each other, bringing each other incredible joy."

She looked at the closed drapes and stood, stretching to reach the cord and open them. Light burst into the room through the privacy curtains, causing her to blink as the warmth of the sun engulfed her nude body. "Lovers want to be with each other and know each other. You don't qualify, but you were watching me last night?"

"Oh yes. You had my undivided attention. I visualized you naked."

"In the bikini you left for me it wouldn't take much imagination." She paused. "You got me out of bed. Are you watching the window now?"

"Maybe. What do you wear to bed?"

"You'll have to depend on your imagination."

"To paraphrase Marilyn Monroe, you're wearing a scent. I wear musk to bed."

She smiled. "That's more information than I want." *You're coming to the surface. I feel it.*

"The silence of the listening devices tells me you found my toys."

Santiago took a deep breath. "Yes."

"We all have to be careful about talking on the phone, what we say, but I really enjoyed your last call and the bath that followed."

"So you know some of my secrets.... I've been asking myself what you want. You didn't plan Lindsey's kidnapping. She didn't come to the same end as the girls on the coast or the dancer at the Bramble Bush. It's like this was a crime of opportunity, nothing more. And whether you disappear or not, I'm gone in a few days. So why are you still around?"

"I want you. I want to take a bath with you, make love to you."

Santiago was quiet for a moment. "It'll never happen, Yancey."

She heard a gasp through the receiver.

"That's very good, Michelle. You caught me by surprise. I wasn't sure they knew my name."

"I had a lot of resources at my disposal."

"I know you're looking for me."

"I was looking for Lindsey. Now she's home and I'm out of it. You have the cops and Feds on your tail. They're looking for you."

"So you were really here just to find the kid?"

"The Brauns are close friends. I took a leave to help them, maybe think about a new job. Little did I know we were just touching the tip of an iceberg."

"You really want me to believe that line?"

"Believe what you want. I'm relaxing for a few days before heading home or possibly accepting a new position with DataFlex. We both know the Feds and local cops don't want some outsider nosing into their investigations. Hell, they don't even like to work together."

"That is true."

She noticed a small cobweb in the corner of the room. *Housekeeping is getting lax.* "I have other things I want to do."

"So you're just doing a vacation thing?"

"That's about it. By the way, have you contacted Veteran's Trust?"

"Should I?"

"We tracked the money transfer."

"Impossible."

"Not if you have the right people working on it. Like I said, they'll get you, Yancey. It's just a matter of time. They don't need or want my help. If I were you, I'd be heading to new pastures."

"Cut and run?"

"That's what I'd do. For me, it's hangout at the pool, soak up some rays and relax. Maybe get to know a few new people. Now that you've got me completely awake, I'm going to take a bath."

She hung up and waited a minute, wondering whether he'd call back. The phone remained quiet.

* * *

At 9:17 Santiago was enjoying breakfast in the Oasis coffee shop. Sam Evans approached her with bloodshot eyes and deep lines in his face. "God, you look like someone who was up all night. What time did you leave the Bramble Bush?"

He sat down and exhaled. "Half-hour after you. Ran out of money."

"You don't look like you slept much."

"How about not at all?"

"Young babes cavorting. That'll do it every time," she said.

Evans' eyes were intense, and moisture covered his upper lip. "Quarterman called my house last night. He threatened my family."

A waiter approached with an empty cup. "Breakfast, Sir?"

"No thank you, just coffee."

The waiter filled the cup from a carafe on the table and left.

"Quarterman wants two more bugs placed in your room and me to keep him advised of the investigation."

"What did you tell him?"

"That we're out of it, I've been reassigned."

"Good," she said. "He called me about an hour ago and got the same story." She looked around and leaned toward Evans. "I told him I'm going to do a little relaxing for a day or two, then leave for home unless I accept a position with DataFlex."

"Did he buy it?"

"I don't know, but I told him we knew where the money was and used his name. He's definitely our man."

"So how do we draw him out?"

"We already are. We know he's stalking me. I'm here and untouchable. I just hope the man Stone brings in fills the part of young hunk love interest. Given the call this morning, Quarterman's more than a little interested."

"How so?"

"He watched me in the spa last evening. He was more taken with what the bubbles were doing to me than with our looking for him. He said he wants to make love to me. I'm sure he feels some rejection that he's not my primary interest."

"Jealous?"

"That and confused, but the cover is plausible. He knows the Feds and cops don't like interference in their workings whether from each other or outsiders. He has to be staying here. It's just a matter of picking him out."

"You make that sound simple."

"I know, but it's a good opportunity and it's all we've got."

Evans patted the breast of his blazer. "I have the bugs with me, one for the bathroom, and one for the lanai. They were at the office when I got there this morning."

"We'll go up when we're done. If he's watching, let's make him wait."

They spent the remainder of breakfast chatting about Santiago's next few days.

Evans checked his watch. "Stone said the new man would be at the office at 10:30."

"Give Stone a call and have him show up here, alone. I'll greet him as a long-lost friend when he comes to the room. You'll just be leaving when he gets there." She smirked. "We'll play it by ear, but let Stone know what we're doing so his man doesn't blow it."

Evans called Stone while Santiago signed off on the breakfast tab. "Thank you, Claude. You are generous."

Evans patted his pocket. "Bug time."

She looked back at Evans and shook her head. "A girl needs her privacy. Let's put the bathroom bug in the toilet tank and open the valve so the water just dribbles all the time. After a day or two housekeeping will find it when they fix the toilet."

"Good call. Housekeeping will send maintenance up when they hear the water. Quarterman will get that on his tape."

"Sam, does anyone else know about the threat?"

"No. I wanted to talk to you first."

"Good."

"Mitch, do you think we have a leak at DataFlex too?"

"It's possible. Either that or Quarterman's also a hacker. We're not even going to tell House or Braun. No leaks, just keep the danger level down."

"For the first time in my life I'm scared. I've never had anyone threaten my family."

"You're not alone. How much longer before Stone's man gets here?"

"He'll be here in about forty-five minutes. His name is Alex Patton, former Air Force intelligence officer. He's been with the Agency for the last four years."

"How old is he?"

"Thirty-five."

"Married?"

"Don't know."

She stood. 'Well, let's go plant the bugs. We can't keep Yancey waiting forever."

Santiago and Evans went to her suite where he installed the two bugs and she looked up the number of the U.S. Marshall's office while soaking in the morning rays on the lanai. A light knock drew their attention.

Evans said, "That should be Alex Patton"

Santiago darted to the door and checked the peephole. The man waiting was a fit-looking mid-thirties with a dark complexion. She opened the door slowly.

The man looked her over from head to toe and smiled. "Hi Michelle."

"Alex, what a surprise! Come in!"

She stepped aside opening the door wide. He reached into the blazer and she shook her head while holding up a hand. Evans stepped to the entry. "This is a friend I've been working with at DataFlex for the last few days... Sam Evans."

Evans extending his right hand and mouthed the word bugs. "It's a pleasure to meet you, Alex."

Patton nodded while pulling out an FBI identification holder for them to view.

Santiago said, "This is great. What are you doing here?"

"Vacation," Patton looked around the room. "I saw you downstairs, thought we might hook-up... you know, like old times."

He's good. "How'd you find my room?"

"Bribery, Darlin', good old bribery. Works every time."

"You'll never change, Alex. God, you look great, overdressed for the desert, but we'll get you out of that blazer, tie and slacks. How long are you going to be in town?"

"Just a few days, then back to the grind."

"Sam was just leaving. He brought a job offer over from DataFlex. They're trying to steal me away from the SPD."

"It would be their gain," Patton said. "You look great, Mitch. The sun agrees with you."

Evans stepped to the door. "We'll talk later. I can see you two have some catching up to do. Let me know about the position."

"I will, Sam. It's very generous. Thanks for bringing it by. I appreciate your help."

Evans stepped out and closed the door.

Patton moved to the center of the sitting room. "So what do you have planned for the day? I'm free."

"Are you staying at the hotel?"

"Fourth floor, suite, 4007. It's got a splendid view of the pool."

She grinned. "You always did like things easy on the eyes."

"True. Your plans?"

"I have a few errands to run. I'll be back around 1:30. How about we meet at the pool and do lunch?"

"Works for me, and how about dinner tonight?"

"Love it. Then we can go to a club. When's the last time you visited a strip joint?"

He said, "It's been a while, certainly a different idea than I had in mind."

She handed him a tube. "And Alex, when you come to the pool, bring this. The desert rays are tough on northwest bodies."

"Really? It doesn't show."

She motioned him toward the lanai door, wrapped him in her arms and kissed him hard. "It's so good to see you. Like old times."

Still holding her hands, he said, "I hope so. This sure beats Seattle."

They walked to the front door, and she gave Alex another quick kiss on the cheek. "I'll see you at the pool."

He stepped into the hallway. "With lotion in hand, but I may need some help putting it on. See you then."

"Wait. I'll walk out with you," she said while grabbing her purse.

Patton checked her bronze flesh against the pink low-rider shorts and crop top. A questioning look crossed his face.

"We're in the desert, Alex. By this afternoon you'll be in shorts too."

They left the room together and walked hand in hand to the elevator. Inside, it was empty.

Once out of the room he said, "That was quite a greeting."

"Didn't Evans tell you the rooms are bugged?"

"Oh yes. You think Quarterman is following you?"

"I don't know."

The elevator stopped on the third floor and a couple joined them. All four rode to the lobby in silence.

They exited and she went toward the parking lot. He said, "I'll walk you to your car."

"Okay. So tell me, Mr. Patton, have you worked undercover before?"

He chuckled as her cheeks reddened. "Is that a professional question?"

"Of course."

He arched his eyebrows. "Yes, but not in a situation like this."

"You're a flirt."

"Guilty, but I'm in good company. So you don't know if he's following you?"

"No, but he's definitely been observing me at the hotel."

"That wouldn't be too difficult," he said.

She glanced at Paxton. *You're pretty easy on the eyes yourself.*

He sniffed as the air. "Stroganoff... must be today's special. Just what is our relationship supposed to be?"

"We're former lovers. Quarterman is obsessed. He makes obscene calls, kills women during sex and wants to make love to me. I think the quickest way to force his hand is to let him see things he can't have. Do you like hot tubs?"

He smiled. "Who do you want to turn on? But in answer to your question, yes."

"Good. He's been fantasizing about the spa. We ought to spend ample time with the warm bubbles... that is, if you don't mind."

He grinned. "It's a dirty job but somebody's gotta do it. My colleagues will never believe this assignment. I mean forced undercover with a beautiful woman? Hell, even I don't believe it."

"I think we'll handle it just fine."

He opened the door of the Sebring. "Oh yes."

Santiago started to get in the car but Alex stopped her with an embrace, pulling her close to him. "Just for show," he whispered in her ear.

She slid onto the seat and started the engine. "I like a man who thinks ahead. Later."

"Michelle?"

"Call me Mitch, all my friends do."

"My room isn't bugged."

She smiled. "I'll see you at the pool."

She pulled out of the parking place.

He watched as she turned onto Baseline. "Focus, Alex, you need to focus."

* * *

It was 12:56 when Lisa Fargo looked up to see the silhouette of a man's head lost in the noonday sun looking at her over the pool fence at the Borderline Motel in Yuma. He spoke in a soft voice. "I knew I'd find you here."

She sat up, straining the straps holding the tiny triangles of the fluorescent lime bikini top in place. "Yancey, is it time to head for Mexico?"

"It is for you." He walked around the fenced area and came through the pool gate carrying a flight bag. "You have no idea how much a man appreciates it when you sit up like that."

She straightened the halter top. "Oh yes I do."

"Yeah, right."

Lisa looked at him for a long moment, head tilted. She wet her lips with the tip of her tongue. "You're lookin' pretty dapper today, like a golf pro or something."

"The Oasis has a way of encouraging a change of appearance for people like us, but you look more natural here."

"I feel comfortable here."

He pulled a chair over near Lisa's lounge. "You're the only one at the pool? An outfit like that ought to attract more than a few admirers even if some of 'em are only caught in youthful fantasies."

"It's pretty quiet here. Right now I'm the only guest."

"Not for long. Acapulco is nice this time of year. I want you to go on a trip with a tour group, stay with them at their hotel for a few days, then find a condo and rent it."

"Am I goin' by Brooke?"

"No, you can use your own name."

"If anyone is lookin' for me I'll be a lot easier to find."

"Probably, but they have nothing on you. Believe me, it's better not to deal with the Mexican authorities where falsification is involved. As far as they're concerned you're just another tourist who's done nothing wrong while helping the local economy."

"Where are you gonna be?"

"I don't know yet and neither will you."

"Will you join me?"

"Can't say for sure. If things go that way I can find you easy enough."

Lisa looked at the flight bag. "You could've left it in the room."

He patted it. "Before you leave Yuma I want you to get a safety deposit box and put the money in this bag in it."

She shifted her gaze to the bag. "How much is there?"

"Three-hundred thousand dollars."

"Cash?"

Quarterman smiled at Lisa as she gulped air. "Cash. It's yours, but use it wisely. Take small amounts across the border, just a few thousand at a time. You can always come back for more."

She caught her breath. "That's a lot of money. Mine?"

"It's all for you. It'll last a long time."

She broke into uncontrolled laughter. "Yeah, like for life."

"Just don't tell anyone about it."

"You're makin' this whole arrangement sound really permanent, Yancey."

"That's possible. I just don't know. I've been coming and going for years. Is that a problem?"

"Not anymore."

"Not anymore?"

"I've found someone, or maybe he found me. It's very exciting after all these years."

"Sort of sudden isn't it? I mean, you've never mentioned anyone before."

"Sudden? Yes. Wonderful? Yes. Love? I think so. Anyway, you're pretty taken with that woman detective too."

"That's different, unique."

"So is Aaron. He's coming to join me."

"He knows you're here?"

"No. He knows where I live. We'll go to Mexico after I pick him up tonight."

"Where?"

"At Jake's in Eloy. He knows where my hidden key is. He'll be waiting."

"So he knows your real name?"

"He knows all about me, even my past... some of it."

"Does he know about me?"

"No. I thought it better to leave you out. What he doesn't know he can't spill by mistake."

"You're sure he's not a cop?"

"Positive. We met at the hotel, did dinner, you know the routine. He's the man who had dinner with your bitch cop the night before. You wanted me to check him out. Well, we've really connected. When you had me leave so suddenly my heart ached. After checking in here I called him."

"From here?"

She shook her head. "On my cell. Yancey, you look confused. Aren't you happy for me?"

"Very happy," he said. "It just never crossed my mind each of us would find someone special at the same time."

"Well, at least Aaron knows me. Ours is a two-way street."

Quarterman looked at the pool. "Mine will be too. You really think you love this guy?"

"I know it. I've never been so happy."

He smiled and patted her hand. "You deserve better than you've had for the last several years."

"We both do."

"I just want you safe and able to take care of yourself if need be. Maybe in the months to come you can start that craft business. I remember how you talked about it as a kid."

"A lot has happened since then."

He patted the flight bag. "I know, but you'll have ample time to consider your future, maybe even with the love of your life. Think of this as your nest egg."

"Is the money part of the ransom?"

"No, it's totally clean."

"So why aren't you comin'?"

"I have to play out my hand."

She looked into his eyes. "No, you don't."

"It's what I do... what I've been doing all my life, taking chances."

"They're gettin' close."

"Yes, but that's the thrill, the rush. I want one last victory over them, one last time to put it to the Agency. Then I'm out."

Lisa looked around, stared at the water, eyes welling. "Are you abandoning me?"

"No. Right now I'm just going in a different direction. You're my family, Lisa. You're all I have. I want you safe at all costs."

She grinned. "What you want is Santiago."

"She wants me too, in jail on death row." He paused. "I enjoy the sight of her, the sound of her voice. I want to know her."

"You want to sleep with her."

"Yes, that too."

"You sound like a teenager with a serious crush."

"Maybe I am. You know, second childhood and all that."

Lisa said, "She's poison, Yancey... pure poison."

"She's the most fantastic woman I've ever encountered. I just wish things had been different."

"So why go panting after something you can't have?"

"She's a tool for them. She is for me too, but much more. I guess we're both using her."

"Lust, Yancey. Lust is driving you."

"Maybe, but I think it's revenge... getting even."

"How will it end? It can't be good."

His voice was soft. "I don't know. She's just... different."

Lisa changed the subject. "I have time right now if you have a special need."

He shook his head. "Have to get back to Chandler. That'll take three hours even taking Highway 347 through Maricopa." He bent over Lisa's face and kissed her on the cheek.

"That was just a peck."

"Maybe after all these years we're moving on to new chapter for each of us, still good but different." He stood. "'Bye Lisa." He stood and walked through the gate without looking back.

Quietly, Lisa said, "You're in love with an image, Yancey. She's untouchable." She rolled over, inviting the warm rays of the sun to bake her backside. "Will I ever see you again?"

* * *

Sam Evans was in his office drumming fingers on the cluttered desk. He glanced at the wall clock and shook his head. "1:17." His stomach turned in retribution for the tacos he should have left in the cafeteria. He rubbed his belly, dialed the secretary of the security office and asked for the number of the Seattle Police Department, then punched in the number and waited. A receptionist answered and directed his call to Chance Stewart's line.

"Stewart."

"Detective Stewart, I'm Sam Evans. I've been assisting Miss Santiago for the last few days."

"Hi Sam. She speaks very highly of you. What can I do for you?"

Evans shared the background information Santiago had given to the FBI and Marshall's office.

Stewart nodded. "So the Bureau has provided an agent to work with her undercover?"

"Yes."

"What's he like?"

"I beg your pardon?" Evans said. "He's an experienced agent."

"No, I mean is he a good match for Mitch or just some dusty bureaucrat?"

Evans smiled. "An excellent match... they make a perfect couple for this assignment."

"That's good. He's experienced, knows what he's doing?"

"Oh yes. Patton's been an agent for years."

"Well, you know, undercover can be delicate work."

"He was in Air Force intelligence before joining the Bureau. I'm sure he has more experience in covert operations than most of us."

"Mitch said you had a background that included secret operations and undercover work."

"I was with the Agency for many years before joining the private sector."

"Well, I appreciate the background data and you letting me know she has a good agent working with her. You know Mitch and I talk, so please, why did you really call?"

"I thought you might want to come down and work with her during the last part of the investigation. Mr.

Braun could arrange a leave for you. I know you two are... close."

"I'd like to, but too many things are piling up around here. They even called me back from vacation. You did say Patton was a well-trained professional, right?"

"Yes."

"Mitch is a beautiful woman. I wouldn't want him distracted from the primary task if you get my drift," Stewart said.

"I got your message loud and clear." *You're not coming down to help her.* Evans snapped a pencil in two.

"Besides, I doubt my boss would take kindly to two of us being on leave at the same time again, much less down there. I'm sure your boss could pull it off, but my boss wouldn't like it."

"Maybe not, but he'd do whatever the brass told him even if he didn't like it," Evans said.

That took Stewart aback. "B-but my turning up now could jeopardize the cover Mitch and Patton have established."

Evans hesitated only a moment. "Possibly, but dueling lovers might also add to the pressure for Quarterman to surface. I just wanted you to know it could be arranged. I want her to feel as comfortable as possible during these next few days."

"You think it will end that fast?"

"Yes, and so does Mitch. Yancey is obsessed with her. He'll either surface or he'll leave, and I really doubt it'll be the latter. Even the reunion with one old friend should inflame Quarterman more than enough to tip his hand."

"From what she's told me, I agree." Stewart paused and looked around the office. "Sorry, Evans, I have a priority call coming in."

"I understand. Just wanted to let you know an option is available that you might not have considered."

"Thanks again. Say, ah... how about we keep this conversation just between us? I don't want Mitch worrying about anything else."

Evans said, "Of course."

"Duty calls," Stewart said and the line went dead.

Evans put the phone down and took a deep breath. "I hope you do relocate after this case, Mitch. You deserve better than Stewart... much better."

* * * * * * *

By 1:30 in the afternoon Santiago had met with a deputy marshal in Phoenix, completed a workout at the DataFlex gym, talked with Mario Spears and done some shopping. Once again in the tiny red bikini she was embracing a lounge in a sunny corner of the Oasis pool. "I hope you're lurking in the shadows somewhere, Quarterman. I want you turned on and jealous."

A waiter approached. "May I get you something? Perhaps a cocktail?"

She glanced up. "No thank you."

She propped herself up on an elbow and looked around. "Come on, Alex. Its show time and I want a good look at your bod... a real good look." She put her head on a rolled towel and relaxed, keeping her attention on the entry. The sun warmed her flesh.

Alex Patton walked through the pool security gate wearing a print pair of board shorts, an unbuttoned short sleeve cotton shirt, and low-cut canvas shoes with no socks. She whispered, "This man is gorgeous. Too bad this is all work"

Patton waved. "Hi Mitch."

She pushed herself up, resting on her elbows and smiled. "Hi, Honey. Join me. It's been a long morning."

A smile creased his rugged face as he approached. "Join a bronze goddess in a red bikini? I'd love to."

"Thank you."

He tossed a towel on the nearby table, pulled over a chair, and looked around. He gave Santiago a long, appreciative look. "Nice pool. Not too crowded."

"It will be later," she said. "I think most of the guests are business types but they play hard at night."

"And you?"

"I'm on vacation just like you. We can play easy and hard 24/7 for the next few days if we want."

"So we can. Are you going to burn? This sun is a little more intense than anything I'm accustomed to."

She handed him a small brown plastic bottle. "Just in case you forgot your lotion."

"I did."

She said, "You could put some lotion on my back. Rub it in really well." She pressed her body to the lounge.

Patton began spreading the lotion on her back, taking care not to come too close to the spaghetti strap.

"Your hands are a little rough but strong. I use a lot of lotion down here. The air is so dry. Do you have any lotion on?"

"Not yet."

"You will. Without it your skin will begin to crack and become scaly."

Patton sat back on the chair, looked around and laughed. "So we just play at the pool. Nice duty."

She rolled onto her side. "Could be worse."

"I'll let you do your own front side." He looked away after a brief glance at her bronze frame.

She smiled. "Afraid I'll burn you?"

"Afraid of my quivering hands in public. You're a beautiful woman."

"You're more of a gentleman than most of the guys I know."

"Subconsciously I'm a masher but each of us deserves respect."

"A man not in a rush. I like that. Most men would work tirelessly just to get under the strap."

"We're working," he said. "Whatever happens between us, if anything, will come naturally. Intimacy can't be forced."

"I agree."

"So tell me," he said, looking at her near naked form, "do you always dress so formally for the pool?"

"This is the gift from Quarterman. He insisted I wear it at the pool the first time he called. Now I want to rub his nose in it." She licked her lips. "But in answer to your question, yes."

He laughed. "Nose rubbing, that's graphic. I know men who would line up for the opportunity."

She looked at his muscular frame and pulled another lounge close to hers. "Why don't you stretch out on a lounge? I wouldn't want you fading away."

"Neither would I."

She watched Patton stretch out on the lounge. "I'm going to like this. I hope we can be friends... close friends."

He said, "Are you always so forward?"

"Sometimes, when I think the chemistry is right."

"And how is our chemistry?"

She glanced at his trunks. "It's building."

A cell phone rang. He took it from his rolled towel. "Patton."

Cops... we all answer the same way. She looked around the pool and noticed a statuesque redhead coming through the gate. The woman surveyed the area, then dragged a lounge chair to a spot near two well-chiseled hunks chatting over drinks. *You're shopping, lady.* The two men watched her. She stood straight for a moment, then stretched out on her belly. *Show 'em what you've got, Honey.*

She noticed Patton watching the display out of the corner of his eye while taking his call. The woman reached behind her back untied the strap, letting it fall as she pressed her torso hard against the lounge. Nobody missed the fullness of her breasts as she opened a paperback book. Santiago whispered, "You've got 'em."

Patton tossed the phone on the towel. "That was Stone's secretary. Quarterman has a cousin living in Eloy. She works at a truck stop."

"Eloy is about forty-five miles south of here. Shall we do a late lunch?"

He glanced one last time at the redheaded woman reading. "Just what I had in mind."

"Really? I thought you were ogling the babe over there."

"She's hard to miss but she couldn't hold a candle to your looks, and I'll bet she's not nearly as bright."

She grinned. "And you're working?"

"If I wasn't I'd be hitting on you. Ready for lunch?"

"Let's give it a few minutes. If Quarterman is watching we don't want to leave too soon."

They both sat and watched the redhead reading and working the hunks.

"So tell me, Alex, what do you look for on a first date?"

"Someone who likes the same things I do."

"Such as?"

"I like going out to dinner, catching a lounge act of easy listening music where you can talk to each other and hear. I like most kinds of music; rock, pop, jazz, big band, but I'm not much on rap although the poets of the street have their place."

"Poets of the street? That's nice way of putting it. Do you read much?"

He glanced at the redhead again. "Sometimes. I get into mysteries and sometimes I just like a trashy romance. Strange for a guy, huh?"

"No. Do you think of any singers other than rappers as poets?"

"Some of the old guys: Paul Simon, Paul McCartney, Bob Dylan, Kris Kristofferson, hottie Cheryl Crow. How about you?"

She squinted into the sun while looking into his face. "I read Kerouac, Fitzgerald, Twain and DiPrima. I also enjoy history, political science and philosophy when the mood hits me, and sometimes the occasional mystery."

"Any particular mystery writers?"

"Elmore Leonard, Bob Parker, Clive Cussler, Judy Jance."

Patton took another look at the redhead. "Yeah, I like a thriller once in a while." He stretched his legs. "We're going to burn out here."

In a slightly louder voice she said, "Enough gawking and small talk. Lunch it is. Let's change and go for a drive."

They stood and gathered their things. Patton took her in his arms, pulling her body close against his torso and kissed her. "Just in case he's watching."

Santiago smiled and continued to press against him. "Lunch," she said. "I think we just had dessert... either that or you're really into this assignment."

She pulled a cover-up around her and they walked to the gate.

The two young men watched them for a moment, then turned their attentions back to the redhead.

* * *

Greg Rich's office door opened, and an attractive young woman around twenty stepped into the reception area with tears in her eyes. Mavis Lupino glanced at the clock on her desk. "1:56... a short session," she said. "You're dressed for the club scene, Miranda. Are you going out this afternoon?"

The young woman stopped in front of Lupino's desk. "No, I'm going home. May I have a tissue?"

"Of course. Are you all right, Dear?"

"Yes, but Greg said he wanted me to begin seeing a new doctor. I don't want to. I love him."

"That may be why, Miranda. He's a very smart man and if he notices a client becoming too attached he'll find a way to restore patient-doctor objectivity. Perhaps, after a period of time he'll have you return as a client. You've been with him for a long while."

"Do you think so?"

"Anything is possible, Dear."

"I hope so. I don't know what I'll do without him."

Lupino held out a box of tissues. "You'll be fine, Miranda. You'll be just fine. Here, you might need another."

She watched as Miranda left the office, still sniffling. "You're the third one since yesterday. What the hell is going on?"

Claude Braun had called during the brief last session. Lupino picked up the message slip, walked to the office door, knocked twice, and stepped in.

Rich turned and looked up from his computer on a credenza behind his desk. "Mavis?"

Lupino crossed the office, stopping in front the desk. "Mr. Braun called and left a message."

Rich spun around, the blood draining from his face. "A message?"

"Are you feeling all right, Greg?"

He snatched the message slip from her hand. "Yes, I'm fine. The last session was somewhat traumatic for Miranda."

"You're shaking, Greg."

"Too much caffeine this morning." He forced a smile, pressed the note firmly against the desk and quickly glanced at it. A chill ran down his spine. "He wants me to call him ASAP."

"I know. I wrote the note."

"Of course. Cancel my afternoon sessions. I have some special tasks to do."

"You only have one appointment. I'll call her now. Anything else?"

"Yes. I'm going to need complete privacy today. After you're done with the call, lock up and take the rest of the day off. Just turn the answering machine on before you go."

"Miranda was crying when she left and—"

He looked away. "I know. I've arranged for her to see someone else."

"She's the third client in the last two days you've transferred."

He spun around in his chair, looked at the screen and pressed Delete. Without looking at Mavis, he said, "Sometimes you just have to clean house."

Mavis watched the client file disappear. "You tense, Greg. I always help you relax."

He shook his head while turning back toward her. "Not today. Everything will be fine. Go have lunch. Don't worry."

She stepped back from the desk. "Will be? I'd better make that call but I could come back in a few hours. You know how you like to go home free of office tension."

"On second thought, come back around 3:30 if you're in the neighborhood. I think I'd like that. I know I'd like that."

"So would I."

He looked at the message slip on the desk again as Lupino left the office. He waited another fifteen minutes while drumming his fingers on the piece of paper until the auto answer light on the phone flashed. He picked up the receiver, pressed directory, stopping at *Braun* and punched Dial.

A strange man answered. "Braun residence."

"Mr. Braun, please. This is Doctor Rich returning his call."

A moment later, Braun came on the line, his voice harsh. "Greg, you bastard! You dirty fucking bastard!"

Rich was quiet for a moment. "Claude, I apologize for my unprofessional behavior. Lindsey is so physical, so wanton, a beautiful, irresistible young woman who's enjoyed many men beyond her years, so mature. I just don't know what came over me."

"She was young and defenseless. You've been bangin' her since she was fifteen years old you pervert!"

"I'm doing as your representative suggested, Claude. I'm retiring."

"Not good enough, Greg. We've talked with Lindsey and she's going to prefer charges."

Rich felt his throat swell. He choked. He wiped a hand across his forehead. Sweat covered the palm. "That's not really necessary and it would be embarrassing to her, to you."

"I've embarrassed myself before and probably will again, Greg, but I'm not a criminal. I don't seduce defenseless children. You were entrusted to help her."

Rich sat up straight stiffening his back. "Sierra is Lindsey's age."

"True, but I wasn't doin' her when she was fifteen. You might consider getting things in order before the authorities become involved."

Rich's legs shook beneath the desk. "Has Lindsey already been in touch with them?"

"She will be tomorrow after a good night's rest at home. You know, Greg, you should just count your lucky stars. My first thought was to strangle you, and my second was to beat the crap out of you and then strangle you. But now I like the idea of your public humiliation." Braun abruptly broke the connection.

Rich looked around the office, the pictures of himself, the leather bound books and stuffed couch.

Taking a letter opener from the desk he walked to the couch and repeatedly stabbed the cushions. He burst into loud laughter and looked at the torn fabric. "This is nuts! Why was I so weak?"

He returned to the computer and deleted the remaining client dossiers, all labeled *Personal Notes*.

He looked again at the desk and focused on the only picture of his family in the office. He went to a painting on the wall. It was hinged. Pulling it away from the wall revealed a small safe. He turned the combination and, after a muffled click, he pulled the small thick door open, and removed several cassettes, CDs and a chrome-plated snub-nose .38 revolver. Re-crossing the office he tossed the cassettes and CDs into the wastebasket, then placed the revolver on the desk in front of the picture. He paused for a moment, then removed the items from the wastebasket.

Looking around the office he began picking up and crumpling any papers he could find and placed them in the wastebasket. Going to the outer office he retrieved the morning newspaper, crumpled it by sections and placed them in the wastebasket along with the cassettes, CDs and DVDs. Opening the bottom left-hand drawer of the desk he removed nine videotapes and tossed them into the container one at a time. "I'll burn the evidence. Thanks for the warning, Braun. At least I won't have self-incriminating files for jurors to watch and listen to. It'll be my word against hers, maybe a few others. Kids stick together, sometimes."

The revolver came into focus in front of the family photo. He shifted his gaze to his wife's face in the photo. "I'm on the edge, Ice Princess. You made me do these things. No, lust made me do what I did. How many more angry dads are going to call, come looking for me?"

Standing, he walked to the window overlooking Mill Avenue with its bustling people and traffic. The image of his former mentor came to mind. "Well, Doc Steckler, did you see this coming when you kept repeating 'A doctor's job is to heal?' or were you just paying lip service to a personal mantra?"

Rich returned to the desk, sat down, and called home. His wife answered. "Helen, how are you doing today?"

"Greg, it's after two in the afternoon. Is something wrong?"

"No no, Darling. Everything is fine. I just thought I'd call like the old days, see how your day is going. Remember back when I called every day?"

She took a deep breath. "Yes, I remember. It was always very nice until you stopped. That was when you went 'uptown,' as you put it. Will you be home for dinner or is it another late night session?"

"I'll be a little late. Don't wait dinner. Eat with the boys."

"The yard man is at the door. I have to go. I'll see you tonight."

"Until tonight," he said. "Helen... I love you."

Breaking the connection he again looked around the office. "You're a coward, Greg. You couldn't even tell Helen, and it'll be all over the news in the next day or two, maybe tonight."

Opening the lap drawer he removed a book of matches, his hands trembling almost uncontrollably. Pressing his elbows against his ribs he lit a match, then the book and tossed both into the wastebasket. A smile crossed his red, sweating face. The paper began burning, and smoke filled the office making his eyes water even more. "Yes."

The smoke alarm triggered followed a moment later by the overhead sprinkler system. The flames died down, sizzled, and ceased. He struck the desktop. "No! No, don't do this to me!"

People could be heard leaving the building. Fire engine sirens wailed in the background, getting louder and louder, then stopped. Rich looked at the family picture again, the wastebasket, the office. He was trembling all over. He could barely breathe. The acrid smoke filled his lungs and eyes. Someone was breaking in through the outer office door. "Damn firemen... I need privacy."

He picked up the .38, cocked it and placed the muzzle in his mouth just as his office door burst open. Two firemen rushed into the room.

Rich held up one hand, then squeezed the trigger.

* * *

Santiago and Patton followed Highway 87 to Eloy, coming into town from the east. Patton surveyed the nearly empty main street. "This is sure different than D.C. or London."

"You're a name dropper," she said.

"No, just reflecting how different various places can be."

"It's pretty quiet here, but his cousin lives around here someplace. We should've come down I-10. I don't see any truck stop signs."

He said, "It was a nice drive. I've seen more open country today than in the last three months."

"Me too."

He watched Santiago's hair as the wind teased it. "You like driving a convertible?"

"It's different than Seattle: sun, fresh air, no coat."

"It is nice. So tell me, is there someone special in your life?"

"There was. It's amazing how fast things can fade away. How about you?"

"No. I've met some wonderful ladies, but my work always comes first. I guess that's how I'll know when I meet the right one... work will come second."

"Method in your madness. You're doing better than I am," she said. "I've been gone four days and he already has a little friend helping him."

"That's not a good sign. So what's the plan after we talk with Lisa?"

She laughed. "Go back to the hotel, catch some rays for the next day or two and wait. If Yancey's coming out it won't take too long and we don't want your spray tan to fade away."

Driving west toward Exit 208 on Sunshine Boulevard they searched for Jake's Truck-O-Rama. They crossed railroad tracks and kept looking from side to side.

She said, "The town has really wide streets."

He said, "Looks like a farming community, that's for sure."

"Cotton."

Patton frowned. "Cotton?"

"When Eloy was first established, cotton was the primary business. Might still be for all I know. Agriculture is the primary money maker here even as the town works to establish an industrial base."

"You're quite a source of information."

"Mario did the work. He looked it up on the 'net when I told him we wanted to check out Quarterman's cousin, Lisa."

"Mario... the same guy who tracked the money?"

"That's him, a computer whiz of the first order. He's still monitoring the money just in case it moves again."

"Eloy... that's a strange name," he said.

"That's a funny story too. It seems the original founders called it Cotton City, but when they applied for a post office around the end of World War I the name was turned down. Someone in the postal service changed it to Eloy, and that's been the name of the community ever since."

"What does Eloy mean?"

"Mario says it's Spanish for, 'My God, why hast thou forsaken me?' and originated with a railroad worker."

"Interesting." Patton looking around. "It's really flat except for over there."

"That's Picacho Peak. The blue and gray fought a battle there."

"You've got to be kidding. What was there to fight over?"

"Politics," she said. "Arizona became a Confederate Territory in 1862, and a United States Territory in 1863."

He said, "Some big signs are coming into view. Must be getting close to I-10."

She nodded toward her left. "I see 'em and there's Jake's."

He pointed to the large truck stops populating both sides of the road as Santiago eased the Sebring into a parking place. He said, "Bet it's tough competing with these big operations."

She shook her hair as she got out of the car. "It's got to be rough."

He smiled. "Hair didn't get enough movement coming down here with all the sun and air?"

"Guess not."

He gestured toward the door. "Lunch time."

"I'm starving, late lunch today."

They walked in and took an empty booth near the back. Patton looked across the table at Santiago. "You blend in better than me although you're much more exotic than just Hispanic."

"Island and European too."

He looked at her smooth flesh, delicate nose, and full lips. "Your eyes sparkle when you talk."

"Sometimes. It depends on what I'm saying, who I'm with."

"They're sparkling now."

Crimson crept up her neck as a young waitress approached and placed two menus in front of them. "Afternoon folks. I'm Vicki and I'll be your waitress today. Coffee?"

"Diet soda, please," Santiago said.

"Make that two."

After the waitress left, Santiago said, "You look like a surfer, tanned with a touch of sun bleach. I know about the spray job, but the hair?"

"I was once a blond, no jokes please. San Diego was home 'til I grew up."

"Surfer?"

"Beach bum according to my parents until I joined the Air Force. Dad was Navy and disapproved of that too, initially. But let's skip that. I'm hungry too." He picked up one of the menus.

Vicki returned with the sodas. "Have you decided, yet?"

"Mitch, ladies first."

"I'll have the jumbo frank with the hot mustard on a sesame bun and chips."

"They're really good," Vicki said. "And for you, Sir?"

"Double-meat cheeseburger with all the garnishes on the side and fries."

Vicki jotted down the order. "They'll be out in a few minutes."

Santiago said, "Ma'am, Vicki, do you know Lisa Fargo? We understand she works here."

The young waitress said, "She does, or did. Haven't seen her for almost a week. She hasn't called in sick either. Jake says he'll fire her when she shows this time, but I doubt it."

Patton looked up at Vicki. "This time?"

"She probably ran off with another trucker. She always says, 'If the money's right,' and Lord knows she'll sleep with anyone."

Patton said, "Are there any special men she goes with more often than others?"

"Yancey, a big stud. Kind'a old but she sure likes him. Says he's the best. She even wanted me to take a tumble with him. Are you guys friends of hers, 'cause I don't want trouble."

Santiago said, "No, we just wanted to see her about a personal matter. Anything you've said here stays here."

Patton said, "Are Lisa and Yancey related?"

Vicki blushed. "I hope not. The way they sleep together and talk about it all the time would be even more disgusting if they're related."

"So you'd say Lisa is a party girl?" Santiago said.

Vicki waved a hand around the café. "See those guys out there? They'd all tell you she's a party girl. Truth is, she's a whore. They ride the highway and park on Lisa."

Santiago watched the young waitress. "Do you know where she lives?"

"She might be in the berth of pretty much any truck, but she has a trailer parked out on the back lot. Jake let's her stay there because she's good for business."

"Jake?" Santiago said. "Is he the manager?"

"Owner, manager, you name it. He works really hard to keep this place going. It's hard competing against the big stops. That's why he won't can Lisa. Whatever else she may or may not be, she brings in the truckers."

Santiago said, "Prostitution is illegal."

Vicki shrugged. "She's a waitress here. What she does on her own time Jake doesn't control."

Patton said, "You sound close to Jake."

"He's my uncle. My mom is his younger sister."

Santiago said, "Is he around? We'd like to talk with him for a minute if we could."

"I'll see if he's free."

Santiago watched Vicki walk away. "Well, she doesn't hold anything back, surely not a fan of Lisa. Waitress, hooker—Yancey's cousin by adoption sounds like she's more than a little messed up too."

"Could be. Remember what Hughes said about Yancey's mom? Maybe it just runs in the family."

A heavyset man approached the booth. "Vicki said you wanted to see me about Lisa? I'm Jake Cisco."

"I'm Alex Patton... my associate Michelle Santiago."

Santiago said, "Please join us for a minute."

Jake sat down beside Santiago.

Patton said, "We're trying to locate Lisa Fargo about a small inheritance, nothing huge but a tidy sum."

"She hasn't been to work for four or five days. Hasn't called in. Haven't heard from her."

"Has she worked here long?" Santiago said.

"About six years. I hate to admit it, but without her this place would be tits up." Jake's face turned red and he looked at Santiago. "Sorry Ma'am." He looked back to Patton. "You say the money she has comin' isn't real big?"

Patton smiled. "All things are relative, Mr. Cisco. Your niece said she had a trailer parked out back somewhere. Maybe we could leave a note on the door."

"Sure. It's the ugly mustard yellow one in the southwest corner of the lot. It would have a pathway beaten to the door if it wasn't sittin' on asphalt."

Patton said, "That popular, huh?"

"Sad but true. She's proud of it. Look around. I'm sure she's bedded almost every man in here except you."

Patton looked at Santiago, then Jake. "That covers a lot of territory."

Jake's face turned red. "Yes, it does."

After Jake left the booth, Santiago and Patton finished lunch, then walked out of the café accompanied by several smiling faces turned in Santiago's direction. She said, "I think those guys spend too much time on the road."

"Could be, but from a man's point of view it's hard not to notice a beautiful woman."

"It works both ways," she said.

They drove the short distance to the back lot. She said, "He was right, it's ugly."

Patton opened the screen and tried the door. "It's locked."

"I'll get some note paper."

He reached into his pocket, extracted two small instruments and placed them in the keyhole. "Wait, I must have been mistaken; it's open now."

"Did we just break and enter?"

"Not according to the Foreign Surveillance Act of 1978. With permission from a secretive court targeting terrorists we can break into homes, offices, cars... we can do all kinds of things."

She raised an eyebrow. "And Quarterman fits into that category?"

"Absolutely."

He pulled the door open. "Miss Fargo?" A cat rushed out the door as Santiago followed Patton into the shadows of the interior. His eyes became slits, lips pursed and nostrils flared. "Whew! Well, they said she's been gone about a week."

"It's bringing tears to my eyes," she said. "This place is a mess."

He pushed a foot through garments and fashion magazines scattered on the floor. "First time I ever saw a floor used completely as a closet."

Santiago went to the small combination TV/VCR and scanned the tapes stacked around it. "She liked chic flicks and porn if this is any indicator."

Patton shook his head. "I can't tell whether she packed for a trip or not. I'll check the bedroom." A moment later he called out, "Mitch, you've got to see this."

Santiago stuck her head into the bedroom. One wall was covered with posters. "They're well hung. Everything else is mirrored."

"And the room is neat compared to out there."

Santiago chuckled. "Her guests weren't much interested in the other room."

He pointed to a video recorder attached to a tripod. "Check this out. Maybe some of the guests wanted film of their prowess."

Santiago pulled the bedspread back. "Not much on sanitation. Let's see if there's anything on the redial." She picked up the receiver. "Dead."

"It's a cell phone world, Mitch. Let's get out of here."

As they left the mobile a large man in his late forties approached. "Is Lisa here?"

Patton said, "Not right now."

The man looked at Santiago and wet his lips. "Are you takin' her place?"

Santiago blushed. "Not hardly. Just visiting."

"Too bad. You could make some real money here." He turned and headed toward the truck parking area.

Santiago looked back at the trailer. "Wait… was there a tape in the video camera?"

"We better go back and check."

She said, "Isn't this a moment for chivalry?"

Patton took a deep breath, shook his head and went back in the bedroom. A moment later he called out, "Yes there is. We'll take it with us. Let me see if there are any other homemade videos." A few minutes later Patton came out gasping for breath. "Man, it stinks in there but I found a couple of tapes. We can watch 'em after dinner."

"Dinner? Come on, Alex, we just finished lunch and it's already 3:15. How about before dinner, the pool or whatever? If Quarterman's on these I want to know."

"No strip club tonight?"

"Not tonight. I want faces to put with the names... especially his name."

* * * * * * *

Claude and Nikki Braun tiptoed into their daughter's bedroom. Shadows surrounded Lindsey's quiet face as she huddled fast asleep in the king sized waterbed. He said, "She looks so peaceful."

Nikki put an arm around his shoulder. "She's home. She feels safe."

"She looks like a small child. I feel like we've lost the years of her youth, her becoming a young woman, all of it. I pushed too hard."

"Maybe, but she's cut from the same cloth as you, Claude. She's like you in every way."

He said, "She has the beauty, passion, and people skills of her mother. She's never been the egomaniac I am."

"Well, she has her father's stubbornness."

Lindsey stirred and opened her eyes, stretched and sat up. "I have visitors."

Braun stepped to the bedside. "Here, let me prop a pillow behind you. We didn't mean to disturb you. We just wanted to look in, see how you were doing."

Lindsey took a deep breath. "You didn't disturb me. What time is it? I feel like I've slept for a week."

Nikki said, "About 4:00 in the afternoon. You slept all night at Doctor Yount's clinic and went to sleep again as soon as we got you home. It's not surprising considering the medication and what you've been through."

Braun said, "How's the hand?"

Lindsey held it up in front of her and shook her head. "Sore but not throbbing or anything. If I was a guy I could claim something neat like losing it working on an engine or a hunting accident." She looked at her dad. "You know, a badge of honor kind'a thing."

He said, "We'll worry about badges later, Kid. Right now we just want you to get well."

"I'm not sick, Dad."

"You know what I mean. Then we'll do something together like a real family."

Nikki looked at her husband, surprise lighting her face. "What do you have in mind?"

"I don't have a clue, but it's obvious I've been ignoring my responsibilities as a dad." He looked at Nikki. "I haven't been a very good husband, either."

"Dad, are we talking quality time here, or some splashy vacation tied to a business trip?"

"Quality time, no business. In fact I'm thinking of retiring or at least taking a year off, a leave of absence, something."

Both women said in unison, "It'll be a leave" and all three of them laughed.

He said, "That's the first time we've laughed as a family in a long time."

Nikki nodded, her eyes welling. "We won't let it be the last. We have the opportunity for a new beginning."

Lindsey sat up. "Yeah, a fresh start. I love you both so much."

Braun wrapped an arm around Nikki's shoulders. "And we love each other."

Nikki's wiped her eyes. "Yes, we do."

Lindsey said, "I have an idea. How 'bout we take a long cruise, just the three of us?"

Braun smiled. "Good idea, and maybe go to Europe for a few months."

Nikki wrapped an arm around Braun's waist. "What if we chartered a boat to a south sea island and just took some time together, just the three of us without the bustle of other tourists and all the sightseeing?"

Braun said, "And a crew of at least two. I don't sail."

Lindsey nodded. "That's a neat idea. We could regroup as a family, like Dad said."

He said, "Reconnect yes, but first we have a few other things to take care of. The man who did this to you hasn't been caught yet. When he is we'll have to be around to testify."

"Right, Dad."

Nikki said, "If they catch him. A trial could be a year in the future with postponements."

Lindsey grinned. "Hopefully we'd be back before a year."

Braun said, "That's true. It will only take a week or so to get my office in order. They've run the company without me before."

Nikki said, "Lindsey, what about Doctor Rich? You said earlier you wanted to bring charges against him. Are you still so inclined?"

"Yes, if you two will go along with me. I'm sure the press will have a field day with that and I don't want to embarrass the family."

Braun said, "Good. I'm proud of you, and yes, of course we'll back you all the way."

Lindsey yawned. "It's nice to be home. I didn't think I'd ever see either of you again."

Nikki said, "We had the same fear. Now we're the hunters, or more exactly your Aunt Michelle is. She'll catch him."

Braun bent and stroked her hair for a moment. "You get some rest, Kid. We'll be here." He straightened and looked at Nikki. "I'm serious about changing my habits." He turned back to his daughter. "I guess you were right, Lindsey. It did take something serious to get my attention. I just wish it wasn't so damned harsh on you." He turned and headed for the door.

Lindsey watched her dad leave, then said to Nikki, "I'm sorry. I didn't want to hurt you two."

"Oh, you didn't. You made us better. Now get some sleep. Do you need another pill?"

"No, definitely not a pill. But I could really eat something... anything."

Nikki smiled. "Let me see what I can do about that."

* * *

Midday traffic was light when Santiago and Patton pulled onto Interstate 10 heading toward Phoenix. They'd stopped at several larger truck stops to ask about Quarterman and Fargo. "Lisa seems well established even if Yancey is still a mystery man," Patton said.

"They all seem to know her," Santiago said.

"Have you noticed drivers are more inclined to go the speed limit here than up north today?" he said.

"More police cruisers. See?" Santiago nodded toward a Department of Public Safety vehicle in the median.

"And there's another one going the opposite direction," he said.

"I have it on the highest authority— one of the desk clerks—that Eloy is a speed trap," she said with a grin. They covered the next thirty-five miles at a steady seventy-five miles per hour.

Her cell phone rang. "Santiago," she answered over the road noise.

"It's Sam, Mitch. Where are you?"

"We're just south of Chandler coming up on Exit 167. Why?"

"It's been a busy day here. Mario is taking his assignment seriously. He thinks he's found Lisa Fargo, or at least where she was yesterday."

"Where?"

"Yuma."

"How did he find her?"

"She used a credit card at a gas station on Interstate 8 just before the California border. Stone has a team flying down there now."

"Good." She glanced at Patton.

Sam said, "Have you heard the news in the last half-hour?"

"No. We haven't had the radio on today," she said

"Doctor Rich committed suicide sometime around noon. Authorities just released his name."

"Oh God!" Santiago swerved onto the shoulder running over several warning bumps.

"Hey, take it easy," Patton said.

"Sorry. Here, talk to Evans." She passed him the cell phone.

"What's going on out there?" Evans said.

"Nothing, Mitch just swerved a little," Patton said. "You pushed her buttons. What's happening up there?" Evans filled him in about Rich.

Patton said, "Jesus! Why?"

Evans said, "Mitch and I visited him yesterday. She told him we knew about the sexual abuse of Lindsey. I think he took the easy way out, no inquiry."

"And no jail," Patton said.

"That too. Strange what surfaces when you open Pandora's Box, Alex."

Patton said, "Well, guilt pushed him over the edge, not Mitch. So much for humiliation."

"That's cold, Alex."

"It's a cold world, Sam."

"What are you two doing when you get back?"

"A workout at DataFlex, catch a bite and watch videos."

"Videos?" Evans said.

"We found them at Lisa Fargo's place. We'd like to see if Quarteman is in any of them."

"Whose room?" Evans said.

"What do you mean whose room?" Patton said.

"Yours or hers?"

"Mine. You bugged hers. Besides, her absence might pull Quarterman out from under his rock."

"We'll talk later," Evans said. "I have Spears on another line."

"Right." The connection broke and Patton turned to Santiago. "Evans will probably see us at the gym. Then I guess we just watch dirty movies, eh?" He chuckled.

"Been there and done that on my last investigation. The workout sounds good." She nudged the accelerator and pushed traffic to the Baseline exit. "I think you're right about Quarterman. He'll come to us." Then she thought about Dr. Rich and shook her head. "Suicide... very strange. There must have been more girls involved than just Lindsey."

"It's not your fault, Mitch."

"I know. I was just thinking."

Patton said, "Well, Doctor Rich doesn't appear to be involved with Quarterman. I wouldn't concern myself with him too much."

Santiago said, "You're right. Maybe I'll give Alexandria Hughes a call. It will be difficult for Lindsey to bring closure to Rich. Maybe she'll have some suggestions."

"Could be. Just remember that she's a pipeline to Stone. Some folks think they're having a thing." He chuckled.

Santiago said, "You never know what goes on behind closed doors."

* * *

On his way back to Phoenix from Yuma, Quarterman called Veteran's Trust and spoke with his personal banker. "I want to transfer some funds. Half a million to the business account and another half-million to the Mexico City account just as we've done in the past." He provided the necessary account numbers and identification codes. "Will that be a problem?"

"Of course not, but we've had inquiries about your new account and deposit."

"I thought you might get some questions. Who knows, the money may sit there for a long time. I have other resources."

"So you do. Consider the transfers done."

"Thank you."

"And Yancey, we can always make other arrangements, as we have in the past."

"Yes. I'll be in touch." Quarterman broke the connection and glanced at a road sign coming up. "Highway 84, one mile." He checked the rearview mirror. "Lisa will be okay. All she has to do is watch what she says and keep quiet about the money." As a

Porsche passed him at a high rate of speed heading toward Interstate 10, he thought of Vicki again and laughed. "What's in your trailer, Cousin? Pictures? Videos? It's going up in smoke."

He passed the exit to 84 and continued east on Interstate 8 until it connected to Interstate 10, then headed to Eloy. *I want a new life with Santiago.* He passed a young couple hitchhiking. "Not today, kids. I have things to do."

He got off the interstate at Exit 208, drove east on Sunshine Boulevard, crossed the railroad tracks and pulled into a mom and pop hardware store next to a gas and go grocery. The faded sign over the front entry read *Founded 1925.*

An older man behind the long-outdated counters said, "Afternoon. Nice day."

Quarter man nodded. "That it is." He walked through the store, selecting a fifty foot length of half-inch rope, an eight-inch grappling hook and a one-gallon gasoline can. He approached the counter placing the items in front of the elderly clerk.

"Odd combination. Haven't sold one of those hooks in a couple of years."

"My kid left our pickup in a field when it was irrigated. This'll work and maybe he'll learn something crawling around in the mud." Both men laughed.

"Surprised he didn't want you to call a tow truck."

"He did, but he wanted me to pay the tab."

The clerk shook his head. "Kids today."

"Yeah," Quarterman said. "Boy has to be strong enough to solve his own problems, be a man."

"This here rope ain't gonna pull the truck."

"It's for a different task. The hook goes on a chain."

Quarterman paid for the goods, took them to the Caddie, opened the trunk and tossed them in, except for the gas can. He walked next door and filled the can at the gas and go. Walking back to the car he placed the can on the floor of the back seat, then drove west, backtracking toward Interstate 10. He pulled into Jake's parking lot and drove to the back area where Lisa Fargo's small trailer was parked. Three forty-foot trailers were resting on jacks nearby. "Nice cover." He drove around behind them and parked.

He carried the gas can to the door and tried his key. "Damn things been picked." He pushed the door open. The cat ran up to the door, sniffed the can and stayed on the porch. "Smart animal."

Quarterman stepped inside. "A lot of happy truckers bedded you in this little den in iniquity." He splashed gasoline around the living room. "What a mess." He went to the bedroom and repeated the process. He saw the empty shelves. "Shit... someone took your videos, Lisa." He walked back to the doorway where he encountered a heavyset middle-aged man.

In a gravelly voice the man said, "Lisa in there?"

"No. She'll be back in a while. Check back in a half-hour or so."

The man smiled. "Wait... are you Yancey?"

Your dumb luck, Pal. Quarterman paused for a moment, trying to place the man, then stepped to one side. "On second thought why don't you wait inside?"

The man stepped through the door and said, "Smells like gasoline."

Quarterman grabbed his head and chin and twisted hard. *Crack!* The man slumped to the floor as Yancey looked down. *Like I said, your dumb luck.* He pulled the body to the center of the small living room and splashed it with gasoline. He carried the can outside and put it in the Caddie, then returned to the doorway of the trailer. He looked around, then lit a match and dropped it on the gasoline. He walked to the Caddie, started it and drove away. Just as he started up the on-ramp for I-10, the trailer exploded. He glanced in the rear view mirror in time to see men running from Jake's toward what was left of the trailer.

He slowed for a moment, taking a last look toward Jake's through the driver's side window, then headed for Phoenix, paying careful attention to the speed limit. "There are ways to bring you around, Michelle. Tonight you're mine."

* * *

Santiago and Patton walked into his fourth-floor room, walked over to the lanai and checked the pool area. She said, "That was a great workout. It's nice to have someone involved at the same level of intensity."

He laughed. "Office types aren't into self-defense so much as trying to look good. You achieve both."

"Well, thank you. I try. Otherwise I'd be wearing those burgers and fries right here." She patted her backside.

"I do a lot of greasy food too. But hey, we're surrounded by luxury here. What better way to have a reality check than a workout? Anybody down at the pool?"

She looked out the lanai door. "Not that I'd be interested in but maybe a few who could catch your eye."

Patton walked over to the stack of videos they'd picked up earlier at Fargo's, inserted a cartridge in the VCR, and waved toward the couch. "Shall we? Then we can go downstairs and put our nose to the grindstone."

"Yes, let's see if we can spot Yancey." She sat down beside him, squinting at the screen. "My room doesn't have the sun reflection."

"No, but your room has bugs."

"True."

Patton flicked the remote and a blurry picture came on the screen. "That guy is a porker." He turned it off.

"No, leave it for a minute. Let's see if we can ID Lisa."

He flicked it back on and they watched for a long moment. "The camera seems stationary. No panning or close-ups... very fixed."

"Yeah, aimed right at the bed. Very romantic." She pointed. "There she is."

"She has a great body for a middle-aged woman. She obviously works out."

Santiago laughed and crossed her ankles. "Well, we both know where her gym is. Did you know a man's pupils double in size when he sees a nude woman?"

"Really? I'd better get some shades. There!" He hit the freeze frame. "Do you recognize the face? I don't."

She said, "Yes, I think I do. I've seen her around the hotel."

"Think she's the one who dropped off the package?"

Santiago nodded. "Could be. She's built for distraction. What did the bellman say? Money and cleavage, right?"

"Something like that, but this guy isn't Quarterman. I'm sure of that."

Patton hit the fast-forward but only the one couple appeared throughout. He inserted second tape and punched Play, then hit the Stop button. "This guy is too young for Quarterman."

She licked her lips. "No, no, not yet. Let's see if anyone else is on the tape."

Patton hit Play again. "Do women's eyes do the same thing when they see naked men?"

She laughed. "Not for the first specimen. I like to think we're more subtle and discreet."

"Are you sure that's the way you're looking now? It appears your subtlety and discretion are experiencing a momentary lapse."

She bit her lip while the tape played for another minute or two. "Maybe... let's move on."

Changing tapes and sitting back down, he pushed Play again. "What's number three got to offer?"

Santiago sat up. "Well, well... two men. It's getting more interesting to say the least."

Patton said, "One of them definitely isn't Quarterman. The other guy I'm not too sure about."

"Maybe he'll turn around."

"Hope so. Can't tell much from the back."

She smiled. "I wouldn't say that. He's firm, muscular."

"Clinical, Mitch. We're working here."

"Is that what's causing those intense looks and big pupils?"

His face reddened. "Maybe a brief distraction here and there. I haven't got a lot of experience watchin' this stuff. Are my pupils really giving me away?"

"Let's just say that so far you've had the best of it. There, he's turning around."

"That's not his face."

She continued to watch, then pointed. "No, but that is."

Patton hit the Pause button. "Too young."

She said, "Maybe for Quarterman."

Patton moved to the VCR. "Let's try another tape."

"Would you like something to drink? There's a vending machine down the hall."

He said, "Ice water would be good. Do you have change?"

"The machine takes bills. I'll be back in a minute."

Santiago returned a few minutes later with a diet soda and a plastic bottle of water. Handing the water to Patton she said, "How will you note tonight on your report?"

"Video surveillance sounds good. Besides, anything else would require too much explanation, especially when I have such a beautiful partner. What about your report?"

"I don't have to write one. I'm just keeping are notes for when Quarterman comes to trial."

"You think he will?"

"Yes. Don't you?"

Patton rubbed his temples. "I don't know, Mitch. Stone says we look at him as a terrorist because of his post-Vietnam activities. Military courts are different, not public, but save your notes. You could be called for testimony." He cleared his throat. "Anyway, let's check the fourth one." He hit Play.

An older, muscular man appeared underneath a writhing young woman. "That could be him. All we can see is the top of his head and longish hair with a lot of gray in it."

"I'd be surprised if he let himself be photographed, much less filmed."

"Maybe he didn't know. Look, there's another woman coming into the picture."

Patton hit Pause. "Are you sure it's a woman?"

"Look at the hands: thin, both rings are feminine, a woman's watch. Turn it back on."

"What's she holding?"

Santiago groaned. "It looks like a scarf. Jesus, is she gonna choke her?"

The young woman continued to straddle the man, holding her head high, body erect rhythmically rocking, her mouth alternating between wide smiles and wide open, teeth showing, her tongue wetting her lips.

The other figure came into view again, straddled the legs of the man and pressed against the back of the first woman. Then she wrapped the scarf around the younger woman's neck and leaned back, pulling hard. Patton stood. "Look, her face is getting red... *really* red. Oh, Mother of God!" Sweat appeared on his forehead and upper lip. He sat down again. "Jesus."

Santiago said, "But she's still rocking. No, she's choking now. Look at how she's grabbing at the scarf. And he's become even more agitated beneath them. Look at the way he's thrusting. This is sick."

Patton's breathing became harsh. "She's shuddering, Mitch. Is she fainting? Having an orgasm? Dying? What?"

Santiago looked away as the young woman collapsed on top of the man. "I'm going to be sick."

The man reached around the young woman, embracing her limp form, then kissed her. Santiago ran to the bathroom and vomited.

Patton remained on the couch, his attention riveted to the screen, a white-knuckled grip on the remote. Cold beads of sweat ran down his forehead and arms. "My stomach is turning too." He paused. "Mitch, she's not dead! Come here!"

Santiago returned to the room wiping her face with a washcloth. "What?"

He pointed at the screen. "She's not dead. She's moving, sitting up. My God, this is perverted."

She said, "They call it rough sex, but I've never heard of anything quite so bizarre."

"Me either."

She shook her head and continued to wipe her face. "Strangulation during orgasm?"

Patton's breathing returned to normal. "Sick bastards. Thrill seekers." The video continued to run, and soon the screen went blue.

Finally Santiago raised her eyebrows. "Do you think the murdered women were victims of rough sex? All of them had sex before death but showed no signs that it was forced."

"It sounds really gross, Mitch, but do you think he was literally mixing revenge with pleasure?"

"He's a sociopath, why not a sexual sadist too? Anything is possible. Pervert." She looked at the empty screen. "We still don't know if this guy is Quarterman or what he looks like."

"No, we don't, but I'm going to give Stone a call when we finish here. His people are looking for Lisa Fargo in Yuma and this video opens up a whole new line of questioning. She could be an accomplice to murder."

Santiago nodded. "Very possible."

They watched the remaining two videos without further incidents of violence, and Patton tossed the remote on the coffee table. He said, "At least we got to regain our composure after that one freaky tape. The last two were just good old fashioned sex."

She laughed. "Now you're sounding like an expert. They weren't even erotic."

"So what's next?"

"You call Stone while I run up to my room and change. We're going to the salt mine, remember?"

For a moment he frowned, then smiled. "Ah yes, the salt mine... the pool. Sorry, my mind was elsewhere. I've come to think of it as showtime."

"Show and tell, Big Boy."

"Don't you wish?"

"Your eyes dilate easier than mine. I'm subtle, remember?"

They both laughed.

"Yeah, subtle in a red string bikini."

* * *

The agent in charge answered his cell phone. "Stone."

"Patton here. Thought I should check in."

"Are you just taking a break from your sexy playmate or do you have something concrete?"

"She's a good cop. You know that from yesterday's briefing. She surprised us as I recall."

"Yes, I suppose, but I don't like interference."

"Do you think we can draw Quarterman out on our own?"

"No, probably not. The only possibility I see for us on our own is using his cousin, Lisa Fargo. We have some operatives trying to track her down in Yuma."

Patton smiled and took another look at the pool. "Yes, we know. Evans called us earlier today. He told us Spears, Santiago's whiz kid, had tracked her just as he had the money."

"We would have found the same data. He was just a little ahead of us... lucky."

"Santiago and I visited her trailer in Eloy today."

"Find anything?"

Patton filled in the details of the day's search. "One of the tapes was a rough sex number, strangulation. At first we thought the woman was dead. We think Lisa might have been the other woman in the tape. Thought it might open a new avenue for questioning when you locate her."

"But the woman wasn't dead?"

"No."

"Another line of questioning is good thinking. Did you do anything else at her place before you left?"

"Other than taking some videos the only thing we disturbed was the lock when I picked it. Why?"

"Someone torched the trailer this afternoon. Evans called and said his people picked it up on the net."

Patton said, "Probably Spears again."

"Yeah, well the body of a man was found in the ruins, burned beyond recognition. A trucker reported a man and woman at the trailer earlier, maybe an hour before the fire."

"That would be us. A man asked if Lisa was home."

"The owner of the café also commented on a couple looking for Lisa."

"Definitely us. We talked with him but he had no information we could use other than she's every trucker's friend and where the trailer was located. Do you think Quarterman is following us?"

"Could be. He's complex to say the least. Hughes says he's volatile, ready to pop. Watch out for yourself and your new toy."

"Detective Santiago," Patton said firmly as the connection broke.

* * * * * * *

As they walked into the pool area Santiago said, "This ought to be easy on your eyes. There's enough skin showing to cause a few heart attacks."

Patton surveyed the area. "It's a photo shoot for one of the skin mags doing their annual swimsuit edition. I saw the announcement on the lobby events board. The photographer and his crew will be working for the next few days with these glossy ladies."

She nudged him with an elbow. "Maybe you should check your pupils at the gate. Your recognition skills are working overtime."

"Dilation is good. I only have eyes for you. So pool or spa?"

"I feel like lounge-chairing my way into the evening."

Patton looked toward the far end of the pool at the woman they had observed the day before. "The trawler is back."

Santiago nodded in a young man's direction. "So she is, and she has a new target."

"What would a beautiful woman her age see in a guy that young?"

"Does the term cougar mean anything to you?"

"Yeah, and she's succeeding."

They found two lounge chairs near the spa, opened them full length and stretched out. "With all due respect, Alex, men aren't all that hard to attract."

He laughed while watching the trawler work. "I know. Give us a little skin, a smile and a soft voice and we think it's an invitation. But under that easy exterior we're much more challenging than women expect."

She glanced at him. "Really?"

"Do you think I'd be that easy?"

"Is the Pope Catholic? But I will give you high marks for perseverance in the line of duty."

He watched the photographer work. "That's what I like, an honest, down to earth woman. Do you think they're all models?"

"That and wannabes... which reminds me, I'm supposed to call my sister, Jill. I'll do that when we go in."

"Seeing a bunch of models reminds you of your sister? Sweet."

"She's in the business. This is what she does, model."

"Do you think all these guys are photographers?"

"The guy with the cameras, the lights and the assistant is the pro. Think of the others as prospectors. They've just found the end of the rainbow."

"I see," he said. "But it appears there is a bit of an estrogen imbalance as well, perhaps more localized than some of us would admit."

"Perhaps, but it was a long afternoon in your room even with the disturbing tape. This is more appealing."

Patton continued to look around. "I don't see any candidates for our guy. Do you?"

"Not yet. Most of these guys are twenty years too young to be him."

"There's a fair amount of gray in here too, but they look like executive types."

She nodded. "Drooling executives... but he's here somewhere. I can feel him looking at us, watching. Let's put the lounges closer together, rub a little, kiss a little, play a little, and fantasize a lot. Jealousy is as old as time."

"Show him something he can't have... I like that."

* * *

Quarterman passed through the gate a few minutes after Santiago and Patton had. He looked around the pool area and spotted her near the spa, stretched out on a lounge. "There you are... and you're in good company."

He took a chair near a young woman sitting on the edge of the pool, her feet in the water. who was seated alone. "Ah, another beautiful day in paradise... just beautiful."

She looked over the top of her sunglasses at him for a moment. "Yes, it is."

"Have you been in the water yet?"

"Yes. It's very nice... sensual."

"Sensual, I like the sound of that. I'm going to have some refreshment." He waved to the poolside waiter. "Would you like something?"

She looked at him in silence for a moment. "Is that a pickup line?"

"Do you want to be? It's kind of like sensual."

She looked him over and smiled. "It's a good way to meet people, and yes, a large OJ would be nice."

He held out his hand. "I'm Lance."

She stood and leaned toward him taking his hand. Her full breasts strained the top of her bikini. "Rachel. How do you do?"

He gestured toward an empty chair by his table. "Please, join me."

"Thank you."

The waiter arrived and Quarterman ordered two large OJ's.

"Yes, Sir."

"With ice."

"Of course." The waiter left.

Rachel said, "So what brings you to Phoenix?"

"Business and pleasure."

"In that order?"

"Not necessarily. And you?"

"Just a short break from the cesspool of everyday life."

"Cesspool. That's pretty strong coming from such a beautiful woman."

"Sometimes I just take myself on a little vacation, cut the stress."

"You don't look stressed."

"I'm not, really. I just want what I want."

"And what would that be?"

"Fun, meet new people, maybe find the right guy for a few days, maybe forever."

"I'm sure there are many men here who would like to make your acquaintance."

She shrugged. "But I've already met you and I like what I see."

"You're direct."

She teased her lips with the tip of her tongue. "Does that scare you?"

"Should it?"

"Those young studs...." She gestured toward the men hanging around the models. "They go for the skinny little hard-bodies. They have no experience. Most of 'em don't know how to really make love to a woman. An older man knows how to treat a woman, satisfy her."

Quarterman's looked at Rachel as the waiter arrived with the orange juice. He said, "You're somewhat worldly. I like that." He glanced at the waiter, signed the slip charging the drinks to his room and then glimpsed across the pool toward Santiago and Patton.

Rachel looked in the same direction. "They seem to be enjoying themselves."

"Yes, probably old friends."

She said, "They look more like lovers to me. They came in together nuzzling and chatting. Nice chemistry."

He shifted his weight and tapped the table. "Yes, it is. Maybe she has a bit too much skin showing."

Rachel watched Santiago and Patton kiss. "Skin works for me. It got your attention, and I think he likes it too."

He looked back at Rachel. "So it seems. Tell me about yourself. How does a nice young woman like you end up in a place like this?"

She laughed. "Now that's a pickup line, but I'm here by choice. In my real life I'm a grocery clerk. Once in a while I just want something different. Up until three years ago I was a biker bitch."

"A what?"

"Biker bitch."

"You really are direct."

"My boyfriend was a biker, one of the outlaw crowd. He liked the package." She looked at herself and smiled. "I liked sex, and we were young and dumb. Life was an adventure. Eventually I got tired of it."

"What, riding around the country and being free?"

"Getting banged by everyone in the club. From the time I was eighteen until I split I was everyone's piece of meat, sex toy, whatever."

"Sounds ugly."

"It got to be. At first I kind'a liked being banged all the time, but it got old. Finally I decided there are better things in life, even for a nympho. I wanted the big house, the flashy car, trips... you know. So after six years of being their bitch I just packed up and left one day with a trucker while they were out doing something that was probably illegal."

"And the big house?"

"Haven't found it yet but I've met some great men on the journey."

"You meet a lot of people being independent."

"So tell me, Lance, did you really want someone to just chat with or were you thinking bed?"

"Since we're being so direct, maybe a little of each. I didn't think someone you're your looks and age would be interested in a man my age, not with all the young guys around."

"You never know 'til you try."

He looked over her shoulder toward Santiago. "Nympho, huh? Have you been diagnosed as having nymphomania?"

She shrugged again. "I just know what I know. It doesn't bother me. What it means is I'll never have a permanent relationship. That may not be all bad, at least for me."

"Men could take advantage of you."

She nodded toward the redheaded woman Santiago and Patton had seen the day before. "I'd bet she's in the same boat."

Quarterman looked at the red headed woman. "Why do you say that?"

"It's just a feeling. She's a cougar. See how different she is from the couple across from us?"

"What couple?"

"The couple you keep looking at, the lady in the red bikini."

"Oh, her. She could never get my interest with you around."

"You are a silver-tongued devil. Anyway, she's occupied. So tell me, would you like to sleep with me?"

His eyes widened. "Yes, I think I would, but would you want to sleep with me?"

"Among other things. I don't think sex should be rushed. Foreplay is everything. And you?"

"We're like soul mates for a day."

"The last man I spent a whole day with was an artist. He used me as a model. Two weeks later he brought the painting by my apartment. It was beautiful. I took several pictures of it. Who knows... maybe someday I'll be famous like the Mona Lisa."

"She's not what comes to mind when I look at you."

He looked at Santiago and Patton again. They were kissing and touching each other.

She said, "And what comes to mind when you look at the woman in red?"

"They're being much too public in their display of affection. Her red bikini is even smaller than yours."

"Not really. We wear them to get a guy's interest, give him a hard-on. It usually works, wouldn't you agree?"

"The right bikini on the right woman can push a man's lust button, even more so if she's in the shape you're in."

"You've got me figured out. So what's your story? I can see you're middle-aged and in great shape. You must take care of yourself, and I like guys with dark hair."

"Why dark hair?"

"Men with dark hair are usually, you know, hung."

"I didn't know that. More is better?"

"Trust me, more is better."

"Well, as for my shape I'm a gym rat. Uncle Sam taught me many years ago the value of taking care of myself. My family is scattered around the country. No wife or kids, at least none that I claim. And about the brown hair, I don't want to lead you on too much, there is some gray. We live in a cosmetic world." He looked at her breasts. "I was just thinking...."

"Yes, they're mine. All of me is real... just another bikini body."

"And nicely presented if I do say so. I'd guess a size six to eight, five seven, one twenty-five give or take."

"You have the eye of experience."

"Speaking of eyes, yours are beautiful. I can see why the artist wanted to paint you. They're large, light green... a striking contrast to the dark eyebrows."

She laughed. "I don't think my eyes were what initially attracted him. I was in a bikini the day we met at another pool doing pretty much what I'm doing right now. So tell me, Lance, what was the first thing you noticed about me?"

"You're right, it wasn't your eyes."

"So you were thinking sex, right?"

His face reddened. "Probably. What was your first thought?"

"The same thing. We were both thinking of having a good time with a well-built partner. I still am."

He nodded toward Santiago and Patton. "Likewise, and those two aren't doing much to help matters."

"They'll end up in bed."

"Really?"

"That or they'll be doing it in public. I think the redhead has the right idea."

They both watched as the cougar and her new catch headed for the building.

He said, "I think we ought to finish our drinks and go inside."

She moved her hand onto his thigh, then reached above the waist of his trunks, touching the flesh just above the drawstring. "I think we should skip the OJ."

He looked across at Santiago. "Rachel, remind me later that I have someone to call... much later."

They stood and walked to the pool gate hand in hand. She said, "You place or mine?"

He watched Santiago and Patton embrace. A burst of heat surged through his loins. He paused and looked at Rachel. *It's almost our time, Michelle.* "Yours. I'll join you in a few minutes. I have to get something first. You're in...."

"3007, and I'll order up some champagne."

"A good plan. I'll be there in ten minutes."

He walked into the building catching an elevator just before it closed.

Rachel was left standing, waiting for another. "Must be after his little blue pill."

An older couple were waiting beside her. The man smiled at Rachel while the woman glared at the elevator arrows.

* * *

Lisa Fargo drove into Jake's Truck-O-Rama at sunset. She drove behind the restaurant, passing several news vans and police vehicles parked near the charred remains of what had been home. Her breathing was forced more with each step. Yellow plastic tape surrounded the area. A Pinal County Coroner's van was parked nearby. A sheriff's deputy kept curious onlookers away from the scene. Two television news trucks from Tucson and Phoenix were parked off to one side where a half-dozen men and women were drinking coffee from paper cups.

She searched the surrounding faces for Aaron Martin but didn't find him. Tears welled in her eyes as she looked on. A chill ran through her body. The acrid odor of the fire became stronger the closer she got. She shook her head as she neared the yellow tape. "What on earth has happened? This is terrible." She called out, "Tabby? Tabby?"

A man behind her said, "Can I help you, Ma'am?"

She turned to face a deputy. "What's going on?"

"A fire, Ma'am. A man died in it. We're asking folks to stay back and let the coroner's people finish their work."

She blinked her eyes. "A house fire? This looks like a crime scene from some TV show."

"It could be, Ma'am. Do you know the woman who lives here?"

She looked at the ground and swallowed. *They'll be looking for me.* "No, no I don't. Nobody lives here, not any more. I just saw all this activity... kind'a unusual for Eloy."

The deputy turned toward another couple coming toward the scene. "Please folks, just stay behind the tape."

Fargo said, "How'd it start?"

The deputy turned and faced her. "Don't know, Ma'am. What we have has been on the news."

Two men approached waving identification card holders and said something to the deputy without stopping. The deputy turned to another officer near the burned out trailer door. "FBI, they want to talk to...."

Lisa Fargo turned and began to walk away. She jumped as warm fur brushed against her right leg. "Tabby, thank God you're safe."

She looked back toward the FBI men and watched. One of them men asked a woman in a white lab coat, "Do we know who the man is?"

The woman took off a pair of latex gloves and tossed them into a special trash bag. "Not yet, but his neck was broken. That's all we've got. The place is a mess. Fortunately they got the fire out pretty fast or we'd have even less to work with."

Fargo walked to her car with Tabby following. She opened the door and got in, brushing the cat back. Tears filled her eyes. "Jake will take care of you."

She tuned in the radio as she pulled away. "Nothing but damned music when you want the news. I have to get out of here."

She drove through the parking lot to Sunshine Boulevard and headed west toward the freeway. Rather than turn toward Phoenix she drove across the Interstate 10 overpass and pulled off into a gas station near the Tucson on-ramp on the other side took out her cell phone and called the restaurant.

"Jake's Truck-O-Rama."

"Hi Vicki. This is Lisa. Is Yancey around?"

Vicki paused for a moment. "I haven't seen him. Where are you?"

"On the road."

"Have you heard about the fire?"

"What fire?"

"Your trailer went up in smoke this afternoon, fast and furious. I'm so sorry. They found a man's body in it."

"Yancey?"

"I don't know. Jake doesn't think so. He saw something like a class ring on the guy's hand when they brought the body out before they covered it."

Fargo said, "Well, Yancey didn't wear jewelry, but—"

"I can't hear you, Lisa."

"Nothing. You're breaking up a little too. Has anyone been asking for me?"

"Several. You've been gone for awhile."

Tears ran down Lisa's cheeks. "Yeah, I know. I mean today, this afternoon, not a trucker?"

"A couple was in around lunch, then one guy early this afternoon. The last one said he'd wait around for you."

Fargo said, "He said he'd wait?"

"You don't suppose he's the one in the fire?"

Fargo swallowed hard. "Could be. We're still breaking up here, Vicki."

"When will you get back?"

"I don't know for sure. It doesn't sound like there's much to come home to."

"Your friends are here and Tabby is running around. Want to talk to Jake?"

"I'll have to call back later."

She cut the connection and threw the phone on the passenger seat. "Damn you, Yancey. Why? After all we've been through and done together, why this?"

She wrapped her arms around her body and twisted in the car seat. "I loved him."

A truck rolled by, its air horn breaking into her world. She looked up and saw a familiar face, his arm waving as he passed.

She waved back as she muttered, "You'll pay for this, Yancey Quarterman."

She slammed the car into gear, pulled back onto Sunshine, passed the Tucson on-ramp on her right and re-crossed the freeway overpass, then made a left turn at the I-10 on-ramp to Phoenix. "You'll pay dearly."

* * *

Quarterman was standing at the open lanai slider door of his bedroom looking down at the pool. "You're beautiful. What in hell do you see in that guy?"

Patton took Santiago's hand and kissed it while looking into her face. She smiled at him and Quarterman moaned. "You lucky bastard. I should be doing that. She'll love me. I can make her love me."

He went to the bathroom sink, filled a water glass, took two aspirins and returned to the slider. He sipped the water, his gaze never leaving Santiago and Patton. "Do you sleep with him? Of course you do... for now."

He felt a little lightheaded, dizzy. He spit the mouthful of water back into the glass and set in on the table. "Tepid, foul tasting stuff. I'll be a few minutes late, Rachel... just a few."

Patton looked around the pool area smiling, continuing to talk with Santiago. He looked in the direction of the models, occasionally pointing.

Quarterman made a fist. "You should be concentrating on her, you fool, not the bimbos with the photographers. You'd have my undivided attention, Michelle. I'd be like Rachel's artist lover, sketching you, painting you, loving you. No interruptions."

Santiago ran a fingernail down Patton's thigh and a chill ran up Quarterman's back. "Christ, do all women do the finger thing? I feel the electricity surging through my body, Michelle." He shifted his gaze to Patton. "Damn fool, you're still watchin' the bimbos."

Santiago and Patton continued to chat, smile and gawk.

"You could be a model, my model, Michelle. I would paint us side-by-side, touching, loving, having fun, sharing. You don't need him."

Quarterman checked his watch, then glanced at the phone. "6:51... I'll be a few more minutes, Rachel."

He stretched while taking one more look at Santiago, then stepped away from the curtain. "Man, I am tired."

He bent over the table, reaching for the water glass, then quickly straightened up. "Wow... must'a come up too fast." A prickling sensation raced over his body for a few seconds. He shook his head. There was a spinning sensation, and then it ceased. "Damn malaria... you haven't visited in years. I'm gettin' too old for this shit."

He turned and sat down on the bed, then took a deep breath and turned on the television with the remote. A picture of firefighters and policemen filled the screen as the commentator said, "Sheriff's office is treating the Eloy fire death as a homicide. The victim's name has not been released. Authorities are looking for Lisa Fargo, the owner of the trailer."

Quarterman hit the Off button. "This'll piss you off, Lisa, but you'll get over it."

He took another deep breath, then stood and walked through the sitting room to the doorway. He looked at the well-traveled backpack sitting on the floor of the open closet. "Old habits die hard, but they do die."

He walked out the door empty handed. "Rachel, room 3007," he hummed. "Later tonight I'll be seeing you, Michelle."

* * *

It was after eight when Lisa Fargo exited Interstate 10 onto Chandler Boulevard and pulled into the Freedom Estates Motel on 54th. The parking lot was sparsely filled. When she entered the lobby a young man wearing a blue blazer with the name of the motel on his breast pocket was behind the counter.

"I'd like a room for the next few nights."

"Yes Ma'am." He handed her a registration card and watched as she completed it. "Will that be cash or charge?"

"Cash."

He looked at the registration card. "I'll need a deposit of $75.00, please, Miss Martin."

She handed the man a hundred dollar bill. "Of course."

He set her keys and change on the counter. "Room 211 is just around the corner and up one flight of stairs. If there is anything further I can do for you just ring the front desk."

"Thank you," she said.

Once in the room she sat down on the bed and took a deep breath. "God what a day." Taking a note pad and pen from the nightstand and wrote, *Call the cops. Yancey and Santiago.* She put the pad down. "No, I'll just find you, Yancey. Why did you kill Aaron? Bad enough you burned up my stuff, but to kill him... you'll have to kill me too."

She sat up and dangled her feet over the edge of the bed. "If I wasn't with you on some of those killings I'd call the cops right now."

She went to the window and looked out into the parking lot. "I could call anonymously. That would frost you... but no, you'd know and turn me in too. God I hate you." She looked down and kicked the flight bag. "Why did you give me so much money? Of course, you didn't know about Aaron then."

Sitting down on the bed she called the front desk. The clerk answered on the first ring. "Yes, Miss Martin, how may I help you?"

"Where is the nearest library?"

"The closest is the Sunset branch on 49th and Ray Road, but the downtown Chandler branch may have more selections."

"Would it have computer access for the public?"

"Both branches do."

"Thank you."

She hung up. "I could tip off Braun to your whereabouts. You're gonna pay for this, you bastard."

She looked up the number of the Oasis Hotel and dialed.

"Thank you for calling the Oasis Hotel and Golf Resort. My name's Yvonne. How may I help you?"

"Room 5004, please."

The woman sounded young. "One moment.... I'm sorry, there's no answer. Would you like to leave a message?"

"Yes."

"Record your message at the tone; press one when you're finished."

A faint beep sounded in her ear. "Yancey, why is Aaron dead? I'm angry, very angry. My hands are trembling. I hate you." She pressed one, then hung up, rolled over, buried her face in the pillow and sobbed.

* * *

Evans and Spears walked into the Oasis Lounge at 8:45. Patton pointed. "There they are." As they approached the table, Evans said, "Mitch, Alex, it's been quite a day."

Santiago looked up at them. "That it has. Sorry Mario, I know you thought this would be a social occasion but duty calls. This is Alex Patton, a friend and associate."

Patton stood, extending his hand. "A pleasure. Mitch tells me you're a genius with a computer."

Spears smiled. "Thank you, dear lady. And you, Mr. Patton, are you with the FBI?"

"Yes. All of us are working together on this case. Please, sit down."

A waitress came and took their orders.

Santiago said, "Good job on tracking the money, Mario. Has he tried to get it yet?"

"Not exactly. He moved some money from another account to Mexico City, then again to Switzerland. The Swiss system is so far impossible for me to breach. I don't have a clue what's going on. It's my understanding the government can get some information."

Patton shook his head. "Not much of a chance on that. This is a clandestine operation."

Evans said, "Too bad. We already know Quarterman's a killer. We also think he broke that man's neck in Lisa Fargo's trailer and set the fire. So far we haven't been able to connect the man to Quarterman, but there's got to be a link."

Santiago said, "Do we know who he was?"

Evans nodded. "His name is Aaron Martin, a salesman with a history of some small time cons."

Santiago's face became pale. "Aaron Martin?"

Evans said, "Yes. Why?"

"I had dinner with him a couple of nights ago. We shared a table in the dining room when it was crowded. I called you for a background check."

Evans said, "Yes, you did. Mario was setting up a possible tracking scheme for the ransom when you called."

Patton said, "Was he trying to get information from you?"

She smiled. "No, we simply ate dinner and parted company. We had separate checks. He may have been hunting but I wasn't in the game plan. If he was a con it would figure I just didn't look wealthy enough. You know, no sparkly things."

Evans frowned. "So how did he end up with Lisa Fargo?"

Patton said, "We may never know. Do we have anything new on her?"

Spears shook his head. "Not since the credit card was used in Yuma."

Evans looked at Patton. "Your people didn't find anything down there today, either. Stone called and said it was an automated gas pump. Nobody saw her, nothing. He'll be getting some video to check but that'll take time. Furthermore, she has no criminal record."

Spears shrugged and looked at Santiago. "Maybe he just met her and liked her. It happens."

Evans laughed. "Yeah, and I believe in the tooth fairy too. I just don't like this setup. Quarterman is as dangerous as anyone can be."

Santiago said, "Maybe when we find her we'll get some information."

Patton shook his head. "*If* we find her. She could be dead too."

The drinks arrived and a pale Mario Spears sipped his scotch water. "This man really is dangerous, isn't he?"

Santiago said, "Very, but you're safe. He doesn't know who you are."

Mario sighed and looked at Santiago. *It wasn't me I had in mind.*

Santiago looked at Evans. "Does he?"

Evans said, "No. In fact I haven't heard from him since, you know. It could be he's so focused on Mitch he's just not giving Stone much attention. I'm sure he plans on disappearing again."

Santiago said, "We don't have much, do we?"

Patton looked around the table. "No. You're our only link to this guy."

She said, "Too bad we're in such a big hotel. Even the computer generated picture hasn't helped. You can bet he's altered his appearance since the kidnapping. It's another way for him to demonstrate that he's in charge. He lets us see what he wants, and nothing more."

Patton nodded. "I agree."

"Sam, if he contacts you like he said, let him know Alex and I are sharing a room. I want to push his buttons." She looked at Patton and smiled. "Tell him it's Alex's room."

Evans smiled. "And if he should ask about your room?"

"I'm keeping it for appearances and DataFlex is paying all my bills."

"Will do, but Mitch... any chance you would consider dropping this case and leaving it to Stone?"

"No."

Evans stood and tossed a fifty on the table. "I didn't think so. I have to get going, late dinner with the wife. Drinks are on me."

Patton stood too. "I need to make a stop myself. Excuse me for a minute."

Santiago looked across the table. "Right now it's all work, Mario."

He laughed. "I thought I was coming here for a social drink with you, maybe a bit of clubbing. Then old Evans is saying he'll meet me here, something about the next level of security operations. Not what I had in mind but it's what you do, isn't it?"

She grinned. "This isn't what I had in mind when I came down here either, but look around. I see several available young women. Maybe you should come by tomorrow at lunch. Another day of picture taking is on tap for some skin mag's swimsuit edition."

He finished his drink and grinned. "Maybe I will."

"You're a new friend, Mario. There's too much at stake right now. Maybe you can show me around some other time."

"I think I've heard that line before. At least you didn't say you're too old for me."

"If I go to work for the company you'll probably hear that line too." They both laughed.

Patton returned to the table. "You two seem like a jovial couple."

"Mario's trying to decide which babe to hit on."

Patton said, "Anyone but the lady across from me."

Spears looked at Patton. "This man... Quarterman... he kills on impulse but he also seems selective in some way."

Patton shook his head. "Anyone, anytime."

Spears said, "Not Mitch... I don't think he'd kill her. If he wanted to do that it would already have happened."

She said, "That's why I'm still here, Mario. It's a game of conquest or something to him. My job is to draw him out."

Patton said, "It's an obsession. He's a sociopath. He's capable of killing whenever he wants, and he'll continue to until he's stopped."

Mario finished his drink and left. Santiago and Patton stayed at the lounge and enjoyed the piano bar for another hour. Patton frequently looked around the room.

"Take it easy, Alex. If he's here we want him to see us as a couple, not a team looking for someone."

"I'm usually not that obvious."

They touched hands across the table. "Let's head up to my room. I need to pick up some things for morning. The rest of the night we'll spend on your turf. We don't want any calls interrupting us, do we?"

"No, but wouldn't impulsive lovers skip packing?"

She smirked. "Yes, but my bathroom and lanai have the bugs, remember?"

"Always working, aren't you."

When they reached her room, Santiago ignored the blinking message light and pointed toward the lanai. They stepped outside and embraced. "It's a beautiful night, Alex." They kissed.

"It is. I can hardly wait to get to my room."

"It'll only take me a minute."

Patton waited on the lanai.

Santiago quickly returned carrying a small bag. "A thong and a tooth brush."

"A toothbrush in the bedroom?"

She teased her teeth with the tip of her tongue. "An extra. You never know when you'll need it."

Patton pointed at the phone.

"Oh, give me a minute. Looks like I have a message. Probably someone from DataFlex. I have a job offer."

"Hello, Aunt Michelle. I see you're still out for the evening."

She looked at Patton and mouthed, "It's him."

"I'll call tomorrow morning around 9:30. Maybe I'll catch you on your cell if you're answering it these days. We have much to talk about." There was a static pause. "I'm a different man, Michelle. Sleep well."

Patton watched as Santiago swallowed and cradled the phone.

She placed an index finger over her lips and stepped to the open lanai slider. In a husky voice, she said, "Shall we? I'm hot to trot." She closed the screen door.

DAY FIVE

Quarterman called Evans' home just after midnight. He answered on the fourth ring in a gruff, tired voice. "Yeah?"

"Is it too late for you, Sam?"

Evans recognized Quarterman. "It's late. What do you want at this hour?"

"I can't seem to find Michelle. I have her on tape from earlier this evening saying she was going to stay with her friend."

"That's correct. His name is Alex Patton."

"Is he staying at the hotel?"

"Yes, but I don't have his room number."

"You've provided more than enough information, Sam. Perhaps I'll call her in the morning; wouldn't want to bother them." Quarterman laughed. "I wouldn't want you to bother 'em either. It could be bad for everyone. You understand?"

"Yes." The connection broke.

Quarterman walked to the door of the lanai overlooking the pool. Two late night swimmers were bathed in shadows and pool lights. "Nobody is home in your room, Michelle. You always leave your slider open five stories up. Who would bother you?"

He chuckled to himself, went to the closet, retrieved the grappling hook and rope, and tossed them across the room to the slider. He picked up his worn backpack and walked to the dresser, stuffed a change of clothes into it and fetched personal items from the bathroom, packing them into a shaving kit. He pushed the shaving gear into the pack and dropped it on the floor near the slider, then placed his old but reliable .45 automatic on top.

Turning off the room lights he dragged a chair to the opening of the lanai and sat down. He secured the rope to the hook. He noted the grounds security guard walking through the courtyard and talking briefly with the swimmers at 12:30. "When is your next pass?" he said, his face hidden in the shadows of a palm.

He went to the closet and changed into tan slacks and shirt. He would blend in nicely with the stucco walls even if someone was outside later. He returned to the chair. At 1:00 a.m. the security guard passed through again. A few minutes later the swimmers retired for the night. He checked his watch and waited.

At 1:31 a.m. the guard made a third pass through the courtyard.

Quarterman smiled. "Right on time." Picking up the hook and rope, he stepped to the lanai, took another look around the courtyard and tossed the hook to the roof. Pulling the rope firmly to ensure the hook was secure, he checked the grounds one last time, then climbed to the roof, wearing the backpack and with the .45 automatic stuck in the back of his pants. It took less than thirty seconds. He pulled the rope up behind him and moved across the building to the opposite side, positioning himself above Santiago's room. He saw a pipe running across the building near the edge of the roof bulkhead. He pulled it with both hands, testing its strength. "Good." He looked over the edge of the roof into the parking lot between the Oasis and Baseline Road. "I had a better view, Michelle...."

He untied the hook, then slid the rope under the pipe pulling the strands even, doubling their thickness. "This will work beautifully."

At 2:07 a.m. a grounds security guard passed through the parking lot riding a golf cart. At 2:18 a.m. another security guard on foot came through the parking lot walking along the sidewalk. He watched the golf cart pass by again at 2:35 and the security man on foot again at 2:46. Same route.

Quarterman slipped the doubled rope over the edge so it passed Santiago's lanai. He climbed over the edge, gripping the doubled strands, and began to descend.

A loud voice said, "It's a beautiful night, eh?"

Quarterman froze, suspended just below the roof, his body pressed against the building. He looked over his shoulder. *Shit! They're back. It must be break time. Don't look up.*

One of the men said, "You got a smoke?"

The other man took a pack out of his shirt pocket. "You gotta start buying your own, man. These damn things are expensive."

Quarterman watched, sweat covering his face. *Give him the damn thing.* One of the men lit a cigarette. Then they both climbed into the cart and drove off. "It's about time." He slid down the remaining fifteen feet to Santiago's lanai, swung onto the deck and pulled the rope after him.

The screen was locked but it easily gave way. The lanai door was wide open. Entering the sitting room he scanned the area, then moved to the bedroom. He returned to the sitting room, checked the bathroom and the hallway door. "A woman of your word... gone for the night."

He took the backpack off and put it beside a chair near the lanai facing the hallway door. "Ah, this feels good. I can wait, but not too long."

He touched his groin.

* * *

By 9:00 a.m. Quarterman was pacing Santiago's room. Housekeeping had roused him an hour earlier and he'd sent the middle-aged Hispanic woman on her way with a good tip and instructions not to come back until after lunch. At 9:04 he called Santiago's cell phone.

She answered on the second ring, anticipating that he'd call early.

Quarterman's voice was soft. "Michelle?"

A chill ran down her spine as she looked at Patton and mouthed, "It's him."

Patton focused on Michelle.

"Yes. You're early."

"I missed you yesterday. Did you and your friend get together?"

"We did at the pool, twice. He likes the red bikini."

"Most men would."

"I'm sure of that. So you missed our little poolside encounter. Too bad, he rubbed lotion into my skin, touching me all over."

"I bet his hands were firm."

"Actually they were firm, and inviting and gentle. So what's on your mind this morning? Is it time for another obscene call?"

"No. I don't want to offend you."

"That's a change from yesterday. I'd never have guessed."

"That was a different me... a me I want to leave in the past."

"Really? What a difference a day makes. Or are you getting a little nervous?"

Patton sat down beside Santiago tilting his head to hear what little he could from the cell.

"Can we just talk?"

"We are."

"I mean in person. I want to be different. I want you to know me in a different way."

"How so? Flat on my back, maybe with my neck broken?"

"You know I've done bad things... terrible things."

"That's not exactly news."

"But I have changed."

"How?"

"To normal... I want to be like other people... other men."

"With your track record, that's a reach."

"Please, just listen."

Santiago looked at Patton, raising an eyebrow.

He mouthed, "Let him talk."

"The killing in Vietnam wasn't evil. It was my duty to kill the enemy." He waited a moment in silence. "Are you there?"

"I'm listening."

"Good."

"And what about the women?"

"I know it was wrong. They made me do it."

"Who made you do it? How?"

"The women. Anger. They made me angry, something I can't always control."

"That's a heavy price to pay for putting out," she said. "How did they make you angry? What did Barbara Ratafia do to make you kill her?"

"Who?"

"God, you don't even know your victims' names. She was the girl at Seaside, Oregon."

"She teased and taunted me. She made men want her. She demanded things. She was like an auction item, going to the highest bidder."

"So she wanted more from you than you wanted to pay?"

"So you *do* understand. She was young, beautiful, and available, but demanding."

"How much did she demand?"

He said in a husky voice, "She didn't want money. She challenged my manhood. Could I keep up with her, satisfy her like younger men and other older bulls she'd been with?"

"She taunted your ego?"

"Yes, always commenting on liking mature men with stamina."

"And your stamina... did it make the grade?"

"Of course!" he snapped. "I have more energy than most men any age."

"So you don't need any little blue pills. Bravo. But really, killing a woman during sex can't be that hard, not if she's a willing player. She just didn't realize how sensitive you are. The whole thing seems cowardly to me."

"Nobody has ever called me a coward. Nobody."

"Barbara never had the opportunity. What about the girl at Pismo Beach?"

"Same thing, the challenge, can you make the grade."

"Spokane?"

"Your sources are good, but those are all in the past, a different me."

"So why not find playmates who aren't as demanding and challenging? Perhaps a more experienced woman?"

"You mean older?"

"There seems to be a lot of experienced women around, and not all of them are older." She smiled. *You should know Sierra.* "It's not like you're some young guy groping his way through life."

"Women in their early twenties to mid-thirties are the most beautiful creatures on Earth. Why do you think your friend Braun keeps changing wives? He's been in the tabloids for years."

"He doesn't kill them."

"No, but he wants the same thing: a beautiful woman—*his* beautiful woman—on his arm."

"Women, all women, have brains. We're not just eye candy even if some men think we are."

"I know. Women learn at an early age how to manipulate men to get their way."

"That's not what I mean, Yancey. Men and women, normal men and women, are much more to each other than a trophy. When two people love each other they share… they support, trust, and nurture each other."

"I don't understand, but I'm trying."

"Real couples don't play masters and slaves. They work, play and help each other grow as individuals and as couples."

She paused and looked at Patton.

He was smiling.

"Why didn't you go to the rehab clinic after Vietnam rather than becoming an MIA?"

"It was a nuthouse. They wanted to send me away. I knew it."

"It was a place where people would have helped you get to where you now say you want to be. So why the sudden change?"

"You're going too fast for me, Michelle. Just listen. I admit I've had problems. I've enjoyed revenge killing. Sometimes I can't control myself."

"No shit," she said. "So what are you willing to do about it? Turn yourself in?"

"Last night I made love to a woman, a demanding sexual creature. She did many of the things those others did."

Santiago looked at Patton, the blood draining from her face. "Did you kill her?"

"No. No I didn't. I wanted to. It would have been easy, like the others, but I didn't do it."

"That's a start. Did you do anything else to her?"

"No. We made love and parted company, both smiling."

"You mean casual sex, don't you?"

"There's a difference?"

"Huge. That's what I've been talking about."

"I've never thought about it. I guess I've never had that kind of feeling... not until now."

"Now?" She looked at Patton.

"I know it sounds strange but I have feelings... for you."

"You don't even know me. You're a killer. I'm a cop. It's not a good mix."

"I know, I know. I just want you to know me before I leave."

"Where are you going?"

Quarterman chuckled. "Now that's a cop question. I've been giving the CIA and FBI fits for years. I'm ready to retire. Where? Someplace they'll never think of looking."

"So how do you plan to meet me?"

"I'll get back to you on that later today."

"You know I'll report this call."

"I know. I just want you to wait until we talk this afternoon."

"Will you give yourself up?"

"No, but I won't hurt you. I promise." The connection broke.

Santiago looked at Patton. "This guy is getting stranger by the hour. Obsession, fixation, and now he thinks he loves me?"

"Just keep in mind what Hughes said about him. It added up to psycho-unstable. I'm going to shower so we can be ready when he decides to get in touch again. And we need to let Stone know about the call."

"Get your shower. I'll call Stone."

"Thanks, that couch killed me last night."

"I think the thought of my being here is driving Quarterman up a wall. I'm sure he was watching us yesterday, especially in the afternoon. I just felt it."

"So why would he lie about it?" Patton called from the bathroom.

"I think it was a test to see whether I'd tell the truth. I think he's still trying to figure out our relationship, yours and mine."

"He's not necessarily alone on that issue either."

Quietly, she said, "No, he's not...."

"When I'm done shall we eat in the room or down in the coffee shop?"

"We're supposed to be high profile; downstairs. While you shower I'm going to run up to the room and get my phone charger."

"Wait a couple of minutes and I'll go with you."

"I'll be back before you're done." She left the room.

* * *

After talking with Santiago, Quarterman stored his gear in the closet by the entry and went to the bedroom. He sat down on a chair and faced the bed, looking at himself in the mirror on the far wall. "You'll drop in sometime today. When you do, you're mine. Jesus, I need a shave."

He was on his way toward the closet by the exterior door when the lock clicked. He stepped back into the bedroom and pressed his back against the wall. As the door latched shut Santiago came into the bedroom.

With her back to him he pointed the .45 at her and said, "Sit down and be quiet."

Santiago spun around. Her mouth dropped open and her eyes bulged. A chill shot up her spine. Her left leg began to shake at the knee. "Quarterman?"

"We finally meet. I suggest you do as I say. We don't want any innocent bystanders getting hurt, do we?"

"No." She sat down as directed. "You called from my room?"

"Yes. I spent the night waiting. Where is your friend?"

She rubbed her fingertips against the palms of her hands. "Downstairs in his room."

He gestured for her to stand. "Good. Let's go before he misses you. I'll do whatever is necessary to get you out of the hotel."

She swallowed, pressing her hand against the thigh of her trembling leg. "This is a strange way to get to know me."

"Momentary. I meant what I said. I do want you to know me as a different man... a changed man, a normal man."

"We could talk here. I could call Alex and tell him I'm busy for a little while."

"He wouldn't buy that any more than I would. It would be best if we left before he comes up here and you live to regret the outcome."

He gestured toward the door. "When we leave I'll be holding your arm. We'll go downstairs and through the lobby. When we get to my car you'll get in and fasten the seat belt. I'll also tie a length of rope around your waist to the seat. Don't try to attract anyone's attention. They'll get hurt."

She nodded. Quarterman slung the backpack over his left shoulder and placed a towel over the hand holding the automatic. They both jumped as the alarm radio went on. "Turn it off."

He gestured toward the bedroom door and watched as she walked to the nightstand.

"I set it for 9:30, but my plans changed."

"Let's go."

* * *

Sam Evans arrived at Santiago's hotel room within minutes of Alex Patton's call. The room was undisturbed except for the forced screen. Evans called Braun while Patton contacted Stone's office.

"Sam, what's up?"

"She's gone. Disappeared in the last twenty minutes."

"Mitch?"

Evans choked. "Yes."

"How?"

"She left Patton's room while he was shaving, ran up here for something and vanished."

"Any signs of a struggle?"

"None. My bet is he was waiting for her. The screen on the lanai was forced. Patton says Quarterman called her only minutes before on her cell. He wanted to meet with her and talk, said he'd call back later today."

Braun said, "That bastard. I'm sure you're right. He had to be waiting for her. What now? Ransom? I'll pay it."

"This isn't about money. This feels sinister... even evil."

"Quarterman's obsession?"

"Exactly."

"What does Patton recommend?"

"He's talking with Stone. They'll send a team to go over the room. Stone will review what little he has and try to get a line on where Quarterman would take her. They don't have much."

"I want you to work with them."

"No," Evans said sharply. "I'll keep in touch with them but I want to work independently. I know how this guy thinks, how covert players work, and I'm not bound by red tape."

"I understand. Your background is why I hired you in the first place."

"I want to come out and talk to Lindsey. She might know something none of us is aware of, not even her. Maybe something he said or did. Who knows? If we don't find him fast he'll disappear and Mitch along with him."

"Have you called the police?"

"Stone still insists on calling the shots, no local interference. I think Patton would take any help we could get right now."

"I'll have Ray House file a missing person's report with the Phoenix police and the county. Considering she's already tipped 'em about a serial killer they'll recognize her name."

"Thanks, Mr. Braun."

"Lindsey will be awake when you get here. We're waiting on you and I know you'll find Mitch."

"I'm on my way."

"And Sam, I'll call Mitch's detective friend in Seattle. Maybe this will change his mind about coming down."

* * *

Lisa Fargo left a message on Quarterman's room phone at 10:15 a.m. from the lobby of the Oasis Hotel. "I know you killed Aaron at the trailer. You destroyed my opportunity for happiness. Aaron and I deserved the chance to become the family I never had. You'll pay for this."

She then called Santiago's room. Patton answered.

"Miss Santiago, please."

"May I say who is calling?"

"A friend."

"Are you Lisa Fargo?"

"Yes."

"Please, don't hang up. Miss Santiago has disappeared."

"Then he has her."

"I'm thinking the same thing. We need to find him before he harms her. Would you help us?"

"Try room 5004."

"Please stay on the line, Miss Fargo."

He shared the information with Evans and Stone.

"Are you helping us because of the man in your trailer?"

"Yes. His name was Aaron Martin."

"I know. I'm very sorry."

"Just get Yancey."

"We have some people checking his room now."

Evans came back into Santiago's suite shaking his head.

Patton said, "Apparently he's gone."

"Then you've lost 'em both."

"Do you have any idea where he'd take her?"

"Someplace private that you wouldn't expect."

"Where does he live?"

"Nowhere in particular. When he was in this area he stayed with me."

"We need to talk. Where can we meet?"

"We can't. If I need you I'll call DataFlex."

The phone went dead.

Fargo sat for a few minutes. *You paid me off and then you killed Aaron. I shouldn't have told you about him.* She went to the coffee bar in the lobby. *Always do the unexpected, that's what you said all the time. Motel? Eloy? Where?*

Two men at a nearby table were talking about the purchase of vacation property.

Of course, the ranch. She left a $5.00 bill on the table, went to the lobby and asked to use a phone book. The clerk sent her to the public phone booths. She thumbed through the pages, found a feed and grain supplier in Apache Junction and dialed.

A man with a crusty voice answered. "Travis Ranch Supply."

"Good morning. I'm up here visiting from Yuma, trying to find a local ranch. Could you help me?"

"Maybe. What's the name?"

"Broken Spur."

The man laughed. "Hell, that ain't no ranch. That's a fancy home in the middle of nothing. Hasn't been a working ranch since some city guy bought it years ago."

"Then you know where it's located?"

"On the Old Apache Highway."

"Thank you. I thought that's the one I'm looking for, but the one I want is a working ranch."

"Then it's not the Broken Spur. Best you check with someone else first, Ma'am. There's a lot of ranches around here with Broken in their names."

"I'll do that. Thank you again."

"Not a problem."

Lisa Fargo purchased a map of Arizona at the gift shop and left the hotel. She studied the map in her car, following the colored lines with a finger. "Apache Highway. Wish I had my GPS." She found Goldfield. "Now you and that bitch will pay."

* * *

Quarterman had Santiago taped to the same kitchen chair Lindsey Braun had occupied. "Nice place your friends have here. We won't be here long. but it'll do for a few hours while I make some new plans."

"I take it we're not here to talk."

"No. I have other plans. You know, it doesn't have to be this way, Michelle. You're beautiful and smart. We're more alike than different. I don't want to hurt you."

He moved around in the kitchen, taking a half-full bottle of frozen water from the freezer and walking to the sink. He topped it off with water from the faucet.

Keep calm. Watch. No expressions, nothing.

He turned and faced her. "Your plan was good, almost believable. It was easy buying into your dismay with that Seattle cop. He's a bed-me-tonight type, maybe some lingering loyalty."

"We knew about the bugs."

"The first set."

"Both."

"You knew about the second go 'round? I'm impressed. Evans is a better soldier than I would've guessed."

"Too many people were in my room. A man of your skill could find a way to gain access. It was a no-brainer."

"My cousin—my adopted cousin—thinks you're an obsession with me."

"She's not alone. How else would you explain my being your prisoner? All things being equal I would've been back in Seattle tomorrow or the next day. You put this plan in place."

"Maybe, but I have strong feelings for you... desires. I'm not obsessed."

"Desire to do what? Not talk. We did that on the phone."

"Demonstrate my superiority over those suits who are trying to nail me. And I'm taken by you."

"So you keep saying. You have a strange way of showing it."

"I mean it."

"But you'll kill again with the slightest pretext."

"I'm a survivor. I'll kill when threatened. I've faced down my anger at demanding women. A lady at the hotel can attest to that."

"It's very uncomfortable talking this way taped to a chair."

"It's a necessity. Only a fool would let you loose at this point."

"Afraid I'd make a break for it?"

"Worse. Afraid I'd hurt you when you did, and you would try. I really don't want to hurt you."

"How many women have you killed while screwing their brains out?"

"Please, don't talk that way. It doesn't become you."

"Really? Perhaps I should just say fucked."

Quarterman stepped from the counter to the table and slapped her face with the flat of his hand.

Her eyes welled.

"I didn't mean to do that. I'm sorry. Sometimes it's necessary to punish even those you care about."

"You hurt me."

"I said I was sorry."

"Slap me 'til I see lightning bolts and say you're sorry? You get any more feelings for me and I'll be a bloody pulp. They'll be looking for us."

"I'm sure they already are."

"You said you wouldn't hurt me. You just did."

"No, I disciplined you."

"What is it you really want from me?"

"Truthfully? I think I'm in love with you."

"So you tie me up and slap me around?" She laughed. "That's a really odd way of showing affection. If you really mean it, let me help get you into that hospital."

"You're resourceful, a danger to me. You're not ready yet."

"You're nuts."

Quarterman slapped her again. "You're like her."

"Who?"

"That girl, Lindsey. You're both very strong. I like strength. My father should've been strong and controlled my mother but he was weak."

"And you're not?"

He smiled. "You're the prisoner."

"You said we'd talk a few hours and then you'd be gone."

"My plans—our plans—have changed. I want you with me."

"I'd rather be dead."

"Stranger things have happened."

She glared at him. "Pavlovian things."

He walked around the table and stood behind her. "Prisoners have become close, even defensive of their captors. It's happened in Stockholm, militias, POW camps, crazies out to reform the world, religious orders."

"You mean they were forced."

"No, I mean real bonding."

She looked at the table top. "That's Lindsey's blood."

"Her father had to be punished. It's old news now."

"As long as I have a choice, I guarantee you we won't bond, it just won't happen."

"Your words, not mine. By tomorrow we'll be gone, out in the desert. I think you'll like what I have planned."

"Putting you away I'd like."

"That's today. We'll see about tomorrow, a month from now. I want to make love with you, and by then you'll want me."

Santiago stared at Quarterman. "You said you've never raped a woman in your life."

"I haven't, but I know you want me. You'll want me even more then."

I need to get out of this chair somehow. "My choices do seem limited. Maybe in a month I'll have a changed point of view."

"Exactly. You see? We've had a very nice first chat. Everything considered I thought it went well, although I'm a bit stiff and tired. But look at the bright side: you're not gagged yet."

He looked at the pool. "I'm going to get out of these clothes. Sit tight."

A few minutes later Quarterman returned to the kitchen wearing a robe monogrammed "CB" and sat down across from her. "I don't suppose you'd like to join me in your friend's spa?"

She made no response.

"No, I didn't think so. Maybe later."

He walked out the back patio door, leaving it open and dropping the robe as he went. "You don't mind naked men do you?"

He immersed himself in the swirling bubbles. "This feels good!" he shouted. "You don't know what you're missing, Michelle!"

Santiago tried to move her arms, but nothing would give. *Sam, Alex, find me, please.* She continued to twist in the chair. The kitchen was heating up with the door left open. Sweat covered her flesh.

After twenty minutes Quarterman returned. He'd put the robe on again, leaving it untied as he came through the door. "That felt good even if the water was too warm. The bubbles felt like grains of sand, needles hitting my legs. It's enough to take your breath away.

Christ, I need some water. I'm sweatin' like a pig." He went to the sink and filled a plastic cup.

Tap water? "Water would be nice. You're red as a lobster."

He tilted his head back and gulped. His eyes swelled as he grabbed at the edge of the counter and crashed to the floor. The plastic cup bounced across the kitchen.

He was stretched face-down on the tile floor, unconscious, his right leg bent at the knee, his left leg straight, his face hidden by one arm wrapped around the top of his head, the other arm reaching out. The house was silent except for the pump in the shed by the pool. She twisted and strained but to no avail. She tried jerking to the side. She looked at the man on the floor. "Quarterman? Quarterman?"

He remained motionless. She tilted the chair but was stopped by her legs under the table. "Damn it!"

After a few minutes Quarterman stirred, groaned, braced himself on his hands and knees, and looked at Santiago. He laughed as his legs buckled. "When we're done with this I have to see my doctor in Vera Cruz. Damn malaria hasn't bothered me in years. Guess neither one of us made it. You're still here and I couldn't get through the kitchen without takin' a dive. Man, I hafta get some rest; then I have a couple of errands to run."

"You fainted. You need to see a doctor. I could help."

He walked down the hallway, bracing against the wall. "It's not even noon yet. Jesus."

* * * * * * *

Sam Evans arrived at the Braun residence and the guard waved him through the gate. A local Phoenix radio station began its 11:15 sports report as he parked at the front door. "Damn, I won't know what the D-backs are doing for another hour."

He rang the doorbell and Nikki Braun answered. "Mrs. Braun, I thought we had personnel out here for this?"

"Lindsey's home, Sam. We wanted privacy. The man on the gate will suffice. Come in. Claude and Lindsey are expecting you in the living room."

"Thank you."

As he walked into the living room, Braun stood. "Sam, my daughter, Lindsey. I don't know that you've met."

"Not formally. Hello, Lindsey. It's been a long week. I hope you're recovering from all that's happened."

"I am. Thank you for helping rescue us. It was a horrible experience. Dad says you have something to talk to me about."

"I do. Are you up to talking about what's happened to you?"

"I'm okay. Dad said the guy that hurt me has Aunt Michelle."

"He does. His name is Quarterman... Yancey Quarterman. I need to find him as quickly as possible, or even worse things may happen to Mitch. Did he say anything that would hint at where he'd been staying, or where he might go?"

"Not really. He was mean. He talked about how he liked individual strength, defiance even when directed at him. He's a very odd man. Control of me seemed to be his big thing, like he was happy breaking people down. Weird."

Evans said, "He's weird all right, and dangerous."

"He implied he'd killed other women but he told me he'd never raped anyone."

"I know. It was on the tape."

"Definite control freak. His way is the only way, or he'll hurt you. I think he liked hurting people physically and emotionally. It seemed to make him feel good."

Braun said, "He's an animal."

Evans raised an eyebrow.

Braun said, "Sorry. I didn't mean to interrupt."

Lindsey said, "He liked the cabin. You could tell by the way he looked at it, like it was something he'd never seen before."

Evans said, "Is there a pool at the cabin?"

Braun said, "Yes, with a spa built into it. Why?"

"One of his fascinations has been watching Mitch in the hotel spa. I think his obsession is built in part around the bikini and the pool."

Lindsey laughed. "Yeah, mom told me about the bikini."

Braun said, "Are you thinking maybe he went to the cabin, Sam?"

"Maybe. He's trained to disappear, go deep. Given the location, his background, and training, it's a good possibility, at least initially."

Braun said, "He wouldn't stay there?"

"He wouldn't stay anywhere for long. He'd head for the desert if he had no other option. He could survive out there indefinitely, even with a prisoner."

Braun looked confused. "Then why do you think he'd go to the cabin?"

"He knows we've already been there when the kids were released. It should be safe for a few days while we look at other leads and information."

"T.J. and I did the same thing, Dad. We were at his place for two days before we went to the cabin. We figured your people would go there early on."

Braun said, "And we did. We never went back after the first visit."

Evans said, "It wouldn't be a bad place for the short term. From what Patton tells us, Quarterman only wanted to talk with Mitch. If that's correct, he's flying by the seat of his pants until he figures out what's next now that he's snatched her."

Braun nodded. "He's crazy."

Evans said, "We're all in agreement on that. Lindsey, if I went out there today would the pool be up and running, ready to use?"

"Yes. T.J. and I cleaned it and turned on the heat. But why would the guy want to kidnap Aunt Michelle?"

Evans said, "To reinvent her as he wants her to be."

Lindsey squirmed. "Like a cult?"

Evans said, "Yes, something like that."

Braun sat up straight. "You're talking about brainwashing."

"That or some other form of dependency. He knows how to do the unexpected in behavior and treatment of prisoners. He's been in the field since Vietnam."

Braun said, "Are you going to the cabin, Sam?"

"She sooner the better."

"Don't go alone. I'll call Stone."

"No, call Patton. Have him meet me at the Green Chili Bar. We'll take a look together. Stone's a bureaucrat."

"Is Patton the hunky agent mom says Aunt Mitch is hangin' with?"

Evans smiled. "You *are* feeling better. The answer to your question yes. It's been her cover."

Braun said, "Be careful, Sam."

"Oh yes, very careful. Did you get hold of Chance Stewart?"

"Yes. He's going to see about coming down. Damn fool. I'd already be here."

Evans said, "My thought exactly. So much for Mr. Wonderful. Now, please call Patton. I'm heading out."

* * *

Lisa Fargo followed Highway 88 out of Apache Junction heading toward Tortilla Flat. She passed Goldfield and a housing development. Then the landscape became barren and scruffy, dotted by cacti, an occasional house, and gateless entry markers with dirt roadways leading over rolling crests.

A faded sign over an open gateway came into view. "Finally, Broken Spur Ranch. This looks like a toll gate to nowhere."

She pulled off the highway and looked at the dirt roadway leading to the crest of a hill. "Tire tracks... somebody's been here, all right. They might be here now. You always said watch and wait, Yancey."

She looked back down the highway toward a rest stop she had just passed and made a U-turn. When she pulled in she parked in the shade of the only tree in the area. "This must be one of Arizona's finest havens: a portable toilet, a cement picnic table and a bench, and a garbage can. Have a smoke, Lisa, set the AC and wait."

Two cars drove past the rest area but didn't turn off at the entry to the ranch. She checked her gauges. "Oh shit, the engine's overheating. Great. No more air or radio." She turned off the ignition. "I hate waiting."

Fargo squirmed when a buzzard flew overhead. "Hang around fella. I think lunch will be just over that hill in a while. Jesus, I'm as sweaty as if I was bangin' a trucker in the sun."

A stream of dust appeared over the crest of the ranch entry. "It's the Caddie and I'm a sittin' duck. He'll pass in less than a minute. And now I gotta pee."

A motor home rounded a curve on the highway approaching the Broken Spur road. The Cadillac waited at the entry while it passed. The coach's turn indicator began to blink.

"Yes, please pull in, please, please," she said peeking over the dashboard.

The Caddie swung into the oncoming lane to pass the lumbering road-box. "Only a driver. It's gotta be you, Yancey."

She watched the car until the motor home pulled in front of her and stopped. "Thank God."

She opened the door and raced to the portable toilet as an elderly man exited the coach.

Afterward she started the car. "One more smoke. Let my heart slow down; then I'll see what you have hidden over that crest, Yancey. I'm betting on the bitch cop."

She drove to the entry to the Broken Spur Ranch and turned in. As soon as she cleared the crest the cabin came into view. "Not bad. If I were you Yancey, I'd find a way to stay at a place like this. No parked cars in the driveway and you were alone in the Caddie. The bitch has to be here. You'll be back, and I'll be waiting."

She passed the paved driveway in front of the cabin and followed the dirt roadway around a small hill beyond the compound. She stopped, out of sight. Then she climbed a small hill toward a cluster of desert brush and cactus to watch the cabin. She knelt at the base of a saguaro lost in sagebrush.

The temperature began to drop. A breeze kicked up, and then a strong wind. Within minutes a cloud of dust had covered the entire area. Fargo closed her eyes and hid her face. "So much for fashion. My hair will be a mess when this is over."

The wind lasted several minutes, then stopped as quickly as it started. The dust began to settle. "Good deal. No tire tracks. You won't even know I'm here until I want you to know."

Fargo looked at her dust-covered car. "I don't even have my .38 thanks to you and your damn fire, Yancey. A bag full of money doesn't buy much out here. I hope you heard my message." She thought for a moment. "Maybe I can sneak in and get a kitchen knife... slit your damn throat, stab you in the back, something. You always have a gun in the backpack. Just maybe...."

As she stood, she saw the Caddie parked in the shaded garage area away from the front door. "I'll be damned. You're back. Must'a come in with the dust storm."

A helicopter flew overhead. She ducked down. "Might be looking for us. I gotta get into that house."

She backtracked from her car to the compound's stucco sidewall and looked in through a small gate. *Smart construction... no windows on the sunny side but it's hotter'n hell out here.*

She quietly opened the gate and ran to the side of the house. On the backside of the compound was another wall separating the backyard and pool from the front. Fargo waited in the sun, peaking around at the front door every few minutes. A light breeze started. "Thank you, Lord. Now tell me how I get in."

* * *

Quarterman checked the tape holding Santiago in the chair. "Sorry I was gone so long. Hope you missed me."

"Can I use the bathroom or am I supposed to go in my shorts?"

Without a word he tore the tape from her arms and legs, never looking away from her face. "I'll give you some privacy, but don't bother goin' through the cabinet and drawers. I've cleaned 'em out."

She started to go to the first door in the long hallway.

"Use the one in the bedroom at the end."

He followed and waited. The toilet flushed. "Don't forget to wash."

Gladly, maybe the tape won't hold as well. She soaped and scrubbed, then walked back through the bedroom, her hands damp.

He was standing by the door naked when she came out. "Better?"

"I am, thank you. What's—"

"Good. Now strip."

"What?"

He tore off her blouse and bra and tossed them on the bed. "You heard me. A little humiliation goes a long way. Now get rid of the shorts and panties."

She covered herself and turned away.

"Face me. *Never* turn your back on me." His voice was harsh, his eyes narrow slits.

Santiago turned, gritting her teeth, and looked him in the eyes. "You're a strange man, Yancey: kind then mean; loud then quiet; brutal then gentle."

She slid the tight shorts over her hips and let them fall to her feet, then stepped out of them like a stripper. "I can tell you're no stranger to watching this."

"Yes, now the panties."

Lip licking, heavy breathing, never looking above the waist... horny old bastard. In a soft throaty voice she said, "I haven't done this in years, not since college."

Leaning forward, her legs straight, she slid the high-cut garment down, her long fingers teasing her thighs, her breasts dangling free. When the panties reached her ankles she stepped out of them and assumed a sensual pose. "Can't get any women on your own?"

He slapped the side of her face. She said nothing.

"You'll understand pain. You'll know shame and humiliation. I can treat you like a goddess or I can treat you like a bitch."

She licked her lips. "I could help you in so many ways."

"You are. I'm remaking you into the woman, the partner, I want. You're beautiful. You take my breath away."

Don't I wish.

Santiago walked naked into the kitchen followed by Quarterman. She looked at his groin. "You're feeling stronger than earlier."

"Yes."

"You've got a big need, Yancey."

He began to sweat. "I do."

She teased her teeth with the tip of her tongue. *Stay out of the chair.* "Are you up to the spa again?"

"Oh yes. Go ahead, I'm right behind you." He looked at his watch. "It's almost 1:00. Will it be too warm for you?"

"Never. The hotter the better. I like everything hot. Anyway, it feels like a breeze is starting up again." She stepped into the spa.

Quarterman pulled a patio chair to the side of the spa and sat down. He watched Michelle in the bubbling water and began to masturbate.

I haven't had a guy jack-off in front of me since I worked the club scene. "Some music would be nice. It's really quiet out here."

He stopped pleasuring himself and stood. "I'll get the radio from the kitchen. I can tell you're not going anyplace."

"Then maybe you'll join me?"

A loud crash broke the quiet. "What the hell was that?" Quarterman moved to the side of the slider. Across the kitchen and living room he saw the front door rubbing against the wall, wide open. He moved into the living room, checked the jam and closed the door. "Somebody broke in here at least once. A man of Braun's means should take better care of his property." He pressed the door hard, making sure it was latched. Going back through the kitchen he patted the backpack. "Gun's still there. Must be getting' paranoid."

He picked up the radio and went to the pump house, pulled out an extension cord, plugged it in, shortened its reach by tying a knot in it and walked to the table. "Country?"

"Sure. What was the noise?"

"Didn't get the door shut tight. No big deal."

He sat down and looked at Santiago. "Don't think I'm buying into this sudden change of mood. I like it, but don't even think you're gettin' away."

"It'd be hard running around the desert naked. Why don't you join me? It's really nice."

He stood. "I'd rather be warm in there with you than hot out here."

He slid into the spa. "Feels hot to me."

She nodded at a bottle of cold water he had just set on the patio table. "Want something cool to drink?"

"Love something, love a lot of things."

Santiago stepped out of the spa and leaned across the table. She grabbed the radio and flung it at the spa.

He jumped up. "You'll have to do better than that, Bitch. Short cord."

She ran into the pump house, slammed the door and grabbed the first tool she saw, a pipe wrench. She pushed it through two hooks fastened to the inside of the door just as his fist hit it.

He laughed. "It's gonna get warm in there."

She blinked. The only light in the shed came through the crack at the bottom of the door. Sweat covered her body. Crystals crunched under her feet. The smell of chemicals made her nostrils flare. Breathing became a chore. He banged the door again.

Her eyes adjusted to the darkness. The outline of plastic bottles, a skimmer net, and a small container came into focus. She moved closer to read the labels and kicked a glass one-gallon jug. *I thought people kept glass away from pools. Hydrochloric Acid. I need a small glass container; a jar, anything.* She searched the shelves.

"I'll wait a while, Michelle, but when I get tired of it I'll bust the door down. You'll be punished this time. You failed my trust test."

He banged the door one last time. Then everything went silent.

* * *

Evans parked just before going over the last crest to the cabin. "Let's take a look over the hill."

They walked to the crest and knelt. Patton pointed down to the cabin. "There's a car parked in the garage area out front. Wait... take a look in the back yard. A naked man standing by the shed."

"It's got to be him," Evans said. "Let's get down there while he's busy." He stood and ran toward the driveway.

Patton said, "We should call this in and—" He stood. "Oh, to hell with it."

He raced after Evans and caught up. Both men crept up to the front window and looked in. Patton said, "I can see all the way through the house. Those are Michelle's clothes on the floor by the table."

Evans pulled out a Glock. "Quarterman must still be by the shed. No sign of him in there. Let's go!"

Patton pulled out his weapon.

From the back yard, a man shouted, "Open the damn door!"

Evans pushed the front door open. Patton darted in first, surveying the living room. Evans followed. The man in the back yard continued to shout.

Patton and Evans moved to a living room wall out of sight from the kitchen and patio door. There was a splashing sound followed by Michelle running naked through the kitchen and going down the hall. She didn't see them or pay attention to the open front door.

A moment later Quarterman came into the kitchen. He grabbed the backpack, dropped it on the floor and crouched. "You can't get away from me."

Evans stepped around the corner into the kitchen. "It's over Quarterman. Stretch out flat, arms out straight. Wiggle and I'll blow your fucking head off."

Quarterman looked Evans in the eyes, cold, dead, unblinking. The gun was steady. He did as ordered. Patton came around the corner, holstered his weapon, kicked Quarterman's legs apart and began patting him down.

"I'm naked, man, I'm not carrying. You already got to my pack."

Evans looked at Patton.

Lisa Fargo appeared with Santiago. "No, they didn't."

Patton looked up. Evans began to turn around.

"Don't move or the bitch dies first. Drop the gun."

Evans looked at Quarterman, who was beginning to stand, and dropped his gun. "Sorry, Mitch."

Lisa said, "Shut up! Now kick it over here!"

Patton, standing nearer to Quarterman, dropped his gun.

Quarterman said, "I'll get it."

"Move and I'll shoot your nuts off!"

Quarterman frowned. "Lisa?"

Fargo's hands began to tremble. "You killed Aaron. You didn't have to do that."

Quarterman swallowed. "Careful, Lisa. That thing has a hair trigger."

Patton and Evans were standing far apart. Fargo was pressing the barrel of the .45 against Santiago's neck. "Why did you kill him?"

"Lisa, we've killed lots of people."

"Women. Why Aaron?"

"He was a threat. He didn't love you. He wanted your money."

"I loved him the same way you love this bitch. I'll kill her first so you'll know the pain I'm feeling, why I'm here."

"No!"

"She doesn't love you! She just tried to kill you! I saw the radio hit the hot tub. I saw her throw something on you and run into the house while you jumped in the pool."

"Don't matter. Let's do these two and get the hell outta here before their backup arrives. We can work out our differences later."

"How do you work things out with someone who wanted to kill you in a motel? I don't think it's possible."

She moved the gun under Santiago's chin.

"No... no... Lisa, I just wondered how close we could get. A thought, that's all it was."

"Easy for you to say. It was a bad idea." She waved the gun at Quarterman.

Santiago grabbed at Fargo's arm. Fargo pulled away, falling and the .45 fired. Santiago took her down. Evans jumped Fargo, taking the gun and placing a knee in the small of her back. He stretched her arms behind her. Patton leaped at Quarterman, who had fallen to the floor holding his stomach when the gun fired. A pool of blood was seeping from under him. Quarterman turned his head, a hand beneath him covering the wound, blood pouring over his lips.

Patton said, "Gut shot. We need medics."

Evans scooped up the .45 as Santiago ran down the hall. She returned in a bathrobe and handed the waist tie to Evans. "Use this. It'll hold her 'til help gets here. In my other life I'd have cuffs."

Patton stood. "Sorry. I wasn't thinking, Sam." He tossed Evans his cuffs, then looked at Santiago. "I was scared. I thought I'd lost you."

"So did I. Did you retrieve your gun?"

"No, I thought you'd—"

Blood bubbled over Quarterman's lips and chin as he waved Patton's Glock. "You're dead, Lisa." Quarterman fired and the top of Lisa Fargo's head exploded on the floor. Evans fired at Quarterman, hitting the center of his right cheek. "He's dead now."

Patton retrieved his weapon. "Jesus... I almost got us killed."

Evans picked up Santiago's clothes from the kitchen floor and handed them to her; then he bent down remove the cuffs from Fargo's hands.

Santiago said, "Leave her the way she is. This is a crime scene."

"Of course. I was just gonna—"

"We need to leave everything the way it is."

Evans said, "You best get dressed."

"Thank you." She went down the hallway.

Evans looked at Patton. "Was it really a mistake, Alex? Stone wanted him dead."

"I wouldn't risk Mitch to kill him."

From the bedroom Santiago called out, "We'll never know how many women they killed. There's no closure to this."

Stone came through the door followed by four men in SWAT gear. He stared at Quarterman's body. "Is he dead?"

Patton said, "Yes. He killed the woman and Sam saved our bacon after I screwed up."

Stone said, "Good riddance to both of 'em. Good work, very good work. I'll call the sheriff's office and let them know we have their serial killer." He glanced at Santiago as she came into the room. "Evans, I want you to take her in for a quick checkup."

Santiago looked at Evans and Patton. "The Sheriff will want your weapons and our statements."

Patton held Santiago. "It wasn't a setup, Mitch."

"I know."

Stone said, "They'll get your statement through my office. This is a national security case. Get her checked out. We'll talk later."

The two men gave Stone their weapons.

Evans put an arm around Santiago. "Come on, I'll get you outta here."

"Take me to Brauns'. I don't need a doctor and the Oasis just doesn't sound good. Maybe I can e-mail my notes from Claude's den. All I want right now is a bath and some sleep."

Evans said, "I'll get the car."

They walked out the door as Stone's team was searching the Caddie.

"No," she said, "let's walk up to it. I just want to be away from this place."

* * *

The Braun Family and Santiago were sitting at the patio table. Nikki looked around and smiled. Her eyes were wet, buried in dark circles. "A week ago I wasn't sure we'd ever get to sit down as a family again. Now we're here. I don't think the grill ever smelled as good as tonight."

Braun said, "It's a nice evening. It's been too long since we sat down as a family. You made this possible Mitch. Thank you." He raised a wine glass.

Santiago said, "Thank you. Lindsey was the catalyst. There was no way of her foreseeing the events that accompanied her plan. I just hope only good things come from now on."

Braun looked at his daughter. "We're together now and we'll do better this time. How's the hand tonight?"

"The finger's fine... I guess, numb. It's nice being home and to finally get to know you a little, Aunt Michelle. Thank you."

"Just call me Mitch."

Braun said, "So what are your plans, Mitch? Back to Seattle and catching the bad guys? You could have a great future here in the valley. I'd hire you right now. Just give me a number."

"It's tempting, very tempting, on all accounts."

Nikki said, "Have you heard from your detective friend?"

"Not so much. I think he's got a new roommate."

Braun nodded. "He said he might be coming down."

"I'll believe it when I see it. Don't get me wrong. Chance is a good cop and a good partner. For a while I thought it might be more." She shrugged. "I was wrong."

Nikki smiled. "Alex?"

"Maybe."

Braun changed the subject. "Did my system work okay for your report?"

"Great, and thanks for having my stuff picked up. I needed a different oasis, at least for now."

Lindsey said, "So Mitch, what's Alex doing tonight? I thought he'd be here."

"I think he's debriefing with Stone. We're all supposed to meet tomorrow somewhere."

"My conference room: us, Sam, Ray and Stone."

"No local cops?"

Braun shook his head. "They'll have to go through him, I guess."

Santiago said, "Too much hush-hush for me. I didn't like Stone's attitude the first time we met, the terrorist thing in particular."

Braun said, "I know, but at least it's a closed matter now."

Santiago said, "Lindsey, where's your young man?"

"We're like you and the guy in Seattle, not an item any longer. He gave me an uncomfortable feeling after I told him about the money. I can't really explain it. Anyway, Dad's taking a year off. We're going on a vacation, no distractions for any of us."

"That sounds nice. After what you've all been through you deserve it."

Braun handed Santiago an envelope. "Mitch, we want you to have this. What you did in the name of friendship was extraordinary. You gave us something we'd lost. We want to give you something in return, the flexibility to control your own destiny wherever and whatever you decide to do in the future."

"I came down to help out. I don't need anything."

Lindsey said, "Open it, please,"

Santiago opened the envelope and her eyes swelled. "One million dollars? I don't know what to say. I can't accept this."

Nikki said, "Yes you can. You changed our lives. We want to change yours, if you want."

"Sam deserves this. He's the one that was shot at and had his family threatened."

"Sam's been taken care of, the same bonus. I just hope he stays on. Think of it as a token of our appreciation."

"Claude, you've given too many speeches. If this is a token, I've been saving the wrong stuff."

They all laughed. Braun looked at the pool and sniffed. "I still need maintenance service. Can't you guys smell chlorine or something even over the smell of the grill?"

Santiago said, "It's late, and I'm beat. Think I'll get hold of my folks tomorrow after we're done. They don't even know I'm here yet. See you in the morning." *A million dollars... what's next?*

Day Six

Braun's team and Santiago were in the conference room early. His receptionist called. "Mr. Stone is on his way in."

"Good," said Braun.

Santiago was on Braun's right. Sam Evans sat next to her. Ray House was at the far end in his normal spot. Jessica Rodriguez was on his left. Braun was the only man in the room dressed in a polo shirt and slacks. The DataFlex people wore dress shirts, ties, blazers and slacks. Jessica was in business attire. Santiago was in a yellow mini, a white blouse and five-inch stilettos.

Braun leaned toward Santiago and whispered, "I have to change the dress codes. It's far too formal."

John Stone rushed into the room dressed in his standard issue black suit. He looked at Ray House, then took a seat on Braun's left and opened an attaché case. He took out a single type written page and handed it across the table to Santiago. "Sign this, please."

"What is it?"

"Your notes. I've edited a few of your comments for security reasons."

She read it. "A few comments? Other than our names these notes as you call them are bull."

"Just sign it."

"And perjure myself? Not a chance in hell."

"It was a simple open and shut case, nothing more."

"I don't work for you or follow your orders, Mr. Stone."

"You refuse to sign it, is that correct?"

"Yes."

"Very good. I'll note you were unable to sign."

"Unwilling, Mr. Stone, not unable. Unwilling."

She took a pen and wrote across the center of the page in page bold letters Report Fabricated. "Jessica, can we get this photocopied?"

Claude Braun nodded and Rodriguez left the room.

"Mr. Stone, Mitch and my staff have performed far above any expected standards. I will not have you attempt to intimidate them with anymore of your disrespectful boorish behavior. Let's get on with the business at hand, shall we?"

Stone said, "My Director will hear of this."

Braun said, "So will the president."

Stone stood. "In that case this meeting is over."

"Wrong again. You're welcome to remain or leave, but we have other business to attend. Sam, you've written a detailed report including Mitch's contribution for our friends in Washington?"

Stone remained seated.

Evans handed Santiago some papers. "Yes. Please, take a copy of this report and pass the others around the table. What you are receiving is a composite of the events of the last several days, outlining the actions taken, details, and personnel involved. Please review it, append if needed, and initial. Jessica will collect all copies before we leave. I will also attach a copy of the bogus Santiago report to the document and have it delivered to Washington as per our operating protocol involving government matters."

"Thank you, Sam. Mr. Stone, I note that Alex Patton is not attending?"

"He's meeting with a deputy sheriff. He'll be along shortly."

"Good. Sam, make sure he reviews the document too."

"Will do, Boss."

House arched an eyebrow. Braun smiled. "Relax, Ray. Sam and I have reached a new level of informality based on our very close association over the last several days. I've come to the conclusion that we've been a little stiff in security."

Stone said, "I do believe this meeting over and I have important matters to deal with. My team already has a new assignment. This has not been a pleasure, Sir."

Braun said, "I agree wholeheartedly. Please, don't forget to give Miss Rodriguez the document on your way out."

As Stone stormed from the room the receptionist poked her head in the door. "Mr. Braun, someone to see Miss Santiago. You said to come in and tell you."

"Yes, thank you. Gentlemen, Miss Rodriguez, our guest has a guest. May I suggest we leave the room to them? Our work here is done."

Everyone except Santiago and Evans stood and began leaving. She glanced out the door and saw Chance Stewart waiting.

Sam Evans was placing the documents into a sheaf when she rounded the table and returned her signed copy to him. "Thank you, Sam, for everything. You and Alex saved my life yesterday."

"Mitch, I know you have someone waiting, but I have to tell you, this has been one unique and unforgettable experience. I sincerely hope we get to work together again someday even if we don't earn another bonus."

They both laughed and he left the room.

Chance Stewart peeked into the conference room. "Is the meeting over?"

"Before it ever started. Claude told me last night you might come in."

"You've had a tough week."

"For sure, but I'll be home in a few days."

"Coming back to work?"

"No, I don't think so. Too much has happened, so many things have changed. I don't know what I'll be doing next."

"Sounds like we're both at crossroads."

"I know we are. I felt it when I left so suddenly. It just wasn't our time... not then, not now."

"I think I wanted something I couldn't commit to. I thought maybe I was too old to change my ways. When you came down here I realized how different we are from each other as people."

"I know. I've had the same awakening. We were a good team."

"The best."

"I can't come back, Chance. It would never be the same. You know that as well as I do."

"I do. I came down here because I have to be up front with you. It's been really stressful trying to keep tabs on you, almost nerve wracking. Amber has provided me with strength."

"Knowing you and Amber I'd bet she's provided more than strength. That's good for both of us."

"You don't understand."

"I understand only too well. The question is, do you? Commit to her, Chance. Tell the girl you love her. Be honest with her. Trust me. Every woman wants to hear that."

"And you?"

"My life has had a few changes this week."

"Patton?"

"Maybe. I'm going to give it some time."

"We're still friends?"

"Always."

He looked around the conference room. "Nice place. Well, I'd best get going. I have to get back."

"You're going back tonight?"

"Not exactly. Amber is here with me. This is really awkward. She said I should come down here personally, not call. She came with me."

"Well, there you are... you'd best get going."

"Yeah."

The door opened and Alex Patton walked in. "Sorry, they told me the meeting was in here."

"It's all right. Come in. Alex, this is my partner—my former partner—Chance Stewart. Chance came down to see how I was doing. He was just on his way back to the hotel and Amber."

Patton extended his hand. "A pleasure, Detective."

"Thanks for taking care of her. Mitch is a very special person."

Stewart stepped out of the room and closed the door.

"So... I didn't mean to interfere," said Patton."

"He's a close friend."

"You said former partner? You're being reassigned?"

"Quitting. I need some time to sort things out."

"Don't we all?"

"Do we have closure with the sheriff?"

"Best as they'll get with Stone. The forensics team found seven severed fingers in Fargo's freezer. They're running DNA tests trying to match them to the victims we know of and hopefully identify the other three. Stone's people found three-hundred thousand dollars cash in Lisa's car. None of it was from the accounts we've been monitoring, so we're not sure where it came from. Quarterman probably had other accounts. Why she had the money we'll never know, but it may explain Aaron Martin."

She said, "Mario told us about Yancey moving money into other accounts."

"Yes he did. Stone will love hearing about Mario again."

"Do we know anything concrete about Martin?"

"He was a salesman, married but separated, has a history of playing around. Whether it was the real thing with Fargo or a money grab, we don't know."

She said, "Perhaps a little of each. Lisa was definitely taken with him."

"I want to look at this case as a win-win. The government kept its secrets buried, we caught a serial killer we didn't even know about, and we met."

"That's true. Stone said his team have a new assignment. Are you part of that?"

"No. I was on loan, but I am going to Washington tonight for training starting tomorrow on a new assignment here in Phoenix. I'll be back in about two weeks. I thought I'd fly up to Seattle and see you. I want to spend some time with you and I don't even know where you live."

She placed a finger over his lips. He stopped talking and they kissed.

"I'll be here in two weeks, permanently. You'll have to call Nikki or Sam to find out where because I don't know yet." Her stomach growled.

He said, "Lunch?"

"Love to, and I've still got to call my sister, Jill."

Walking out of the conference room they both spotted a copy of the morning paper on the receptionist's desk. The headline read *Sex Killers Die in Gun Battle with FBI*. He said, "Have you read it yet?"

"No, I get my pulp fiction at the book store."

"So what are you going to do down here?"

She patted her purse. "Haven't decided yet but I'll think of something. Girl has to pay the rent. Can we stop by a bank on the way to lunch?"

"Sure, but I'm buying."

"I know. I just have to open an account."

~ Ends ~

In *Killer Disc*, the third title in the Santiago mystery series:

An industrial accident paves the way for Michelle "Mitch" Santiago, former homicide detective now working for DataFlex Laboratories into the dark side of white collar crime and industrial espionage. Shari Stiletto steals research files for a multiple virus detection process from a Thomas Grant's, President of Virus Detect, free standing computer. But she also unknowingly takes files previously stolen from the Venezuelan government for an unpatented synthetic fuel process by Grant. In quick succession the files are stolen again.

Grant discovers an electrical surge at the lab has destroyed backup files. Needing both sets of research for very different reasons he connects with the underworld to retrieve them offering a substantial reward. The result is warfare between bounty hunters.

He goes to DataFlex, for help in finding the virus data. He does not want the police involved or investors know. The Venezuelan government has a team seeking the fuel research while both intimidating and protecting Stiletto.

Santiago deals with the underworld, foreign espionage, and murder after rescuing Stiletto in Algodones, Mexico and hiding her. As Grant's world crumbles he seeks revenge, takes Santiago prisoner and tortures her. He has Santiago, he wants Stiletto. His rage kills him.

About the Author

Ron Wick is a retired teacher, principal and poet from the Seattle area, now living in Arizona. As an educator he also worked with police and court authorities involving many criminal issues, ranging from juvenile delinquencies to suspected pedophiles. One of his students was alleged to be a Green River murder victim. He is dedicated to improving the quality of life for all humanity and will donate 10% of his royalties to Lions Clubs International Foundation, the charitable arm of the association of which he has been a member and officer for 35 years.

If you enjoyed *Desert Kill*, be sure to look for the first title in the Santiago mystery series, *Gold Coast Murder*. It's available through all major ebook venues and in print at Amazon.

Talk to me at peterputter@juno.com

Made in the USA
San Bernardino, CA
27 September 2018